All of Me

A LOVE BETWEEN THE BASES NOVEL

JENNIFER BERNARD

AVONBOOKS

An Imprint of HarperCollinsPublishers

This is a work of fiction. Names, characters, places, and incidents are products of the author's imagination or are used fictitiously and are not to be construed as real. Any resemblance to actual events, locales, organizations, or persons, living or dead, is entirely coincidental.

AVON BOOKS
An Imprint of HarperCollins*Publishers*
195 Broadway
New York, New York 10007

Copyright © 2015 by Jennifer Bernard
ISBN 978-0-06-237216-1
www.avonromance.com

First Avon Books mass market printing: June 2015

Avon Trademark Reg. U.S. Pat. Off. and in Other Countries, Marca Registrada, Hecho en U.S.A.
HarperCollins® is a registered trademark of HarperCollins Publishers.

Printed in the U.S.A.

10 9 8 7 6 5 4 3 2 1

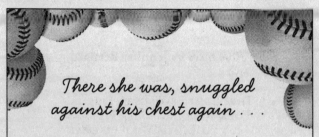

*There she was, snuggled
against his chest again . . .*

"There, that's better," he said with satisfaction, the words rumbling against her ear. "I kinda like this whole fishing thing."

"No fair, I got distracted," she protested, turning her body in the circle of his arms so she could see his face. Water streamed from his hair, down his neck to his wide shoulders. "I'd forgotten how much I love swimming in this lake."

As he watched her something shifted in his expression. His goofy smile vanished, replaced by an intent, hungry look. His head lowered, eyes glittering.

Oh wow. He was going to kiss her.

His lips burned against hers, sending pure shock throughout her body. Kisses didn't feel like that. They didn't turn your lips to fire, they didn't liquefy your lungs so you could barely breathe.

Sadie pulled away with a gasp. He looked just as stunned. Water lapped against her hips, and a breath of air kissed her shoulder. Everywhere her body touched Caleb's, heat seared.

And then they were on each other again.

This book is dedicated to everyone who
has ever spent a sunlit day at the ballpark,
and to the players who make that joy possible.

Acknowledgments

I'd like to thank Sierra Dean, Kristy Birch, and LizBeth Selvig for their help with baseball and other key elements of this story. Thanks to Tessa Woodward and Elle Keck for seeing this manuscript through to completion, and to Alexandra Machinist for her early support. My baseball memories go way back to childhood, so special thanks to my father for introducing me to the greatest game in the world. My reader group continues to amaze me with their generosity. Lastly, much love to my family for their unswerving support and patience. I couldn't do any of this without you.

All of Me

Chapter 1

IN **C**ALEB **H**ART'S first start as a Kilby Catfish, he set a minor league record—and not the good kind. By the top of the fourth inning he'd given up seven runs, five homers, three walks, and nearly taken El Paso Chihuahua Steve Hunter's nose off with a wayward fastball. Sweat was running down his back in rivulets of failure, and under his brand-new cap, with its cartoonish blue catfish logo, his head felt as if it might spontaneously ignite.

He stepped off the mound and swiped his arm across his forehead. Mike Solo, the catcher, called for time, the pitching coach jogged onto the field, and suddenly his new infielders surrounded him. Apparently they thought he needed some support. What he really needed was . . . well, he hadn't quite figured that out yet.

"You can take this guy," said the tattooed first baseman, Sonny Barnes. "He can't hit the changeup for shit."

Caleb didn't bother mentioning that he couldn't *throw* the changeup for shit.

"Just keep 'em down," said Mitch, the pitching coach, clearly some kind of baseball genius. "And get 'em over the plate."

"That's right, you're overthinking it," said the fast-talking shortstop, who looked about twelve. "I saw you pitch with the Twins. Over three games you had an ERA of 2.78, average of five strikeouts per game. 'Course, then you had that crazy fourth game. Whatever you do, don't think about *that game*. Do what you did during the first three. Forget the fourth. Easy peasy."

Caleb stared at the smaller player, trying to remember the last time he'd heard a baseball player say "easy peasy." Never, that's when. And why'd he have to bring up the worst game of his entire life?

Solo, the only guy on the team Caleb had played with before, gave a wolfish grin and a wink. "Yeah, easy peasy, big guy. The natives are getting restless. And since it's Texas, they're probably armed."

Caleb looked at the half-full stands, where the crowd of maybe three thousand diehards was starting to shout catcalls. For a painful moment he remembered the noise level at Target Field in Minneapolis. It was like comparing a 747 jet to a mosquito. But the Twins had traded him to the San Diego Friars, and the Friars had sent him down to their Triple A team in Kilby, and here he was. Blowing it.

The pitching coach headed back to the dugout, with an air of having done all he could. Caleb glared at the remaining players. "What is this, a damn committee meeting?"

The baby shortstop looked offended. "Excuse me for trying to help you resurrect the correct firing of your synapses."

Caleb looked incredulously at the other Catfish. "Is this kid for real?"

"He was studying brains before he signed on," explained Mike Solo.

"Not brains. Neurophysiology," piped up the shortstop as everyone scattered, jogging back to their positions.

Christ. He'd heard the Catfish were a little . . . odd. So far that seemed to be an understatement.

Caleb settled himself back on the mound, inhaling a deep breath of humid, grass-scented air. *It's just a baseball game. Pretend you're back home, when baseball was the only fun thing in life. When you ruled the diamond, any diamond.*

Solo called for the fastball, low and away. Good call, since an inside pitch might hurt someone, the way he was pitching, and his changeup wasn't doing shit today. He went into his windup, lined the seams up just right in his hand, and let fly.

Boom. Home run number six cracked off the bat with a sound like a detonation. Maybe it was his career blowing up, come to think of it.

Just to torture himself, Caleb swiveled to watch the ball soar high overhead, winging toward the right field bleachers like a bird on speed. Lowering his gaze, he caught the shortstop's reproachful stare. The Chihuahua batter cruised around the bases. The guy ought to send him a thank-you note, the way he'd served up that pitch with extra biscuits and gravy.

Someone cleared his throat behind him. He turned to find Duke, the Catfish manager, facing him, hand outstretched. He wanted the ball. Wanted him out of the game. But as much as Caleb hated giving up home runs, he hated giving up the ball more. How could he turn things around if he got yanked from the game?

"I'm just trying to get my rhythm going, Duke," Caleb said in a low voice.

"And how's that working out for you?"

Sarcasm. Ouch. "My last pitch had to have been in the upper nineties."

"Yup. It sure went over the fence fast." Duke, a barrel-chested former catcher, didn't sugarcoat things. "I'm taking you out before your ERA looks like a Texas heat wave. Let's talk after the game."

A sickening sensation made Caleb's gut clench. In the minor leagues, being called into the manager's office was either good news—you were being called up to the major league team—or bad news of a variety of kinds. Caleb was a hundred percent sure he wasn't being called up.

"Nothing bad," Duke assured him. "Just want to talk."

Caleb nodded, and handed him the ball. It felt like handing over a piece of his heart. He needed the ball, needed to pitch. Because the only chance he had in life was when he had that ball in his hands.

Walking toward the dugout, he caught a "shake it off" from the third baseman, along with a rumble of boos from the stands. His replacement, Dan Farrio, ran onto the field from the bullpen. Farrio was, theoretically, his rival for one of the spots on the Friars pitching staff. But after today that rivalry might be history.

From someone's radio, he heard the color announcer saying, "We're checking the history books, but one-time blue-chip prospect Caleb Hart just had possibly the worst first start ever on a Triple A team. He should have been pulled after the second inning, but the Catfish bullpen's about as ragged as my kid's blankie. If the Caleb Hart trade was supposed to add some juice to the Friars pitching staff, maybe they should have gone with a shot of the cactus instead. How much you want to bet Crush Taylor's squeezing the limes already?"

At the mention of the owner of the Catfish, Caleb groaned. No one cared what most minor league owners thought, since the major league front office culled all the *chura But Crush Taylor* was a legend, a Hall of Fame pitcher who had purchased the Catfish shortly after his retirement. Not to mention that he was Caleb's childhood idol.

He'd just had a record-setting horrendous start for the team owned by his childhood idol. And he'd been lectured by a shortstop barely out of high school. Could things get any worse?

He reached the dugout and grabbed a drink of water at the cooler. Man, it was hot today. All he wanted to do was hit the showers and get the hell out of this stadium. But since it was his first game, he ought to stick around and support the team. Before he could sink onto the bench, Duke caught his eye and gave him a jerk of the head, releasing him to retire to the clubhouse.

First break he'd gotten all day. He seized the opportunity and stalked out of the dugout. He'd get to know his fellow Catfish sometime when he didn't want to knock someone's head off.

As soon as he entered the rabbit's warren of back corridors that wound through the stadium, his tightly maintained control disappeared. He ripped off his sweat-soaked uniform shirt as if he could ditch the sense of failure along with it.

"Damn," he bit out, slamming a fist against the wall. "Get it together, Hart." He usually kept his emotions under tight wrap, but . . . *damn it*. If he screwed this up, he'd be letting down his sister and brothers, and they'd all been through enough. His entire family was depending on him, and he'd just given up six home runs in about five minutes. His frustration boiled over.

"What the hell is wrong with you? You can't afford another freaking fuckup." Veering around the corner toward the home clubhouse, he nearly tripped over someone standing at the double doors that guarded the entrance.

The someone pushed an elbow into his stomach, making the breath whoosh out of him. It wasn't a hard blow, probably accidental, but still, not what he normally encountered on his way to the shower.

Struggling to get his breath back—and his composure—he steadied his attacker. A woman, a young one. Though he still hadn't gotten a good look at her, she felt soft and shapely under his hands.

"Geez, you should watch where you're going." Her voice had a drawling, husky cadence; a local girl. She stepped out of his grasp and spun to face him. He received a quick impression of brilliant but wary dark eyes, quicksilver slimness, and a haphazard ponytail. He was six feet five inches, but he didn't tower over her as much as he did most girls. He guessed she was at least five-ten, with a lanky, slim build, all arms and legs. She held a manila folder filled with papers about to spill out. "You must be one of those crazy Catfish players."

"What clued you in? The uniform or the overuse of profanity?" He gave her a rueful smile, remembering his exuberant cursing. He should have waited until he was *inside* the clubhouse, but he hadn't expected to run into anyone. Let alone someone like her.

Something sparked in her eyes, and her lips quirked. "Well, I guess it must be the profanity, since I don't see much in the way of a uniform." She glanced down his torso. He remembered he was bare-chested, having ditched his shirt.

"Yeah, well . . . had to let off a little steam."

"So that was you cussing up a storm? I thought I was about to get trampled like a barrel of grapes."

"No trampling, I promise." From the gleam in her

eye, she was probably teasing, but just in case, he took a step back. Again her gaze flicked down his chest, as if she couldn't help it. "I'm not coming on to you either. Too sweaty. But if you want to hang around until after my shower . . ."

He said that mostly to get a rise out of her, since something told him she'd be fun to get all riled up.

But her face changed, the playful sparkle vanishing. She took a big step back and narrowed her eyes at him. "No, I do not. I want to deliver this message and get on with my day. Can you tell me where to find Mr. Ellington?"

Ellington—that was Duke's last name. Most baseball guys had a nickname, though not many were named after jazz greats. What did this girl want with Duke?

"He's busy bossing around baseball players. I guarantee he wouldn't want to be interrupted." He folded his arms over his chest. Excellent. Now those lively dark eyes were taking in his forearms as well as his torso. Usually, at this point, a girl would do something to signal her willingness to spend intimate time with the hotshot pitcher who'd gotten half a million dollars for signing with the Twins.

Not this girl. "I can see you want to be difficult, which is exactly what I would expect, given the contents of this document." She tapped the folder. "Fine. In the interests of moving on with our lives—you to your shower and probably a six-pack and a groupie—why don't you give me a hint about where Mr. Ellington's office might be? I'll wait for him there."

Holy RBI. This girl could certainly talk. Her face moved as she spoke, her eyes danced; every bit of her seemed alive and in motion. She looked to be in her early twenties and had a sort of student-gypsy vibe about her. Her lips curved in a way that suggested she liked to laugh . . . and talk, and tease. She wore a tight white T-shirt molded to high, pretty breasts, and a flowery skirt that ended just above her knees. And red cowboy boots. Damn. How could he resist red cowboy boots? Those things ought to be banned.

He plucked the folder from her hand. "Got a pen? You seem like the kind of girl who would have a pen."

"What's that supposed to mean? And yes. But no. Why?"

"Want to clarify any of that?" He raised an eyebrow at her, while trying to get a surreptitious peek at the typing on the document inside the folder. *Whereas we, the residents of Kilby County,* it began.

She snatched the folder back. "Yes, I have a pen. No, you can't write on the petition. And why do you want to?"

He put on a wounded expression. "I was going to draw you a map. These passageways can be superconfusing. It's completely understandable that you got lost and found yourself at the place where the guys get undressed." He winked, watching the flush rise in her cheeks. Yes, she was definitely fun to get riled up.

Then her words sank in. "Petition? What petition?" He tried to take the folder back, but she whisked it out of his reach. He barely missed grabbing her breast instead.

Before he could apologize, she stepped back with an exaggerated gasp of outrage. "There you go again. You Catfish really are a menace to decent society. Just like the petition says."

"What?"

"That's right." She waved the folder. "They say you're completely out of control."

Caleb had heard the talk about the Catfish too. They liked to party a little too much, and they indulged in the occasional bar-clearing brawl, but then, they were fun-loving young baseball players, so what could you expect? Anyway, it wasn't his problem. He intended to put Kilby in his rearview mirror as soon as possible. "I wouldn't know. Can't say that I care either."

"So the stories are true? Did you guys really fill the community pool with rubber catfish? I heard the senior exercise group had quite a scare and had to call the paramedics."

He snorted.

She shook her head sadly. "Things sure have changed since I came to games as a kid. And to think I thought it was safe here for a nice, civilized girl like me. Next time I'll make sure to bring a bodyguard."

A *bodyguard*? Now that was taking it a little too . . . He caught the gleam of mischief she hid under the sweep of her eyelashes. Damn. He'd been right before. She *was* teasing him.

Whether it was the incredible frustration of the last two hours, on top of the preceding frustration of being sent down, then traded—throw in the never-ending worry about his family—whatever the cause, all his emotions boiled over in that moment. In two quick steps he crowded her against the wall—no contact, just heat and sweat and closeness.

He growled in her ear, his lips almost brushing the delicate skin there. "There's only one way to find out if the stories are true. But you have to want it. Bad. You have to be so hot for it, you come chasing after me and beg for it. Then you have to prove you can handle it. Put that in your petition."

She stared up at him, her pupils dilated so far her eyes looked black, with a rim of glowing amber. The little pulse in her neck beat like a drum.

All of a sudden his cock was so hard his vision

blurred. *Damn.* Where had that come from? She wasn't even his type. In fact, she was on the irritating end of the female spectrum.

He let her go as if she was a grenade about to explode. "Duke's office is down the hall to your right."

Pushing open the clubhouse door, he headed directly for the shower. It was going to have to be a cold one.

Chapter 2

AFTER WATCHING THE baseball player walk away—the rear view just as breathtaking as the front—Sadie Merritt took a full two minutes to wrestle her breathing back to normal. Normal-*ish*. Good Lord, that was one sexy man. It wasn't just the muscles, though those were hard to miss. She'd never seen anything like his sculpted, rippling torso. But really, it wasn't about his looks. It was the way he talked, the things he said, the way he looked at her. As if he wanted to rip her clothes off right there in the hallway.

The best part—he didn't know who she was. He hadn't heard any of the nasty gossip. Probably none of the ballplayers had, since they tended to come and go. And she'd *flirted* with him, sort of. And blatantly ogled him. She hadn't done anything remotely flirtatious since Hamilton Wade had decimated her reputation before the entire town of Kilby. She'd avoided guys since then, and definitely hadn't teased any. But something about that Catfish player brought out her mischievous side, which she'd thought was dead and gone forever.

What had he said about the manager's office? Down the hall somewhere. She hurried down the corridor, which smelled faintly of dirty socks. Forget the ballplayer. Had she learned *nothing* from her experience with Hamilton Wade? Rule number one: no spoiled, good-looking boys. Actually, make that no spoiled, good-looking, *athletic* boys. No boys at all would be the smartest way to go.

The baseball player was no boy, however. He was entirely, one-hundred-percent *man*.

Didn't matter. He was probably one of the bad boy troublemakers who'd gotten her boss, Mayor Wendy Trent, and the Ladies' Auxiliary of Kilby, so upset. She wasn't here to ogle baseball players, she was here to do her job. A job she was extremely lucky to have. After Hamilton's nasty smear campaign, no one had wanted to hire her. She'd fought tooth and nail for this job. Doing it well meant everything to her. Self-respect, sanity, pride . . . everything.

She heard the distant sound of clapping and the occasional thump-thump of feet overhead. Spying a door, she cautiously opened it, only to encounter a warm rush of air carrying the summery sound of laughing male voices. Blinking in the sudden sunlight, she got an eyeful of green grass, dotted with a blur of white and blue uniforms.

Oops, she must have taken a wrong turn. Everyone was running off the field, so the game had to be over. Quickly, she pulled the door shut and nearly ran in the other direction. The last thing she wanted was to run into that ballplayer again. That half-naked hunk of a ballplayer. Annoyingly, he hadn't even smelled bad, despite his sweaty state. He'd smelled like sun-heated flesh and oiled leather. He'd radiated furious energy, a kind of restless power, as if he wanted to shake up the world and put it back the way he wanted.

She felt exactly the same way.

Finally she spotted a door marked MANAGER. It stood

ajar. She knocked lightly, then stepped in at a "Yeah" that could have been the bark of a Chihuahua.

The man at the desk scowled at her from under a Kilby Catfish cap. Geez, did everyone on the team have a bad attitude? This man, with the build of a bloated pit bull, looked nothing like the blue-eyed god outside the locker room.

Actually, the god's eyes had been more gray than blue, like the sky reflected off steel.

Forget him. "Hi, I'm Sadie Merritt. I'm here representing a group of local residents who have prepared a petition."

"I don't sign petitions." He waved her off and turned back to the pile of papers on his desk.

She set her teeth. Mayor Trent hadn't sent her here to get dismissed like a pesky schoolgirl. "Well, sir, you definitely wouldn't want to sign this one, unless you're just as fed up with your team as the rest of Kilby is. If even half the stories are true, you must have your work cut out for you. How *do* you keep up? Do you read the daily police blotter?"

His head snapped up. "What the hell are you talking about?"

A-ha. Now she had his attention. "The petition. I work for the mayor of Kilby, who is quite concerned about your team."

"Did you say you work for the mayor?" A drawling voice cut in from across the room. She swung in that direction and saw a man in his late forties lounging in a chair, legs crossed at the ankles. She recognized him at once. Crush Taylor, legendary playboy pitcher and owner of the Catfish. He looked like he had a hangover.

"Yes. I'm Mayor Trent's assistant."

The manager surged to his feet. "Let me get a look at

that thing. Petition, huh? This team is going to fucking kill me. Where are my goddamn glasses?"

He fumbled around the desk until finally Crush said, "In your pocket, Duke."

He snatched them up, said, "Give me the highlights. It's not like this day could get worse. Do you know what it's like to lose by eleven runs? And to have your star pitcher set a record for a first-start shellacking?"

"No." She wondered if the baseball god with the killer ass was the star pitcher in question.

"Start at the beginning. Who are you again?"

"My name is Sadie Merritt. I work for the mayor."

"You know the one, Duke. Always looks like she's chewing on ice cubes," said Crush with a yawn.

"What does this have to do with me? I'm running a baseball team here. Well, most days. Today I'm not sure what the fuck I'm doing."

"Maybe I'd better just read the petition," said Sadie. Before either man could object, she raised the page to eye level. " 'Whereas we, the below-signed residents of Kilby, are shocked and appalled by the reprehensible behavior of the Pacific Coast League baseball team known as the Catfish, we hereby demand that the team relocate to another city or prove their fitness to reside in Kilby.' "

Duke held up a hand to stop her. "Hang on. You're saying Kilby wants us out? That's stupid. Kilby loves us."

"Not all of Kilby loves you." She rattled the paper at him. "We have hundreds of signatures here."

"And I have thousands of people at the games. I got every business in town wanting a promotional night. Know what today is?"

She shook her head.

"Kilby Fire Department day. We had a fireman throw out the first pitch in full turnout gear. This town loves us. The whole county does. Kilby's the smallest town in the country with a Triple A team."

"I know that. Maybe it's time the team moved to a bigger city, one that won't mind the unruly—"

Duke flung one arm toward a whiteboard positioned in the corner of the room. "Baseball is all about numbers, Ms. Merritt. My guys are here to put up numbers that will get them to San Diego. The team could play in Pig-Fuck, Nebraska, for all they care. What matters are ERAs, slugging percentage, on base percentage, RBIs . . ."

"I'm not here to argue, Mr. Ellington." Truthfully, she couldn't really argue. The petition was pretty ridiculous. Who didn't love baseball? Sure, the Kilby Catfish were a little rowdy. But she used to love coming to the games, and she'd mourn if they actually left town. Not that her personal opinion mattered.

She turned to Crush Taylor. He was the team owner, after all. "A portion of the Kilby community is appalled by your team's behavior. You know, if they cared about their reputation, they shouldn't have detoured the team bus to that nude beach. Or maybe they should stop holding player meetings at Charlie's Showgirls. Or—here's a thought—maybe they shouldn't have filled an entire hot tub with beer for some guy's birthday."

"St. Vincent," Crush Taylor muttered.

"What?"

"Nick St. Vincent. Best young prospect I've seen in thirty years. Guy like that turns twenty-one, you gotta celebrate."

She stared at the owner. He didn't seem too concerned about this situation, and it was starting to irritate her.

"Mr. Taylor, this is a petition to 'Can the Catfish.' I think you should take it a little more seriously. Don't you think it's going to be a little embarrassing to the San Diego Friars when this story gets out?"

Can the Catfish. The words seemed to echo through the cluttered room. The two men stared at her for a long moment. Someone let out a gurgle of a laugh.

Just then the man from the hallway poked his head around the door. He must have showered. His damp, slightly shaggy, tawny brown hair clung to his temples, setting off a strong-featured face with the sort of cheekbones that belonged on a billboard somewhere. Those steel-blue eyes held a troubled, stormy expression.

His big hand wrapped around the edge of the door. When he caught sight of her, his knuckles whitened.

"I can come back," he said, and made to withdraw.

"No," Crush said quickly. He rose to his feet and ambled toward the door. "Come in, Caleb. Duke has a job for you." The owner stuck out his hand for Sadie to shake. "Ms. Merritt, I appreciate you coming in today. We're going to work on finding a solution to this . . . uh . . . dreadful impasse. Is your number somewhere on here?"

"Yes, it's on the press release attached to the petition."

"Good. I'm sure we can find a way to make the mayor happy." Smoothly, he dropped a pair of designer aviator glasses over his eyes and made his exit, while the baseball player stepped inside the office.

Duke clutched his head as if it were about to explode and clenched his teeth. "Ms. Merritt. Would you mind very much if I spoke to my pitcher for a moment? We'll be in touch. Guaranteed."

"Of course. Thank you for your time." She got to her feet, offering both men a wide smile.

The baseball player—Caleb—held the door open for her exit, and she ducked under his arm. She shivered as she passed by, as if some sort of force field surrounded him. Something electrifying and confusing and . . . *Sigh.*

She headed for the parking lot and looked for her old Corolla. As requested, she called Mayor Trent to let her know the deed was done.

"Did you speak with Crush Taylor or just the manager?"

"Both." Along with the sexiest man she'd ever witnessed. "Mr. Taylor didn't seem too worried, but they said they're going to call. My guess is that they will. I think I got their attention. What do you want me to do next?"

"Come on back. They got the message, and that's all I wanted. If we can reform the Catfish even a little bit, we'll have done good work." The missionary zeal in the mayor's tone made Sadie chew on her bottom lip. Reform the Catfish? The testosterone-loaded men in that office hadn't looked very reformable.

But Mayor Trent hadn't hired her to argue.

Caleb reluctantly took a seat in the chair just vacated by the girl in the red cowboy boots. It was still slightly warm, and he beat back the image of her tall, slender body perched there.

"Before you say anything, I already talked to Mitch. I'm going to throw a few bullpens so he can check out my mechanics."

"It's not your mechanics," said Duke bluntly.

"I think I'm throwing across my body a little too much."

"It's not that."

Caleb pressed the heel of his hand into his forehead. "It's like someone cursed me," he muttered. "That's the only thing I can come up with. One day I'm throwing missiles, the next I'm a pinball machine. That game last season—"

"We're not talking about last season. Can't do anything about that. You know what I thought when I heard they traded you here?"

"How can I get out of my contract?"

Duke let out a raucous laugh. "Hell no, you don't scare me. How long have I known you?"

"Five . . . six years." Duke had been Caleb's very first manager back in Double A. Back then he'd been a wild flamethrower with zero control and a bloodthirsty competitive urge.

"I always knew you were a special player. And your family situation . . . well, that lit a fire under your ass."

"Is there a point here?" The last thing he wanted to do was talk about his family. Duke knew about his father because he'd had to ask for an advance on his signing bonus when both twins broke their legs playing ninja on the roof. No one else knew, and that's the way he liked to keep it.

"You always threw like your life depended on it. Whatever fueled you, it was working. Something's changed inside your head. I don't know what it is. But if you don't figure it out, you can forget San Diego. Hell, you can forget Wichisaukee low A. Maybe you don't need it anymore. Maybe you're done with baseball and want to go race cars or something."

Caleb bolted to his feet. With this kind of bullshit coming at him, he couldn't sit in that chair one more second. "I'm not done with baseball." Even the thought made him sick down to the bone. "I'll get it together, Duke. It's a new team, new league. It's a new day. You'll see."

Duke popped a giant hunk of gum into his mouth, where it bulged in his cheek. "There's nothing you want to tell me about your home life? Something that might shed a little light?"

"No. Absolutely not."

Nothing he would ever, *could* ever, mention to his manager or anyone on the Catfish.

Duke squinted at him. "Fine. We'll see how it goes. I'm keeping you in the lineup. Work with Mitch. And call this girl." He pushed the petition across the desk. "If you can't be the pitching star you're meant to be, at least you can do some PR for the team."

"Call her for *what*?"

"Figure something out. It's a bunch of ladies who have their panties in a wad over those nasty, rowdy baseball players. Pour on the charm. Use that smile of yours. Or come up with some charity thing that'll make them happy."

"No."

"This'll be a good distraction for you. Maybe you're overthinking things out there."

Caleb ground his teeth. "It's a waste of my time."

"You want in my lineup?"

"Yes."

"Then you're doing this."

If Duke took him out of the lineup for too long, the San Diego farm director would be on his ass. His semi-big-money contract meant they expected him to produce at some point. But he didn't need a feud with Duke, who was actually his favorite of all the managers he'd played for.

"I'll think about it," he said, and to lighten the tension, gave a slight wink. "But not overthink it."

Chapter 3

As a lifelong resident of Kilby, Sadie knew its good points and horrible points. On the plus side, it was a lovely, family-oriented town known for its Spanish-mission-style architecture and plentitude of parks. The city had originated as a ranch owned by the Wade family back in the late 1800s, which brought her to the worst aspect of Kilby. The Wades still acted like they owned the place. Gossip ran rampant, and the Wades had their fingers in every pie.

Including the pie of Sadie Merritt, the only girl reckless enough to dump a member of the Wade family. After their breakup, Hamilton and the rest of the Wades had spread disgusting rumors about her, posted private things on Facebook, and convinced the entire city of Kilby she was a heartless, conniving slut.

And then, the final mortifying blow—the "Birthday Sex Tape."

For weeks before Hamilton's twenty-first birthday, he'd begged her to do a striptease for him. With real stripper clothes and music. She'd given it her best shot, dirty-dancing to "Don't You Wish Your Girlfriend Was Hot Like Me" in nothing but a thong—even though she hated both the song and thongs. She had no clue that Hamilton had secretly set up a video camera and recorded the whole thing. Including what came after the striptease. The tape didn't show *everything*, thank God. It ended with her naked on the bed, posing like a wannabe porn star, while Hamilton's bare quarterback ass moved across the screen; people could pretty much imagine what came next. The tape made her look sleazy, porny, and also embarrassingly uncoordinated.

She didn't even know it existed until it started appearing in e-mail in-boxes all over town and someone forwarded it to her. Why would anyone believe that she didn't *do* that sort of thing? That it was a one-time thing, a girl trying to please her boyfriend, with no clue it was being taped? Especially when Hamilton was also busy with the S****y Sadie Facebook page, filled with embarrassing photos and nasty posts. Mortified beyond endurance, she'd barely left the house for a month, afraid to face the mocking eyes of her former friends.

Her mother, always teetering on the edge of depression, had taken a medical leave from her job at Kroger. Sadie moved back home to take care of her, which meant coaxing her mom through crying jags about the callousness of males. Only a combination of humor and stubbornness—and the need for a job—had pulled Sadie out of the pit.

It had taken her over a year to land this position as the mayor's assistant. Mayor Trent, a school friend of Sadie's mother, had been elected on a platform that promised a fresh start while preserving the best of Kilby. Sadie was a hundred percent behind the "fresh start" part.

When she got back to her tiny cubicle in the Kilby City Hall, with its ornate bell tower, it was nearly 5:00 P.M. and Mayor Trent was in her office with the door closed. Sadie sank into her seat and pulled out the bottle of iced tea and tuna sandwich she'd grabbed at the 7-Eleven. Taking a bite, she logged onto her computer and scanned through the e-mails that had come in. The usual requests for appointments with the mayor, complaints about potholes in the roads, and invitations to charity events.

Sadie loved working for the mayor, even though the job was easy—taking calls, filing, keeping track of her schedule. Mayor Trent had recently started giving her more responsibilities, such as drafting press releases and leading meetings. She woke up every day determined to prove herself and put the "scandal" behind her. By giving her a chance, Mayor Trent had won her undying loyalty.

She still remembered how much her heart had pounded as the mayor, stern and blond, like a Norwegian ice queen with extra hair spray, silently examined her résumé while she sat in the "supplicant" chair, as she thought of it, slightly lower than the desk. "I shouldn't even consider you for this job. You know how much heat I'll get if I hire you."

"Yes. I know that, Mayor. But your whole campaign is about fresh starts, right? That's all I want. A fresh start. A second chance. I made a mistake getting involved with Hamilton. But doesn't everyone deserve a second chance?"

"Not in the Wades' view. That family knows how to carry a grudge."

"I know," Sadie said miserably. "And no one wants to go against them. They're too powerful. I have a college degree, *with honors,* and I've had exactly one job offer. Charlie's Showgirls. They like scandal." She saw the mayor's mouth twist, and added quickly, "But I don't. I despise scandal. I just want to find a job I care about, keep my head down and work my butt off. If I get this position, I swear I'll pour my heart and soul into it."

"Well . . ." The mayor tilted her head, her smooth cheekbones catching the light like marble. "All right. I'm going to hire you. I despise the way the Wades are handling this situation. It's shameful. And your mother and I are old friends. But I want you to keep a low profile. Your behavior must be impeccable. We can't give them any ammunition."

"I won't," said Sadie firmly. After the trauma of becoming the most notorious girl in Kilby, she never wanted the spotlight again. "I promise. I'll be the best assistant you ever had, I swear."

"I'm sure you'll be the most interesting." Finally, a smile ghosted across the mayor's perfectly pink lips.

Employed! That fact still made her giddy, nearly six months later.

Sadie had barely taken two bites of her sandwich when the red button on her phone lit up. Mayor Trent needed her. Quickly brushing the crumbs off her hands and taking a swig of tea to get rid of tuna breath, she collected her notepad and joined the mayor in her office.

Her heart sank when she saw who was in the "supplicant" chair. Brett Carlisle, a raging stoner from high school, someone who'd partied hard with Hamilton and his friends. What if he was here to badmouth or humiliate her in some way? Hamilton was very creative in his revenge tactics. Once he'd sent seven orders of Marie Callender's honey-glazed ham to her house. A picture had gone on Facebook with the caption, "Slutty Sadie gettin' ready to suck down some Ham."

She gave Brett a cool, professional nod and sat down, poised to take notes.

"Sadie, this is the head of Kilby's new Save Our Slugs campaign," said Mayor Trent warmly. "It's a group dedicated to preserving the habitat of the horn-toed slug."

She smothered her involuntary laugh behind a fake cough. "Good one," she muttered under her breath.

"Excuse me?" the mayor asked, her smile slipping.

"I said, that's a good cause. I'd love to hear more about it."

She shot Brett a suspicious glance, but he looked nothing but innocent. Too innocent? Dread lanced through her belly. When would Hamilton move on from his stupid vendetta?

"The Kilby area is one of the few remaining population centers for the horn-toed slug," continued the mayor. "Places like Lake McGee and the Kilby River are essential for their survival. And they happen to be iconic landmarks for longtime Kilby residents. This fits in perfectly with my campaign promise to preserve the traditional Kilby way of life. Not only that, my niece Katie did her science project on the horn-toed slug. I intend to put the full support of the mayor's office behind this effort."

Sadie had a bad feeling about this. "But Mayor, what about the group working on more humane treatment for immigrants at the border, or the healthy school lunch—?"

"No controversies. I like this project. Horn-toed slugs are unlikely to become a hot button issue. They're local, they're harmless, and they're boring. Win-win-win."

"Well, then, that's great news," Sadie said with her widest, fakest smile. "Maybe I can ask Brett a few questions about it before he goes."

Brett spread his hands apart with a vague wink. "I'm all yours."

The possible double entendre almost made her gag. If this was a Hamilton prank, he'd really gone too far.

"Sit down with him and brainstorm some ideas, Sadie," Mayor Trent said. "I have dinner at the Elks Lodge tonight, but I'd like you to report back to me next week."

She nodded at them both in dismissal.

As soon as she and Brett were safely out of the office with the door closed, Sadie wheeled on him. "This better be real. And if it isn't, you'd better start caring about some poor endangered slugs, like *now*."

"Babe, babe . . ." He made to put a hand on her shoulder, but she shook it off. She'd rather shoot herself than let anyone connected with Hamilton put a hand on her body. "It's real. See?" He tugged at his T-shirt, which she now saw had an urgent S.O.S. printed on it in bright orange, with the *ave . . . ur . . . lugs* in smaller letters.

"Since when do you care so much about slugs?"

"I did some 'shrooms out at the lake, had a vision. The slugs starting singing to me, begging for help. Said I was the chosen one."

"The chosen one of *the slugs*?"

He shrugged. "When you get the call, you can't turn away."

"Seriously, is this some kind of joke? Is Hamilton behind this?" Her stomach was still roiling with anxiety—exactly how she'd felt ever since the breakup.

"Ham? Nah. I haven't partied with him in a while."

Still wary, she scrutinized his pleasant, vacant face. Come to think of it, he'd never been part of Hamilton's inner circle. He was more of a hanger-on, in it for the constant flow of weed and money.

"Okay. I'm choosing to believe you. Let's set up a call in the next couple of days."

"Listen to you, all professional. Sure, let's set up a call. Right on. Oh, and Sadie . . ." He bumped against her and whispered in her ear, "If you ever want to do that thing Hamilton said you liked, you know, with the chocolate syrup and the licking and—"

She shoved him aside. "Hamilton is a *liar*. Everything he said is a lie. Why can't anyone understand that?" Brushing past him, she went to her desk. She wouldn't let him see that he'd upset her.

"Fine, fine." Brett trailed after her. "No skin off my nose. I'm not part of that scene anymore. I stopped smoking a year ago. I'm serious about the slugs, Sadie. I know it sounds different, but I've been working hard to put this group together. We're trying to get the horntoeds on the protected list, and we're getting real close. The more positive attention we can bring to the issue, the better our chances."

"Good." Well, maybe he did know what he was talking about. Briskly, she picked up her day planner. "How's Thursday?"

After Brett left, she walked quickly down the hall to the ladies' restroom, which fortunately was empty. Her hands shaking, she ran the water in the sink, sucking in deep, shuddering breaths. This was a trick she'd clung to during the worst of the Hamilton Disaster. The sound of running water soothed her, and washing her hands made her feel less dirty.

Oh, fireballs. She refused to let Hamilton and his friends shake her up like this.

"It's okay," she muttered to herself in the mirror. "I'm okay. He can't hurt me worse than he already has." She didn't actually know if this was true, but it sounded good. Her eyes looked huge and worried, and a few flecks of mascara had migrated to her cheekbone. For a silly moment she wondered if she'd been this disheveled while talking to Caleb Hart, the baseball player.

Why would he care? Why would she care if he cared? If she knew one thing, it was that spoiled rich athletes were poison. Hamilton was a star high school quarterback and came from the richest family in town, after all. Never again. *Never* again. No boys. Even if Caleb the Catfish did make her feel alive again. Alive and fizzy and fun. As if the moment he'd knocked into her had woken her up from a coma.

Forget him.

Her phone rang. She dried off her hands and answered.

"Hey bestie. I have to get out of here. What are you doing tonight?" Donna MacIntyre, the only friend who had stuck by her after the "scandal," was a live-in nanny for a wealthy family. She was allowed to go out one night a week, and she made the most of it.

"What I always do."

"You can't hide in your cubicle forever."

"Are you sure about that?"

"I'm picking you up at eight. We're goin' out. Have you forgotten it's my birthday?"

Sadie smacked her forehead with her palm. "Oh *crap*. I'm so sorry, Donna."

"Yep, it's my birthday, and I'm going to get wild tonight. I need a wing woman."

"N—" Sadie snapped her mouth against the automatic no. She owed Donna so much. Without her, she would have been utterly friendless during the worst time of her life. "Fine. I have to go home and change, and check on my mom."

"I have a dress for you. It's a birthday present from me to you."

More guilt stabbed at her. "A present? I didn't—"

"You can buy me a drink, or several. And come out with me. And have fun like the young, gorgeous thing you are. I'm tired of you hiding away like you have something to be ashamed of. You *don't*, Sadie. Let people talk. Fuck 'em."

"How many drinks have you had already?"

"A little sip of Mr. Gilbert's whiskey, s'all. The Shark took a billion hours to put to sleep tonight."

Donna called her eight-month-old charge the "Shark" because he required constant motion.

Sadie sighed. "I'll pick you up. See you at eight."

"Or a little sooner."

"Soon as I can."

Back at her desk, she called her mother to let her know she'd be home late. From the sound of her sleepy voice, she knew her mom was already dozing off to the sound of a mystery book on tape. When she wasn't on her medication, her mother found life overwhelming, and tended to fall asleep at every opportunity. During the worst of the post-Hamilton drama, she'd refused to even answer the phone; she'd done nothing but listen to the entire Stephanie Plum series on tape. "All right, sugar. You be careful, hear?"

"I will."

"I mean it, Sadie. Stick with your girlfriends. Don't trust any of those boys."

"I think I've learned my lesson. Get some sleep, Mom. And don't forget to eat. I left some spaghetti in the refrigerator."

Her mother yawned. "You shouldn't worry about that. At my age one meal a day is more than enough." After she hung up, Sadie heaved a huge sigh, wondering if she should skip her date with Donna and hand-feed her mother some french fries instead.

She propped her chin on one hand, heart aching for her mom. Brenda Merritt had always been fearful of men—possibly because she'd gotten knocked up by a married pharmaceuticals salesman who conveniently lost his ring when he went on the road. Her whole life, Sadie had been warned about the male gender. The Hamilton Disaster had made it so much worse. Her mother never blamed her for the fiasco—always Hamilton, which made Sadie feel funny. She wasn't sure she liked being lumped into the "screwed over by a man" club.

Mayor Trent came out of her office dressed in a black dress and discreet pearls, her hair teased and sprayed into camera-ready perfection. With her briefcase in one hand and an umbrella in the other, she looked like everything Sadie wanted to be. Cool, poised, untouchable—the mistress of her universe.

"Good night, Sadie. Thanks for all your hard work."

Sadie wanted to bow down before her like a devotee before a goddess. A former Miss Texas and the first female mayor of Kilby, Wendy Trent was someone she had always admired from a distance. She seemed cool and aloof, the opposite of her mother.

"I can do more," Sadie said eagerly. "If you have any other projects you'd like me to handle, I have the time—"

"You need a life too. I'll see you tomorrow."

Sadie swallowed back her protest. Instead, she made her umpteenth vow to prove that she deserved the incredible break the mayor had given her.

On his way back from the ballpark Caleb made his daily phone call home. Teddy, one of his thirteen-year-old twin brothers, answered. "Did you blow 'em out of the water?"

"Next question."

That was code for a game he didn't want to talk about. His brothers and sister knew the routine, and Teddy immediately launched into a long explanation of why his karate teacher must have been an assassin in his last job. "He has a tattoo on his rib cage, like a rifle target. Why else would he have that?"

Caleb felt the tension of the day release as Teddy rattled on. During the off-season, he took care of the boys while his sister Tessa accumulated college credits toward a degree. During the baseball season it was her turn to play head of household. It worked, but he missed them all terribly when he was away from Plano.

"Don't you think an assassin would have enough money so he didn't have to coach idiot suburban kids?" he asked when Teddy finally paused.

"I think he's scouting us, looking for his successor," Teddy explained in a hushed voice.

That laugh carried Caleb all the way to the front door of his newly rented apartment. "Just got home. Gotta go."

"Have you seen him yet?"

No need to ask who Teddy meant. Until two weeks ago their father, Thurston "Bingo" Hartwell, had been inmate number 14-893 at the minimum security federal correctional institute at Three Rivers, serving a sentence for fraud. Now he was Caleb's brand new roommate. "Of course I've seen him. He's living with me."

"Does he have, like, shivs and shit?"

"Stop that. And don't say shit. Or shiv, come to think of it. Talk to you later, bud."

He stood at the front door for a long, long moment, mustering the will to walk inside. Bingo had betrayed them all and messed up their lives, but nonetheless when he got out of prison, Caleb had felt compelled to offer him a place to live. Since he tensed up at the mere sight of his lying, ex-con father, this didn't make for the most harmonious living situation.

Bingo must have heard him drive up; he was wait-ing with an ice pack. His eager expression made Caleb want to throw up.

"I already iced in the clubhouse."

"Right, right." Bingo slung the ice pack over his shoulder and stuck his hands in the pockets of his chinos. With his blue button-down shirt, nice leather belt, and expensive haircut, he could have illustrated a Forbes Magazine "How to Retire Wealthy" article. Caleb forced back the choking resentment that his father looked so good after six years in prison, when he'd struggled every minute of those same six years to take care of the kids Bingo had left behind.

"Well, how'd the game go?" Bingo asked.

"One for the history books."

"That's my boy," he said proudly.

Caleb pushed past him, through the bare-bones, furnished apartment. As an up-and-coming baseball player, he was used to anonymous furniture, whether in hotel rooms or short-term apartment leases. In the kitchen, he opened the refrigerator door and stared blindly into its depths. Nothing much there besides beer and leftover pizza. Worked for him.

He cracked open a Budweiser and glugged half of it before he even closed the refrigerator door.

"Did you see your probation officer?" he asked his father, who'd followed him into the kitchen.

"Of course. It's my check-in day."

"That's why I'm asking."

"Well, you don't have to ask," Bingo said testily. "I'm a grown man. You think I want to go back to prison?"

"Did you want to go there in the first place?"

"Of course not."

"Well, there you go." And there went the rest of the beer. His words echoed back to him, mean and irritable. He didn't like talking to his father that way, but he couldn't seem to stop himself.

When he emerged from behind his beer can, Bingo was staring at him reproachfully. "That chip on your shoulder isn't hurting anyone but yourself, Caleb."

"Thanks, Dr. Phil."

"You know, a good attitude gets you a long way in life. Try smiling a little more. Be more upbeat. People will like you better." Bingo gave him his famous megawatt grin, the one that had fooled hundreds of marks. The one Caleb had inherited. "If you learn nothing else from me, that's enough."

Caleb crunched the can into a flat disc and sent it winging across the room toward the trash. Nothing but net. Glad to see he still had some skills. "Why should I learn anything from you? I'm a ballplayer, not a con man."

His father, generally a good-humored man, winked. "Maybe it's not as different as you think. Don't you try to fool the hitters and the guys on base?"

"Men on base."

"That's what I said."

"We don't say 'guys on base,' they're 'men on base.' And sure, I try to fool the batters, but I stay within the rules to do it."

"No cheating, no going after that extra little advantage? What about the one I read about, with the tar on his neck. Brushes his hand against it, gets a better grip. You don't ever do that?"

"No." Caleb pulled out the pizza and stuck it in the microwave. He pushed the Start button with about twice the necessary force.

"Really? The way the article made it sound, all the big-league pitchers do it. Maybe you should give it a try. Get you back where you belong, on a major league team."

"You don't know what you're talking about."

Bingo laughed, that jolly, intimate, life-is-wonderful laugh that had reeled in countless marks and three wives—all of them ex-wives now. "When it comes to cheating, I might know a thing or two. Everyone cheats, son, one way or another. Only difference is, some get caught."

Caleb stared at the pizza going round and round inside the microwave. Maybe when the timer went off, his father would be gone. When the timer went off, he'd have a father who wasn't a con artist, who hadn't gone to prison, and who *freaking left him alone*.

Ding.

Nope. Still there. Caleb spun around and stalked out of the kitchen. "I forgot, I'm meeting the guys for some food. Pizza's all yours."

"Maybe I could come along . . ."

But Caleb was already out the door, striding into the warm evening, with its sunset the color of flamingo feathers. There ought to be some Catfish players out there chowing down and getting plastered. If that petition was right, there was bound to be all kinds of trouble to get into. He'd call Mike Solo, see what he was up to.

He was supposed to call that girl, he suddenly remembered. Hauling out his phone and the petition that he'd stuffed into his pocket, he dialed quickly. As it rang, he inserted his long legs into his Jeep Wrangler. He couldn't remember the last time he'd called a girl. He'd been so focused on baseball and taking care of the family that girls had taken a backseat. Occasionally he hooked up with someone, they had fun for a night, and if they mutually decided on more fun, they texted each other. The texts were just informational: where are we meeting, are you wearing underwear, that sort of thing.

Actually calling someone on the phone felt . . . old-school.

Her voice mail clicked on. "You've reached Sadie. Leave your number at the tone." Quick and to the point. And that name, Sadie—both soft and sexy—suited her.

"Hi, this is Caleb Hart from the Catfish. Duke asked me to call you to discuss some ideas for the team. And the town. So . . . er . . . call back any time. Here's my number."

Now that called for a drink.

Donna held tight to Sadie's wrist as she cut a path through the crowd of dancers at the Kilby Roadhouse. A bluegrass band in jeans and loose flannel shirts was playing onstage. Some people were doing a line dance up front, others had paired off into couples. Most crowded around the small round tables dotting the edge of the dance floor.

Donna was already flying high, buzzing with the joy of being out of the Gilbert house for the night. "I tell you what, Sadie, I'm lookin' to get into some trouble tonight. Six days a week with the Shark, I'm about ready to gnaw my arm off. I need some adult company, like whoa, you have no idea."

Sadie, feeling very exposed, glanced nervously around the bar. This wing-woman job was going to be a challenge. The good news—for her—was that no one was looking in her direction. They were all too busy staring at Donna.

Her friend wore skintight alligator pants and a

white leather sleeveless top. She would have been a walking PETA outrage if it weren't all fake. Her thick ruby-red hair was teased, then sprayed into place. She'd smoothed glittery body lotion over every exposed inch of skin, so whenever the light caught her, she glowed. If the Gilberts could see their nanny now, they might take the Shark and run. In high school Donna had gotten top grades without blinking an eye. Sadie still didn't understand why she hadn't applied to college. Donna flat-out refused to talk about it.

Under pressure from her friend, Sadie had ended up in a fitted, spaghetti strap, above-the-knee dress in burnt orange, with snaps up the side. She'd drawn the line at the four-inch heels Donna wanted her to wear. At five-ten, Sadie always wore flats, sandals, Converse sneakers, or cowboy boots. End of shoe story.

"Here." Donna waved her over to a tiny round table with no chairs. "We can just perch on the table, like so." She sat on the edge and crossed her legs so the light slid across the silver patterns on her pants. Underneath the pants, she wore purple snakeskin boots. "Eye-catching, right?"

Sadie grabbed the other edge of the table before it could tip over. "That's one way to put it."

"Go get us some drinks, wing woman. White Russian for me, double for you. You have some catching up to do, missy. I'll rustle up some men for us. These girls work better than a lasso." She adjusted her halter top to expose more cleavage.

Sadie took a deep breath and headed for the bar. A year ago she never would have come in here; too much risk of being publicly mocked. She caught sly glances from a few people, but she held her head high and ignored them. That stupid tape showed a private moment no one should ever have seen. So she was going to pretend they hadn't.

She knew the bartender, Todd, from high school, where they'd been on the yearbook committee together. Back in those days, she'd been a goofy, fun-loving good girl, verging on dork. Then she'd tutored Hamilton in history senior year and he'd shocked everyone by asking her out. So much had happened since then.

Todd gave her an embarrassed smile. "How've you been, Sadie?"

"Oh, peachy."

He leaned closer, speaking intimately as he poured Kahlua into two glasses. "You know, I never believed half the things people were saying about you."

"Really? Which half?" Was it the merely embarrassing half, or the excruciatingly mortifying?

He turned red. "Drinks on the house."

"That's not necessary." She pulled out her wallet and threw down a twenty. It was more than she owed, but her pride was at stake here. "Keep the change."

"Hang on," he said, as she took the drinks. "Is one of those for Donna?"

"Yeah, why?"

"She looks like she's already had a few." He added extra ice to one of the glasses to water down the drink. "You need help, let me know."

"Thanks." Sadie felt her face heat as she gathered up the glasses. Good grief, her paranoia was getting the better of her. Todd was trying to be nice, and she'd assumed the worst. Not every guy was a jerk.

A glass in each hand, she forged her way through the milling crowd. In the shifting gaps between dancers, she saw that Donna was now sitting squarely in the middle of the little table, one alligator-sheathed leg sliding provocatively against the other, her chest arched in the direction of a tall, fit-looking man. The man's hands were shoved into the back pockets of his jeans. Those jeans covered a rear end that, even in the land of tight cowboy butts, screamed "outstanding hottie."

Could she call her wing-woman's job done? Maybe she could deliver Donna's drink and skip out of here before any awkward encounters ruined the night.

"Here you go, birthday girl. Sorry it took so long." She reached past the strange man, who turned and looked down at her.

It was Caleb the baseball player. He looked just as good here as at the ballpark. Maybe better, in those crisp blue jeans and cowboy boots, along with a tight blue T-shirt that made his eyes stand out. Of all the guys Donna could have found, why this one? Why the only man she'd been attracted to since the Hamilton Disaster?

As she met his startled gray gaze, she bobbled both glasses, sloshing white liquid onto his pants.

"Maybe I should have brought a bodyguard," he teased, grabbing the drinks—or trying to, anyway. He and Sadie ended up in a sort of tussle over them.

"What are you doing here?" Silly question, but she was completely rattled . . .

"Right now? Wrestling chick drinks." Caleb tried to steady the glasses, splashing Kahlua across his hands. Another man, who stood on Donna's other side, laughed out loud. Sadie noticed dark curly hair, mischievous green eyes, and a dimple.

Donna eyed the creamy liquid on Caleb's hands. "Want me to lick that off for you, handsome?" She gave a goofy, exaggerated wink.

Caleb's friend snorted. "I'm getting a beer. Be right back, handsome." He slapped Caleb on the back, then headed for the bar.

Sadie finally managed to wrangle the two glasses onto the table. Donna looked like she wanted to jump

Caleb right there on the floor of the Roadhouse. She couldn't tell what Caleb wanted. Donna was beautiful, after all, and a fantastic person, even though she was a little out of control at the moment.

But Donna could get away with it. She had a fun, kooky way about her that made everyone like her. Sadie knew if she threw herself at Caleb like that, all the talk would flare back up. Her life would become hell all over again. And who knew what Hamilton would do when he heard?

No, she couldn't afford any sort of misbehavior, which was why she was the perfect wing woman. She snatched up one of the White Russians and took a long sip.

"What's your name, cowboy?" Donna was saying. She lifted one boot and ran it along Caleb's leg.

Sadie gripped her glass as if it were a hand brake on a runaway train. Then she drained it, grateful for the sudden fuzziness it granted. If ever a moment called for alcohol . . .

"Caleb Hart."

"I've heard of you. You're from the Catfish. I'm Donna and this is Sadie. You should really ask her to dance, because even though she's acting kind of strange right now, she's super cool. Like, the bestest of the bestest."

Caleb shot an amused glance at Sadie, who made a little face to indicate Donna's buzzed state.

"Besides, she doesn't go out much anymore." Donna leaned forward, nearly toppling off the table. "She had a *bad experience.*"

"*Donna.*"

"It's my birthday and I can say what I want. Besides, I can see the sparks flyin' here." She waved her hand back and forth between the two of them as the curly-haired guy returned with two Lone Stars. "And I think your friend's a hottie. I've decided to put my money on those cute little dimples."

"Now that's an interesting bet," said Caleb. "We'll leave you to it. Let's go, Sadie." Eyes gleaming with laughter, he grabbed Sadie's free hand and tugged her toward the dance floor.

Chapter 4

As soon as they hit the dance floor, and Caleb drew Sadie against him, he regretted it. Her dress had no sleeves, and the back was cut to expose her shoulder blades as well, so he couldn't avoid touching her skin, which felt like silk in firelight. Her hair kept brushing against the back of his hand too. He'd never felt so *aware* of another person.

It unnerved him.

"It's her birthday," Sadie was saying. "She wanted to cut loose. I really should get back to her."

"Mike can handle it. He has a couple of sisters." He directed his words toward the delicate shell of her ear, which looked pinker than it should. Was she embarrassed? She kept darting glances around the dance floor, as if she was avoiding someone.

"Is he a Catfish too?"

"Yes. Catcher. Good guy."

She peered up at him doubtfully. "But . . . he's a baseball player. Emphasis on *player*."

He stiffened. "We're not all like that." Sure, girls came on to him all the time, but he, for one, was pretty careful about who he hooked up with. He liked to keep his personal life private, and didn't trust the baseball groupies not to tattle. "Mike likes to flirt, but he takes a strict vow of celibacy during the baseball season."

"A vow of celibacy?"

"Yes. Literally. He visits a Catholic church right before spring training and takes a vow of celibacy. Says it keeps him sharp."

"Does it?"

"It seems to work for him. He's batting .322 this season. He'll probably be called up in September, if not before."

She laughed, a low, throaty sound that seemed to reach into his pants and stroke his cock. "So you left your friend, who took a vow of celibacy, with my friend, who wants to get laid for her birthday. That's either genius or a little mean."

The breath from her laughter fluttered against the skin of his throat, making him swallow hard. *Sadie.* Sexy Sadie. And Lord, was she sexy. Especially in that dress. Although the dress couldn't compare to the red cowboy boots.

Tightening his grip on her upper body, he swung her to the left to avoid a passing waitress. The scent of her hair—some sort of spice, like cloves?—made him want to bury his nose in the thick dark locks. He actually leaned down, just a little, to inhale a deeper breath of it. The Kilby Roadhouse, which at first glance had seemed a generic, dreary place with a lackluster band, pulsed with energy around him. He swung her past an awkwardly placed table, noticing how smoothly she matched his movements.

Sadie was still talking. "She's my best friend, and I swear she's not usually like this. Believe it or not, she works in child care. Normally she has Cheerios stuck to her hair and diaper bags on both shoulders."

He laughed. He liked this girl, her sparkly eyes

and hot body. He wouldn't mind knowing more, even though he had no intention of actually getting *involved*.

He noticed that people were watching them and exchanging the occasional whisper. Had he already been recognized?

"Is Sadie your full name? Not short for anything?"

"No, it's just Sadie." She tilted her head back to meet his eyes. Hers were dark, brilliant, sparkling in the dim roadhouse light. "Why?"

"I read the petition and looked at all the signatures. I didn't see any Sadie. Does that mean you don't have it in for the Catfish?"

"I don't have it in for the Catfish, no." She leaned toward him, as though sharing a secret. "But don't tell my boss. She has nothing good to say about you guys."

"Now that's just all kinds of unfair. She ought to get to know us better first." He winked at her. "Maybe you can do that for her."

"No," she said quickly. "That's not a good idea." She made to draw away from him, but he took the opportunity to swing her in a little dip, so she couldn't escape.

"Shouldn't you gather more information before you pass judgment?" he asked her. "Seems only right."

When she didn't answer, he wondered if maybe he'd gotten out of the habit of talking about anything not baseball-related. Even the girls he met wanted to talk about the game.

Maybe she did too. "You said you went to Catfish games when you were a kid, right?"

"Good memory."

"Yes, I have a good memory," he said simply. "I can remember all kinds of shit. Ask me what pitches I threw to Derek Jeter the one time I got him out. Fastball low and inside, fastball low and away, that one got fouled off, slider down the middle, he almost got a piece of that one, but he missed. Strikeout. Highlight of my career."

She smiled at him, a wide grin that made her eyes tilt at the corners. "So far."

At this point he'd rather talk about anything than his career. "What about you? How long have you been working for the mayor?"

"About six months. But I'm hoping to go to law school someday."

"Nice. Gotta love lawyers. They make contracts that keep us ballplayers from getting screwed." He chose not to mention his father's lawyer, who'd been a lifeline during his trial and imprisonment.

Sadie raised her chin with a flash of disdain. "Is that all you can think about? Rich baseball players getting good contracts?"

"Well, it does come up a lot in the clubhouse. What kind of lawyer do you want to be, then?"

"Probably a civil rights lawyer. I want to fight for people whose rights aren't being respected. Especially if they're female. I'd also consider environmental law." She gave a little hiccup. "Plants deserve respect too."

He laughed. He couldn't help it. She was just so appealing. Sexy too, with all that tanned skin peeking out from her tight dress, the shadows hinting at curves. He'd been semi-aroused this whole time, and now he felt himself harden even further. Her combination of sexy and feisty really did it for him.

She shook out her hair so it flowed over her shoulder. "Are you laughing about the plants?"

"No. I never laugh about plants."

That got her. She burst out laughing too, her eyes sparkling at him.

"You know," he added. "I think you'd be a great lawyer."

"Why?"

"Because of the way you talk. Every lawyer I've known can talk up a storm. My fa—" God, he'd almost let slip something about Bingo's lawyer. "Just an observation."

As if to prove him wrong, for a moment they danced in silence. The temporary lull wasn't quiet though; something electric pulsed through it. He felt the muscles of her back shift under his hand. This girl did something to him, and if he was smart, he'd run the other way.

"What did your friend mean about the bad experience?" Where had that come from? He never asked personal questions like that. It was hard to tell in the lowered light of the dance floor, but he thought she turned a deep red.

"She's a little buzzed."

Her reluctance to answer made him more curious. Actually, everything about her made him curious. He liked talking to her. He liked how quickly she responded to his jibes, and the sparkly energy she gave off, and the occasional wariness that flitted across her face. He *really* liked how she felt against his body.

"You know, I called you earlier," he told her.

"You did?" Her eyes widened. There was so much life in those eyes, as though a million thoughts were flying through at the same time.

At that moment he made a snap decision. He wanted to work with her, for real. Even if that petition was insane. "Yeah. I have some ideas for the team. I think we should get together sometime and talk about them. We're going on the road after the game tomorrow. What about when we get back?"

The band shifted into an up-tempo number, and she drew away from him. "I don't know."

"Hey, you don't want to get me in trouble with my manager, do you?" He gave a mock shudder. "You saw how terrifying he is."

"Fine. We'll talk about it when you get back. I'd better find Donna."

He watched her walk off the dance floor, her long legs sleek and quick, her dark hair tousled from their dance. What would it look like after a tumble in bed, after he'd stripped her naked, licked every bit of her silky skin, made her bright eyes go sleepy with pleasure? She was all eyes and skin and fire and heart . . . and look at the way her hips moved under that short dress . . .

Just like that, he knew there was only one thing for it. He wanted Sadie. And he'd have her, even though every bone in his body told him she'd be a huge distraction. She already took up more space in his brain than most girls did *after* he'd taken them to bed.

Not that he was proud of that.

"Hey, aren't you the new pitcher for the Catfish?" Two guys in backward baseball caps had approached while he'd been staring at Sadie's retreating ass.

"Yep."

They handed over a beer. "Tough loss, man. Looks like you're overthinking it out there."

He clinked the bottle against theirs. For some reason, that comment didn't bother him nearly as much anymore. "You may have a point there."

When Sadie glanced back over her shoulder, Caleb was chatting with two guys who must be fans, the way they were staring up at him in awe. She let out a long breath, grateful that she still had the ability to inhale and exhale. Caleb Hart was completely outside her experience. She'd known plenty of guys, of course. Boys at high school, boys at Kilby Community College. And the boy who'd ruined her life, Hamilton Wade.

But not even Hamilton had caused her heart to do this crazy cartwheeling Caleb inspired. She'd been swept off her feet by Ham, but in an awestruck, what-does-he-see-in-me way. He hadn't made her hands damp and her thoughts scurry every which way like an anthill someone had stepped on.

Caleb had caught her at a vulnerable time in her life, that was all. There was a rational explanation for this crazy sensation, as if the ground wasn't quite stable under her feet. Maybe there was a medical explanation, like vertigo. Or maybe Donna had spiked that White Russian. For sure, she couldn't risk another devastating humiliation at the hands of a man.

She found Donna leaning on the bar, talking to Mike. Thank goodness, she still had all her clothes on. "Donna, I have to go home. I told my mom I wouldn't stay out too late."

Donna turned a beaming, blurry smile on her. "Mike was just explaining the benefits of celibacy to me. Did you know it could raise my batting average by fifty points?"

Sadie smiled at Mike, who winked. "Thanks, Mike. It was nice to meet you, but I'm going to take Donna home now."

"Good idea." He gave them a salute, then leaned against the bar while she steered Donna toward the red exit sign.

Sadie couldn't help looking for Caleb as she herded Donna toward the exit. As one of the tallest men in the room, and the one all the girls kept checking out, he was hard to miss. By the time she reached the door, three girls had joined the two other fans. He leaned against the wall, listening patiently to the little knot of admirers. The low light created shadows under his cheekbones and made the stubborn line of his jaw stand out. A slight smile tugged at one corner of his mouth.

His eyes shifted so he caught her gaze in a sudden flash of steely silver. The half smile turned into a full-voltage grin that transformed his face into something that belonged on a movie screen. Her knees nearly buckled, but she couldn't for the life of her stop the smile that spread across her face.

She gave him an awkward little wave, then nearly tripped over Donna, who had stopped to adjust her halter top.

Donna staggered, then grabbed onto a nearby table. Sadie hauled her back to her feet and then, her face burning, glanced again at Caleb.

His smile broadened even further. He put his hand to his ear in a "Call me" gesture, then pointed from himself to her.

He was going to call her. Already, her phone was burning a hole in her pocket because she knew there was a message waiting from him.

Donna whispered in her ear. "I know I told you to dance with him, but I just have to say this, as your friend. He's a Catfish. And you're Sadie Merritt. You know what people will say."

"You don't even know him." What Caleb had said about getting to know him before judging him had really struck home. She'd been the target of such harsh judgments, most of which were completely undeserved.

Donna gestured in his direction. "I know enough. He's gorgeous. A man like that's a born heartbreaker. He makes Hamilton look like a child, bless his spoiled heart. You didn't give him your number, did you?"

"He already had it." They reached the exit door. The bouncer stepped off his stool and pushed it open for them. "I'm supposed to help the Catfish figure out a way to improve their image.

"Well, sign me up for that," said Donna enthusiastically. "Get him naked, that would improve his image. That man is sex on a stick."

A group of girls on their way into the Roadhouse giggled and whispered to each other as they passed. Sadie felt her face heat. She wondered if they were talking about her, and what shameful lie they were repeating.

"You know, I just changed my mind again. Go for it, Sadie. You've been doing the celibate thing too long. That Mike doesn't know what he's talking about. You deserve a hot ballplayer, not that I'm not jealous, you gorgeous bitch." She slung her arm around Sadie's neck, so she nearly staggered.

"That's not going to happen, Donna. I'm not going to sleep with him. He's going to call about the Can the Catfish petition. That's all."

"Well, that's just a tragic waste of chemistry. Seriously, the air was crackling between you two. Even Mike noticed."

"Sorry, Donna. There's no chance of sex here."

"Didn't you see that man? The chance of sex is two thousand percent."

Sadie cast her eyes toward the sky, where stars glittered peacefully. The more Donna talked about Caleb that way, the more quivery her insides felt.

"Sure, he's sexy, but he can probably sleep with any woman in the Roadhouse if he wants. This is going to be strictly business."

"You keep telling yourself that, Sadie. I'll keep laughing my ass off." Donna gave a huge yawn and looked around the parking lot. "I might have to nap in the car. I never get to nap in the car. That's the Shark's job. Do you mind?"

"Of course not."

No, she didn't mind; it would give her a chance to relive every word of her conversation with Caleb Hart, star pitcher and sexiest man she'd ever met.

Caleb had to admit the Kilby Catfish had one great thing going for them. They had a killer bus. When he'd been with the Twins, ever so briefly, he'd flown on charter planes and stayed at five-star hotels. Luckily, he hadn't had much chance to get used to it, since he was traded after that disastrous last game. The major league life hadn't ever sunk in—he'd always felt like a wide-eyed newcomer who didn't yet belong.

Now it was back to charter buses, the occasional commercial flight, and an endless string of motels. But Crush Taylor had done his time in the minors and knew what it was like, so the Catfish were lucky enough to ride in a deluxe, air-conditioned bus with plush seats and plenty of leg room. Each seat had its own entertainment system, though most guys listened to their own iPods, watched movies on their iPads, or caught up on their sleep. The Catfish even had a bus version of a flight attendant, a hot young thing who made the rounds taking drink and sandwich orders.

"Now this is traveling in style, right?" In the next seat over, Mike Solo stretched out his legs with a sigh. He had a typical catcher's build—muscular and solid—and a head of wild black curls. "The Friars ain't got nothin' on us."

"Yeah, you keep telling yourself that," Caleb answered. "One call from San Diego and you'll be gone so fast we won't remember what you look like."

"Except when you see me on TV." He winked.

Across the aisle, Sonny Barnes, the lanky, glasses-wearing first baseman, who had two full sleeves of tattoos, was breathing on the window and drawing hearts in the steam left on the glass.

"Newlywed," explained Mike. "Got married last month. They spent their honeymoon in the Econolodge in Albuquerque. One time we stole his cell phone, and me and Dwight did a dramatic rendition of the texts he and his wife send. Fucking hilarious."

"Dwight is . . ."

"Dwight Conner. Big black guy, the funniest center fielder you're ever going to meet. He's sitting up at the front of the bus right now. Says the back of the bus gives him genetic flashbacks."

Duke stepped on board, followed by the bus driver, and a few minutes later they were on the road. Across the aisle, Barnes nearly broke his neck trying to wave to his wife until the last possible moment.

Caleb settled back in his seat, iPod buds at the ready. He'd intended to nap—he hadn't slept well last night, hadn't since his father arrived—but he liked this way of getting to know his fellow Catfish. Like most Triple A teams, they were a mix of up-and-comers, rehabs, and players who'd reached the limit of their talent.

"Who are the prospects?" he asked Mike. The blue-chip prospects were the money players who'd been picked first in the draft and were expected to head up to the majors and become stars.

"Besides you?"

Caleb winced. Sure, he *had* been a prospect. He'd done well in Double A, even better in Triple A with the Rochester Red Wings. He'd missed a season thanks to injuries, but come back even stronger. Then he'd gotten the Call. He'd experienced the incredible feeling of pitching in a big league park for a big league audience. Three games he'd pitched, and he'd been on top of the world. Then, for no reason, he'd crashed. Now he wasn't so much a prospect as a headache . . . or a head case . . . someone everyone was trying to figure out.

"Yeah, besides me."

"Well, we got our rehabs. Don London broke his toe kicking a cooler. Bad move, but he'll be gone soon. Should heal up good. Ramirez won't be here long. He's hitting .343 with twenty homers so far. Got call-up written all over him. He's the Latin guy with the Bose earphones and the sketch pad." Mike gestured up ahead a few rows.

Caleb raised an eyebrow. "Sketch pad?" You didn't see that every day on a Triple A bus.

"He likes to draw. Doesn't say much. He expresses himself through home runs and his art."

Now that was unusual. Then again, there were all kinds of characters in baseball.

"I heard the Friars are trying to get Trevor Stark in a trade," Mike continued. "That oughta be interesting."

"Think they'll send him here?"

"Probably. He just got out of rehab and he's pretty shaky. Hasn't gotten a hit yet. He'll probably get sent down no matter what team he's on."

Caleb had actually pitched to Trevor Stark during his second major league start. The mighty slugger had hit a triple off him. And halfway between second and third base, as Caleb waited helplessly for the outfielder to catch up with the ball, Stark had fucking *slowed down*. He'd looked directly at him, slowed his pace and shot him a cocky grin. Then he'd scooted into third with a stand-up triple.

Caleb hated the guy's guts. If they ended up on the same team . . . well, watch out, Kilby. Things were guaranteed to get ugly. "Hell," he muttered under his breath, then decided to change the subject. "So listen, is there anything to the stuff they say about this team?"

"That we're mad, bad, and dangerous to know?"

The rookie third baseman poked his head over the top of the seat in front of them. "It's not our fault. Go to one of Crush's parties and you'll see the problem."

"Throws a good party?"

"The best," said the guy reverently. He managed to insert his hand between the seats. "I'm Tommy John Gates, but they call me TJ."

"Tommy John, huh? Your parents were baseball fans?"

"Surgeons. But they come to every game they can," he said proudly. Caleb steeled himself against the automatic sense of envy. For so many of the guys, baseball was something shared between father and son, something passed down through generations. Not for him. He'd learned baseball at the Boys and Girls Club where his dad used to park him while he was "taking care of business."

"Anyway, yeah, Crush wasn't called the Playboy Pitcher for nothing. He's divorced now. Almost seems like he bought the team so he'd have some ballplayers around. He likes it when the team gets rowdy. I think he might have a grudge against the Friars because they traded him to a last place team back in '04. Maybe he likes making trouble for them."

Caleb's phone vibrated in his pocket. He pulled it out and saw that a text from his sister Tessa had just come in. *Dentist says the twins need braces. Ten freaking thousand dollars. Can u do it?*

He used his thumbs to tap back a message. *I'll put some more money in the account.*

Awesome. Guess I won't jump into the Rio Grande yet. How's Bingo?

Tessa refused to call him "Dad," as did Caleb. He texted, *If the Rio Grande was closer . . .*

LOL. Don't like that joke, but LOL.

He smiled to himself, and stuck the phone back in his pocket. When Bingo had been sent to prison, Caleb was nineteen, Tessa seventeen, and the twins seven. He'd done about five years' worth of growing up in the week after Bingo's guilty verdict. He'd immediately called up the agent who'd told him he could get a big signing bonus if he'd leave college right away. Done, and done. Two weeks later he was a member of the Minnesota Twins system instead of a freshman at Texas Christian University. They'd all been living off his bonus ever since, while Tessa took on the role of big sister-slash-single parent during the baseball season.

He didn't want to tell Tessa, but that bonus had shrunk to an alarmingly small amount since he received it. His minor league salary wasn't enough to keep them going for long. He *had* to get back to the majors. Had to prove himself and win a big money contract.

Had to.

Chapter 5

SADIE WAS COMPLETELY wrong about the chances of Caleb's calling. He called on the second day of his road trip, from Austin. She happened to be on her lunch break, on her way to meet Donna in the little park near City Hall.

"This is Caleb Hart," he said casually, in his rugged baritone, as if hotshot pitchers called her every day of the week.

"Hi Caleb." Her voice sounded weirdly fluttery to her ears; but hopefully he wouldn't be able to tell.

"I've been thinking up a bunch of ideas to make the team look good."

"The mayor will be happy to hear that." Then, on a devilish impulse, "Not that you guys don't *look* good already . . ." Seriously, Caleb definitely brought out her flirty side. Had from that first moment in Catfish Stadium. It felt good, like exercising muscles that had atrophied.

"Mmm. Will you sue me if I say that sounds like a come-on?"

On its own, her mouth quivered into a broad smile. *Bad Sadie.* "You're reading between the lines, Catfish."

"Hey, I'll take what I can get. It's tough out here

for a ballplayer. Show a little mercy." The teasing note deepened his voice so he sounded like a late night DJ introducing a Marvin Gaye song.

"Oh really? I've never heard that things are tough for baseball players. The fans, the adulation, the big money . . ."

"The injuries, the long road trips, the lonely nights, the generic hotel rooms . . ."

"Poor baby." In the green patch of park up ahead, she spotted Donna waiting at the edge, and waved.

"My sad story's working, I can tell. You want to kiss it and make it all better."

No flirting, Sadie. You know this is a bad idea. She wrenched the conversation back to the original topic. "So what have you been thinking about the team?"

"Well, what about a baseball clinic for underprivileged kids?"

She snorted. "Cliché. Anyway, the Catfish already do one every year. It's a blatant photo op."

"So harsh. What are you doing right now?" With his voice low and intimate like that, he might as well have asked what she was wearing.

"Not much. I'm meeting Donna for lunch." She reached her friend, who raised an eyebrow at her while jittering up and down, bouncing the Shark in his backpack.

"What about you? What are you doing?"

"Icing my shoulder, munching on nachos. The glamorous life, you know."

At Sadie's giggle, Donna looked at her askance. She sobered quickly. No need to get Donna curious. "Your shoulder hurts?" she asked Caleb.

"No more than usual. I ice it after every game. What about something with summer school? Literacy or arts in the schools." The speed of subject change made her head spin. "I can run that one by Duke and the PR chick. It would make us look warm and fuzzy."

"Did you just say PR 'chick'?"

"Sure did." His voice got that low, teasing tone again, the one that made the palms of her hands tingle. "Got a problem with that? Tell you what, why don't you hop in your car and drive out here to Round Rock and give me a good old-fashioned tongue-lashing."

"You are *bad*."

"Oh, I can be very bad." His voice dropped another octave, and she shivered down to the soles of her feet.

Still, she couldn't help but notice that he'd managed to shift the subject away from his pitching. The guy might be a big, strong ballplayer, but he also had a quickness that really appealed to her.

"I gotta go," he told her. "Someone's at the door. It's probably the rest of the team. We have a plot to kidnap the mayor of Round Rock and tie him to the front of our bus like a figurehead. We want to make Kilby proud. Will the Can the Catfish ladies give us points for that?"

She laughed. "No, but the hunters would love you, and they vote too."

"Mind if I call you again tomorrow? I might think of something brilliant. You never know."

"Sure. That would be fine."

Actually, that would be much more than fine. Talking to him on the phone was almost more fun than talking to him in person, because she wasn't so distracted by his knee-weakening physique.

After she hung up, and while she was still laughing over the image of the bus figurehead, Donna bumped against her. "You look like the cat who ate the catfish."

Her cheeks burned.

"I knew it was that baseball player! I haven't seen

you laugh like that since junior high. It's nice to see my fun best friend again."

"He's funny. He makes me laugh. But it's just business," Sadie assured her, stuffing her phone back in her pocket. "It's part of my job, like I told you."

"That crazy Can the Catfish petition?"

Sadie groaned. "I thought if I delivered it and they laughed in my face, that would be the end. But they're actually taking it seriously. The owner called Mayor Trent and promised his full cooperation. You should have seen her face."

She'd gone all pink and flustered, as a matter of fact. Sadie had never seen her like that.

"If you get a hot ballplayer out of it, why are you complaining?" Donna said. "I'd deliver a petition to send the team to the moon if it got me a date with a hunk like that."

Sadie peered behind her at the sleeping baby's face. "So sweet and innocent. You'd never know his nanny was psycho."

"He'll find out soon enough," said Donna cheerfully. "I should get him out of this heat. I slathered him in SPF one thousand, but even so."

"You know something, Donna? You're really good at this nanny thing. You're a natural."

A stricken expression twisted Donna's face, gone so quickly Sadie thought she'd imagined it. She stared at her friend as she veered toward the path that would take them to the downtown strip.

"Yeah. Well. Back to the Hot Pitcher Dilemma. Let's go get some cold drinks and figure out how to hook you up with him."

Hmm. Something was going on with Donna. But Sadie knew her friend well enough to know she'd only share it when she was ready.

"I have no plans to hook up with anyone," Sadie said as she followed Donna out of the park. "I got too burned the last time. It's not worth it."

"You don't know unless you give him a chance. You can't just give up on men forever. What's the fun in that?"

They turned a corner, reaching downtown Kilby, admiring the prom dresses draped in the window of Kilby's Happy Days Boutique and the dusty old Coca-Cola bottle display in the window of the hardware store.

"By the way, I watched your new boyfriend on public access the other night. He struck out two and walked eight. Didn't seem like a good balance to me."

Sadie had watched the game too, although it would be more fair to say she'd watched Caleb. The rest of the players had all blurred together. "I know. I felt bad for him. Everyone's saying he's a brilliant pitcher, and they can't figure out what's wrong with him." She shivered. "Not my problem. Remember how Hamilton wanted me to go to every single practice because I was his 'good luck charm'?"

"I remember. I always thought he deliberately screwed up when you had to miss a game, just to make you feel guilty. But Caleb is a pro, Sadie. He wouldn't pull shit like that."

"It doesn't *matter*. I'm not dating him. He hasn't asked, and I wouldn't say yes if he did."

Donna grumbled but didn't argue anymore. While Donna paced outside in little circles, Sadie went inside the Sacred Grounds, a new organic, New Age café, and bought them both sweetened iced tea.

When she came out, LucyBelle, a girl she'd known in high school, was chatting with Donna. When Lucy-Belle spotted her, her eyes widened, she made a quick good-bye and continued her jog, her hot pink spandex flashing down the sidewalk.

"Lucky me, I guess I'm still the town slut," Sadie said, hiding her bitterness behind a joking tone.

"Ignore her." Donna made a furious gesture at LucyBelle's back. "We're going to get out of here, Sadie. We're going to save our money. You'll become a Supreme Court justice and pass a law against stupid gossip. And I'll . . ."

"Yeah?"

"I'll figure something out." Another shadow passed over Donna's face, but then she tossed her gorgeous red hair and took Sadie's arm. "Something really good, you'll see."

The next time Caleb called, Sadie was at home. Her mother was experiencing one of her occasional bursts of energy and had begun a weird decoupage project that involved cutting out photos of movie stars and pasting them onto high-heeled shoes. Sadie offered to help, in the spirit of "whatever made her mom happy."

When the phone rang, her heart leaped and she nearly cut off Angelina Jolie's head with her scissors. "Hello?"

"It's Caleb."

Excitement jolting through her, she scrambled to her feet. "I have to take this, Mom. It's for work."

Brenda Merritt nodded vaguely and wiped a hand across her forehead, leaving a streak of glue along her hairline. Sadie took the phone and a glass of iced sweet tea into her bedroom and closed the door. She sat cross-legged on the bed, tilting her face toward the ceiling fan lazily moving hot air around the room.

"That was your mom?" Caleb sounded out of breath, and she heard outdoor noises around him.

"You're calling kind of late, aren't you?"

"Sorry, the game just ended. I'm walking back to the hotel. Are you about to go to sleep?" His voice deepened in that way that turned her to Jell-O.

"No. How was your game?"

"You don't want to know."

"Why wouldn't I want to know?"

"Christ, I don't even want to know. It was a train wreck out there. So you live at home?"

"For now. My mom's kind of . . . needy." She'd tried living on campus for a while, but then the Hamilton Disaster had happened—a huge setback for her mother's mental state. Brenda was slowly coming out of it, but Sadie couldn't leave her alone until she was stronger. "If I moved out, my mom might eat nothing but peanut butter crackers," she added, trying to make light of it.

"To be honest, I see nothing wrong with that. I like peanut butter crackers."

She smiled and reached for her iced tea. "Good to know."

"Yes, you'll know what to make me when you invite me over."

She nearly choked, and spurted iced tea onto her bedspread. "Excuse me?"

"You know, to talk about the Catfish image problem. Strictly business."

"Riiiight." She grabbed a towel from her laundry hamper and blotted the spilled tea. "Because hanging out with me will definitely help the Catfish image problem." As soon as she said that, she winced. Caleb knew nothing about "Slutty Sadie." And she wanted to keep it that way.

Unfortunately, he didn't miss a trick. "What does that mean?"

"Oh . . . nothing. Just . . . you should be working with

kids or animals. Not a plain old assistant to the mayor."
She tossed the towel back in the hamper and wandered
to her desk, where everything blurred together because
all her attention was on the voice in her ear.

"Sadie, the last word I'd use for you is 'plain.' The
last."

"I didn't mean it that way. You don't have to compli-
ment me."

"I'm not. I'm just telling it like it is. You're . . ." He
seemed to be struggling for the right words. "You're
like a fastball with a lot of juice."

"A lot of 'juice'?"

"Yeah. Movement. Life. Energy. When a pitch has
that, we say it has 'juice.' "

So he thought she had movement, life, and energy.
Maybe before Hamilton she had. Now, not so much.
"Do your pitches have juice?"

"Yes. Too much."

His gloomy response made her smile. "Better too
much juice than not enough, right?"

"Maybe. The hell if I know. So what does your mom
do when she's not eating peanut butter crackers?"

"She works at Kroger. Collects tabloids. Tells me
to stay away from boys. Sleeps. A lot. She has trouble
coping with the modern world."

"Sorry."

She shrugged, as if he could see her. She smoothed
her hand across the bedcovers, thinking of the nights
she'd spent huddled under them, hiding from the world,
with only her giant stuffed panda for company. Juice?
Yeah, right.

"And your mom is right. You should stay away from
boys. I know, I have twin brothers and they're pesky
little monkeys."

"Really?" Images of two mini-Calebs swam across

her vision, towheaded and gray-eyed. "Do they look like you?"

"When they stand still. I take care of them during the off-season. I'm a stay-at-home brother. My sister has them when I'm playing."

"What about your parents?"

"Long story." His voice dropped away for a moment, while she thought about the fact that he took care of his twin brothers. That didn't sound like something a spoiled athlete would do. She heard a horn blare as a car sped past, then a door opened and closed. "Sorry, just got to the hotel. I have to go, the guys are waiting for me. Just one more thing."

"What?"

"Stay away from *boys*."

She snorted. "Don't you dare say I need a 'man.'"

"Absolutely not. I was going to say 'you *deserve* a man.'" And without giving her a chance to get the last word, he hung up. She uncurled her hand from the receiver. It had gone numb and tingly from gripping so hard.

Then again, the rest of her was just as tingly.

Over the course of the next endless road trip—Albuquerque, Reno, Las Vegas—Caleb had more ups and downs than a bouncy castle. Each game, he'd begin well. In his first outing against the Isotopes, he struck out five before anyone could touch him.

But the second he started feeling good about his groove, something would change. All of a sudden his fastball would lose its edge, his control would slip, and the batters would jump all over him.

He'd spend the rest of the game in the dugout, watching one ridiculous promotion after another. They didn't lighten his mood much, not even Bubble Wrap Night, in which every fan got a piece of bubble wrap so they could attempt to set a world record for simultaneous bubble-wrap popping.

Against the Albuquerque Isotopes, he pitched four outstanding innings, walking only one and striking out five. Then he gave up six hits in a row, the last to a guy with a .100 batting average. His performance gave him plenty of time to brood in the dugout during the seventh inning mooing competition staged by the Isotopes.

Maybe he should polish his mooing skills and win himself a free steak dinner.

He wasn't the only one who noticed the pattern. Mitch, the pitching coach, videotaped him during each game, then edited together those key moments when things started going downhill. The two of them watched the results on Mitch's iPad in the visiting clubhouse of the Reno Aces, the coach on the bench, Caleb toweling off next to his locker, watching over his shoulder. The overhead TV was tuned to the Friars-Dodgers game. The rest of the team was finishing up their showers, wandering past the long table loaded with the postgame meal, and texting their wives, girlfriends, or hookups.

"You know what it looks like to me?" Mitch asked. "Like aliens took over your body in the sixth inning. Aliens from a planet without baseball."

Caleb rolled his eyes. "I might use that one on the press next time. Don't blame me, blame the aliens. Is that really all you got?"

"I could read the big profile of you in *Sports Illustrated,* but I'd rather eat glass."

"Profile? On what a disaster I am?"

"I didn't read it. The PR girl told me about it, but she didn't look too happy."

Wonderful. Just what he needed, *SI* on his back.

"We could order another MRI, but I don't see the point, since you're not feeling any pain. It's something else. It's either something in your head or it's invisible aliens."

The annoying baby-faced shortstop zipped over to them. Caleb had since learned that his name was Jim Leiberman, and that he had a lightning-quick glove and an adequate batting average. He seemed to be everywhere and know everything. The only way to get rid of him was to use his nickname, Bieberman, after the pop star. That was guaranteed to drive him crazy. "I read the *Sports Illustrated* article," he said, "and I think it's baloney. I'd put my money on aliens. I used to go searching for ET in the woods behind our house."

"When was that, last year?" Mike Solo asked, snapping a towel at him. "There's no such thing as aliens. And if there were, why would they pick Hart? If I was an alien looking for a body to inhabit, I'd pick a curvy blond one. Like the announcer for the mooing contest. Did you see her? Imma ask her out."

Caleb shook his head. Mike's vow of celibacy didn't mean no girls at all. He seemed to attract them like honey.

"Too late," said Dwight Conner, slinging his bag over his shoulder. He beckoned to the clubhouse attendant. "You got that reservation, dude? Table for two, in a corner with a river view? Champagne chilling?"

"Yes, sir."

Dwight, with a smug smile at the rest of them, tipped the attendant five bucks. "Good work, man. See you slackers tomorrow." And he strolled out of the room as if accompanied by his own personal slow jam soundtrack.

"That's just wrong," Mike shook his head with a disgusted look. "I really liked that girl."

"She wasn't even blond, dickhead," Caleb pointed out. "She's a redhead." And now that he thought of it, she resembled Sadie's friend, Donna.

"You noticed her too, did you?"

"Only because I watched every damn second of that mooing competition. Don't worry. Not interested." And to be honest, he really wasn't. He hadn't pursued any of the invitations that had come his way this road trip. None of them seemed as entertaining as calling Sadie and joking around with her. In fact, that was his plan for tonight. Grab some grub, hit the sheets, and press speed dial. Yes, he had her on speed dial now. He was about to ask if they could Facetime.

He really didn't want to think about the implications of that.

"Can you assholes clear out of here?" Mitch waved his arm at the other players. "We got work to do."

"What's to figure out?" Mike said. "Next time he pitches, make him wear a tin hat to keep away the aliens."

That got big laughs, so big that Mitch put away his laptop in disgust and stalked off.

Caleb wasn't at all surprised when he found a base-ball cap covered in tin foil taped to the front of his locker the next day.

The only thing that saved his sanity on that crazy road trip was talking to Sadie every night. He'd spend an hour or so on the phone with Tessa and the twins, who kept asking him questions about Bingo, when they weren't talking about karate or their endless games of Clash of Clans. Then he'd call Bingo to make sure he hadn't skipped town. With his family responsibilities completed, he'd settle in for a long, satisfying conversation with Sadie. Mostly he teased her and told her

funny stories from the clubhouse. The tin foil hat totally cracked her up. But they also talked about movies
and cars and her fear of spiders and his obsession with
the X-Men comics and whether blueberry pancakes
were better with or without whipped cream. Normal,
silly, fun stuff, but when it was Sadie's husky voice
talking about whipped cream, he nearly came in his
pants.

A few calls in, holed up in yet another bland hotel
room after another lackluster outing, he got more
personal than usual, and asked her if she was seeing
anyone.

"No. No. No, no, no."

"Okaaaaay."

A long pause. When she spoke again her voice
sounded strained. "Has no one said anything to you
about me? Anything . . . um . . . well, anything at all?"

"No. I don't talk to other people." True story. He
talked to the team members, Bingo's probation officer,
and that was about it.

"Okay." The relief in her voice made him wonder.
"Anyway, no, I'm not seeing anyone. I was, but I broke
up with him a year ago."

Good thing they weren't Facetiming, because she
might see the satisfied smile he couldn't hide. He didn't
like thinking of her with someone else. "Sorry about
that," he said insincerely.

"No need. It was a disaster. Not at first. When we
first started dating, he seemed really sweet. He used to
slip me chocolates in study hall."

Really sweet. No one would ever describe him that
way. No problem. He'd just have to convince her that
"really sweet" was all wrong for her, and a big nasty
ballplayer was what she needed. Because every time he

talked to her, the feeling grew; they *would* go to bed together. It wasn't an "if," it was a "when."

"Was this the 'bad experience' your friend mentioned?"

"Yes. He turned out to be a jerk. On an epic scale. So if you ever hear anything . . . about me . . . don't believe it, okay? Or at least ask me about it."

The pain in her voice made him want to tear the guy apart, whoever he was. "I don't listen to other people. I like to form my own opinions. I've driven a few coaches crazy that way. You don't have anything to worry about, Sadie. Unless you try to tell me how to pitch."

She laughed. "I do have one suggestion. You could try taking your shirt off. Maybe all that fabric's getting in your way."

Oh, man.

His cock stirred as he pictured stripping off his shirt and rolling around the sheets with her, all hot and tumbled and juicy and laughing. He took hold of himself, feeling his shaft harden in his fist. Yeah. Probably a really good thing they weren't Facetiming.

"Anyway, that part of my life is over for now," she said, all stern and back to business, as if her little slip into flirtation had scared her. "I'm completely focused on my job now."

His smile dropped. Well, he'd just have to convince her there was more to life than work. "What happened at the mayor's office today?"

"Meeting about the slugs."

"The slugs?"

"The horn-toed slug. They're endangered. Probably because boys like to drop them down girls' shirts."

Damn, why'd she have to mention her shirt? He could see her, so slender and sexy, her long torso begging for his tongue. He gripped his cock tighter and dragged his attention back to what Sadie was saying. She was talking in a kind of laughing, husky voice that seemed to have the same effect as the hand wrapped around his dick.

"The girls were supposed to scream and try to take their shirts off to get rid of the slugs. It was a game, but I used to feel sorry for the slugs. They didn't ask to be dropped down some kid's shirt."

"You felt sorry for slugs?"

"Yes, of course! I started rescuing them, because the boys would stomp on them to impress the girls."

"After they dropped them down their shirts."

"Exactly."

"You have a soft heart, you know that?" Maybe it was wrong, but he wanted her to use that soft heart on him. Not to mention her soft body, her soft cool hands . . .

"Anyway, it turns out the slugs are a special kind only found in our area of Texas. And the population is dying out. There's a conservation group, Save Our Slugs, and the mayor's gotten involved. For some reason she loves the slugs."

"So let me get this straight. The mayor loves the slugs but she hates the sluggers."

"Cute, Catfish. Very cute."

There was that flirty tone again. When she talked like that, he wanted to jump up and down like a kid with a new toy.

"Call the reporters. Sadie Merritt thinks I'm cute."

"I bet all kinds of people think you're cute."

"Maybe I don't care about them." He could practically hear her blush over the phone. Then his own words flashed back at him. *Slugs . . . sluggers.*

"That's it!" In his excitement, he took his hand off

his dick and sat up against the headboard, banging his head. "That's how the Catfish can look good."

"What are you talking about?"

"Save the Slugs."

"But they're . . . slugs. They're slimy."

"So are catfish. It makes sense that we'd try to help other slimy creatures."

She giggled.

"You're not taking this seriously. We'll call it 'Sluggers for Slugs.'"

"Sluggers for Slugs. Actually, that's kind of cute." He heard her scrawl something on a piece of paper. "It looks good written out too."

"Anyone can do a campaign with cute puppies or abandoned kittens. It's about time the slugs got some support."

"Now I know you're joking."

"Well, maybe. But maybe people would love it. It's funny and unique. Goofy, like all the other promotions in the minors. A major league team wouldn't touch it, but it's perfect for a team like the Kilby Catfish. We can do some events at the ballpark, like . . . um . . . Dress Like a Slug Day. Or . . . everytime a slugger hits a home run, the team donates money to the campaign. Maybe we can even add another mascot. Slimy the Slug. Or Doug the Slug. Whatever. Kids would go crazy for it."

"Do you think the team would go along with it?" From her serious tone, he could tell he'd gotten her attention. Good, because he intended to keep it.

"Word is that Crush Taylor wants to get on the mayor's good side. And believe me, the team is always looking for new promotional ideas. It's got to be better than the mooing competition they held in Albuquerque. Slugs don't make any sounds, do they?"

"No."

"Good. Because that mooing contest just about killed me."

"I guess I can run it by Mayor Trent. Any chance you big macho ballplayers would dress like slugs for a promotional photo op?"

He chuckled. "Get enough beer in us, we'll do just about anything."

"The costumes will be skintight, you know."

Flirty Voice was back. He was getting to her, slowly but surely. He wondered what it would be like to see her again after all these phone conversations. Strange? A little awkward? Or would he get his wish and they'd fall right into bed together? "Whatever brings in the crowds."

"*Sluggers for Slugs*. You know what, I think this is a great idea!" He imagined her dancing a happy little end-zone dance in her bedroom. Then realized that imagining her bedroom was risky. "I'll talk to the mayor first thing tomorrow. I'll try to come up with some more promotional ideas too, and maybe write a press release. This is brilliant, Caleb! Totally brilliant! Give yourself a big kiss from me."

"You know what, I'll take a rain check on that. I'll collect when we get back to Kilby."

"We'll see about that, Catfish."

After they hung up, he tossed the phone to the end of the bed and took his cock back into his hand. Give himself a kiss . . . hell, he could do better than that. He closed his eyes, the effect of her voice still sending ripples up and down his spine.

Sluggers for Slugs. He'd done it—found an idea that would keep Sadie close. Give him an excuse to call her. To see her.

Moving his hand loosely up and down his cock, he let a satisfied smile spread across his face. Things weren't so bad. He might not be able to hit the inside corner, but he was going to get Sadie Merritt into bed if it killed him.

Chapter 6

CALEB DREAMED ABOUT the Game that night. The game that had been worse than any nightmare he'd ever had, including those after Bingo had gone to prison. First inning, no problem. Second inning, no problem. And that was maybe the worst part, the way disaster sucker-punched him in the third. Facing the bottom of the Orioles lineup.

The first batter singled. So did the second. The first runner stole third. Caleb overthrew his pickoff attempt, the ball zipped into the dugout, and both runners scored. The next batter hit a double. The manager came out to talk to him, give him a chance to settle down. Caleb knew the manager was trying to calm him, but instead of helping, it filled him with rage. What was he, a child to be talked down from a tantrum?

In the dream, unlike in real life, he pushed the manager out of the way, violently, so he crumpled to the ground and incinerated into a wisp of smoke. With the manager gone, he focused on the next batter, who was huge. A terrifying giant with arms the size of tree trunks. He had to get the ball under those arms, somehow, but there was no room. He squinted and peered, trying to find a spot of open air to aim for, but it was impossible, and when he finally threw the ball anyway, it shattered into a million pieces, which the giant started eating with great snaps of his jaws. Then he swung the bat in circles over his head, around and around. Caleb watched, hypnotized and helpless, as the giant released the bat and it went winging across the infield right toward his head.

Caleb woke up in a hot sweat. He rolled out of bed and shook himself like a dog, trying to get rid of the feeling of the dream. When the sense of failure and helplessness still clung to him, he headed for the bathroom. Dwight, his roommate for the road trip, hadn't returned last night, so there was no one to chase him out of his hot shower before he was done.

He took a long time in there, letting steam fill the shower stall and scalding water sluice across his skin.

What if the Game had spooked him? What if that one outing had been so traumatic that he would never fully recover?

He shook his head. That was *bullshit*. He was a baseball player. A flamethrowing fastballer who enjoyed the mental aspect of the game even more than the physical. He was mentally tough, everyone always said so. He'd pitched out of hundreds of jams. Thousands. He was an intimidator. An elite prospect. He'd get past this little bump in the road.

On impulse, he fired up his laptop and went to the *Sports Illustrated* site. He typed in his own name. Right away the latest article popped up. "Hart of Darkness. What's wrong with Caleb Hart?" Written by John Firestone.

Oh for Chrissake. He shouldn't read this. It would mess with his head even more. *Don't read it. Don't read it.*

But now that he had it open, he couldn't stop himself.

Ask any knowledgeable baseball fanatic about major league baseball's most intriguing pitching prospects, and Caleb Hart will be one of the first names mentioned. He's known as a ferociously intelligent, intensely competitive, wildly talented young fastballer whose changeup, when it's working, can make a batter's eyes cross. His fastball has been clocked at 97 miles per hour. His ERA coming out of Triple A was 1.23, and he averaged six strikeouts per game. That's an average. So why is this phenom now in Kilby, Texas, dodging the tumbleweeds and playing for the always-quirky Catfish?

The process of figuring out "What's wrong with Caleb Hart?" started as an academic exercise, but soon became more like a journey into the heart of darkness.

Struck with sudden horror, Caleb scanned quickly through the rest of the article, looking for the name "Bingo" or any mention of his father. But no, the writer had stuck to interviewing coaches, managers, other pitchers, and even one of the batboys who'd been at Target Field for that epic game. Phrases like "loss of confidence," "weirdest thing I ever saw," and "psychological *Apocalypse Now*" screamed past his eyeballs. He logged off his laptop, slammed it closed, and threw himself out of the chair. Strode to the window and looked down on the grim little parking lot of the Econolodge.

Breakfast. He needed coffee, some fried eggs and bacon, and maybe some toast. And he needed the ball. More workouts, that was the answer. He'd work out his legs, that might help him pushing off the mound. He'd build up his core strength too.

He checked his watch. No time for a run. He barely

had time for breakfast. Quickly, he packed his bag, shoved his laptop in its case, then texted Tessa.

Kids get to school okay?

Just dropped them off. Text you later. Guess what? I got into med school. Got the news last night too late to call you.

Awesome, Tess! Knew you'd do it. Dr. Hart. Nice.

It's expensive.

Good thing you have a million-dollar ballplayer for a brother.

He could practically hear her snort all the way from Plano.

Medical school. Hundreds of thousands of dollars in tuition fees. Endless hours away from the twins. Taking classes at the local college was one thing, but med school was different. It would take all her time. They'd have to figure something else out for the kids. Aunt Mary had offered to live with them, but the boys paid no attention to her. The house might get burned down if she was in charge.

Whenever Bingo mentioned seeing the twins, Caleb hit the roof. As far as he was concerned, Bingo had lost his rights as a parent when he went to prison. No way did he want the kids around him. He'd quit baseball before he let that happen.

Out in the hallway, he ran into Mike Solo, and they headed downstairs, catching glances from the other guests.

"You missed a hellacious party, dude," Mike said, jamming sunglasses over his bloodshot eyes.

"I'm not worried about it. There's always another party."

"What did you do? Snuggle up with your ERA? Stick pins in a voodoo doll of your pitching arm?"

"Get off my back." They clattered down the steps,

their steps echoing in the stairwell. "Why can't everyone talk about something else for a while?"

"I want to, but when my good buddy gets profiled by
Sports Illustrated, I gotta read that shit."

Caleb stopped dead and pinned Mike against the
wall with one hand. "Don't mention that piece of crap
story around me. I'm serious."

"Okay." Mike nodded, but as soon as he was a few
steps away, he started whistling. Caleb wasn't a hundred percent sure, since he hadn't seen the movie in
years, but he was pretty sure it was the theme of *Apocalypse Now.*

Brett Carlisle loved the Sluggers for Slugs idea; Mayor
Trent had some doubts.

"I don't want any controversy. This is the Catfish
we're talking about."

"But they're trying to improve their image. And they'd
help us get more press attention," Sadie pointed out.

"I don't trust the Catfish not to make a joke out of it.
I want to make sure the positive coverage is worth the
risk. Feel out the local press on the topic. But discreetly,
in case I nix the whole plan."

So a few days later Sadie caught up with Burwell
Brown, reporter for the *Kilby Press-Herald,* outside the
newspaper's downtown offices. A year ago the Wade
family had tried to use him to plant a libelous story
about Sadie. He'd refused, and ever since then Burwell
had been her favorite reporter. Now that she worked for
the mayor, she fed him tidbits of news, like a wild bird
she was trying to tame.

"Please tell me you have a tip about a big exposé that
will get me a Pulitzer," Burwell said to her. "Or at least
the front page."

"Sorry." Sadie shook her head regretfully. "I don't

have anything reportable right now. I liked your last scoop, though."

"Riiiiight. Another 'Goofy Antics of the Minor Leagues' story. In this town, they're my bread and butter. Did you hear what the Catfish did on their last road trip?"

She shook her head, wondering what he would think if he knew she'd talked to a certain Catfish pitcher every night for the past week.

"They kidnapped a cow and got it into the home clubhouse of the Isotopes. Dressed it in an Isotopes uniform and a tiara. Ellington nearly blew a valve."

She shook her head, thinking about how fun it would be to tease Caleb about his rambunctious team.

"But what can I do for you, Sadie? I know you're not here about baseball."

"Actually, I am. Partly. Have you heard of the horn-toed slug?"

"The fate of the poor doomed horn-toed slug keeps me up at night," he said dryly, adjusting the horn-rimmed glasses on his dark cocoa face. "Why?"

"It's not a sure thing yet, but I wanted to gauge the media's interest. What would you say if a new and very prominent member of the Catfish became the spokesperson for the Save Our Slugs campaign? What would you think if they called it Sluggers for Slugs? Do you think readers would be interested? And do you think the Catfish could get some positive coverage for a change?"

"Is the player Caleb Hart?"

She gave a start. "You've heard of him?"

"Kid, everyone in Kilby's heard of Hart. Most fascinating new player we've ever had here. And he won't talk to the media, not since he got sent down."

Now that part, Caleb hadn't mentioned. This was even better than she'd hoped. "I might be able to con-

vince Caleb Hart to talk." He certainly hadn't mentioned anything about *not* talking. "About the slugs,
anyway. Theoretically, would you be interested in that
story? I can keep some elements exclusive to the *Press-
Herald*, of course."

Burwell Brown looked like a kid at his first birthday
party. She'd never seen him so excited; so that's what
he looked like when you weren't pestering him to cover
school lunches. "That's a big ol' Texas hell yes, Sadie.
You aren't just teasing me, are you? Because that would
be cruel, after everything your boss has put me through
lately."

She brushed off that little dig. "I'm not teasing, but
like I said, nothing's for sure yet. I'm testing the waters."

"The waters say come on in."

"Great."

He gave her a fist bump. "You take care now, Sadie.
If you need anything, regarding those Wades . . ."

"I'm good. I'm moving on," she said, her face turning the temperature of a brick oven. "Don't people in
this town have anything else to talk about?"

"When Kilby's founding family throws dirt around,
people tend to pay attention. Call me when you have
this nailed down, you hear?" And he hurried off, a
bounce in his step she'd never seen before.

Her feet, on the other hand, felt like lead. Every time
she thought she'd moved past the Hamilton Disaster,
someone mentioned the Wades and it all came rushing back. The Wades were . . . She didn't want to call
them evil, but they protected their own, no questions
asked. One of Hamilton's uncles was the police chief
of Kilby, and his father owned the biggest ranch in the
county. When oil was discovered in their backyard,
they'd become instant millionaires. Apparently all that

money had gone into spoiling their blond, blue-eyed, football-hero oldest son.

Actually, all the Wade cousins liked to get their way. And they liked to party. And they *did not* like to be broken up with. Sadie was the first, in fact.

The breakup itself wasn't difficult. Half stoned, Ham went through an entire bag of sour cream and onion Ruffles while she presented her carefully rehearsed speech about going in different directions and not wanting to hold him back. Of course, she didn't mention the real reasons—his growing drug habit, regular cheating, and general incompatibility.

When she finally finished, he held up one hand, fingers splayed apart, and peered through the gap between thumb and forefinger, framing her face between them. Then he snapped them together, making her jump. "Hasta la vista, babe. See ya, wouldn't want to be ya."

That was it? She left his bachelor pad condo, practically running past the members of his entourage lolling around the pool, so relieved to put the breakup behind her that she didn't analyze Hamilton's last words.

But they came back to her with a vengeance the first time she stopped in at Starbucks to grab a coffee. Everyone looked up when she walked in, and the barista could barely take her order for laughing. While she waited for her iced mocha latte, the whispers echoed around her like the hissing of snakes. "Sadie . . . did you see . . . Facebook . . . slutty . . . Sadie . . ."

And then the barista called out her name, not just "Sadie," but "Slutty" buried inside a cough. Smothered laughter spread across the room, but no one would meet her eyes as she walked out, face burning. With the bile of fear tightening her throat, she tossed the mocha latte in the trash outside. As soon as she got home, she went on Facebook and tracked down a new page called S****y Sadie. It already had five hundred likes. Revoltingly sexy photos, some of her, some of other people, populated the page. Her full name was never mentioned, but anyone who knew her and Hamilton couldn't possibly mistake her.

Horrified, she scanned the photos, which just skirted the line between sexy and likely to be banned. When had Hamilton taken that blurry picture of her in the shower? She didn't remember that. When had he snapped a shot of her in bra and panties, standing in front of an open refrigerator door? And then a zoom-in on her butt as she bent over to reach inside? Judging by these photos, she spent most of her time half naked. Some of the shots must have been taken by someone else—like the one of her sitting on his lap at a party, putting her hand on his zipper . . . she didn't remember doing that, but she remembered that party. She'd had a few too many margaritas. There had been body shots . . . Yup, there was a photo Hamilton squeezing lime juice on her navel.

Oh God. Maybe the photos wouldn't look so bad, so "Girls Gone Wild," if he hadn't added gross captions, like "Slutty S***e likes a licking."

Sickened, she'd shut down the computer. All her embarrassing moments caught on camera and posted in one place. With sleazy captions.

What should she do? she'd agonized. What *could* she do?

Ignore it, she decided. *He's mad right now, but he'll stop soon. He'll forget about me.*

The problem was, he *hadn't* forgotten. Hamilton and his entourage made it into a game. A mean, vicious game. They'd treated her reputation like a fumbled football up for grabs, tearing at it like dogs. She'd broken the cardinal rule of the Wade family: they always had the upper hand. And she'd paid. Oh, how she'd paid. So had her mother, who'd been so traumatized that she still avoided the Internet, not to mention large swaths of the gossip-loving population of Kilby.

And then someone forwarded the "sex tape" to her, and all her recent job rejections made sense. At least Caleb would never see that horrible tape, because it wasn't posted anywhere public. No—Ham held onto it for special occasions. Like when she went for job interviews.

Something brushed against her cheek. Surprised, she realized it was a tear. *Oh fireballs.* She wasn't about to cry over this again. She wasn't going back to that hell. Those days were over. Her life was in her own hands now. *The slugs.* Focus on the slugs.

Wiping away that stupid tear, she plucked out her phone. She should call Mayor Trent and let her know what Burwell Brown had said. But her finger wavered over the list of phone numbers, somehow, on their own, finding Caleb's.

Caleb, with whom she'd talked on the phone nearly every day for the past week. Caleb, who spoke like a grown man, not a spoiled boy. Caleb, who only had to answer the phone to send excited tingles shooting to her belly.

He was probably busy pitching, or working out, or on the team bus, and she'd have to leave a message. Still, she stared at his number, longing to hear his voice. Talking to him made her feel *good*, that's all there was to it. It honestly seemed as if they'd developed a real friendship. Friendship, nothing more, even though they sometimes strayed into flirtation. Well, more than sometimes. Still, this was just a project. Business. Save Our Slugs. It was safe. Perfectly safe.

She pressed his number.

"I was just thinking about you," he answered in that deep, rugged, sexy voice—the voice of a man who knew how to spin a girl around a dance floor and make her melt in his arms.

"Really?" she said faintly. *The slugs. Focus on the slugs.* "I have good news."

"Great. You can tell me over dinner. We just pulled up to the stadium."

"Oh. Well . . . uh . . ." Dinner sounded too much like a date. And someone might see them; she didn't want word getting back to Hamilton. She had to keep this safe. *Focus on the slugs.* "How about if I show you the slugs' habitat?"

"The slugs' habitat," he repeated.

"Sure. You probably want to know all about the slugs, since you're going to be dedicating yourself to their survival."

"Good point. All right. You're on. Bring on the slug habitat. Where should I meet you?"

"Can you go now? I'll pick you up."

"Sure thing." He still sounded a little bemused. The corners of her mouth quivered.

"Oh, and make sure to bring swimming trunks."

A pause. "Does that mean you'll bring a bikini?"

"I guess you'll find out. I'll be there in fifteen minutes."

She grinned as she ended the call. It was her turn to tease the unflappable Caleb Hart.

Swimming trunks. Now that was more like it. If the slugs' habitat included a girl in a swimsuit, he was all for it.

At the stadium, the usual gathering of wives, girlfriends, and baseball groupies waited in the parking lot. As Caleb scanned the crowd, he got a shock. Bingo stood off to the side, hands in his pockets, a jaunty smile on his face.

He nearly fell off the bus in his rush to get over there. "What are you doing here?" Grabbing Bingo's elbow, he spun him around toward the parking lot. "I told you to stay away from the ballpark."

"I missed you, son. I thought we could go grab a bite."

"How did you even get here?"

"Took the number seven bus, then walked a mile."

"Bingo . . ." He checked back over his shoulder, but the team was already dispersing and no one was paying any attention to him. "Nice thought, but I have plans. You should have called."

"You never answer my calls."

"It's a road trip. I've been busy."

"When you're home you're busy, when you're away you're busy." Bingo pulled his sad face, and for a moment Caleb got tugged in. His father must be lonely. He didn't know anyone in Kilby. Then he hardened his heart. It was a damn good thing Bingo didn't know anyone in Kilby, or he'd get up to his old tricks. And he'd warned Bingo that he couldn't babysit him; he'd offered him a place to live rent-free while he looked for a job. That was as far as it went.

"Yeah, well, I'm trying to revive my goddamn baseball career. It takes a lot of my attention."

"But . . . I could help. If we talked more, maybe I could understand more about baseball, and—"

"I really appreciate the thought. I do. But you should have called first. I'll see you back at—"

"Hi Caleb." He spun around. Sadie stood right behind him, out of breath, as if she'd dashed across the parking lot looking for him. With her bright eyes and smile, her presence felt like a fresh breeze in the desert. "I was afraid I'd missed you."

"Nope. Still here." He gave her a tense smile, trying to think of a way he could avoid introducing her to Bingo.

Too late. Bingo stuck out his hand. "Hi there, pretty girl. I'm Bingo, Caleb's father."

"Bingo," Sadie repeated with a faint smile. "I like that. I'm Sadie." She glanced in Caleb's direction. "Should we do this another time? The slugs can wait. They're not going anywhere very fast."

"No. This is the perfect time. We don't want them to go extinct on us, do we?" He dug out his car keys and tossed them to his dad. "You can drive the Jeep back. I'll see you later."

Bingo's crestfallen expression made him want to scream. He wished he could block it from Sadie's sight, because a soft-hearted thing like her would be guaranteed to fall for it.

Sure enough, "I promise I won't keep him long," she assured Bingo.

Caleb hustled her away, guiding her so quickly across the lot that she nearly stumbled.

"What the heck?" she protested.

"I missed you. We haven't talked in nearly a full day. I need my Sadie fix."

Despite her skeptical snort, she allowed him to drag her to her Corolla. Caleb had to push the passenger seat all the way back, and even so, his knees pressed against the dashboard. For a while they drove in silence.

"Want to tell me why you needed rescuing from your father?" Sadie asked as they cruised through town.

"Nope."

She shot him a narrow-eyed look but didn't pursue it.

"And by the way, it's damn good to see you, Sadie." She had no idea how good. After all their phone conversations, they'd gotten sort of cozy with each other, but being with her was about a thousand times better. She looked like a long-legged tomboy in denim cutoffs and a tight red T-shirt. He turned the full force of his widest grin on her, and saw her creamy cheeks turn pink.

"I gotta tell you, I really like the way you wear the color red," he told her. "Like those cowboy boots the first day I saw you."

"I can't believe you remember my boots."

"I remember everything. I told you."

She colored even more, until she practically matched her shirt.

Oh yeah, rattling Sadie was the best possible way to spend a Tuesday afternoon.

After about a fifteen minute drive, at the outskirts of town she pulled onto a gravel road that wound through a grove of tender-leaved river birches. The big Texas sky arching overhead, and a few late season bluebells scattered along the roadside, made Caleb feel, for the first time in a while, that he could take a deep, free breath. Soon the road petered out at the shore of a small, brownish lake.

"Slug home base?" he asked Sadie.

"This is it. One of the few remaining spots you can find horn-toed slugs. Of course, most people come here to fish. If only slugs were more fun to fish for," she added thoughtfully. "That's the problem with slugs. They don't really *do* much. And you wouldn't exactly call them cute."

"That's why you're bringing in the ballplayers." He winked. "According to the girls, we're a bunch of cutie patooties."

She rolled her eyes and got out of the car. He followed, strolling to the shore, where gentle little waves pitter-pattered against the muddy margin. Slimy, neon-green algae coated the gravel, and a stench of rotting vegetation wafted toward them. Caleb gazed at the unappetizing shoreline. "Uh . . . you were joking about the swimming trunks, weren't you?"

"What? Too icky for the big strong ballplayer?" Her eyes danced.

He looked from her to the murky lake, which looked more unappealing by the second.

She burst out laughing. "Sorry to get your hopes up. Believe it or not, you *can* swim in this lake. But unless you grew up here, it's probably too gross for you. Anyway, the slugs live along the shore, not in the water."

He gazed at the lake. Damn. He'd really been looking forward to that bikini. A devil's impulse seized him. "Well, it's just as well that I don't have any swimming trunks."

She quirked an eyebrow at him. "What do you mean?"

"I prefer skinny-dipping." And he ripped off his Catfish T-shirt in one smooth movement. The warm air felt good against his bare chest.

"*What?*" Her gasp was loud enough to wake up a few doves roosting in the river birches. He laughed and put his hands to the waistband of his jeans.

Chapter 7

"**Y**OU'RE NOT SERIOUS." Her voice came out kind of breathless—no surprise, since she suddenly had a hard time drawing a breath.

"Serious as a clambake." Caleb unbuttoned his jeans and pushed them down his thighs. His incredibly muscular, powerful, golden-haired thighs. Underneath, he wore gray briefs that nestled against the taut muscles of his rear like a needy girlfriend. "But you don't have to watch."

He winked at her, or at least she imagined he did. She couldn't tear her eyes away from his body long enough to find out. Lord almighty, those chest and arm muscles, tightening and stretching under all that tan, firm skin. And what about that ridge of pure iron that ran down his side, from his underarm to his hip. What was that called?

"Turn away, and I'll be underwater before you know it."

"Okay," she squeaked. It was rude to stare. But what were you supposed to do when someone started taking off his clothes right in front of you? Someone who looked like a Greek sculpture stepping out of his jeans? Since he was turned to the side, she couldn't really get a good look at the front of his . . . Good grief, what was she doing! She spun around so she was staring at the trunk of a river birch instead of the underwear of a Catfish pitcher.

She heard a few squishy footfalls, then a big splash and a "Whoop-whoop."

"You should come in," he called out to her. "It's refreshing, in a putrid kind of way. You sure it's safe?"

Peeking over her shoulder, Sadie saw him backstroking through the brown lake water as if it were the pristine Caribbean ocean.

"Now you ask me? Yeah, it's safe. It gets tested all the time because so many people fish here." She stepped closer to the edge, then bent to take her sneakers off before they got too muddy.

"Come on, Sadie. Live a little," he called. "Come swimming with me."

"Are you really naked?"

"Come and find out," he teased. He shook his wet hair away from his eyes, which shone with a wild blue light. "I dare you."

"I haven't swum here since junior high."

"Why should kids get all the fun? Come on." He splashed water at her, and she jumped back, nearly tripping over his pile of clothes, which, she noticed right away, didn't include his briefs. He must still be wearing those, the sneaky bastard.

"You tricked me," she called. "You're going to pay for that. Turn around!"

"Nope." Eyes glittering, he kept his gaze fixed on her. "Scaredy-cat."

"Fine, but I'm keeping my underwear on too."

"I'll take whatever I can get."

Oh, that deep, teasing note in his voice was so . . . irresistible. Just to check, she pulled out the waistband of her cutoffs. If she was wearing her backup underwear, the ripped pair she'd been vowing to throw out, no way was she stripping down. Fortunately, she'd put on her favorite light blue boy-cut panties.

Before she could lose her nerve, she unsnapped her cutoffs and stripped them off. Caleb gave a wolf whistle from his spot in the lake. "Keep going," he called. "You don't want to get that shirt all wet, do you?"

She made a face at him, then teasingly pulled off her tank top. Her bra didn't match her panties, but at least it wasn't a total disgrace. It actually fit, with no loose straps, and it even pushed her boobs together for a little cleavage.

"Ah yeah," Caleb catcalled. "You make slug-hunting look goooood. Anything else?" he added hopefully.

"No! Now scoot over."

"Oh no. I'm a gentleman, I'm all about helping the ladies out. May I?" He waded to shore, water streaming off him, his briefs clinging to every impressive inch of his middle section. She made herself stare higher, at his broad chest and those magnificent shoulder muscles.

He held out his hand with a bow. Like a duchess, she laid her hand in his. Bad move. Next thing she knew, she was being whisked through the air and spun into the deliciously cool water.

The two of them splashed in, getting all tangled up together. Caleb's firm grip on her never wavered, and she clung to his mighty shoulders, spluttering and coughing to get the water out of her eyes.

"Sorry about that," he murmured in her ear. "Slipped on the mud."

"Yeah right."

"Or maybe it was a slug." He had her scooped against his hard chest as if she were a babe in arms.

Against her hip, she felt the nudge of something rising from his midsection.

She laughed up at him. "There's either a fish poking me, or, um . . ."

"That would be an 'or . . . um.'" He grinned at her. "What do you expect when you strip off all your clothes and jump into my arms?"

Strip off all her clothes . . . . Good Lord, she'd just stripped down to her underwear in front of a man for the first time since the Hamilton Disaster. And she hadn't thought about that stupid tape once.

Caleb made her lose her head, plain and simple.

She rested her forehead against his chest, amazed all over again by the firmness of his toughened muscles. The heat of his body contrasted with the cool water in the most heavenly way. "Maybe I didn't think this all the way through."

"Are you telling me a dumb baseball player got the better of a brilliant future law student? Nah." He bent his head so he could nuzzle her hair. "You smell nice. Like water lilies."

She smelled hot man, mixed with lake water and sun-baked mesquite. Somehow they'd drifted away from the gravelly edge, so the stench of mud wasn't as prominent. She felt so dreamy and secure, held tight in Caleb's arms as they floated aimlessly in the lake.

"I used to come here with my father when he was in town," she told him. "We'd bring a little rowboat and cast a line. Sit for hours, just drifting and fishing. I never got bored. I thought it was heaven." She tilted her head back so it rested on his shoulder. "You like to fish?"

"Never really fished much. But I must be a natural, because I caught myself a nice one." He grinned down at her, the light reflected off the lake water turning his eyes a soft, clear blue. Sun glinted in his hair, spangled

with crystal drops of water. He really was a remark-
ably beautiful man. Everything seemed to still while
she soaked in the details of his powerful physique, his
rawboned handsomeness, the flash of vulnerability in
his eyes.

She could really lose herself in him. Completely and
utterly. Never before had she felt anything close to that.

"Dream on," she told him, and flipped out of his
arms. She dove under the surface, letting the slide of
water through her hair and across her body wash away
the effects of that alarming moment.

She'd always loved to swim, and it took only a few
moments to put distance between herself and Caleb.
But he wasn't a professional athlete for nothing, and
within moments he was splashing in her wake.

She dove deeper, down to the muddy bottom, then
veered in a different direction. When she surfaced, he
was swimming the opposite way. She let out a hoot of
laughter. "Where are you going, Catfish?"

"Nice move, Sadie. But I don't give up easy." He
spun around and butterfly stroked after her, churning
the surface with his wheeling arms. After a taunting
laugh, she filled her lungs with air and slipped underwater again, swimming this way and that, like a fish.
Much as she loved to swim, she hadn't done it in years,
except when she swam laps in the on-campus pool. But
this was an entirely different kind of swimming, free
and wild. In her delight at being in the water, she lost
track of Caleb's location, and when she surfaced, gasping, he was only a few strokes away.

Shrieking with breathless laughter, she flung herself
backward, as if onto a watery couch. He grabbed an
ankle, and she flipped to her stomach, kicking hard. But
it was no use; she felt herself being inexorably pulled
toward him, his wonderfully big hands reeling her in.

And then there she was, snuggled against his chest again. It rose and fell with his rapid breaths. "There, that's better," he said with satisfaction, the words rumbling against her ear. "I kinda like this whole fishing thing."

"No fair, I got distracted," she protested, turning her body in the circle of his arms so she could see his face. Water streamed from his hair, down his neck to his wide shoulders. His eyelashes clung together, so his eyes looked bluer than ever. "I'd forgotten how much I love swimming in this lake."

"It's starting to grow on me too. Or at least something is. Hope it's not that green stuff."

She giggled, and then, as a grin split his face, started laughing. As he watched her something shifted in his expression. His goofy smile vanished, replaced by an intent, hungry look. His head lowered, eyes glittering. The rest of the world receded, so only his face remained, coming closer and closer to hers, his mouth reaching for her . . .

Oh wow. He was going to kiss her.

And then he *was* kissing her. His lips burned against hers, sending pure shock throughout her body. Kisses didn't feel like that. They didn't turn your lips to fire, they didn't liquefy your lungs so you could barely breathe. They didn't make you dizzy.

She pulled away with a gasp, still in his embrace, their faces close enough so she felt his quickened breathing. Caleb looked just as stunned as she felt, his eyes gone dark and gray as a hurricane. For a long moment the two of them just stared at each other, poised on the edge of the unknown. Water lapped against her hips, and a breath of air kissed her shoulder. Everywhere her body touched Caleb's, heat seared.

And then they were on each other again. She opened

her mouth to him, meeting his challenge with need and surrender. He seemed to consume her, exploring her mouth with long sweeps of his tongue that left sparkling trails of heat in their wake. He tasted so wonderful, like summer days, like fireflies and bicycling down dusty back roads, like every time she'd laid on her back in a meadow and dreamed about the future.

Little whimpers rose from her throat. She pulled her mouth from his, her cheek brushing across his stubbly chin, its roughness sending more shocks through her. His grip loosened and she slid down his body until she stood on the lake bottom, pressed against him from head to toe. The huge bulge in his briefs made her feel a little faint.

"Sweet Jesus," he whispered as she nibbled on his jaw. She couldn't help it; she wanted to eat him up. "You're making me crazy. We can't do this here."

"Shh." She didn't want to talk. She wanted this all-consuming, crazy conflagration that she'd never even imagined before. Tugging at his shoulders, she rose on tiptoe, brushing her lips against his again.

With a heartfelt groan, he gave in, claiming her mouth with a deep, hot hunger. She pressed against him, electric currents racing through her veins as their tongues entwined, stroking against each other in a wild dance, desire rising with every breath, every touch, every sigh and tremble.

When his warm hand cupped her breast, with its water-saturated bra, she nearly jumped out of her skin. His thumb shifted the edge of her bra to expose her nipple, which tightened in the fresh air. The sensory overload of wet skin and hot touch made her gasp. Her bra slid off her shoulders and Caleb dropped his gaze to her chest, holding her breasts in his big hands. If she didn't faint dead away from pleasure, it was because she

wanted to *keep feeling* that pleasure. It filled her mind
and body in a hot, incredulous rush and—

"Hey, isn't that Caleb Hart?" a voice called out.
Caleb tore himself away from her and swung around,
shielding her with his body. Sadie, gasping at the sudden
shift in circumstances—no, noooo!—covered her chest
with her hands then looked around wildly for her bra.
There it was, floating away with the current. *Fireballs*!

She dove into the water and crouched behind Caleb's
legs so no one could see her. A motorboat floated about
thirty yards away, carrying three fishermen. Well, two
of them were fishing. The other man was holding up a
smartphone. Oh my God. A smartphone. Slutty Sadie
was about to get caught with a Catfish star—topless. If
this got out, all the talk would flare up again. Ten times
worse.

"Hey, man," called Caleb. "Not cool."

"You're the new guy on the Catfish, aren't you?"

"Do you mind? My friend and I are having a conversation."

"Bet you're conversing about that bra that's about
to wash up in the mud." They all laughed and someone
said something about those crazy Catfish.

One of the fishermen chimed in. "Who's that with
you? Someone caught herself a live one."

Caleb growled; Sadie could feel him shake with fury.
She was afraid he'd launch himself at them and her
cover would be gone.

"Don't move," she hissed. "Don't let them see me."

"You have no idea how much I want to maul them
right now," he said through clenched teeth.

"Please. If they find out who I am . . . it'll be bad."

After a short pause, his voice softened. "I won't
let anyone see you. Just stay where you are. But don't
drown." He addressed the men. "Come on, guys. This

is a private moment. I'm not a baseball player right now, I'm just a guy."

"They got hotel rooms for that sort of thing."

Peeking around Caleb's legs, Sadie saw that no one was moving. Something slimy slid against her shin. She wanted to scream and jump out of the water but made herself stay still.

"Are you gentlemen baseball fans?" Caleb was saying. "How about front row seats for the whole family? All three of you."

"Now that's outright bribery."

"Just a little gesture of appreciation for doing the right thing and letting us get back to shore. I'll even throw in some Cracker Jacks. And some signed baseball cards for the kids. Anyone have kids? Grandkids, maybe?"

Biting her lip, Sadie watched, agonized, as the men murmured to each other.

"Fine. You get to stay out of the papers this time." The older man lowered his smartphone. The others craned their necks, trying to see behind Caleb, but Sadie pressed her face to his legs so they couldn't possibly get a good look at her.

Not until she heard the speedboat chug across the lake did she dare leave her protected crouch.

Caleb helped her up, fury still simmering in every line of his body. "I'm sorry about that."

She sloshed toward the shore, her arms crossed tightly across her breasts. "It's not your fault. It's mine. This was a huge, huge mistake."

"I wouldn't go that far," Caleb called after her. "Before they saw us, it was pretty much the best thing that's happened to me in a long, long time."

A thrill shivered through her. But she couldn't afford to soften. She'd nearly gotten shot right back into the living nightmare of the past year.

96   JENNIFER BERNARD

"I need to get out of here," she told him. "This isn't good."

"Why are you so upset? A couple of crazy kids kissing in the lake. It must happen all the time. What's the big deal?"

Sadie reached the spot where her bra had snagged on a low birch branch trailing in the mud. She wanted to grab it, but that would mean revealing her breasts again, and she couldn't risk that. No more exposure—of any kind. "That was my favorite bra," she told Caleb. "Can you get it?"

He plucked it from its muddy nest and picked algae off it. "I have fond feelings for it too."

She wanted to snatch it from his grasp, but kept her hands tightly clamped to her front. "Put it in my car, please."

With a quizzical glance, he tossed the bra through the open window of her car, then snagged his warm-up jacket from his pile of clothes, strode back to Sadie and wrapped it around her. When she gave a huge shiver, he ran his hands up and down her arms, creating warm tingles everywhere he touched. "What's going on here? Are you worried because of your job? Mayor Trent wouldn't like you consorting with a Catfish?"

She stared at him, struck dumb. She hadn't even thought about that part of the situation.

"Yes. That's it," she said in a tight voice. "I'm supposed to be doing a job here. I seem to have forgotten about that. I have to get dressed. Turn around, please."

He turned around in a little circle so he ended up right back where he'd started, looking straight at her, one corner of his mouth quirking up.

"Very funny." It would be funnier if every doomsday scenario she could imagine weren't running through her mind.

"Couldn't resist." He cupped her cheek in his palm. She fought against the comfort that big warm hand offered. "You shouldn't worry so much about Mayor Trent. I think she's cooler than she seems."

When she answered with a stony stare, he stepped away to pick up her little pile of clothing. He handed it to her—she finally took her hands from her chest to clutch her clothes against her body—then turned his back. "I promise I won't look. I've caused you enough trouble for one day. I'll meet you in the car when we're both dressed."

"Thank you."

He didn't break his promise once. She knew, because she stole about a thousand glances from over her shoulder, under her arm, however she could manage. The sight of Caleb Hart, muscles flexing smoothly under his wet skin, pulling on his jeans and T-shirt . . . well, it would have to keep her going for a while, because they really couldn't repeat this mistake anytime soon.

If Mayor Trent found out about this, she'd be severely disappointed. This was bad on so many levels.

But oh, the dreams she was going to have tonight.

In the car, rattling down the gravel road, her clothes clinging to her still-damp skin, she addressed something that had been bothering her ever since he'd said, *I've caused you enough trouble.*

"Caleb, don't feel guilty about this. Promise me."

His jaw set, and she knew she'd hit a sore spot.

"I mean it. It wasn't your fault. If anything, it was mine. I brought you here, I went in the lake of my own choice, I knew fishermen love this place."

"I goaded you into taking off your clothes. Then I got carried—" He broke off, pressing his lips together.

"Carried away. I know. So did I. I don't want you shouldering all the blame yourself."

He stayed silent, his face slanted toward the other window so she couldn't make out his expression.

"You carry the whole world on those shoulders, don't you?" she said softly.

"No. Just the important things, like watching out for the girl I'm with and . . . what's that on your shirt?"

She twisted around. A tiny, slimy brown creature clung to the sleeve of her red t-shirt. She gave an involuntary shriek, just the way she had back in her school days. Before she could take her hands off the wheel, Caleb reached over and plucked it off her sleeve.

He peered at it, turning his palm this way and that. "Horn-toed slug?"

"Yes," she said in a strangled voice.

"Stop the car. I'll find a nice leaf for it."

Speechless, she watched the big ballplayer slide out of her car, cradling the slug in one hand. He walked a few steps, placed it carefully on a nest of fallen birch leaves, then watched it for a moment. Looking up, he caught her eye. "You don't like them hurt, right?"

"Right. 'Save Our Slugs.' That's my motto."

But as they drove away, she couldn't help wondering who would save her . . . from falling for him.

Chapter 8

HER MOTHER WAS already home when Sadie got back; she'd parked her old brown van as if the driveway was just a suggestion. When Sadie was little, she'd loved their little pink house; now it looked dingy and broken-down. But her mother resisted change of any sort, including things like exterior paint and a much-needed new handrail.

"Mom?" Sadie stepped into the front hall, which was lined with boxes of old magazines, catalogues, and newspapers that her mother used in her decoupage and other crafts projects. It was probably a fire hazard, but since her interest in art was the only thing that brightened her mother's mood, Sadie considered it worth the risk.

"In the kitchen, sugarpie."

Evening light slanted through the windows, giving all the appliances a rosy glow. Brenda Merritt sat in her fuzzy bathrobe at the table, her long hair in a loose knot as she sorted through mail, an empty glass at her elbow.

"How was work?" she asked, looking up from a Restoration Hardware catalogue.

"Great," Sadie answered, as she always did. Her mother couldn't handle problems of any sort.

That's nice, sugar. It's good to keep your mind off things. Think about something that's not going to break your heart."

Okay then; not a good day for her mom. "Did any law school catalogues come?" Right away, she winced, knowing she'd picked the wrong question. Her mother hated any mention of law school—it would take her so far away—but Sadie just couldn't let go of that one wisp of a dream. She'd requested mailings from several of the top schools, just because she liked the glossy, studious world they depicted.

"Don't see anything like that, but you can look through here." Brenda sniffed. "I don't know why you think about something so out of your reach. That'd be like me goin' to the Oscars. You should be more practical, Sadie. Stick with what you got."

Sadie set her jaw, shifting her attention to the stack of mail, looking for anything law-school-ish, like brick buildings or serious faces.

"How was your day?" she asked her mother.

"Oh, fantabulous. Mrs. Wade came through my register."

Well, that certainly explained her mother's bad mood. "Did she say anything?"

"Not to me, she didn't. She talked on her phone the whole time about a barbecue they're throwing. Bought a whole buttload of chicken wings."

Sadie briefly imagined the Wades' guests coming down with salmonella, then scolded herself for the mean thought.

"She kept mentioning Hamilton's new girlfriend. Said he's crazy about her. Over and over."

"Good. Maybe he'll forget that he got dumped by a nobody like me."

Brenda picked up her glass, realized it was empty,

and slammed it down with a click. Her chin wobbled. "How many times did I tell you to stay away from boys like that?"

And how many times did she have to admit she'd picked a mean, spoiled boy? Didn't girls have the right to fall in love with the wrong guys? If her mother knew what she'd just been doing at the lake with a here-today, gone-tomorrow baseball player, she'd throw a fit. "You warned me," she repeated, for probably the hundredth time. "I didn't listen. But really, Mom—"

"You'd better be listening now. You're always so stubborn, Sadie Merritt. You think you know everything, and now you keep talking crazy about going to law school. I worry about you, Sadie. I really worry."

Sadie abandoned the pile of mail, and headed for the door. "It doesn't matter what I do, you're still going to worry! About everything! I'll be in the Chevy if you need me."

Brenda called after her, "Do you know how weird that sounds? Who spends their time hanging out in an old car? You're such a strange girl. No wonder I worry so much."

Blocking out her mother's familiar complaints, she hurried out the door and headed for her favorite spot in the world. A 1964 Chevy station wagon sat in the far corner of the yard, shaded by an old live oak tree. It had belonged to her long-gone father. The car, which didn't even run anymore, had been her safe haven when she was little, and again when the Hamilton nightmare unfolded. It held a nostalgic comfort for her even now, at the age of twenty-three.

She threw herself onto the comfy old back seat, which served as a study room, a bedroom when her mom had guests, and a place to dream. She felt horrible for snapping at her mother, after everything she'd put her through—everything she had caused with her bad judgment in dating a Wade. But her mother kept going over the same worries, over and over, no matter what she did or said. Wasn't there more to life than worry?

I'll make it up to her. Popcorn and an AMC marathon later.

Stretching out on her back, her hands folded under her head, Sadie gazed at the graceful, drooping branches drifting in the slight breeze. Sun-warm air curled around her cheeks.

And then she was back in the lake, wrapped in Caleb's arms, his hot mouth on her as if she were the most wonderful thing in the world.

In the Catfish bullpen, Caleb went into his windup, reared back and let fly a 97 mile per hour zinger into Mike Solo's glove.

"That's real good," Mitch the pitching coach called out. "Nice heat."

"Painted the inside corner," Mike agreed. "You still got it, Hart. No matter what *SI* says."

Caleb set his teeth. The guys hadn't stopped ragging him about that story, but he didn't mind too much. At least word hadn't gotten out about him kissing Sadie at the lake. She'd seemed so worried about people knowing, which made him determined to shield her from gossip. She brought out his fierce, protective side, which he usually saved for his family. But Sadie . . . Sadie was special. And if he doubted that, all he had to think about was that kiss.

Hottest thing he'd ever experienced. And it was just a kiss. Talk about a mind-blower.

"Again, Caleb. Fastball low and away this time."

The ball was back in his hand. He threw it again

before he even thought about it, still remembering how her mouth felt opening under his, alive with eager sweetness. Like drinking honey straight from the hive.

Wham. The ball thumped into Solo's glove. He whistled, rising to his feet. "Damn, Hart. What'd you do, kick it up a gear?"

That felt *good.*

"Stop jabbering and throw it back."

Solo tossed the ball back and settled into his crouch. After a glance at Mitch, the catcher signaled for a changeup.

Caleb fixed the target in his mind, adjusted his grip, and let fly the best changeup of his life.

Mike whooped. "That's it, Mitch. We got our boy back."

Caleb grinned. Energy flowed through him, fast and furious. He could pitch all day and all night feeling like this. Kilby might think the Catfish belonged to them, but the whole purpose of a Triple A team was to get players ready for the Show, and at this point Caleb topped the list of guys the Friars wanted back on their forty-man roster. All he wanted was to prove he was ready for that.

Mike slung an arm over his shoulder as they left the bullpen and ambled across the field toward the dugout. "Take that, *Sports Illustrated.*"

"In your *face.*" God, it felt good. The groundskeepers were reapplying the chalk on the lines. Bright white against pure green grass—the colors of summer. He soaked in the sight.

"Word up, dude. Me and a couple other guys got a call from a local reporter about some crazy-ass petition against the Catfish. Funniest thing you ever saw. It calls us morally depraved and some other shit. I think they're making one of those oddball 'life in the minor leagues' stories out of it. Think I should tell them about my vow of celibacy?"

"No way. You'll have every girl in town gunning for you. Everyone likes a challenge."

"Exactly. I'll have my pick come September."

"You dog." They trotted into the dugout, where Caleb sat on the bench to pick the dirt out of his cleats.

"Anyway, they might call you, even though you're new here. Check your e-mail. PR department sent us all a direct order to keep our mouths shut."

"Don't need to tell me twice."

As Mike left through the dugout door, Caleb pulled out his cell and called Sadie. "Word's out about the petition."

"I know. One of the Ladies' Auxiliary members leaked it to the *Press-Herald*." She had her business voice on. Damn. He'd been hoping she'd softened since their lake adventure. "At least it's just local."

"What does the mayor think?"

"She's on the phone with Crush Taylor right now. I think they're negotiating some joint comment."

"Any fallout from yesterday?" His voice went deep and husky at the memory of their moment in the lake.

A pause. "Caleb . . ."

Fuck. She was going to tell him she couldn't see him again. In her tone of voice, he could hear the axe about to fall. She was worried about her job, he got it. But they were two single young people; who could blame them for being attracted to each other? There must be something else going on. Something she wasn't telling him.

Before she could finish her thought, he interrupted. "I bet I know what Crush is telling the mayor. If the petition's going public, he'll want us to get going on Sluggers for Slugs right away."

"Maybe. They've been talking for a long time."

"I'm pitching tonight. Do you want to come? I can leave tickets for you." He held his breath. He had a feeling tonight was going to be a big night. With his groove finally back, all he wanted to do was get out there and humiliate some opposing batters.

"I'll try. I'm working late on budget stuff with the mayor."

"I can leave a ticket for her too. Courtesy of the morally corrupt and depraved Catfish. And the man who ruined her assistant's favorite bra."

She let out a burst of rippling laughter. "Come to think of it, you do owe me, Catfish."

Flirty Voice was back. *Whew.* Dumping averted—at least for the moment.

That night, the first game of a three-night home stand against the Sacramento River Cats, was Dental Health Night, sponsored by a coalition of dentists. The Jumbotron flashed tips about cavity prevention, and the first five hundred fans through the gate received giant foam toothbrushes. Just another day in the wacky minor leagues. Normally, Caleb would have been rolling his eyes, but tonight he had other things on his mind. During the Catfish's at-bats, he kept compulsively scanning the stands, looking for Sadie.

On the mound, things were shaking out exactly as he'd hoped. He was on fire through the first two innings. He only had to throw eleven pitches the first inning, and even fewer the second, as he got a dribble to first, a foul-out, and a strikeout in less than ten minutes.

The fans knew it too. The sound of thousands—well, at least two thousand plus—people clapping gave the pleasant evening air a glow and an addictive buzz. It was one of those wonderful evenings at the ballpark when it seemed that nothing could dampen the mood. The Catfish's hits kept falling in the right places, the River Cats couldn't touch him, the temperature was just right. The only thing missing was Sadie.

Caleb told himself that she was probably stuck at work with the mayor, making up for the problem he'd caused by kissing her at the lake.

Sadie's warning that he shouldn't blame himself had gone in one ear and out the other. Of course he blamed himself. Hadn't he been plotting how to get her into bed for days now? He hadn't planned on getting her into a lake in her underwear, but he sure had seized the opportunity when it came up. Completely his fault.

Besides, he didn't carry the world on his shoulders. Not even close. Just the team. And his family. That didn't count as the "world." And if he couldn't handle that, he didn't deserve to be called a man.

At the bottom of the fifth inning, when the Catfish had two men on base and no one out, trying to pad a 3-0 lead, something in the stands caught Caleb's eye. A man in a straw hat, not cowboy-style, but boater-style, with a ribbon around it. A hat you might see at the Kentucky Derby. The man wore big white-rimmed sunglasses that hid nearly his whole face and made him look ridiculous. He was eating peanuts from a bag and chatting with a group in the row ahead of him, leaning forward to listen. It was the *way* he listened, with his head cocked, as if nothing could be more interesting, that caught Caleb's attention.

It couldn't be. His father wouldn't dare, after he had specifically forbidden him to come to a game. It must just be a weird resemblance.

When the man leaned back in his seat and tossed a peanut into his mouth with a lightning quick move,

Caleb knew without a doubt. That was his father's favorite trick to entertain kids. It had worked on him, and on any number of kids related to wealthy older women. Who didn't trust a man adored by one's grandkids?

No doubt about it. Bingo was in the stands.

Top of the seventh inning. Caleb took the field with the rest of the team, jogging out to the mound. His legs felt like lead. Random unpleasant thoughts stumbled over each other. *What's he doing here? Father son reunion, my ass. He's up to something. Where'd he get those white sunglasses? I ought to alert security and get him kicked out. Everyone's a cheater. Maybe he stole the sunglasses out of some old lady's purse. Yep, that's my dad.*

Someone was yelling. The umpire. Right. First batter up. Pedro Guttierez, righty who liked 'em fast and high. Solo called for the changeup, which looked like a high and tight fastball until the bottom dropped out just as the pitch was crossing the plate. *Focus, Hart, focus. Doesn't matter if Beyoncé's in the stands, gotta get Pedro out. Those look like Beyoncé sunglasses, come to think of it. Maybe Bingo scammed some shades from Queen Bey. Shit. What's that?*

The pitch he'd delivered went flying past him, a little blooper right over his head. He jumped, trying to get a glove on it, but he was a half step too late. He came down stumbling, while Pedro, incredulous at his good fortune, booked it to first.

Caleb tried to shake it off, walking around the mound. One man on base was nothing. All he had to do was get the next guy, Koji Tanaka, to hit into a double play. Or strike him out. Or induce him to fly out. So many ways to get a guy out. *Everyone's a con. Don't you try to fool the hitters?*

Mike put up two fingers for a curve, but he shook

him off. He wanted to throw some hard heat. With
a shrug, Milts set up for a fastball. Caleb went into
his windup, ignoring the blurred faces in the stands,
all of whom seemed to be wearing white sunglasses,
and delivered a fat, juicy fastball right over the plate.
Home run.

Three hits later Duke came to the mound and held
his hand out for the ball. "You're done, Hart." Caleb
took a quick glance at the stands, but the straw boater
and white sunglasses were gone.

"I'm good, Duke. I pitched myself into this jam, I can
pitch myself out."

"No. You're done. You had six good innings, Hart.
Not bad. Things are looking up, big guy. Now go."

The taste of failure bitter on his tongue, Caleb sur-
rendered the ball and loped off the field. His teammates showed no reaction, which he appreciated to the
bottom of his soul.

He slumped onto the bench a good distance away
from anyone else. The familiar scent of sweat and dirty
socks, leather gloves and turf, relaxed him. The smell of
baseball. He loved this game. Baseball had saved him in
more ways than he could count. Baseball was all about
the numbers, and numbers didn't lie. Numbers didn't
cheat. Numbers were cold, hard reality, and he'd take
that any day over finding out your entire childhood was
a bunch of lies.

When the police had first come for Bingo, he'd been
at home, studying for his chemistry final. In fact, he and
his friend Pete—a genius when it came to science—were
on the phone working on a foolproof way to share the
answers. Caleb knew the history stuff cold, so they decided to work out a trade. They'd just figured out a code
system when a knock on the door interrupted them. It
was the kind of knock that meant business. When he

opened the door and saw two police officers, he just about had a heart attack.

Did schools send the police after cheaters?

Hiding his terror behind the famous Hartwell smile, he had answered the officers' questions. When he figured out they weren't after him, but Bingo, his terror didn't lessen.

"He's at Applebee's, I think. With his girlfriend." No, he wasn't at Applebee's. His father despised the place. Stupid lie, because it would be so easy to check. But the lies kept pouring out of him.

They asked about his mother. "She's traveling in Europe." That sounded so much better than "She abandoned us for a race car driver."

"Is your father home a lot?"

"Well, sure, as much as he can be. He tries to work from home as much as possible."

"What work does he do?"

"He's a consultant."

The glance the cops shared was one step from an eye roll. "Well, son, we have a search warrant here. Want to step aside so we can take care of this?" It wasn't a request.

"But . . . shouldn't you call my dad? He's not far. He can be here in a few minutes."

"I'm afraid he's across state lines, kid. We'll have him in custody shortly." Realizing the police knew every word out of his mouth had been a lie, he'd wished a thunderbolt would incinerate him on the spot. "Social Services should be here in a few minutes."

"We don't need that," he said quickly. "I'm eighteen. Two months and three days," he added for extra accuracy, as if that could make up for his lies.

"Not up to us." They pushed past him, flashing the warrant at him, and all he could think was to hide the

chemistry book and don't let them look at his phone
with all those texts. *Do they send people who try to
cheat on tests to prison? What if they're just thinking
about cheating and haven't actually done it?*

After they'd rifled through Bingo's office, filling
several boxes with papers and photos and mementos,
one of the officers paused at the door. "You seem like
a good kid, so let me give you some advice. Remember this moment. Remember how this feels. And try to
do the right thing. Even if you think you're trying, try
harder."

He knew about the cheating. Shame, quick and ruth-
less, filled him the way the creek behind their house
flooded every spring. He nodded, though it seemed to
take a huge amount of effort to move his head. Getting
his legs to move, to carry him to the door, sapped the
rest of his energy. After closing it, he watched out the
window as the officers carried their boxes to the two
police cars parked outside. Every neighbor on the street
was blatantly watching the show.

Even though he'd never, not once, considered cheating at anything ever again, that hot, sickening, debili-
tating sense of shame had moved in and become such
a permanent fixture he didn't even notice it anymore.
It was just there, like red on roses or stink on shit. But
sometimes it crept out of its hiding hole and sapped the
life out of him.

Farrio was pitching now. Bases were still loaded, but
he struck out the next batter. The audience responded
by cheering and waving big foam toothbrushes in the
air. Caleb grinned, feeling slightly better. No matter
what, life went on. So did baseball.

He scanned the crowd. *White sunglasses.* There
was Bingo. He'd moved seats. What was he doing here
anyway? If he was looking for another old lady to scam,

a ballpark wasn't the best hunting ground. He shaded his eyes and squinted to see who Bingo was talking to, and saw red.

Sadie in red. Talking to Bingo.

Everything that happened next was a blur.

Chapter 9

Duke slammed his office door so hard a framed photo of Nolan Ryan fell off the wall and toppled face forward, as if ashamed to be in the room with Caleb.

Caleb winced. He stayed close to the door, not daring to get any closer to his furious manager. Not when he was in this kind of mood.

"What the fuck were you doing up there? If you say helping that man with dental hygiene, I'll bench you for a month."

"Sorry, Duke," Caleb muttered.

"Sorry? *Sorry?* You're supposed to be making the Catfish look good. Not assaulting our customers *in the stands.*"

"I didn't assault—"

"Did I miss an e-mail? Does Sluggers for Slugs mean actually *slugging* the fans?"

"There was no slugging."

Duke flung himself into his chair, shoved a big wad of cherry gum in his face, then bolted to his feet again. "I've never heard of anything like this happening at any other ballpark. A pitcher climbing into the stands and whaling on a fan."

"It won't happen again." He cleared his throat,

scrambling to come up with some kind of explanation without revealing too much. "I was in the dugout, and I thought I saw a crime in progress. My protective instincts kicked in."

"Nice try."

And yet, it was the truth. The only thing on his mind had been getting Bingo away from Sadie. It had worked too. Bingo had slipped through his grasp and scurried out of the ballpark.

"When I realized I was mistaken, I hung out with the crowd for a little while. I signed twenty foam toothbrushes. And one woman's chest."

"Who was it? Who'd you think you saw up there?"

Fuck. Cold fear sent icy fingers down his spine. He couldn't afford for Duke to know that Bingo was in town. "I told you, it was a mistake."

Duke butted his chest against Caleb's. The scent of cherry blasted him in the face. "If you got family shit going on, deal with it *outside* the ballpark."

"Yes, sir."

"I have to put this in my report to San Diego, Hart. What am I supposed to say? He's getting the juice back, but losing his freaking mind?"

Caleb stayed silent, letting Duke get the rest of his rant out. He knew he deserved every spitting word. It was probably nothing compared to the fury Sadie would dish out.

She'd been so horrified by the crazy scene that she crawled behind the bleachers and disappeared even faster than Bingo. He'd texted her and gotten no response. Bingo, on the other hand, had texted him about twenty apologies. His agent had sent him a scathing message saying they needed to talk, stat.

When Tessa and the twins called that night, Caleb had to tell them what happened. Teddy and Frankie kept cracking up and asking if anyone had been filming it. But Tessa said only, "Geez, Caleb. Are you trying to get the Friars to drop you?"

Could he possibly fuck things up worse? Hard to imagine.

The next day, things got worse. Caleb stared at the sports section of the *Kilby Press-Herald*, which featured a crisp color photo of his hand fisted around Bingo's shirt, his father's weird sunglasses making him look like a pinned bug. Sadie stood next to them, mouth open, hands in the air as if she were on a roller coaster. In the background a forest of foam toothbrushes waved.

Bingo peered over his shoulder. "Those sunglasses were a good call, I think."

"Yes, a genius move. Thank you for that, Bingo." *Not.* "You still haven't explained why you came to a game when I asked you to stay away from the ballpark."

"When you were a kid you cried when I didn't make it to a game."

"No, I didn't." Yes, he did. But the hell if he'd admit it now. That naïve kid was dead and gone.

"I'm trying to be supportive, Caleb." Bingo wandered to the fridge, his linen trousers incongruously elegant in the tiny kitchen. "What do you want from me?"

"If you want to be supportive, you could start with the finances. How's the job hunt going?"

Bingo took out a carton of orange juice and poured himself a huge glassful. That orange juice was expensive. The man never denied himself anything, as far as Caleb could tell.

"Well, son, it's not easy when all your job experience is of an illicit nature. But things are looking good over at the Laundromat. It's far beneath my skill level, but my probation officer keeps reminding me not to be so picky. It will give me plenty of time to work on my memoirs."

"Your 'memoirs'?"

"Under a pen name, of course. Don't get so panicky, son. I have a pretty fascinating life story, or so they tell me."

Either Bingo was making this up as a way to get under his skin, or he was serious, in which case . . . well, either way, Caleb didn't want to hear any more about it. He brushed past his father and grabbed the phone book that sat on top of the refrigerator along with other assorted junk.

The white pages listed only one Merritt, first name Brenda, on Brownsville Lane. He snapped it shut and tossed it on the counter. "I have to go see someone. I'll be back later. If you go out, don't wear those sunglasses. They're too recognizable. You can wear mine." He tossed his aviators to his dad.

"Sure thing, kiddo. Don't want to cause any more trouble."

Of course he didn't. He never *wanted* to. It just happened no matter what.

Caleb drove to the address listed, which was in a low-rent neighborhood where every tiny house seemed to have an old truck or junk car parked in the front yard. Not so different from some of the neighborhoods he'd lived in, when Bingo's luck was on a downslide.

Taking a deep breath, he rang the doorbell of a vinyl-sided, salmon-pink house with an old TV antenna sticking from the roof at an oddly jaunty angle.

A woman in her forties, with sleepy eyes and long black hair piled on her head, opened the door. She pulled a white earbud from one ear, and Caleb caught the faint sound of a droning voice. "Well, who the heck are you?"

"I'm Caleb Hart."

"Get out of town."

Did she mean that literally? He opened his mouth to ask if Sadie lived there, but just then she appeared at the end of the hallway, barefoot, in a tight white top over a sports bra. Her ragged cutoff jeans ended just below her ass and left her long legs bare.

"Sadie, can I talk to you for a few minutes?"

"I'm kind of busy," she said stiffly, crossing her arms over her chest. "I'm helping my mom with some important stuff. Which is why I haven't answered the phone."

Sadie didn't seem interested in introducing him to her mother, so he took matters into his own hands. "I'm Caleb," he told her mother. "It's nice to meet you . . ."

She got a look on her face that reminded him strongly of the first moment he'd met Sadie, when she'd elbowed him in the stomach and told him to watch where he was going. "Brenda Merritt."

"Do you mind if I talk to your daughter for a few minutes?"

Brenda Merritt shrugged and reluctantly made way for Sadie, who padded barefoot down the narrow hallway toward him. "If it was up to me, I'd say buzz off. But no one listens to me around here anyway."

"I listen, Mom," said Sadie sharply. "I've done nothing but listen."

"I'll be right inside if things get out of hand," Brenda said, one hand planted on her hip.

"There's no need for that. We're just going to talk." Sadie's firm tone made Caleb want to prove her wrong right then and there. She brushed past him, trotting down the front steps onto the scrubby grass, and gestured for him to follow her. He would have been hard-pressed not to do so, since he couldn't take his eyes off the long, gorgeous legs flashing quickly across the lawn.

"You shouldn't have come here," she hissed at him as she led him away from the house, toward an old faded-turquoise Chevy that sat nestled under a tree. It seemed the most private spot around; he wondered if it was her version of a tree house.

"You wouldn't answer my calls or texts. I couldn't just let it slide."

"I assume you're here to apologize for landing me in the *Kilby Press-Herald*?"

"Yes. I'm really sorry, Sadie."

"Apology not accepted. I need more." She leaned against the Chevy and crossed her arms over her chest. He couldn't help it, his gaze dropped to her breasts. A hint of shadow nestled between them, like a secret begging to be told.

Swift fury swept over him. Why did he care whether she accepted his apology? What was it to him? *Nothing.* He turned on his heel. Two strides took him across the crabgrass lawn toward the broken concrete of the sidewalk.

Fuck this. He was Caleb Hart, star pitcher, and he didn't have to apologize for shit.

About twenty steps across the lawn he hit some sort of bungee-like force field and his footsteps slowed until he came to a halt. Nope. He couldn't leave, not like that. He did a quick U-turn. Sadie was still leaning against the Chevy, watching him with wide, brilliant dark eyes, one long leg crossed over the other.

Those eyes. Fire trapped in darkness. Those eyes wouldn't let him leave.

He strode back to her and braced his hands against the car, with her trapped between. "What do you want from me anyway?" He growled the words like a snarling dog.

She didn't back down. In fact, she got right in his

face. "How about an explanation that makes sense for why you'd leave the field and come climbing into the stands like a lunatic and jump all over your father just for saying hi."

"You need to stay away from him. He wasn't even supposed to be there. He was wearing a freaking disguise so I wouldn't catch him."

"But why? What's so bad about your father?" She poked him in the chest. "You're not telling me something, Catfish. And I don't like that."

His jaw tightened so much he could barely get the words out. "Maybe it's better if you don't know some things."

Her eyes narrowed. With both hands on his chest, she pushed him out of the way. He took a step backward, thinking she wanted to put some distance between them, but instead she did the opposite. She swayed close to him, only inches separating their bodies.

"That's bullshit, Caleb." She slammed the flat of her hand against the car. "See this Chevy? That's the only trace of my father, besides a silly stuffed animal. For the longest time I actually believed my mother when she said he was in the CIA and had to live undercover. When I finally found out he was your garden-variety married man cheating on his wife, I felt like such an idiot. I'd rather just hear the truth. And before you say it isn't my business, you should have thought of that before you vaulted over that railing and scared the living crap out of me."

Her chest heaved with the force of her anger. Color burned in her cheeks. Her slim form vibrated like a plucked guitar string. Another feeling came over him. Crazy as it was, he was getting turned on. He shifted, easing the lump in his jeans. *Great timing, Hart.*

"I told you I'm sorry. That's why I came here, to

apologize." His voice sounded like sandpaper. God, he wanted her. He wanted all that fire and passion directed at him. He'd never felt this way before. Women were great. He liked 'em. No complaints at all. But he'd never felt like this, as if he'd wither away if he didn't have her.

The fiery scorn in her eyes told him his apology hadn't gone far enough.

"I'm very sorry, how's that? How can I make this right?"

Her nostrils flared. It flashed into his mind that the two of them together would be like a nuclear explosion.

"Well, it's a start, but—" But she didn't get a chance to finish because he couldn't take it anymore. He dragged her against him, his mouth on hers, his hands on her ass. Groaning with the relief of it—hot pressure against his hard-on—he barely heard the rest of her sentence.

"What are you *doing*?"

"I want you, Sadie. You don't know how bad. And when you talk to me like that, all fired up and passionate, I can't keep my hands off you." And he couldn't. His hands seemed to have a mind of their own, running free-range along the delicious place where her ass curved into her spine, back down to the sweet globes of her behind, to the tops of the long legs he craved to feel wrapped around his waist. He felt her nipples harden against his chest, her body respond to his touch. Hot words kept pouring out of his mouth. "You feel so fucking good. I want to get you naked right now. Take you right here against this car, so hard and hot you won't remember how we got here. Tell me you want me. Tell me, Sadie."

She tore herself out from his grip. "You know I . . . I'm very attracted to you." It was a ragged whisper. "But I don't know you, and I'm not doing that to myself again."

"What are you talking about?"

"You're not telling me something important. Maybe you were afraid your dad was going to tell me, and that's why you freaked out."

His heart skipped several beats. Did she know the secret he was keeping? Could she possibly? "Like what?"

"Like . . . maybe you have a girlfriend. Maybe you're going to make a fool out of me."

"I don't have a girlfriend." He let out a curt laugh. If she had any idea how much he'd avoided any involvement beyond sex, she'd be amazed that he was even *in* this conversation.

"So you're one of those, then? Love 'em and leave 'em . . . sorry, screw them and leave them? No, thanks." She flung an arm toward the sidewalk, as if gesturing for him to leave. He didn't. He stood right where he was, because his hands still burned to touch her and he wasn't going to leave her side, not yet. "I'm not the right one for you."

"Come on, Sadie. There's some serious chemistry between us. Why would you walk away from that?"

"Because sex isn't enough. Because I'm always going to want to know what's going on in here." She tapped the side of his head. Even after she dropped her hand, he felt the tingling sensation of her touch.

Again she gestured to the open air. "Go ahead. I'm not stopping you. I won't even be mad. We'll keep working on Sluggers for Slugs, or whatever else the team wants. I was thinking about having the players make cupcakes for the local morning news. Brett's sister owns a bakery, and she's offered to donate the space. Everyone loves cupcakes, and it would make you guys look adorable, plus we could sell them for like, fifty dollars a cupcake, and the money would go to the slugs—"

He dug his hands into his hair, feeling as if he were

drowning in her flow of words. Cupcakes? Why was she talking about cupcakes? And she was giving him little pushes, trying to shove him toward the sidewalk, out of her life.

And then, the last words he'd planned to say came pouring out of his mouth.

"My dad is Thurston Hartwell II, he's a con man and convicted criminal. He just got out of prison and he's living with me and no one knows and I don't trust him near another human being. Especially one I care about."

Of all the things Sadie had expected, nothing as explosive as Caleb's blunt revelation had crossed her mind.

"Thurston Hartwell . . ." The name rang a bell. She glanced at the house, wondering if her mother was eavesdropping. This corner of the backyard was the only truly private place on the whole lot, which was why she'd picked it. But sound could carry.

"Come here." Tugging at Caleb's hand, she opened the door to the Chevy and slid into the wide backseat. When the door was safely shut behind Caleb, cocooning them in warm, stuffy, spruce-air-freshener-scented privacy, she asked in a low voice, "Thurston Hartwell is the scam artist from Houston? The one who pretended to marry those widows?"

"That's the one. That was just one of his scams, by the way." His face was a piece of blank stone, absolutely no emotion showing; even his eyes held no expression. She felt terrible that she'd forced him into this confession.

"You changed your name."

"Wouldn't you? I didn't need that kind of baggage."

"Wow." Slowly, Sadie sank back against the cracked ivory vinyl of the car seat. Her mother might be an emotional mess, but at least she hadn't committed any felonies. "So he's living with you?"

"For now." He scratched at the back of his neck. "The other choice was a halfway house, and I couldn't . . . he's not a violent man. Just . . . not trustworthy."

"So you jumped into the stands because you were afraid for me?"

"I don't know. I didn't even think about it. I saw him, I saw you, and the next thing I knew I was clawing my way past a thousand foam toothbrushes." Finally, the faintest hint of a smile animated his face. "Shocked the hell out of me, I'll tell you."

"Does anyone else know?"

"Duke knows a little. Not all. He knows I took over guardianship of my twin brothers. He knows my real name. But I've never gotten into the nitty-gritty about Bingo. If he knows more, it's because he looked it up."

Sadie looked down at the floorboards of the Chevy, where a long-ago mango lip gloss had collided with one of her old journals. All of the fears that had been rattling around her brain were complete fantasies, products of her Hamilton-fueled paranoia. The crazy things she'd been thinking . . . that Caleb was married, that he was trying to make a fool of her.

Caleb's firm hand nudged her chin so she was looking at him. His face filled her field of vision, steel blue eyes gleaming with regret. "It changes everything, doesn't it?"

She stared at him blankly. Of course it did. Now, for the first time, she'd seen underneath the confident ballplayer facade.

"I know what you think when you look at me now," he continued in a low voice. "What anyone would think. Hell, just read the Can the Catfish petition. Morally corrupt. An embarrassment to the town. Depraved—"

Horrified, she put a hand to his mouth. "What are you talking about? Your father committed those crimes, not you. Why should anyone think something like that about you?"

Caleb's expression shuttered again. He shifted his body away from her with a movement that reminded Sadie he was a professional athlete with a champion's grace.

"He raised me. I'm his blood."

"What about your mother?"

"She was no better. One con after another. I knew about some of them, but not all. And I never did anything about it. Just did my thing."

"What were you supposed to do? You were a kid."

He shot her a scathing look. "Kids aren't always that innocent. That saying 'the apple doesn't fall far'? It's a cliché for a reason."

"I don't believe that." She swung her legs onto the seat and rose to her knees. Taking a chance, she moved next to him and wrapped her arms around his shoulders. His chest was a solid wall of flesh, his heartbeat a steady reassuring thump. "If I did, I'd be sleeping half the day like my mom. Don't you think we make our own destinies?"

He turned in her embrace and secured her arms in a circle around him. She linked her hands together. "I don't know."

She snorted skeptically. "You don't know? Didn't you become a baseball player instead of a scam artist?"

His mouth twisted. Caleb, she was learning, was stubborn as hell, even when it came to hanging onto the bad stuff.

"Look, Catfish, I don't know much about baseball," she went on, "but I'm pretty sure you can't con your way into the major leagues."

"If you could, think I'd still be in Kilby?"

She flopped back on her knees with an exaggerated gasp. "Now that . . ." She flung her hair over her shoulder. ". . . was uncalled for. As a member of the mayor's staff, I object."

"Oh no. Don't you go taking that personally." He cupped her face in his big hands, one on each cheek. "Meeting you is the best part of being sent down. No contest."

She frowned. "Is that like saying the best part of Hell is the warm temperatures?"

His laughter echoed through the stuffy interior of the Chevy. With his arms still linked around her, he tilted his head back, his Adam's apple shifting under the slight stubble darkening his neck. "I like the way you make me laugh. I don't know how you do it, but it's really working for me." He pulled her onto his lap, her breasts pressed against the hard musculature of his chest. Tendrils of heat curled through her body. "I told you what you wanted to hear. You said you wouldn't sleep with me because I wasn't telling you everything. Well, now you know. Where does that leave us?"

Chapter 10

THE AIR SEEMED to pulse around them like a living thing. Caleb's heartbeat echoed through her body in a galloping rhythm. The warmth of his embrace made her melt, and his nervous expression made her want to kiss him all over that rawboned face. He might be a big, powerful athlete used to getting lots of attention, but at this moment he seemed to care only about the next words that would come out of her mouth.

The problem was, she didn't know what to say. Logic told her to run, for countless very good reasons. She forced herself to list them. One, he was a ballplayer, and she'd been badly burned by an overindulged jock. But Caleb didn't seem spoiled the way Hamilton was. He seemed . . . lonely. As if he kept a big distance between himself and other people.

Two, Caleb had told her his secret, but she wasn't being exactly open herself. What if they got involved and then someone told him he was dating Scandalous Slutty Sadie and pissing off the entire Wade family? Three, she had a weakness for people who needed her help, and now that she knew Caleb's story, all her instincts were screaming at her to drop everything and fix his problems. Four, he was too damn attractive. If she took a step back now, she still had a chance of avoiding heartbreak. If she went to bed with him, would she have any hope of that?

And that wasn't even including her job, the low profile Mayor Trent had requested, and the Can the Catfish campaign. Reforming the Catfish probably didn't mean sleeping with one of them.

Still, she couldn't tear her gaze away from him, couldn't stop breathing in his scent, like sunshine on fresh-mowed grass. His wary expression tugged at her heart, as if a towline was tightening between them, pulling her closer and closer. But if that line tightened too much, where would that leave her? He'd be gone from Kilby at the first phone call from San Diego.

No.

She scrambled off his lap and slid to the far side of the backseat. "Nowhere, Caleb. It leaves us nowhere. Same as before."

"Why?"

His blunt question sent her scrambling. "You . . . you probably have girls fighting over which one gets to go to bed with you. I've seen the girls outside the ballpark. I saw them when I came to pick you up. Do you know how many were checking you out? Like, all of them. Even the ones with the other players."

"What does that have to do with you and me?" He shifted on the seat, which brought her attention to the healthy bulge in his jeans.

"I just don't think it's a good idea. You're better off with one of those girls."

"I don't agree. I want you."

The quiet conviction in his voice made her shiver. "I . . . I think we should keep things on a friendly basis. It's just . . . better that way."

He stared at her for a long moment, his expression

hardening, then pushed open the door of the Chevy. He stalked out, took a few steps, then stopped. Scrubbing one hand across the back of his neck, he seemed to struggle with himself. Then, as if he couldn't help it, he slid back into the car.

"Just one more thing, Sadie. You're throwing out one excuse after another and none of them make sense. We have this unreal chemistry that practically sets the air on fire, and you're spouting bullshit. You know what I think?"

He snatched her against his body, into the raging heat radiating from him. Tingles raced from her scalp to the base of her spine.

"I think you're afraid of how good it will be with us. You're trying to keep things safe and under control. I'm not safe. And you want that. You want me. But you won't let yourself have me."

His blistering words acted on her system like wind on a bonfire. Sudden lust, beyond anything she'd ever felt before in her life, swept through her. A little whimper rose from her throat. Yes, she wanted him, with every bone in her body. She wanted to dive into his body and abandon herself to this wild, rushing sensation. Giving in to the storm, she sagged against him, telling him silently to take her now, right here, on the backseat of an old Chevy, out on the lawn, wherever he wanted.

He bent his head and fastened his mouth to hers with a possessive passion that made her moan. She clung to his broad shoulders, which tightened into iron. One of his powerful legs pressed between hers, and she couldn't help pushing her groin against the hard, invading limb.

He took the kiss deeper, deeper; it felt as if she were being whisked away by a whirlwind. Need ran through her body in hot streams as his hands pushed up her shirt to touch bare skin.

She practically ignited. His hands were magic, big and callused, moving with sure confidence up the curve of her rib cage. And then he was pushing her bra above her breasts and thumbing her nipples. The sensation made her jump and utter a little cry, which was swallowed by the mouth consuming hers. Her head spun, the Chevy whirled around her, and she closed her eyes, losing herself in swirling darkness. She felt something against her back . . . vinyl . . . she was on her back . . . and then Caleb's hot thigh parted her legs, pressed against her sex. And oh God, it felt so good, all the nerves jumping and screaming for release.

"I'm going to make you come, Sadie. Right now." He growled the words into her neck. His touch and the searing whisper sent shudders through her body. He lowered his head to her breasts and took a nipple into his mouth. Sharp pleasure pierced her.

"Oh God," she mumbled, digging her hands into his thick hair. "Oh my God, oh my God . . ." For a brief moment of clarity she wondered at the way all her other words had deserted her. She, who was never at a loss for words. And then he closed his hand around her other breast, blanketing it in seductive warmth, and she was lost again. Sweet drugging pleasure filled her mind and liquefied her body.

"Come for me," he whispered, snaking his hand between her legs. She still had her shorts on, but underneath she was burning for him, craving him. What she wanted, needed, was flesh against flesh, but at the first press of his hand against her still-covered sex, she exploded. The orgasm rocketed through her, spasm after spasm, sharp and brilliant. Burying her face in his sweat-sticky neck, she tried to hold back her cries. But she had no experience with an orgasm like this one, and it took her in its strong fist and shook her like a rag doll.

Then left her limp and wondering on the backseat of the Chevy.

"Holy hell, that was hot," Caleb muttered, bracing himself above her on one hand. His eyes were twin blazes of blue.

She couldn't find the breath to answer. When he stared at her like that, like she was the only thing that mattered in the world, she couldn't think. She let her head fall to the side, so she was looking at the shabby interior instead of at him. The windows were actually steamed up and her cheeks felt like fire. This . . . this changed everything.

One thing she knew for sure, she'd never experienced anything like that with Ham. It had always taken her a long time to come, and when it happened, it was nothing to get too excited about. Was it Caleb? Did he just know how to do things better? They hadn't even taken their clothes off. Maybe Ham just hadn't known the right way to do it, despite all his boasting.

Perplexed, she looked back at Caleb. He was in the process of shifting himself off her, carefully removing his leg from between hers. A small patch of wetness darkened the front of his jeans.

"You . . ."

"Came in my pants," he said dryly. "You noticed."

She bit her lip to hide her quivering smile. So she wasn't the only one who'd gotten swept away in that crazy hurricane. She sat up, realizing her bra was still somewhere under her chin, but before she could fix it, he brushed her hands away. "I'll do that," he muttered. Gently, he drew the bra cups over her breasts then lowered her shirt. His touch was so light, like a wisp of cotton drifting across her skin.

She gave a helpless sigh.

"I'm sorry," he said when he was done. "I didn't

mean to get so carried away. Again. I just . . . you were so . . ." He ran one hand through his hair, leaving it even more disheveled. With his big body and powerful thighs, he took her breath away. "You do something crazy to me, Sadie."

Heat flamed in her cheeks. If anyone had gotten carried away, it was her. "Maybe we can just forget all about this," she said in a strangled voice.

He narrowed his eyes at her. "Not fucking likely."

Desperate, she tried again. "It doesn't change anything. It's still a bad idea."

"You think so? Maybe I have a weakness for bad ideas." One corner of his mouth drew up, creating a groove in his cheek that would make a grown woman cry. She steeled herself against it. No way was this sexually devastating, emotionally wounded ballplayer going to make her cry. He picked up her hand and turned it palm up, then pressed a kiss into the skin of her wrist, just above the heel. The exquisite sensation made her eyes drift to half mast.

Her mother's voice made them snap wide open again.

"Sadie! Where are you, sugar?" It sounded like she was already halfway across the lawn.

Sadie swore and pulled down her shirt, then dove for the door handle. She yanked the door open so fast she nearly fell out. "Right here, Mom."

Brenda, holding an aluminum baseball bat over her shoulder, came to a dead stop. "You've been out here too long." She peered into the car at Caleb. "What are you still doing here, you?"

"Mom! This is completely unnecessary!"

Her mother ignored her and watched suspiciously while Caleb unwound himself from the other side of the car. He kept his hands in front of his crotch during the entire process; no easy feat. When he finally stood before Sadie's mother, his hair looked as if a ground-hog had made a nest in it. Keeping one hand in place over his jeans, he used the other to straighten the mess. He looked so comical—like an X-rated version of the "rub your stomach while patting yourself on the head" game—that she nearly laughed.

"Sorry to make you worry, Ms. Merritt," Caleb said. "I mean no harm, I promise."

Brenda Merritt looked from one to the other, then back. "What were you doing in the car?"

"Nothing. Just talking." Sadie figured she'd better keep her mother's attention on her, instead of Caleb's awkward stance. "Put down the bat, please. Did you finish that Angelina Jolie shoe?"

Brenda rested the bat on the lawn like a cane. "Sure did. Then I took a nap. I woke up because your phone was ringing and I thought it might be Wendy Trent."

Sadie rounded the Chevy, moving faster than she knew she could. "You have no right to answer my phone, Mom. It's *mine*."

"It wasn't Her Royal Highness, you don't need to worry." Brenda handed over Sadie's smartphone.

If she were as smart as her phone, Sadie thought, she wouldn't have left it anywhere near her mother when she'd been drinking.

"It was a reporter. And don't worry, I gave her a quote."

"*What?* What are you talking about?"

"You, sneaky girl, were in the paper today and didn't even tell me. But that nice ESPN reporter did. We had a long chat. She said the story might be on *Outside the Lines* tomorrow, imagine that!"

Caleb finally spoke. "What story, Ms. Merritt?" The tightness in his voice made Sadie feel terrible. If her mother had overheard the part about Bingo and spilled it on the phone to a reporter, she'd never forgive herself.

"Can the Catfish, of course! What other story is there?" She gave a little yawn. "That petition to make the team move to a different town. Like I told the reporter, when those crazy Catfish players start going after my family, I turn into Mama Bear." She turned to Caleb and lifted the bat off the ground.

"No bat. Put down the bat. And Mom, he didn't 'go after' me. We were just . . . discussing some work-related issues."

She shot a quick glance at Caleb, who didn't look very amused. He still held his hands in front of him, like a superbly fit secret service agent in jeans.

Brenda threw up a hand. The baseball bat glinted in the sunlight. "You don't need to lie. I finally saw that picture of you two in the paper. I know there's something going on. Some things a mother just knows."

"You don't know anything about it," Sadie said through gritted teeth.

"I know you let yourself get taken advantage of, just like me. It's a Merritt family trait, at least on the female side. And I know what ballplayers are like. He probably walked right in here and corrupted you. Just like that petition says."

Sadie pressed her fists into her eyes. If anyone had corrupted her, it was Hamilton. "You should have told them to get lost, Mom. Never, ever talk to the media. Do you know how this will look to Mayor Trent? I could lose my job."

"She only hired you out of a favor to me." Sadie bit back a gasp. It hurt to hear it said out loud, though she'd always known her mother's friendship with Wendy had something to do with her hiring. Why else would the mayor employ someone who'd been the town scandal?

"You keep messing up your life, Sadie. And it's always because of a boy." Brenda picked up the bat and aimed it at Caleb in a vaguely menacing way. But then her usual state of lethargy returned, and she headed back to the house.

Sadie wished she could crawl back into the Chevy, lock it, and curl up to die. A more mortifying scene she couldn't imagine. "I'm sorry about that, Caleb. I hope that reporter doesn't make any trouble for you."

She should say more . . . explain her mother's veiled threats and innuendos. But Caleb was already pulling out his phone.

"It's not your fault," he said grimly. "But I'd better call Duke. He ought to at least have a little warning that we might be hitting ESPN."

"I'm really sorry," she said miserably, trailing after him. "I'll call my contacts at the newspaper and see if there's anything they can do."

"I wouldn't care except—" He broke off, but he didn't need to finish the sentence for her to know what he meant. It would be so easy for the truth about his background to come out. "I told my dad to stay out of the ballpark. This is my fault, Sadie. And I'll deal with it. I don't want you to worry. And hey . . ."

He pulled her to him for a fierce kiss that turned her bones to fire.

"This isn't over by a long shot," he whispered. Then he was gone, hurrying across the lawn, cell phone at his ear.

Sadie watched him go, feeling about as low as she'd ever felt. Her body still vibrated from the aftereffects of that incredible sexual experience. But her mind was busy with a thousand other things. ESPN . . . her mother . . . the mayor . . . Caleb's revelations . . . and then something else surfaced.

"Caleb!" she called, but he was already too far away to hear. At the ballpark, before Caleb came over the railing, Bingo had been talking to someone, and she was pretty sure she'd heard the word "bet" come up several times. Now that she knew who he really was, that seemed a little suspicious. If he'd just gotten out of prison, he was probably on probation, right? She made a mental note to tell Caleb the next time she saw him, then pulled out her own phone to call Burwell Brown and see if she could do any damage control.

Chapter 11

MAYOR TRENT HAD a nervous habit. When she was under stress, she tapped out a pattern with the fingers of her right hand. The more stressed she was, the faster the tapping. At the moment she resembled a concert pianist as her perfectly polished nails danced along the edge of her desk.

"Let's recap. The media knows about the Can the Catfish petition. Right now they're treating it as a kind of joke."

"Yes." Sadie shuffled through the pile of blog posts and articles she'd printed out for this meeting. "Here's an example: 'While most cities are thrilled to land a Triple A franchise, Kilby Texas wants to toss their team, the Catfish, back in the water.' And another one. 'In case you thought *Footloose* was ancient history, get a load of this. One South Texas town says their local baseball team, the Kilby Catfish, has the morals of a tomcat. Are these players too corrupt for Kilby? Are they too depraved for decent society?' And this. 'Town Says Catfish are Blackened and Must Go.'"

Mayor Trent rubbed her temples. "I get the picture. I was hoping to keep this completely local, so Kilby wouldn't become a laughingstock."

"Who cares what anyone says? It's just words." Sadie had told herself exactly that, again and again, over the past year.

"Unfortunately, in politics words have more power than you realize. I don't want my first term in office to be known as the time Kilby became a national joke. Dean Wade will have a field day with that. You heard he's considering running against me, I assume?"

Sadie bit her lip. No, she hadn't heard that. Dean was one of Hamilton's uncles. Normally the Wades didn't bother with politics, except to bribe politicians. Since Mayor Trent wasn't bribable, maybe they'd changed their minds. "He'd never win. That would be a disaster."

"Let's not worry about that yet. Back to our situation. The story is out, and it's gaining a certain amount of traction. Then, on Saturday, *this* happened." The mayor picked up the newspaper photo of Sadie and Caleb and Bingo. "What is this all about?"

Sadie had agonized over the subject of Caleb Hart since his revelation about his father. Should she tell his secret to Mayor Trent? She trusted her boss, but did she trust her that much? Caleb had opened up to her by sharing the story of his father. How could she possibly betray him?

She couldn't. "I don't know. Apparently he thought he saw something in the stands."

"I really wish they hadn't identified you in the article."

"I had nothing to do with that. Neither did Burwell Brown."

"Yes, well, nothing to do about it now. The question is, where do we go from here?"

"That's easy" Hearing a man's deep voice from the office entrance, both women swung around in their seats. The tall, lanky figure of Crush Taylor lounged against the doorjamb. The dark stubble on his jaw and bloodshot eyes made him look disreputable and slightly dangerous.

Mayor Trent surged to her feet. Her dark blue suit, pearls and power-sprayed hair looked even more immaculate in contrast with his dishevelment. "How did you get in?"

Crush raised an eyebrow. "Janitor showed me the way."

"Mayor Trent, this is Crush Taylor. The owner of the Catfish," said Sadie quickly.

"I know who he is. I just don't know what he's doing here." Pink burned high on her cheeks. Sadie had never seen her so energized.

"I'm here to discuss our mutual problem." The way he said *mutual* made it sound as if it belonged in the bedroom. He strolled into the office and lowered himself in the supplicant's chair. Unlike every previous occupant of the chair, he propped his long legs on the mayor's desk, then crossed one extremely expensive steel-toed cowboy boot over the other.

The pink spots on the mayor's cheeks turned fuchsia. "Get your boots off my desk or I'll call security."

"Go ahead. I keep a supply of signed baseball cards in my pocket for such occasions." His eyes, a deep hazel-green, gleamed with a troublemaker's glee. "Don't get your panties in a wad. Why would you want to kick me out when I'm here to offer a helping hand?"

"What sort of helping hand could the Playboy Pitcher possibly offer?" Mayor Trent was still on her feet, as if refusing to sit down while he tainted her desk with his long-boned limbs.

"I'm prepared to offer a substantial cash donation and commit significant resources to the Sluggers for Slugs campaign. I'd hate to see those little guys go

instinct. I still remember the first time I dropped one
down a girl's shirt. It was my neighbor Maisie, and she
sure knew how to squirm and squeal. Of course, she
turned around and squished it on my face. I should have
known not to mess with Maisie." He crossed his arms
behind his head and gazed up at the ceiling, a nostalgic
smile curving across his dissolute face.

"You're revolting." The mayor's lips were pressed so
tightly together they were white at the corners. Sadie
didn't see why she was so offended. Crush Taylor would
hardly be the first to tease a girl with a slug down her
shirt.

"Do you say that to all the guys who offer you a hundred thousand dollars? Or maybe that's chump change
for a lady like you." He gave a quick, nearly invisible
glance down Mayor Trent's perfect figure.

Sadie let out a gasp. "A hundred thousand dollars?"
The fact that he was clearly coming on to the mayor
suddenly paled in comparison to the stunning amount.

"A hundred thousand dollars. I want to prove to the
good citizens of Kilby that the Catfish care about the
community. What's more American than baseball and
swimming holes? I've already got my PR department
working on some great ideas. Your assistant, Ms. Sadie
Merritt here, has done fine work already, and one of
the Catfish stars, Caleb Hart, says he's willing to be the
spokesman."

The mayor sat down abruptly. "That won't do. He
was just photographed attacking a fan."

"He spotted a crime in progress. He's practically a
superhero. Or he will be by the time my PR people get
finished."

Sadie cleared her throat. "Caleb might not be here
for long, right? Everyone's saying he'll probably get
called up soon."

"That's the nature of the minor leagues, kid. They come and they go. But he's the biggest star we have right now, and he's good-looking to boot. If you want press attention, he's your guy."

While he wasn't saying anything Sadie didn't know, it still hurt hearing the raw truth out loud. Of course Caleb would be gone soon. She *wanted* him to go, because that would mean he'd achieved his dream.

"Can he behave himself?" Mayor Trent asked sharply.

"As much as any of us morally depraved baseball players can."

"That's a no, then."

"Ow, that hurts, Mayor." Crush put a hand over his heart. "*Rawr.* Are you sure you're not a wildcat behind those pearls?"

The mayor's nostrils flared, her color rose. Sadie said quickly, "I think Caleb would do a good job. He's trustworthy."

"Far as ballplayers go, he's a straight arrow," agreed Crush. "My other choice is Trevor Stark, and he just got out of rehab. But I'll leave it up to you. The Catfish have a lot of fans in this city. I'd hate to see them get riled up against such a fine mayor."

Again, that teasing double entendre. Crush Taylor clearly knew how to get under Mayor Trent's marble-smooth skin.

"Fine," she said, after exhaling a long breath. "You'll have to speak with the Save Our Slugs leadership, but the mayor's office will be happy to support this initiative."

"Excellent." Crush swung his legs off the desk, took an envelope from the inside pocket of his jacket and placed it on the mayor's desk. She shied away from it as if it might explode. His mouth quirked in a way that Sadie had to admit was appealing. "It's all right, Mayor

Trent. It's tickets to tonight's game against the Round
Rock team. We have some special things going on for
Sluggers for Slugs. Your presence would make it all the
more special."

"Thank you, Mr. Taylor." The mayor rose gracefully
to her feet, like a queen dismissing a servant. "But I'm
one hundred percent sure I have other plans that don't
involve grown men playing a silly boys' game."

If Sadie hadn't been sitting so close to Crush, she
would have missed his flinch. "One of the beautiful
things about baseball, Mayor Trent, is that every once
in a while you come into a situation where you have to
reach down and prove something. Nolan Ryan said that.
But maybe you don't know who Nolan Ryan is, and that
would be your loss. I'll see you at the ball game."

He addressed that last to Sadie, with a quick wink.
When he was gone, so quickly he could have been a
real catfish riding the current, leaving a swirl of ripples
behind, Mayor Trent collapsed back in her chair.

"That man," she ground out. "I don't understand
why people get so excited about ballplayers."

Sadie didn't dare point out that she looked more
churned up than she'd ever seen her.

"No smart woman should go anywhere near them,"
continued the mayor. "If we've learned nothing else,
we've learned that, haven't we, Sadie?"

"So true, Mayor Trent." *So very, very far from true.*
It was embarrassing, the amount of time she'd spent
thinking about Caleb since that encounter in her Chevy.

She cleared her throat. "I'd better get a press release
going." As she stood, the mayor pushed the envelope
across the desk to her.

"You go to the game. I want you to keep an eye on
things for me. But avoid the press, and for pity's sake,
let's hope Caleb Hart manages to stay out of trouble."

Sadie hurried back to the safety of her little cubicle. In her swivel chair, with the familiar smell of ink and vacuum-cleaned carpet, she closed her eyes and made a vow. *No more Caleb Hart. Keep it* professional. *Nothing but professional.*

On his way into the ballpark, Caleb ran into Crush Taylor. The owner held a silver flask in one hand, which gave Caleb a shock. No member of the team or the coaching staff would consider drinking this close to a game.

"Nice to see you again, Hart," said Crush.

Caleb nodded and shook his hand. They'd met a few times, and he always had to overcome a moment of being starstruck. Crush was probably about fifty, and looked fit enough to be twenty years younger. The first scouts who'd watched Caleb pitch had compared him to Crush Taylor. They were both big, rangy Texas kids. They had the same fiery competitiveness, even a similar windup.

"Listen, I'm sorry about the thing in the stands—" he began. If the owner wanted an explanation, he'd decided, he would give him the truth. He respected the man too much to lie. But instead, Crush waved him off.

"Just another wacky day in Triple A. It's being played as a goofy kicker on the newscast. I'm not worried about it." Crush offered him the flask. "Like a drink?"

Caleb shook his head no. He rarely drank. And especially not with the thunder of the fans in the bleachers overhead. It felt deeply disrespectful.

"Good man," said Crush approvingly. "Take care of your body. Very important."

"I do my best."

Crush took a swig. "I always had to let off steam. Might have taken it overboard on a few occasions.

Managers always lectured me, but I won games for them, which pretty much shut them up. And now well, it's a good thing not to answer to anyone. I'm enjoying the hell out of it."

Caleb nodded, though to him, it didn't look as though Crush was enjoying life much. As the legendary pitcher tilted the flask to his lips, Caleb noticed the deep grooves alongside his mouth and the bloodshot weariness in his eyes.

"How's that Can the Catfish fiasco going?" the owner asked.

"Well, they haven't dropped the petition."

"That damn pain-in-the-ass woman."

Caleb bristled. "Sadie Merritt? I wouldn't call her that, sir."

"No, not her. That mayor." His frustrated exhale carried a whiff of whiskey.

Caleb relaxed a bit. "Mayor Trent. I haven't met her. But you can't blame her for the petition."

Crush beckoned him to follow as he crossed the parking lot toward the owner's reserved spot. "Maybe not, but she could stop it if she wanted. Those church ladies put her on a pedestal. They'll do whatever she says. I'd tell them all to go fly a kite, but the Friars already hate my guts. They'll jump on anything to get rid of me. But I'm not going to go, Hart. I'm stubborn that way. It's why I didn't retire until I was forty-two. I like to do things in my own time, in my own way, and to hell with everyone else."

He gave a rude gesture, as if flipping off the universe, as they approached an immaculate sports car gleaming in the late day sun. Caleb's mouth practically watered at the sight. So that's what three Cy Young Awards and a twenty-year pitching career could get you.

"Saint Wendy," scoffed Crush. "I saw her today,

walked right into the lion's den. She looks like she's been carved out of salt. I don't see the fuss, to be frank,"

"I know Sadie has a lot of respect for her."

Crush stopped and shot him a sharp look. "Sadie, is it? Listen to me, son. You're a single guy, right? Never been married? Divorced?"

"No, never been married."

"I've been married three times. It's a fucking wonder I have any money left. Always wanted kids, but instead I got a baseball team. I could have bought into a major league team if I hadn't lost my head *three times*. Why does a guy get married three times, Hart?"

Caleb shrugged. Just what was in that flask, he wondered, and how much had Crush imbibed?

"I got carried away with ideas of love and family. Load of bull. They just wanted the fame and the cash. Real life didn't match up with their ideas, and they got out with whatever they could grab. I'll tell you a hard truth, Hart. You ready?" He clicked the automatic key and the silver Porsche answered with a pleasant beep.

Caleb nodded, debating the chances of Crush Taylor asking him to take his sports car for a spin. Right now he'd much rather have the man's car than his advice.

"Keep your focus on baseball. That's what'll get you to the top. The girls are just a distraction. And you'll get a million of them coming after you. I'm not saying you have to be a monk. Just be smart. And for Chrissake, don't marry any of 'em. Not until you've made your mark. And get a damn good prenup."

He opened the door of the Porsche and tossed the flask on the front passenger seat. God, it must be close to empty.

"I've been watching you. I have my theories about what's holding you back."

"With all due respect—"

Crush held up a hand. "It's your business. You'n and the Friars, I'm staying out of it. But I'm asking you as one lefty pitcher to another. I'm putting a big wad on this Sluggers for Slugs deal. Make sure it doesn't become a circus, would you? I want to prove that ice statue at City Hall wrong."

He slid into the driver's seat, bumping his head on the silver-coated frame.

"Sir, are you sure you should drive? Want me to drop you somewhere?"

"Nice try, Hart." Crush winked. "You do what I say and you'll end up with a Porsche of your own."

"Right."

Chapter 12

THAT NIGHT'S GAME, the kickoff for Sluggers for Slugs, was standing room only. Even the grassy area beyond right field was filled with picnickers and kids running this way and that, blowing bubbles and playing tag. Not only that, but extra media packed the press box. Sadie gave them a wide berth, but took note of the familiar local reporters alongside the better-dressed members of the national press.

Sluggers for Slugs banners adorned the box office. At the gate, she had received a little bag of sour gummi worms with a Sluggers for Slugs sticker on it. Mindful of her duty to report back to Mayor Trent, she took pictures of everything. She pocketed the gummi worms for the mayor's niece.

Sadie's ticket turned out to be for a seat just behind home plate. Donna was supposed to meet her, depending on when the Shark's mother got home from work. Part of Sadie hoped she didn't make it, so she could stare at Caleb nonstop without having to talk to someone.

Excitement buzzed through the packed stadium. The scent of peanuts and cotton candy hung pleasantly in the evening air. The announcer had been stirring up the crowd for a while, leading them in cheers and the

Catfish "clap"—two longs, a short, and a long. A microphone was set up in the middle of the field. The Jumbotron flashed the names of kids who'd been selected for the privilege of standing next to the players during the National Anthem. A flurry of kids dashed down the corridors to the gates that opened onto the field. A slim young woman in a cowboy hat led them onto the diamond. She went straight to the microphone and adjusted it to her height.

"And now, please welcome Ms. Daisy Lynn, a member of the Baptist choir down on Main. She's going to sing our favorite song for us, and your very own Kilby Catfish!" As soon as the crowd erupted into a huge roar, the announcer added, almost as an afterthought, "And give a hand for the Round Rock Express. Hey, they're from Texas too, they can't be all bad."

Sadie rolled her eyes at that, but the thrill was contagious, and she rose to her feet along with everyone else as players streamed onto the field from both dugouts. Right away her gaze arrowed in on Caleb. She'd know that body anywhere—long and tough and rangy. He looked so good in his baseball uniform that her mouth literally watered. She watched him intently as he trotted to the lineup of players and stood next to a thin boy who gazed up at him as if he were the Holy Spirit incarnate.

She couldn't blame him.

Caleb smiled down at the kid and offered him a handshake. A huge grin split his face, and Sadie couldn't help smiling as well. In her opinion, Caleb wore the hero worship well. But she had a feeling she was no longer objective on the subject.

The girl began to sing, her pretty voice floating over the hushed crowd, mingling with the first chirps of the evening crickets and the occasional crackle of feedback from the mike. She was just reaching a full-throated finish when the crowd decided she was done, roaring and stomping their feet with wild applause. She didn't seem to mind. She waved cheerfully, offered a quick curtsey, and skipped off the field, followed by the kids.

"Play ball!" the umpire yelled.

Sadie settled down with a happy sigh and stuck her hand into her box of Cracker Jacks. The atmosphere in the ballpark was pure rowdy fun, and she loved how everyone was getting into the spirit of Sluggers for Slugs. The gummi slugs were a huge hit. The Jumbotron occasionally flashed random facts about the horn-toed slug. "Did you know that the horn-toed slug is a native Texan?" A photoshopped image of a slug in a cowboy hat drew groans from the audience.

All the problems plaguing her faded away as if they'd never existed. What could be better than baseball on a warm summer evening, and a chance to stare at her crush all night long?

She planned to take full advantage of the opportunity. She'd even brought the binoculars her mom once used for watching the hummingbirds on the backyard feeder. The Catfish took the field, jogging to their positions, while the first Round Rock batter loosened up outside the batter's box. She fixed her binoculars on Caleb, who was throwing warm-up pitches to a very well-built player in a catcher's mask. She focused on his face, stern and completely focused. He was chewing something and a little muscle in his jaw jumped and flexed. If he was nervous, it certainly didn't show. He looked cool, calm, and completely controlled. And devastatingly attractive, those silver-steel eyes gleaming with intensity.

Remembering how he'd looked as he made her come,

she had to drop the glasses for a second and take a breath. It didn't seem possible that this confident, unruffled man, the master of the diamond, could have lost control with her the way he had. He'd actually ejaculated in his pants.

She clapped a hand over her mouth to stop an embarrassing rush of giggles.

The elderly black man to her right turned to wink at her. He wore a weathered deer-hunter hat and had a cane propped against one knee. "Don't be embarrassed, chickie. All the girls are mooning after Hart since he got here."

"I'm not mooning," she said, flushing. "I'm just watching the game."

"Well, if you aren't, you're the only one. Lookie over there." He pointed to a group of girls leaning over the railing above the dugout. With their bare midriffs and teased hair, they could have been extras in a music video. Laughing and hooting, they held up a banner that read, HEY CALEB, COME AND GET US, BABY.

"Ever since he jumped into the stands to go after that man, all the girls are hoping he'll do the same for them," explained her neighbor.

Sadie gave an incredulous laugh. "That's ridiculous. I'm sure that was a onetime incident. Players don't make a habit of climbing into the stands."

"Not usually, at least not during a game. But with Caleb Hart, you never know what you're going to get. Man's unpredictable as lightning. It's what makes him so good."

Sadie raised her binoculars again and filled her vision with Caleb's intent, rawboned face. "I don't know that much about baseball. How good is he?"

Blatant ploy to talk about Caleb, anyone?

"That's a million-dollar question right there. He

could be one of the greats. He's got it all. Hundred-mile fastball, pretty accurate placement, and the kind of hunger like you saw in my day. He's got that fire in the belly, and can't no one teach you that. I seen Nolan Ryan pitch, Catfish Hunter, Crush Taylor, and they all had the same characteristic. Know what that is?"

"No, what?" Sadie abandoned all pretense that she wasn't utterly fascinated by what the man was saying.

"Star quality. When they're on the mound, you can't hardly look at anyone else. It's like they hold the entire game in the palm of their hand. Takes your breath away. Like watching Picasso paint, or listening to Aretha Franklin sing the blues. Caleb Hart's got it too. You just try to look away when he's pitching. I bet you a box of Cracker Jacks you can't."

"I don't gamble."

Besides, that was a bet she'd lose, since she couldn't even tear her binoculars away from the man on the mound. Caleb gazed over his glove at the catcher, gave a slight nod, then reared back. Quick as a rattlesnake, he flung the ball toward home plate, ending with his right hand nearly in the dirt. She kept the glasses fixed on his face, where satisfaction echoed the applause from the stands.

"Steee-rike!" called the umpire.

The man next to her clapped once. "Good start. When his slider is on, they can't touch him. Everyone gambles, girl."

"I don't," she said firmly. "I don't like to leave things to chance. Chance might screw things up."

The man laughed. "She does have a nasty habit of messing up your plans. Ever heard of a prop bet?"

At that, the young man in the row in front of them, who was sitting with his pretty blond wife and two squirming boys, turned to face them. "I'll take you up on one of those. I'll put ten dollars on Catfish Bob's first bathroom break. Bottom of the fourth inning."

"Done." They shook hands.

"Are you supposed to do that?" Sadie leaned forward and dropped her voice to a whisper. On the field, the first batter struck out. Caleb tugged at the bill of his ball cap and circled the mound, waiting for his next victim.

"Sure, why not? It don't hurt anyone. These games can get awful long."

The other man winked. "Got another one for you. How long you think our pitcher there's going to last? Will he make it to five innings this time?"

"Now there you lost me. I won't ever bet against a pitcher like Hart."

Just then a mighty crack of the bat pulled everyone's attention back to the field. A batter had just swung so hard at a pitch that he'd ended up on his knees in the dirt, his bat cracked in half. The catcher, who Sadie now recognized as the guy from the Roadhouse, rose to his feet, the ball safely in his glove. It looked like he was trying not to laugh at the ridiculous posture of the batter. The catcher tossed the ball back to Caleb, then offered the fallen batter a hand. He brushed it off, pulled himself to his feet and stalked toward the visiting dugout. Catcalls and hoots rained down on him.

Along the sidelines, Catfish Bob, the mascot, did a hip-thrusting dance and pumped his fists in the air, inciting more cheers from the audience. The girls with the banner jumped up and down and shrieked Caleb's name.

Caleb ignored the crowd, keeping his focus on the ball in his hands, which he stared at intently while the next batter came to the plate. What was going through his mind? How did he handle being the center of attention for so many people? Thousands of people watching every move you made, analyzing it, admiring, second-guessing, envying. The pressure must be so intense.

And what about the secret he was keeping from everyone? Did it make him anxious every time he stepped on the mound, that someone might finally recognize him as the son of the notorious Thurston Hartwell II?

The next batter went down swinging as well. Three batters, three strikeouts. The Catfish fans went nuts as the teams headed for the dugouts. Catfish Bob did cartwheels down the third base line. The Katy Perry song "Roar" blasted over the loudspeakers. The first stars twinkled to life in the deep indigo sky beyond the stands. Sadie shivered as an electric feeling took hold.

Magic. She was in the presence of magic.

Feeling like a spy, she swung the glasses toward the Catfish dugout, and then doubled back to focus on the Jumbotron, where a big Sluggers for Slugs graphic had appeared. *Want to join the Catfish and help save our local Kilby slugs? Sure, they're slimy, but you know how good they are for catching catfish, y'all.*

Sadie winced. Well, if that angle worked for the baseball-game-attending population of Kilby, she could live with it.

So pucker up, Catfish fans! Every time you kiss a slug, it's worth another dollar for Save Our Slugs!

An image of a picture frame appeared in the Jumbotron, along with a cartoonish picture of a slug with giant lips. The camera feed appeared inside the frame, so it would look as if the person in the shot was kissing the slug. The camera panned the crowd. When it settled on the face of a ponytailed young woman in a Catfish cap, she burst out laughing and covered her face. But as the crowd clapped and chanted, she dropped her hands, smiled shyly and pursed her lips so they appeared to kiss the slug's bulging mouth.

Everyone laughed and cheered. Sadie couldn't keep the grin off her face. The campaign was totally working; it was actually cool.

The Express took the field. Sadie shifted the binoculars toward the dugout, where she found Caleb chatting with the catcher, who was unfastening his giant knee pads. Caleb looked relaxed, his legs sprawled in front of him, thighs straining against the white fabric of his uniform pants. His glove perched upside down on his knee, one hand holding it in place. With a sudden flush, she remembered how that hand felt on her body.

Embarrassed, she swung the glasses aside, skipping past a blur of faces to find the Jumbotron but instead pausing at the sight of a now-familiar face. Bingo was back in the stands. He wore a different pair of sunglasses this time—horn-rimmed, like a professor—but she recognized that high-voltage smile. He was chatting amiably with his neighbors, then shook everyone's hands.

Luckily, Caleb hadn't noticed. He was still deep in conversation with the catcher. The announcer said, "Up next we have the top of the Catfish lineup, Dwight Conner, T.J. Gates, and batting third, catcher Mike Solo."

She jumped at a tap on her shoulder. A young kid in a bat boy uniform stood behind her. He handed her a note, then ran off. She opened it and read: *Come out with me after the game. CH.* Looking up sharply, she found him in the dugout, looking straight at her. He winked. Her knees shook, even though she was sitting down.

Oh sweet Lord, she was definitely in trouble.

With the 3-0 victory over the Express, Caleb brought his ERA down to a respectable 3.42. He'd struck out seven and walked zero. A few more games like that and he'd be back in business. He hurried through his postgame shower, stopped at the food table only long enough to shove a burger down his throat, and headed for the exit.

The "Good job" congratulations and jibes of "Where's the fire, in your pants?" barely registered as he stalked out of the clubhouse and into the warm night air. He scanned the small crowd waiting in the parking lot, his gaze lighting on Sadie, who stood apart from the others in simple khakis and a sleeveless purple top, the lamplight creating a ruby halo around her dark hair. Something deep inside him relaxed. The sight of Sadie made him feel . . . better. He couldn't pin it down any more than that.

He strode toward her, drawn by her dark eyes, bright as sparklers on the Fourth of July. Her lovely mouth opened, about to say something, but before he could stop himself, he scooped her up and planted a huge kiss on her lips. Her lithe body melted against his like butter on a hot grill, and he was suddenly hard as a billy club.

Jackass, he scolded himself. Was he going to kiss her every time he saw her? He hadn't forgotten Crush's warning, and he knew it made sense. But when he was with Sadie, nothing else seemed to matter. He wanted to devour her, immerse himself in her bright sweetness. He wanted to make her lose control the way she had in the Chevy.

Out of the corner of his eye he spotted more of the guys filtering out of the big double doors of the exit. A kiss was bad enough, but a kiss witnessed by the whole team . . . she didn't need that sort of attention. With a huge effort, he lifted his head from hers.

"What you do to me," he muttered, running his thumb across her swollen lower lip. "It's crazy."

She cleared her throat, looking equally rattled. "I was about to say, 'Good game.'"

Caleb nodded. "It was fun. I could use a few more like that. Are you hungry or did you fill up on Cracker Jacks and peanuts?"

"I'm hungry, but . . . I shouldn't . . ." She bit her lip. He waited patiently, not wanting to pressure her. "Okay."

Yes. He gave a satisfied grin. Since they'd both brought their cars, he followed her to a tiny Tex-Mex dive called Tico Taco. Over a plate of enchiladas so overloaded pinto beans dripped over the edge, she rattled on about Sluggers for Slugs, as if this were a business dinner. She kept talking about their upcoming event at a local bakery and how excited everyone was.

He was excited too, but not for the same reasons. Under the table, he felt the brush of her leg against his. Oh yeah, he wanted a little more of that. Surreptitiously, he shifted forward so her leg had to press against his. A slow flush rose to the surface of her cheeks. He watched it avariciously, loving how much he could affect her, and knowing it worked both ways.

His Sadie could pretend otherwise, but she wanted him.

His Sadie. A shock ran through him, almost physical in its intensity. What was wrong with him? Sadie wasn't his, couldn't be his. He had a career to save. Younger brothers to support. A father to keep out of trouble. All the reasons he should avoid Sadie ran through his mind, nearly drowning out her words.

". . . keep things on a professional basis . . . nothing but official slug business," she was saying.

He snapped back to attention. "What's that?"

She toyed with her fork, dragging it through the lake of beans on her plate. "What happened at my house was a mistake."

The hell it was. "Have you been listening to Crush?"

"What do you mean?"

"Crush says girls are bad for a baseball career. He gave me a lecture about it."

She drew back. The red light from the fake cactus-shaped candle flickered across her cheekbones. Fire shimmered in her dark eyes. "Oh really? Did you listen? Because I'm pretty sure I got an invitation delivered by a bat boy."

He leaned across the table, taking her chin in his hand. "Hey. I don't care what Crush says. And I don't think what happened at your house was a mistake. If I had my way, I'd be in bed with you right now. I'd make love to you all night, and I wouldn't leave until they dragged me out to pitch the next game. Then I'd come right back and do it again."

"And I suppose I'd be lying there waiting for you?" Her pupils dilated, black against the brilliant mahogany.

"Yes." His raw answer made her draw in a sharp breath.

Even though her mouth was still several inches from his, a current of heat arced between them. He felt her soft flesh under his hand, saw the wild light in her dark eyes, and knew what it felt like to hold a bolt of lightning in his fist.

The click of a camera made him look to the side. A powerfully built twenty-something guy in a Kilby High

School football jacket loomed over them; a slightly smaller clone hovered behind him. The guy held an iPhone in his big fist. "Gotta get this on Facebook ASAP. Slutty Sadie's at it again."

Chapter 13

SADIE COULDN'T CATCH her breath, like one of those nightmares in which she was trying to scream but couldn't make a sound. She jumped to her feet, gulping air like a fresh-caught fish. "What are you . . . don't . . ."

Hamilton and his horrible friend Steve, who had edited the "Birthday Sex Tape," sneered at her. "Heard you were spreading them for the Catfish lately," said Hamilton. "Nice to see it confirmed in the flesh."

Her skin crawled at the way he said the word "flesh." Steve put his hand on his crotch and pretended to rub.

"I'm not . . ." Her blood thundered in her ears. Maybe her head would explode and she would avoid this epic moment of humiliation. She could run to the kitchen and stick her head in the oven. Or in a vat of hot sauce. *Kill me now. Just kill me now.*

Then a big hand shot out and twisted the neck of Hamilton's shirt so his face reddened.

"Delete it," came Caleb's cold and deadly voice.

"The hell—" Hamilton choked. "Steve!"

Steve reared back and punched Caleb in the jaw. The crack of bone on bone echoed through the hushed restaurant. Caleb shook it off, then drove his free hand into Steve's stomach; he stumbled backwards. The waiter whipped out a phone, probably calling 911.

Oh, fireballs. Caleb fighting Hamilton—total disaster. What if Caleb got hurt? What if word got out? One more black mark against the Catfish . . . and Caleb. She was supposed to be keeping a low profile to protect the mayor. She had to get him out of here.

She tugged at Caleb's arm as he lifted Hamilton, whose face was now purple, off the ground. "Come on, let's go," she hissed at him frantically.

He ignored her, completely focused on Hamilton. "You pathetic twit, you take one more picture or say one more thing like that about Sadie and you're going to pay."

"You . . . know . . . who . . . I . . ." Hamilton raged, as much as a guy could rage when held tight in a death grip.

"I don't know who you are and I don't give a flying fuck. Never again, you hear me?"

"Let him go!" Sadie pulled at Caleb's arm. His right arm. The nonpitching arm. Jesus, he was going after Hamilton with his *pitching arm.* "It's not worth it. Let's get out of here. Please, Caleb. Please."

Finally, her plea seemed to penetrate. He lowered Hamilton to the floor, though he kept his grip in place. "You got lucky this time, dickhead." With his free hand, he dug in his pocket for some cash, then tossed it on the table. "There's a big tip in there, mister," he called to the waiter, who snapped his phone shut. "Bring extra guacamole for everyone who had to put up with this scene."

He wrapped Sadie close to his side, where she felt the wild beat of his heart, then thrust Hamilton against the wall, barely missing a giant cactus. Her ex rested his hands on his knees, letting out great gasps of breath.

All her worries vaporized and a primal thrill of satisfaction raced through her blood. Hamilton deserved that. And more. Maybe it shouldn't feel good to see him like this—vanquished, humiliated—but boy, did it ever. She wanted to jump up and down and yell and scream. Instead she skipped to keep up with Caleb as he hauled her out of the restaurant.

"I let him off too easy," he muttered, pausing at the exit to the parking lot.

"It doesn't matter. You need to leave, Caleb. You don't want to be here when the police get here. The chief of police is Hamilton's uncle."

"That was your ex? Hamilton?"

She nodded. "Go. Please."

"You're coming with me. I don't want you dealing with them by yourself."

She pulled out her keys. "I have my car here, remember?"

"Then you leave first. I'm not budging until I know you're safe away from here."

"But Caleb, you don't understand!" She wanted to cry. "If Chief Wade gets here and sees Hamilton like that—"

"I was defending myself. That other guy hit me first."

"But this is Kilby, and Hamilton's a Wade. Please, Caleb." To that plea, she added her entire being's worth of silent begging.

After a visible struggle he gave in. "All right. But you first. Are you safe to drive?"

"Yes. I promise. Please."

"Call me when you get home." With one last scorching look, he waved her toward her Corolla. She started up her car in record speed, gripping the steering wheel tight to stop from shaking.

Caleb had stood up for her. No man had ever done that before.

When he finally got in his car and followed her out of the parking lot, her heart nearly burst out of her chest. She was falling for him, so fast and hard there was no going back. Caleb—her champion. Her defender. And he didn't even know what he was defending her from.

A sense of dread settled over her. She'd have to tell him everything.

But when? The Catfish left on a road trip to Colorado Springs the next morning, and she couldn't tell her story over the phone. It hung between them during every phone call. Their conversations were strained and rushed, as if they were trying to talk around a giant mountain. He didn't press her to explain what had happened at the Tico, but she knew he was curious. Who wouldn't be?

Luckily, the Wade family hadn't said or done anything publicly about Caleb's fight with Hamilton. Maybe Hamilton hadn't said anything. If so, it would be a first. Normally, the entire family closed ranks whenever one of their own screwed up.

She didn't see Caleb again until the day of the big cupcake promotional event that had the fans buzzing.

Brett's sister's bakery, What's Up, Cupcake?, invited the Catfish players to take over for the day to bake and decorate "Slugger's Sweetheart" cupcakes. Word had spread like wildfire that you could purchase an actual cupcake decorated by an actual ballplayer. By the time Sadie arrived, lines of customers snaked around the block.

Her role was to answer questions about the horn-toed slug; she wasn't anticipating much action. In fact, Brett had left the media outreach in her hands.

"You can handle the press, Sadie," he'd said on the phone. "You're a pro."

Now that was music to her ears. If she could get people to see her as a competent professional instead of as Hamilton's scandalous ex, all this would be worth it.

She did a quick tour of the bakery to check on how things were going. What's Up, Cupcake? was crammed full of big, strong, good-looking baseball players—none of whom were Caleb. The space practically vibrated with testosterone. The players were having a ball with the cupcake project, laughing with the customers and joking around with each other.

Dwight Conner, the tall center fielder, had pulled mixing duty. He bent his powerful frame over a big bowl of soupy batter. "Hey, photog!" He whistled to the young PR assistant taking photographs. "Check me out." He tossed a wooden bat in the air like a baton, then pretended to stir the batter with it. With his big grin and goofy pose, Sadie could just imagine the picture on the front page the next day.

Gold. Pure gold.

The decorating table saw most of the action. A long banquet table covered with white butcher paper dominated the seating area of the bakery. The players stood behind it, using tubes of frosting and dishes of candy sprinkles to create their masterpieces. Some wrote their initials with frosting, others made simple slug designs. One Hispanic player had a long line of people in front of him, and Sadie quickly saw why. With trancelike focus and breathtaking skill, he was meticulously copying a photo of a horn-toed slug onto a large cupcake.

"Man, I thought Ramirez was just wasting time with that sketchbook," grumbled Mike Solo, picking up a

tray of freshly baked cupcakes in the kitchen. He wore
a red bandanna and looked like a pirate, except for the
plate of bare cupcakes balanced on his huge palm. "If
I tried to paint a slug on a cupcake, it would look like
my dick."

"You had to go there, didn't you?" grumbled Jim
Lieberman, the shortstop. "A million words in the
English language and the only one you use is 'dick.'"

"Not true. I use 'dickhead' too." Solo flicked him on
the head.

"Do. Not. Flick me." Lieberman waved a tube of
icing at him.

"You're going to frost me?" Mike gave a wide grin
and winked at the PR assistant. "Go ahead. Make my
day. I bet I can convince someone to lick it off."

The PR assistant rolled her eyes and whispered in
Sadie's ear, "I'm used to these guys, but if they get too
rowdy for you, let me know."

"They're fine," Sadie whispered back. "Let's go out
front and get some pictures of the cupcakes. And make
sure they don't look like anyone's . . . you know . . ."

Because now that Mike had mentioned it, the slugs
did look sort of phallic, or maybe they seemed that way
to her because she couldn't stop thinking about Caleb's
hard body against hers . . .

And then he walked in, and every cell of her body
went on high alert. *Caleb's here. Caleb's here.*

Of course, she wasn't the only one who noticed. A
low roar filled the bakery as his fans crowded close,
begging for autographs. The PR assistant began snapping photos, while she hung back, the knowledge of
what she had to say to him ruining the moment.

As Caleb took his position behind the banquet table,
she couldn't help admiring how gracefully he moved.
You'd think that all those muscles might get in the way,

but no. They all synchronized perfectly together, flexing and tightening in just the right ways. He tied an apron around his hips—yes, he made that sexy too—then glanced up and caught her gaze. He looked more handsome than ever—his eyes clear and gray, his face browned from pitching in the Texas sun.

She gathered her courage. Better get this over with as quickly as possible. "Caleb, could I brief you on a few things before you get started?"

"Sure." He left the table and squeezed past the other players lined up with their tubes of frosting. The sense of distance between them made her want to cry, but maybe he was trying to be professional. They were in a public place, after all.

Too public. Everyone wanted to talk to Caleb about the upcoming all-star break, and to ask if he was upset that he hadn't been chosen for the Pacific League all-star team. He patiently answered all the fans' questions, while Sadie's anxiety spiraled higher and higher. Finally they found a quiet corner in the kitchen, where Dwight was rocking out to his earbuds.

"I need to explain what happened at the Tico," Sadie whispered.

Caleb's hand rested on the wall above her head as he bent to listen to her. "You don't have to explain anything. We all have our secrets."

"But I don't want to have any secrets from you."

That bald statement made something flare in his steely blue eyes. "Okay. I'm listening."

She took a deep breath. "When I broke up with Hamilton, he—"

"Hart! What are you doing, flirting while the rest of us slave away in the kitchen?" Mike Solo's mischievous face popped up beside them, an empty tray tilting on his broad hand.

"Get lost, Solo," Caleb growled. "Sadie's filling me in on some stuff."

Her heart pounded, whether from relief at the reprieve or frustration, she didn't know.

"Excuuuuse me. Just thought you might want to know our newest Catfish just showed up."

Caleb lifted his head sharply. "Who?"

"Nope. I'm getting lost now, as ordered." Mike whisked himself to the oven, where Dwight was pulling out a fresh tray of cupcakes. "Fill 'er up."

Caleb refocused on Sadie. "Maybe this isn't the best place."

"It's not, but I need to tell you this, and—"

"Sadie, there you are." Burwell Brown appeared, his notebook at the ready. "Can you give me a quote about the anatomy of the horn-toed slug? Are the horns like toes, or are the toes like horns?"

"Burwell," she hissed through gritted teeth. "Can you give me a minute?"

"Yeah sure. While I'm here, Caleb, do you have any comment on Trevor Stark joining the team? Word has it there's bad blood between you two."

"No comment. And that's off the record."

"How can a 'no comment' be off the record? Why won't you talk to the press?"

Caleb folded his arms across his chest and gave Brown a death stare. The reporter shrugged and turned away, nearly bumping into a stunning man with light hair and crystal green eyes that would make an angel jealous. A thin white scar ran just below one cheekbone, but it didn't mar his beauty at all; it emphasized it.

"Stark," said Caleb, eyes narrowed.

"Hart."

Perking up, Brown poised his pen over his notebook. Sadie wanted to tear her hair out. This must be the infamous Trevor Stark. She had read about him. He was a home-run slugger and a troublemaker who had battled drug and alcohol problems in the past. The Friars had just traded for him, and even though he'd passed all the drug tests, they sent him down to make sure he was clean before introducing him to the home crowd.

With a drama unfolding right before her eyes, she had no chance of telling Caleb her embarrassing story.

Trevor looked from Caleb to her and gave a thin smile. "I heard there were going to be cupcakes here, but I didn't know they meant the brown-haired kind."

"She's not a cupcake. She's the organizer of this event."

"Got it. Thanks for including me in the event, cup-cake."

The two players glared at each other. The air practically vibrated with animosity.

"Yo, dude," Dwight called from the baking area. "Keep it chill."

"I'm chill," said Trevor, his crystal eyes glittering. "Just comin' over to say, What's up, cupcake?"

Sadie felt Caleb's abrupt movement and grabbed his arm. "Caleb, let's go back out front. We can finish this some other time."

"No. This guy's interrupting. It's rude."

Sadie caught sight of Burwell Brown scribbling away. "Burwell, do you mind?"

"Mind what, Sadie? Just covering the news here. If you can call baseball players making cupcakes news."

"Who are you calling a baseball player?" drawled Trevor. "Not him, I bet. Last game I saw him pitch ought to disqualify him for good."

Caleb strained against her grip like a bulldog trying to slip his leash. Trevor braced for action with a look of glee, as if dying for a confrontation. The air crack-led with the lightning of tension. Sadie held her breath, afraid to watch, afraid to look away.

Then something came winging through the air and hit Trevor on the back of his head. He turned, scowling, and whipped a hand up to catch another flying missile. A cupcake crumbled in his hands. Dwight and Mike brandished more cupcakes, ready to fling them.

"You guys ready to get back to business?" Mike asked, smirking.

In answer, Trevor whipped his handful of mangled cupcake at Mike, who ducked the spray of crumbs and launched another one, which hit Caleb in the chest. Caleb started forward, but Sadie desperately hung onto his arm.

"Let me go," he hissed, then shook her off and ran to the door that separated the kitchen from the seating area out front. Good idea, Sadie realized. At least no one else would see the crazy scene unfolding.

And they sure would have gotten an eyeful. Her jaw dropped as four grown baseball players launched a full-on food fight. Within minutes cupcake crumbs were everywhere—in their hair, on their clothes. Chunks of cupcake littered every surface. Mike showed off his catching skills by palming a cupcake whole and whip-ping it back at Caleb. Caleb proved his accuracy with a cupcake right between Trevor's eyes. Dwight threw long. Trevor tagged Mike by mashing a cupcake into his shoulder.

And then the absurdity caught up with them and they laughed until they were hunched on the floor, holding their ribs in pain.

Sadie stood over them, hands on her hips, biting back her own laughter. "Y'all are going to clean this up, right?"

"You look kinda mad, Sadie," gasped Mike. "What's up, cupcake?"

That launched them into another spell of laughter. Sadie shook her head, waited until she got a clear "Yes, ma'am" from Dwight and a "We got this, Sadie" from Caleb. Then she took Burwell by the elbow and hauled him out the back door where deliveries came in.

"You can't write about that, Burwell. Please."

Burwell was wiping away tears of laughter of his own. "Keep dreaming, Sadie. That was gold."

"No. No! Burwell, listen. What will it take for you to write a nice, well-researched fluff piece on the horn-toed slugs and the handsome ballplayers making cupcakes to support the cause? That's a great story. Your female readers will love it. Maybe I can throw in a kitten. 'Bad Boy Slugger Trevor Stark Makes Cupcakes, Adopts Kitten.' How's that?" She knew how desperate she sounded. Too bad. She *was* desperate.

"I'll make you a deal. I'll pretend I never saw the Catfish in a cupcake fight if you get me Caleb Hart," Brown said.

"What do you mean?"

"That exclusive with Caleb Hart you promised. Get me that, and I'll make your slugs look like tiny saints."

"Caleb Hart exclusive. Got it. I'll see what I can do." She knew Caleb hated talking to the press, but he was supposed to be helping improve the Catfish image. A public account of Cupcake Wars wouldn't exactly help matters.

"Soon, Merritt. Make him talk soon." He brandished his notepad. "I want a sit-down with the pitcher who has everyone talking. And I want him to answer some real questions."

Chapter 14

THE FOOD FIGHT at What's Up, Cupcake? had released some of Caleb's tension, but it destroyed any chance of him and Sadie finishing their conversation. He left for batting practice with only a brief "Talk to you later."

Trevor Stark couldn't have arrived at a worse time. Just because they'd had a little fun at the bakery didn't mean he liked the guy. Ever since Bingo came to live with him, Caleb had been irritable as hell. Now it felt like he couldn't turn around without something lighting on fire. The incident in the stands. The fight with Hamilton. The confrontation with Trevor. He felt as if he balanced on the edge of a knife every minute of every day, and sometimes he slipped.

Sadie's odd behavior made everything worse. She had something big to tell him, something to do with Hamilton, something that made her very uncomfortable. And that made him nervous.

He'd told her the biggest secret he had. Was that a mistake? Since he trusted very few people, if any, it was easy to slip back into his usual guarded state. But with Sadie, something felt different. His feelings for her didn't resemble anything he'd ever experienced before. Something about her—her spirit, her intelligence, her vulnerability—brought unexpected impulses to life inside him. He wanted her, yes. But he also wanted to be close to her. Close in a way he had no experience with.

He also wanted to protect her. The anger that had propelled him into confronting Hamilton and his friend still boiled in his veins when he thought of the things they'd said. Why would they talk that way about her? And why had she stood there like a lamb to the slaughter?

At batting practice, he ignored the presence of Trevor Stark while he hefted his own bat over his shoulder. As a former American League player, he hadn't focused much on his hitting. But the Catfish played by National League rules. He didn't want to make an ass out of himself in that ninth position in the lineup.

Lolo, the former coach from Cuba who threw batting practice, flashed him a five-minute signal. He sat on the infield grass and began his pre-practice stretches.

Lolo called out "right field" and tossed Trevor a pitch. Trevor ripped it down the right field line. No doubt about it, the guy could hit. His upper torso rippled with hard muscle. Caleb knew he owed Mike Solo one for defusing the confrontation at the bakery. Honestly, Trevor Stark would have whipped his ass.

"Hey, Hart," Trevor called as he hit a long fly ball. One of the kids who hung around the ball club chased after it, his short legs churning. He flung himself onto the ball, then did a complete somersault across the outfield grass.

"That kid just robbed you of a double," said Caleb. "Better pick up your game, bro."

"Better pick yours up. I found out all about your cupcake girl."

Oh hell. Caleb pulled himself out of his hamstring stretch and bounced to his feet. "Don't go there, Stark."

"Need me to get Duke out here? Any trouble, he'll bench you both," Lolo warned.

Trevor hefted his bat in one hand. "Not looking to cause trouble. I'm done here anyway. Just thought the hotshot might want to know what I found on Facebook."

Lolo, still looking worried, gestured to Caleb to take Trevor's place in the batting box.

"I don't give a crap what you found on Facebook."

Trevor slung his bag over one shoulder and dug inside until he pulled out his iPhone. "You keep telling yourself that. Meanwhile, I'll be scrolling through these photos." He waved the phone at Caleb. "Your girl's a lot more built than she looks. She knows how to fill out a red bikini something fine."

He strolled past Caleb, close enough to display the splash of red on his phone.

"Hang on," Caleb said in a tight voice. Fuck it. If Trevor Stark knew something about Sadie, he'd better know it too. He grabbed Trevor's sleeve; the other player was already slowing to give him a closer look.

Images of Sadie bombarded him. Sadie posing on a beach in a skimpy red bikini, long-limbed and tan. Sadie standing naked in a shower, back to the camera, water cascading over her blurry but definitely bare ass. Sadie sitting in Hamilton's lap while he aimed a can of whipped cream at her barely covered breasts. The photos were sexually charged, clearly taken by someone intimate with her. They danced the line but never quite reached a level that might get them deleted from the site.

"See the name of this page?" S****y Sadie. It has eight hundred likes."

"You shouldn't look at that crap." Caleb's voice didn't even sound like his own. His chest felt tight as a drum. "It's disgusting."

"I'm just concerned for the rep of my new team-mates." Trevor smirked, the scar on his face riding up. "Don't want you getting in over your head, Hart. The girl's trouble."

"Mind your own fucking business."

"Exactly what I'm trying to do." Trevor took his phone back and slid it into his bag. "You're my team-mate now, Hart. It might only be Triple A, and I hope to be gone by tomorrow, but for now I got your back."

Caleb itched to wipe the grin off his face, but Lolo held him back with a meaty hand on his shoulder. Trevor sauntered toward the clubhouse, saying over his shoulder, "I ain't the bad guy here, Hart."

Sadie called that night, while he was on the phone with Teddy and Frankie. He didn't call her back. Two days later the Catfish left for their last road trip before the all-star break. As he did with most troubles in his life, he stuffed the memory of those photos down deep where they couldn't disturb him. Well . . . he tried. But the images from that Facebook page flashed across his vision every time he closed his eyes. They drove him insane. But the worst was getting hit with them out of the blue. He hated getting ambushed by disaster, like officers showing up at his house with an arrest warrant. Or Trevor Stark flashing his iPhone in his face.

Sadie should have told him. And she'd tried. He knew that.

He remembered a comment she'd made early on in their phone conversations, asking him not to believe anything people might say about her. But this wasn't just talk; it was pictures. Pictures he couldn't erase from his mind no matter how much he tossed and turned.

It ripped him apart. He wanted to talk to her, but they'd have to talk about what he'd seen, and he didn't know what to say or what to think. If only he hadn't seen those photos. But he had. And he couldn't forget them.

His only refuge was the mound, where, finally, things were clicking. His fastball was hitting 98 miles per hour, according to the pitching coach. His changeup was dropping at just the right moment. He pitched a complete game against the Fresno Grizzlies, coming away with a 6-2 victory that dropped his ERA down to a sweet 2.23. In the clubhouse, he began keeping a careful eye on the televised Friars games. So far, their pitching staff was healthy and performing well. But in baseball anything could happen.

Not that he wanted something bad to happen to another pitcher. But if an opportunity arose, he wanted to be ready.

At night he'd ride the van back to the hotel with the other guys, have a beer in someone's room, and call it a night. A hundred times he picked up his phone, intending to call Sadie. But the right words didn't come, so he never called.

But he dreamed about her every night, hot, thrashing dreams that left him with a massive boner in the morning. It astonished him how much he wanted her. For Chrissake, he'd never even slept with her, yet couldn't get her off his mind. Maybe that's why she was haunting him like this. If they had sex, maybe he could move on with his life.

Meanwhile, he kept his distance from Trevor Stark. No one liked the guy. Stark kept a calendar on his locker with the days crossed off, as if he was in jail. Granted, no one wanted to stay long in the minor leagues, but an attitude like that didn't endear him to anyone. He disdained the clubhouse food. Instead, every night he sent the attendant out for a steak from the most expensive restaurant in town.

Literally. He'd Google "Most expensive steak," tell the awed attendant the name, give him a hundred dollars and sit back like an emperor waiting for his tribute.

"It's like he's living the major league life whether or not he's in the majors," grumbled Mike Solo as he and Caleb humped their luggage to the bus. Trevor wasn't carrying his own luggage; no, he paid a kid to haul it for him. Every town they played, he'd hire a different kid.

Contributing to the local economy, he called it. Showboating, his teammates called it.

"If he's got the dough . . ." Caleb shrugged.

"He won't have it for long at this rate."

"Not my problem."

"Oh yeah? I heard he's going to ask Sadie Merritt out when we get back to Kilby."

Every muscle in Caleb's body tightened. "Why is that my problem? She's not my girlfriend." He swung onto the bus and stalked down the aisle, looking for a seat where everyone would leave him alone.

"Good to know. That's what I told him, but I didn't know for sure." Mike slid into the seat across the aisle and put his earbuds into place. "Can you turn down that jealous rage? It's drowning out my Yanni mix."

Caleb gave him the finger and settled back for a nap. But he couldn't get comfortable, and when he did finally fall into a restless sleep, he dreamed of Sadie in a red bikini, surfacing from a deep green lake, water streaming off her sleek body. She came close, cupping him, whispering to him, desire turning her gaze sultry and seductive. Then she broke the mood by laughing and splashing him with water. He chased her down but she kept slipping away like a quicksilver minnow. And then she was gone, nothing but a lonely ripple dying on the surface of the water, and terror shook him awake.

Outside his window the humble skyline of Kilby rose up from the flat ranchland that surrounded it. He could just make out the Spanish bell tower that marked City Hall. That's where Sadie was probably working right now. Saving the slugs, or maybe some disadvantaged children, or whoever her soft heart had embraced.

He had to call her. He would. As soon as he figured out what to say.

Later that day, he met with Bingo and his probation officer, Officer Kelly, in her office near the police station.

"Your father's doing very well," said the officer, a young woman with short-cropped blond hair. "He reports in on schedule and has been diligently attending job interviews. I'm guessing it's just a matter of time before he gets a job offer that we can approve."

"Great. So why am I here?" Caleb crossed one ankle over the opposite knee and bounced it restlessly. Conversations with or about Bingo made him want to jump out of his skin.

"You're here because Mr. Hartwell has a request. He asked that I be part of the conversation." She gave Bingo a sympathetic smile.

Fan-tastic. Bingo had managed to reel in his probation officer. The man never stopped . . . being Bingo. Today he wore a sober gray suit with a yellow paisley tie, so he looked like a respectable accountant—the furthest thing from the truth. When it came to Bingo, even his appearance was a lie.

"Well, hit me. What's up?"

Bingo spoke for the first time. "I want to see Tessa and the twins."

"No." The word was out before he even thought about it. "Out of the question."

"They're my *children*, Caleb. What do you think I'm

going to do to them? I just want to see them. Don't you think they miss their father?"

"Maybe if they had any kind of a father, they would. But they have you." The cruelty of his own words made him wince. He got to his feet and paced around the little office. "Why do you want to see them?"

"Because they're my flesh and blood. What other reason do I need to have?" Bingo shrugged, palms facing upward, Mr. Innocent himself. From Officer Kelly's condemning expression, his act was working.

He addressed the young officer. "Look, I'm very protective of my siblings. I became their guardian when he went to prison. I don't want them to get hurt."

"What do you think I'm going to *do*?" Bingo repeated. "I've never hurt anyone. What have I ever done to hurt you?"

The absurdity of that question had Caleb scrubbing his hands through his hair. "You left me with a family to take care of at the age of nineteen."

"I didn't do that on purpose. I made some misguided career choices." That whiny *I'm a victim* tone always made Caleb nuts. "I've been doing a lot of counseling to work through that. But I've never been a violent offender, and I've never been involved with drugs. There's no reason I shouldn't see the boys and Tessa."

Officer Kelly spoke. "What's the reason for your objection, Caleb?"

He's poison. He's toxic. He doesn't do anything without a hidden agenda. He doesn't care what damage he causes.

He's a liar and a cheat.

"He came to the ballpark," Caleb burst out harshly. "I asked him not to, and he did it anyway."

"That's not in the probation agreement," said Bingo quickly. "And I made sure no one recognized me. It

wasn't my fault you jumped into the stands and at-
tacked me."

"You know I didn't attack you." Caleb felt the tendons in his neck throb. "I was trying to get you away
from my friend."

Officer Kelly intervened. "Caleb, have you considered seeing a counselor yourself? It seems clear you
have a lot of residual anger over your father's incar-
ceration."

Before his head exploded, Caleb stalked to the door.
"I think Bingo's getting enough counseling for both of
us. Keep him out of the ballpark, and I'll think about
having the kids come for a visit."

Bingo jumped up and scrambled after him. "It's a
deal. Very fair of you, Caleb, very fair. I only want to
be close to the family again, I don't have anything else
on my mind. That's a sacred promise, son. A sacred
promise."

"I'll see you next week," Officer Kelly called after
them. "Keep up the good work, Bingo."

They emerged from the county offices into the heavy
heat of the afternoon. Caleb felt instant sweat bead his
forehead.

"Why couldn't you just ask me about the kids, Bingo?
Why'd you have to drag me all the way out here?"

Bingo plopped a broad-brimmed cowboy hat on his
head. "Officer Kelly wanted to meet you. I've boasted
about you so much. It's not every day she gets a celebrity in there."

"You wanted to show me off to your probation officer? Why? To impress her?"

"Sure, why not?"

On the sidewalk, Caleb stopped short, then turned
to face his father. Bingo stood only half a head shorter
than him, but he was substantially flabbier, a man who

relied on charm and wits rather than physical prowess. In fact, it had come out at the trial that he deliberately minimized his fitness to look less threatening to his marks. "It doesn't matter who your son is, Bingo. All that matters is how well you fulfill the terms of your probation. No criminal activity."

"Of course not!"

But Bingo's emphatic declaration didn't mean much, in Caleb's experience. "That's what you always said before too. When Tessa and I ran messages for you. You always said it was nothing to worry about, nothing illegal. You used your *kids*, Bingo."

"And I never testified about that. I kept you kids out of court."

"Yeah, you're a bona fide saint. Does it shock you that I don't want you around the twins?"

"But . . ." Bingo pushed his hat back and scratched at the place the headband had left its mark. "All that was before I went to prison. I'm a different man now. Why would I do anything like that now? Do you think I want to go back to prison?"

Logical, sure. Truthful? Alarm bells were ringing all over the place.

A shadow fell over them. He looked over, taking a minute to recognize the guy who'd stopped next to them. The last time he'd seen that smug face, his fist had been wrapped in the man's jacket. The football gear was gone; now he wore a blinding white golf shirt with his sunglasses peeking out of the chest pocket.

Hamilton Wade looked from Caleb to Bingo, then back again. And again. "Sweet Mother Mary, what've we got here? I know you."

Caleb tried to bundle Bingo toward his rental car, but Hamilton followed. "I did a paper on you for my criminology class in college."

"You went to college?" Caleb muttered. "I guess they let anyone in these days."

Hamilton was smart enough to ignore the bait. "Thurston Hartwell II, con artist extraordinaire. And you must be his son. Hart. Short for Hartwell."

Caleb's feet felt stuck to the sidewalk, as if it was coated with tar. He couldn't move, couldn't get away from the smug, smirking asshole.

"You've got it all wrong," said Bingo. "Don't you think if I had a baseball star for a son, everyone would know about it?"

"Good question, old man. Looks like Caleb Hart has something he wants to keep hidden. Don't blame him." His contemptuous glance at Bingo made Caleb's hackles rise. It was one thing for him to be angry with his father, another thing for an ass like Hamilton to insult him.

"Leave him alone," he said curtly. "If you have something to say to me, let's go." Another fight sounded like a perfect plan to him. Sure, it would be another black mark against the Catfish, and Sadie might get upset, but this guy had it coming in more ways than he could count.

"I have a much better idea. Tell you what. You keep away from Sadie and I'll keep your secret."

Keep away from Sadie? Even though he hadn't spoken to her in days, and wasn't sure what he'd say when he did, the hell if he'd let someone else dictate who he saw. "Go fuck yourself."

Hamilton shrugged. "Up to you. Wait'll ESPN gets a load of this one."

"Wait," said Bingo, putting a hand on Hamilton's arm. "Give us some time to think about this."

"I don't need to think about anything," Caleb growled. "This guy's an ass." He wheeled on Hamilton. "What's

Sadie to you anyway? Why do you hate her? You're the one who made that Facebook page, aren't you?"

"So you saw that. Good. Why do you want anything to do with that tramp anyway?" Hamilton took an involuntary step backward, as if just remembering the power of Caleb's grip.

A sort of red mist hazed over Caleb's vision. The guy was dead meat. But he couldn't move his right arm in the direction he wanted, toward Hamilton's face. Bingo had it in lockdown against his chest.

"Let's go," he kept repeating. "Forget him. Not worth it. Come on, Caleb." Bingo dragged him down the sidewalk, away from the face he wanted to smash to bits. "We'll figure this out," he kept saying until Caleb was in the car, gripping the steering wheel so tightly the bones of his knuckles shone white.

Slowly, his vision cleared. Hamilton was gone. He was in his car. Bingo watched him with puppy dog alertness.

"I'm okay," he finally said. "Thanks. I owe you."

"No, you don't," said Bingo, adjusting his hat, which had gotten crumpled. "Not even close. But I'd like to know who this Sadie is. She's sure causing a lot of trouble."

Chapter 15

AFTER DAYS OF no word from Caleb, Sadie came to the conclusion that he'd lost interest in her. Maybe someone had told him about her tainted reputation. Maybe he'd gone online out of curiosity and seen the damning pictures. Maybe someone had sent him the "birthday tape." Whatever the case, things were as dead as the armadillo caterpillar—the last species to go extinct in Kilby.

Yes, she'd been focusing on research lately, since the absence of Caleb made everything else depressingly dull.

On her next night off, Donna once again dragged her to the Roadhouse. Donna seemed so distracted lately; Sadie was starting to worry about her. But every time she tried to ask what was going on, her friend changed the subject.

"I'm thinking of a career change," Donna confided as they pushed through the crowd toward the bar. "I figured out that all this experience being a nanny is perfect training for another job."

"What's that?"

"Think about it. I boss around a helpless being whose happiness depends on me. I'm in charge, and I have to make sure he knows it and doesn't get out of line."

"Hmmm." Sadie waved to get the bartender's attention. It shouldn't be hard, not the way Donna was dressed—in Daisy Dukes and a neon pink halter top. Sadie wore a much more decorous white scoop-neck cotton dress that ended just above the knee. She'd put her hair in a French braid to keep it off her neck, but even so she felt sweat trickle down her neck. "School principal?"

"I'm thinking dominatrix. You don't need a degree for that."

"Unless it's a master's."

"Whoot!" Donna gave her a high five for that. "Good one."

Sadie fanned herself; the sheer amount of body heat in the packed throng was enough to power a small nation's electrical grid. As usual, she scanned the faces in the crowd, trying to identify potential danger before it walked up and tapped her on the shoulder. Only after she'd searched the entire bar did she admit to herself her true purpose: looking for Caleb Hart.

A muscular forearm settled on the bar next to Sadie. She swung around, her heart in her throat, but it wasn't Caleb. It was his friend, the mop-headed, green-eyed Mike Solo, the one who had started the cupcake fight. On her other side, she sensed Donna's immediate reaction to the appearance of such a hot guy.

"You girls are at the wrong party," he told them. "Better come with me."

"We're happy where we are," Sadie said primly.

"Speak for yourself." Donna hopped off her stool. "I'm in, ball boy. Where are we going?"

"Donna! You can't just go off with some guy you've barely met."

"Duh. We bonded last time." Donna rolled her eyes. "I'm almost a hundred percent sure his name is Mark."

"Mike," corrected Mike. "Close enough."

"You don't even know where he's going." Sadie

snatched Donna's wrist, afraid she'd float off like a helium filled balloon.

Mike slung his arm around Donna's shoulders and squeezed. "Sadie's right. Never, ever do what you're about to do. Except with me. I'm the exception. Because I'm an exceptional guy."

His infectious grin was impossible to resist, but Sadie tried her hardest. "Are all ballplayers so full of themselves?"

"Are you asking about one player in particular?" Mike winked. "Maybe the one eating his heart out over you? The one who hasn't cracked a smile in a week? The one sitting alone growling at people at the party I'm about to take you to?"

Sadie's cheeks burned. She put a hand to her forehead to cool herself down. "Really?" she said faintly.

"That's it, Sadie," Donna said. "We are going to this party. No arguments or I'll get out my whip."

"Whip?" Mike asked hopefully as he herded them out of the Roadhouse. "*Rawr.* You girls are kinkier than you look."

"This is a bad idea," Sadie grumbled as he held open the door of a white van with the Catfish logo on the door. "Is this your car?"

"No, I borrowed the team's equipment van. Had to pick up some party supplies for the boss."

Sadie peered into the back of the van, which was packed with cases of beer and a shrink-wrapped submarine sandwich that extended the entire length of the van, from the rear window to the front dashboard.

"The boss? Where is this party, anyway?"

"Party nirvana, babe. Party nirvana."

Ten minutes later they drove through a set of wide-open gates with the insignia BULLPEN RANCH carved into the

wooden blats. A cattle grate rumbled under the tires.
Sleepy, rolling fields of alfalfa and mesquite stretched to
either side of the long drive.

"Bullpen Ranch," said Donna in an awed voice.
"That's Crush Taylor's place."

"Yes, ma'am," said Mike. "Behold and be awed."

Clearly, the place had been designed to strike awe
in Crush Taylor's guests. A sprawling ranch house
made from concrete and steel, with towering picture
windows, looked out on endless pasture land. Strings
of twinkle lights lit up the broad terraces that flanked
the house. A pool glowed iridescent blue under orange
paper lanterns that bobbed in the breeze. At each
corner a tiki torch flamed. Bodies moved like shadows,
drifting toward the bar set up near the pool, merging
together, drawing apart.

Dance music pumped through hidden speakers. The
bass line made the ground throb beneath their feet. Vi-
brations pulsed through the air, turned the atmosphere
electric.

Caleb was somewhere among those shadowy bodies.
She was about to see him for the first time in a week.
Sadie's stomach clenched, and she looked in panic back
toward the faraway front gate.

Mike screeched the van to a randomly angled stop
and jumped out. "Supplies can wait. Let me intro-
duce you around." Holding them both by the hand,
he hauled them down a grassy slope toward the tiled
terrace around the pool. At one end sat a complete set
of living room furniture in a cozy arrangement. Crush
occupied a huge leather armchair that looked over the
pool, as if he were an emperor surveying his domain.
He wore cream linen trousers and a loose summer-blue
cashmere sweater.

Sadie thought Mayor Trent would approve of his

look, though probably not of the nearly topless girls draped on every side of him.

But the girls didn't command nearly as much attention as the abundance of supremely fit men gathered in this one tiny piece of Texas ranchland. Everywhere they looked, a ripped torso caught their eye, or an incredibly fine rear end. Broad shoulders leaned against the backs of chairs, corded forearms rested on knees. Black skin, olive skin, tan skin, every shade gilded by the erotic firelight from the tiki torches. Donna clutched at her arm, pretending to faint.

Or maybe not pretending.

"Dorothy, we're not in Kansas anymore," she breathed. "I think we've died, actually. This is how I've always pictured Heaven. Look at those pecs."

A magnificent bare-chested man wandered past in nothing but swimming shorts. As they watched, he flexed his chest muscles and executed a flat dive into the pool, right into the midst of a game of volleyball. The girls in the pool shrieked and splashed him in revenge.

"Was that Trevor Stark?" Donna asked in awe.

"You girls stay away from Trevor," Mike warned. "Anyone else is fair game, but Stark's on the no-fly list."

Donna gave him a little shove. "You can't tell us who to hang out with."

He leaned his forehead against hers. "Just watch me. Unless you have your whip on you."

Sadie saw Donna swallow hard. She wondered if her friend was in over her head with someone like Mike Solo. Donna talked much wilder than she actually was. But then all thoughts fled as someone took hold of her upper arm. Shivers skittered down her spine.

"What are you doing here?" Caleb asked in a low voice.

"Caleb." Mike clapped a hand on his shoulder. "Should have known you'd come to life sooner or later. I spotted these girls all sad and lonely back at the Roadhouse. They begged to tag along."

"He carjacked us," said Donna. "We were helpless to resist."

Sadie couldn't say anything. The sight of Caleb, with that tense frown creasing the skin between his gorgeous silvery eyes, had reduced her to muteness. As many times as she'd pictured him during the past week, he looked a thousand times better in person. Barefoot, in board shorts and a dark T-shirt, he looked so good she wanted to lap him up like a dish of cream.

Caleb directed his frown toward Mike. "They shouldn't be here. You know how crazy it gets."

"That's what I'm counting on." Mike snagged Donna's wrist. "Come on, pretty lady. Let's dance. It's the next best thing to screwing, and you know that's off the table."

As Mike dragged her toward the house, Donna flashed a smile over her shoulder. "Is it my imagination, or does that sound like a challenge?"

"Knock yourself out," Mike said, his voice nearly lost in the thump-thump of the beat. "I dare you."

Caleb turned back to Sadie and regarded her with hooded eyes. The mark from Steve's punch at the Tico had faded, but she remembered exactly where it was. Her hand floated to his jawbone. "I . . . I'm sorry," she blurted. "I should have . . . You got caught in the middle of . . . I should have warned you . . . I'll leave now." Blindly, she turned to go, desperate to get away from the intense gaze that seemed to delve into the deepest part of her.

"No." He snagged her wrist, whirling her around to face him. "I want to talk to you. Come on."

Oh Lord, she never should have come here. She followed on his heels, not that she had a choice, given his determined grip on her wrist. In a blur of taut muscles and laughing faces, the crowd of party guests gave way to a long, sloping lawn. On the far side of the ranch house, behind a grove of cottonwoods, stood a secluded, six-sided gazebo tucked out of sight behind a thicket of shrubs. He pulled her inside. Benches lined five of the sides, while the sixth served as the entrance. The foliage of the surrounding hedge filtered the moonlight into a mottled pattern of shadows. A spicy fragrance, released by the day's heat, still lingered in the air. The hushed space felt completely private; even the party music was a faint, faraway thump of bass.

Caleb crossed his arms over his chest. "Why didn't you tell me?"

So he *did* know. Someone had told him, or shown him. The injustice of the entire situation made her furious. She whirled away from him. "I tried! And besides, tell you what? That my horrid ex-boyfriend has a vendetta against me? That he's one of those boys who picks the wings off flies, and I'm the fly? Why is that any of your business?"

"It wouldn't be, except—"

"I told you we shouldn't get involved. How many times have I told you that?"

"That's not—"

She spun around and shoved him in the chest. He was so solid he barely budged. "You should just stay away from me, Catfish. I don't have to explain anything to you."

"I'm not asking you to—"

"Oh yeah? You look like a cop right now, interrogating a suspect."

He let his arms fall to his sides. "I haven't said three words! Some Interrogation."

"You said, 'Why didn't you tell me?'" Throwing up her hands, she stalked as far away from him as possible in the small space. "You dragged me out here to interrogate me."

"No."

"Why, then?"

"To understand. Because I care about you."

That slowed her down for a second. But only for a second. "If you care so much, why haven't you called in a week?" She held up a hand. "Let me guess. You were checking out the Facebook page. Wondering how much of it is real. Asking yourself why I didn't seem like that in person, and how I managed to fool you." She turned her back on him, fighting to keep the tears at bay.

"No." Fierce and low, the harsh word was followed by Caleb's iron arms folding around her, pressing her spine against the solid warmth of his chest. "None of that. Don't get me wrong. It was hard seeing those photos. They got me all twisted up, and I'm sorry, Sadie. Fuck, I'm sorry for that. I was wrong. You don't owe me any explanations. That ass is trying to shame you, but he's the one who should be ashamed, not you."

For a long moment she did nothing more than shake in his arms. For him to say those words, hold her close, comfort her . . . it was almost disorienting after everything she'd been through. She drew in a long, shuddering breath while he held her tight.

"My problem is that I hate being blindsided. I kept thinking how I told you about my father. I trusted you, but you didn't trust me. I was hurt and I took it personally."

Her stomach cratered. *Blindsided.* Despite her intention to tell him herself, he'd found out through someone else. She couldn't let that happen again. She had to tell him about the birthday tape. She turned in the circle of his arms to face him. "There's more, Caleb. A really embarrassing tape Hamilton made. I didn't know he was doing it. He emails it to people when he wants to ruin things for me."

"Shh. It doesn't matter. I don't care what Hamilton did or does. I know who you are, Sadie." His mouth brushed her ear, his words less a sound than a hot breath. The sensation made her head spin. "But I'll tell you this. Next time I get into it with Hamilton Wade, I won't be so nice."

A rush of emotion made her knees wobble. She'd felt so alone, taking on Hamilton. In the early days she'd assumed more people would stand up for her. She'd craved that, needed it desperately. Now here was this handsome, strong ballplayer, taking her side without question.

A tear leaked out of her eye and traced a warm path down her cheek. One of his arms kept her firmly clamped against him, while the other shifted. A big thumb brushed against her cheekbone and wiped away the tear.

His kindness made another one swell in its place. She could cry forever over Hamilton, mourn for the naïve girl she'd been, shocked to find such cruelty directed at her. She could hide forever too. Safe in her cubicle at the mayor's office, safe in her old Chevy, safe with her apathetic mother and her one remaining friend.

Instead, she flung her arms around his neck. His thick hair brushed against the back of her hands. She heard his breath catch. His hands went to her waist in a hold that steadied her and simultaneously made her wild. "What are you doing?" he murmured, just before she drew his face down to hers.

"I want you." The raw declaration shocked her, but she knew every word was true. "If you don't mind."

His eyes flashed silver. "Oh, I don't mind. As long as you're sure."

At her fervent nod, he took command, holding her head still in his big, callused hands. He seared her with one long look, while she burned for him. Whatever he saw in her eyes must have satisfied him, because he claimed her mouth in an endless, searching kiss that had her sagging against him.

"God, Caleb," she whispered, pulling away ever so briefly. He snatched her back.

"I know. Crazy, isn't it?" He kissed her cheeks, the fine bone along her eye socket, her eyebrows, his thumbs resting along her jawbone.

"It's never felt like this. No matter what people say, I've only ever been with Hamilton. And I didn't like it much. I know those pictures look bad, but—"

"Shhh." He transferred his kisses to her throat, peppering her skin with hot nibbles. She held onto his shoulders for dear life in the rush of delirious pleasure.

"I was sure I'd just stay alone forever. I didn't plan any of this . . ."

"Woman, you're distracting me." He nipped at her lower lip. The shock went all the way to her toes.

She gasped, finally wordless.

"Are you done now? No more talking?"

She gave a series of quick nods as he kissed his way down the side of her neck to the tender curve of her shoulder, the place where her kitten used to nestle. Caleb, no kitten, clamped his jaws across it like a lion. Hot emotion surged inside her, clamoring to get out.

He released her and soothed the spot with his warm tongue.

"From now on I want nothing but happy sounds.

Moans, whimpers, the occasional 'More, Caleb, more,' "

She giggled breathlessly, riveted to the sight of his big right hand reaching into the top of her sundress. Then her giggle turned to a happy gasp as her breast nestled into his palm. He let out a long groan of appreciation, then extracted the other, so she was entirely exposed to view. The pads of his thumbs brushed across the tips of her nipples. She moaned, clutching his forearms, which felt like twin tree trunks, strong and invincible.

He walked her backward to an upright post at the back of the gazebo, between two benches. Propping her against it, he placed her hands on the latticework of the gazebo wall. "Hold onto that. If you touch me I'll lose it." She didn't even recognize his voice, so low and growling and hot.

Shuddering, her nipples pebbling in the open air, she abandoned all thought of shyness. Instead, she arched her back, urging him silently to touch her, stroke her . . . lick her. A quick glance down her own body gave her an erotic thrill; her breasts were pale, luminous globes, the nipples dark punctuation marks. He took them into his mouth, one, then the other, flicking, teasing, using teeth and tongue and the devastatingly rough skin of his hands to wrest one moan after another from her.

When she was shaking like a leaf, he lifted her skirt and ran a hand up her inner thigh to her panties. He slid one finger inside the elastic and brushed against her aching mound.

"So wet," he muttered, his forehead resting against hers. His ragged breaths made his chest rise and fall. She wanted to touch him, was dying to touch him, but kept her hands tangled in the lattice work. She didn't want this to end. Never wanted it to end.

He was running his hand everywhere under her

dress. His hand said everything with its hungry touch. *You're beautiful, I want you, I could touch you until the end of time*. He molded the arch of her hip bones, brushed across her lower belly, sank his fingers into the flesh of her ass. She burned, craving him like water.

Her hips quivered, her inner channel throbbed. She wanted him inside her body. She wanted his hand on her sex, his fingers on her clit, her mouth, anywhere he wanted. She wanted him everywhere, all at once, urgent as a fire alarm.

"Protection?" It was the first word she'd managed since he'd asked her to stop distracting him.

"Stuck one in my wallet last week. Back when I hoped I had a chance with you."

He took a break from stroking fire across her skin and fumbled for his wallet.

She reached into his pocket, sliding along the imposing ridge of his erection. "Your chances are looking pretty good right now," she managed, her teeth chattering with excitement.

He groaned at her touch, even through his board shorts. "You sure about this?" He looked so serious in the moonlight. "Because I want it more than life right now."

"I'm sure. Just hurry." She was shaking, shivering, panting. She felt like some kind of wild animal, and she didn't even care. All that mattered was following the beat of the need that had taken over her body.

He unfastened his shorts, opening the fabric enough to allow his erection to spring out. Her throat nearly closed up at the sight. Proud and upright, thick and hard, he was beautiful and powerful, all in one. Hands shaking, he rolled the condom down his shaft.

"I'm going to take you right here, right up against this post, and you're going to come so hard you'll have to bury your screams against my neck." He pushed her skirt up and slid his hands under her ass. Anticipating his next move, she wrapped her legs around his hips, so her sex nestled against his erection. The contact nearly made her come right then and there. She rubbed against him, frantic for another taste. Then he was sliding inside her, chasing every last thought to kingdom come. He groaned and muttered in her ear, hot words to match his thrusts. *"Tight . . . hot . . . want you . . . fuck you . . . lose your mind . . . bury my cock . . . fuck, Sadie . . . so good . . ."*

He bent his head to her nipple and drew it into his mouth at the same time as he stretched his thumb across her pelvis just far enough to press her clit. She exploded around him, the pleasure forking through her like jagged lightning, like sexual shrapnel. As he'd warned, she burrowed her face against his chest, feeling his collarbone just above her forehead. He kept up his intense rhythm, deep, deeper, using those perfectly honed ass muscles to drive deep. She clenched around him, aftershocks of her orgasm flashing bright. Or maybe it was another orgasm. Or the same one, still going . . . Then he went rigid, a harsh wheeze squeezing from his lungs, spasms rocking his powerful frame.

"Sweet Jesus," he whispered. "Are you okay?"

She nodded against his chest, unable to lift her head. *Okay* didn't really describe her state of mind. She and a baseball player had just screwed their brains out in a Hall of Famer's gazebo. Not only that, she wanted to do it again as soon as she caught her breath.

She wasn't sure if that qualified as "Okay" or "Holy shit, what have I done?"

Chapter 16

You'd think that the most glorious sex of his life would show in some way. Like it would be scrawled across his forehead in red marker. "Just had mind-blowing sex. Ignore the dumb-ass smile." But luckily no one seemed to notice anything different as he and Sadie wandered through the crowd around the pool. He didn't want her reputation to take any more hits because of him.

He dropped a word here and there to the players he passed, keeping Sadie firmly at his side the entire time. Their experience together had not only blown off the top of his head, sexually speaking, it had also made him deeply protective of her. Feeling her sob in his arms as she spoke about Hamilton made him want to rage against the world and the unworthy men who infested it.

In his view, no one who dirtied a girl's reputation—or even talked about having had sex with her—deserved to be called a man.

Out front, rigs were parked everywhere, in the big circular driveway, on the grass. A few couples were making out, and a couple of the younger players were tossing a football around. The guys right out of high

school had more energy than they knew what to do
with

He knew what to do with his energy. He planned to
spend every extra ounce on the mouthwatering girl at
his side. Leaning against the side of his Jeep, he tugged
her against his hips. He could go again right now, but
he didn't want to scare her off. Or give some horny first
year drafts a show. "When can I see you again?"

Moonlight glinted in her eyes as she tilted her head.
"Aren't you busy with the team?"

"All-star break. That's why Crush threw this party."

"You aren't going to the All-Star Game?"

"No, that would require pitching like an all-star. If
they didn't count the beginning of the season, I might
have stood a chance."

"You're an all-star in my book." She nuzzled his
cheek, rubbing her nose across the stubble.

"Don't get me going again, woman," he warned.
"When can I see you? And where?"

She drew away, and they stared at each other blankly.
"My mom would faint on the hall carpet if she heard
one peep coming from my room."

"I intend to make you do more than peep." Playfully,
he nipped at her chin. The buttery texture of her skin
made him wild.

"She's nervous about me seeing anyone new. When
the stuff with Hamilton happened, she took it really
hard. It was almost worse for her than for me."

He ran his hands up her arms and cupped her shoulders. "I don't want to worry your mother. But I have no
intention of leaving you alone."

Even in the moonlight, he saw the flush darken her
cheeks. "I don't want you to," she said shyly. "But my
mom's home a lot. What about your place?"

Caleb cursed. "I've got Bingo living with me. Like he hasn't caused enough trouble."

Sadie chewed on her lower lip. "What about the ballpark? Are there any secret rooms hidden away anywhere?"

"Sonny Barnes got caught with his new wife in the storage closet of the training room. Bieberman's the one who busted them, and he got so embarrassed he messed up three double plays in the next game. I'm not going to take that kind of chance."

"Car?" she said dubiously. "Not mine, since you barely fit inside it."

"I could spread you open on the hood."

He caught her deep shiver, which echoed his own sudden arousal. "Maybe something more private. The lake?"

"Hell no." He shook his head impatiently. "Let's not worry about it now. Leave the details to me. Don't plan anything for tomorrow night, that's all."

"I won't. Unless the mayor needs something."

"She needs something, all right. I have a feeling Crush has a thing for her."

"He'd better get over it. She wouldn't go out with him in a million years."

"You think not? Ballplayers are pretty irresistible. It's our butts. And the uniforms."

"Oh, I see. Are you saying I can't resist you?" She laughed up at him.

"Tomorrow night, babe. We'll put it to the test."

He put a lot of thought into how he wanted the night to go. Sadie had been through a lot; he wanted her to forget all her stress and worry. "You said your mama doesn't want you to see anyone," he said on the phone when he called to make the date. "I might have a solution to that."

"What is it?"

"Meet me in Room 106 at the Courtyard Suites. I'll be there at ten."

He didn't need to tell her they shouldn't show up at the same time. She was just as anxious to keep things secret as he was. He hadn't forgotten Hamilton's threat to tell the press about Bingo. Bingo kept fretting about it, but since his advice was to find another girl, Caleb tuned him out.

No way in hell was he letting some local dickhead keep him away from Sadie. From the start, he'd wanted to get her into his bed, but now his feelings for her went far beyond that. How far? He didn't want to analyze; he just wanted to enjoy it.

He arrived at the hotel room first, which gave him a chance to think again about what he was doing. Getting involved with Sadie was going to change things. Distract him from his determination to get back to the Show. Disrupt his life. He knew it, and yet . . . he couldn't wait to see her again.

At about ten-thirty a soft tap at the door scattered all his cautionary thoughts. He ushered her inside, after a quick glance down the corridor to make sure no one had spotted her. He pulled her into his arms and felt his tension ease when she eagerly plastered her sweet body against him. Part of him had worried that she'd let her mother's fears stop her.

They kissed, a desperate, thirsty kiss, as if no one had ever before thought of the idea, as if kissing was their own personal stroke of genius.

"Why is the light off?" she whispered finally, drawing her kiss-swollen lips away from his.

"You said your mother doesn't want you to see any boys."

"Ha ha. I don't think a dark hotel room is what she had in mind. Besides, you're not a boy."

"No, I'm not." He was all man, hard and hungry for her.

"And I can still see you a little," she added. "I can see you're wearing only a towel."

He dropped the towel. The tension in the room tightened to a nearly unbearable level.

"I have a plan for that," he whispered. He brought her to the bed and sat her down on the edge. "Do you trust me?"

"Ye-es," she said hesitantly.

"You worry so much. I want you to enjoy yourself completely. I think this might help."

"What?"

He picked up a scarf from the bedside table where he'd stashed it. "Just close your eyes and let Big Caleb handle things from here."

She burst out laughing, which he ignored. He waited patiently until her head stopped bobbing around, then fastened the scarf over her eyes. "Now tell me that isn't relaxing. You don't have to do a thing. We're completely safe in here. Just sit back and relax and let me worship every inch of your gorgeous body." He kept whispering as he unbuttoned her blouse and drew it off her shoulders. Underneath, she wore a fire-engine-red bra.

"Red," he said, touched. "You thought of me."

"Well, only now and then. Like, maybe every two minutes or so." Her lips curved. He traced their circumference with his finger. Now that her brilliant eyes weren't taking up his attention, he could focus on her pretty lips. They had a merry curve to them, as if a secret smile was always waiting, ready to bubble over into laughter. And yet she didn't laugh nearly enough.

"How could anyone hurt you?" he whispered. "I just don't understand."

"Because you're not like him," she said promptly. "You're good."

It was fortunate that she couldn't see his face. *Good.* Good didn't describe him. It didn't describe the wayward son of a convicted con artist. *Good.* The word started a slow boil inside him. "Don't be so sure about that."

He pushed down the sleeves of her blouse, leaving her arms trapped inside, then snapped apart her bra. She strained toward him as he ran a finger between the two mounds of her breasts, where deep shadows lurked. He detoured for a quick fix, cupping her breasts so the hard tips rubbed against his palms. Then he ran his hands down her torso to her pants. She must have come straight from work, since she wore thin silky trousers that could be part of a suit. Didn't matter. They were coming off. He unfastened them, ripped them off her body, then did the same to the scrap of underwear underneath.

Feeling her tense, he knelt before her and put his hands on her upper thighs, caressing the soft skin under his thumbs. Quivers traveled through her, and slowly, with his insistent urging, her legs fell open.

"You okay?" he whispered.

She nodded and let out a soft gasp. He pushed her back on the bed, not gently, but not too rough. Her arms were pinned to the side by her blouse; that and the scarf around her eyes were the only things she wore. Lust pounded through him, blood pumping into his cock. He had to close his eyes for a second to get a grip on himself. She trusted him enough to put herself in this position.

In return, he was going to make sure she had the best orgasm of her life.

"I love touching you. Every inch." He removed her blouse, turned her over on her stomach, and put his hands on the smooth skin of her back. Gently at first, testing how much pressure she liked, he massaged the sleek muscles of her back and shoulders. She sighed, her flesh turning pliant under his strokes. He made his way down her body . . . buttocks, thighs, calves, feet. Slow and steady, giving her all the time in the world, he worked the tension from her frame. When she was boneless with relaxation, he turned her onto her back. A smile parted her lips; she looked so beautiful his heart clenched.

He brushed his thumb across the dainty patch of hair adorning her sex. Wetness glistened underneath. She was turned on; he could smell it, sense it, and her scent went straight to his head. He lowered his head between her thighs, feeling them tremble on either side of him. Her sex beckoned him like the most beautiful flower in the world, fleshy petals unfurling for his pleasure. He stroked the flat of his tongue across her slit, so silky and soft. The hardening knot of her clit welcomed the tip of his tongue as he licked, slowly at first, then faster, more friction, more pressure, until she thrashed from side to side.

"Caleb," she pleaded.

"Yes, sweet," he growled against her clit. The vibration of his lips on her sex tipped her over the edge into a screaming, writhing orgasm. He rode it out, his mouth on her, as if he was mainlining her heat and juice. His cock throbbed, and he took it into his hand, readying himself with a condom. When the pace of her convulsions slowed, he tossed her higher onto the bed and turned her over, so she lay on her stomach.

She immediately took hold of the sheets on either side, her dark hair spilling across her back.

"Want more?" he asked her roughly. She gave a quick nod, her head turned to one side, the scarf still tight around her eyes.

"Tell me."

"Yes. Yes, I want more. I want you inside me." Her voice shook.

His Sadie.

He spread her legs wide and plunged deep and hard. She pushed her ass back against him, as if the friction of the sheets on her sensitized private parts was too much for her. He dragged her higher in the air, mad with desire, needing to lose himself in her fist-tight heat. He dug his fingers into the flesh of her hips and slammed all the way to the hilt, his balls bumping against the soft backs of her thighs.

"Caleb!" she screamed. "Oh sweet Lord."

Two thrusts, three, four, need thundering down his spine, building like a thunderbolt about to strike. And then it hit, picking him up like a frickin' tornado and whirling him into Oz. He went blind with it, blind, deaf, and dumb. No words, no sounds, just endless, blessed release. The orgasm was so intense it could have been a house landing on him.

They crawled under the sheets afterward, like two survivors of a natural disaster. He took the blindfold off Sadie and snuggled her against him. He must have drifted off to sleep, into a warm, happy void where no worries could touch him. A thread of a whisper pulled him back to consciousness.

Sadie was stirring in his arms. He pulled her back

against him, with the loopy idea that nothing could hurt him while they were joined together.

"So that was your big plan?" she was saying in an amused murmur. "Blindfold me so I could tell my mother I'm not seeing anyone?"

"I guess it sounds stupid, now that you put it that way. Also, I figured you wouldn't have any worry about cameras if we kept the lights off."

She put a hand on his chest, conforming her palm to the slope of his muscles. "I trust you, Caleb. I don't worry with you. I'm too busy losing my mind." She fell quiet while he stroked long strands of hair off her damp forehead. "I really didn't know sex could be like this."

Now that was guaranteed to stoke a guy's ego. Except that . . . "I didn't either," he admitted. "I mean, I've always liked sex. But this . . ." He shook his head. "It's different with you, Sadie."

Her soft breath warmed his skin in little puffs.

"Have you been with a lot of people? I only ask because . . . well, Hamilton used to cheat on me all the time. Then he'd accuse me of cheating, but I never did. Every time he threw one of his accusations at me, I knew he'd been with someone else."

Caleb's gut tightened. "I hate that guy."

"Yeah, well, stay away from him. You don't mess around with the Wade family." She gave a soft, bitter laugh. "If I'd known, I would have joined a convent before dating Hamilton. I don't even know what he saw in me. Every girl wanted to date him."

"Maybe he saw what I see. A beautiful, smart, fiery girl worth all kinds of risks."

She raised herself on one elbow, her hair falling like a silk curtain over her shoulder. "Risks? Do you mean the risk of Hamilton finding out?"

He traced the path of moonlight across her skin,

down to the soft nipple, which responded immediately
to his touch. "No. That's not what I mean."

What he meant . . . what he couldn't yet say . . . was
that he meant the risk of falling in love. But something
told him it might already be too late.

Sadie already knew that Caleb wasn't the spoiled athlete she'd assumed. For one thing, he worked his ass
off. *Show up early, stay late*, was his motto. *If you respect the game of baseball, it will give respect back to
you.* He worked out like a fiend, threw extra bullpens
to refine his pitching motion, even mentored some of
the raw newcomers to the team.

"You have no idea how much help I got when I first
came up," he told her. "You have to believe in yourself,
but you need other people to believe in you too. Especially as a pitcher, it's such a mind game. It's one on
one, pitcher against batter, and if you let yourself get
psyched out, the batter wins. You have to stay focused."

"How do you do that?"

"Stay away from girls." He winked at her. She was
spending her lunch break with him at the ballpark.
They sat in the stands watching batting practice. She
picked at a roast beef sandwich, while he downed a
power smoothie.

"Oops." She pulled a mock-sorry face.

"Actually, my ERA has improved since we met."

"You're welcome."

Despite her sassy tone, he narrowed his eyes at her.
"You sound down. Is everything okay?"

Caleb could be frighteningly perceptive. One might
even say "sensitive," if he weren't such a tough, rugged
athlete.

"Fine." She mustered a smile, hoping to throw him
off the scent. The truth was, this new thing with Caleb

made her nervous. Every night, she went to sleep hug-
ging the thought of him close, like a pillow. Every
morning, she woke up with sort of incredulous joy. *Am
I really going to see him today? Does he really think
about me the way I think about him?* Then the wary
part of her, the part that had been so brutally crushed
by Hamilton's behavior, would kick in.

She couldn't shake the sneaky feeling that disaster
lurked around the corner. Possibly in the form of Hamilton Wade, but possibly something else.

Enjoy this while it lasts, Sadie.

She snapped out of her reverie to see that Caleb was
talking on his cell phone. "Okay. I'll tell Bill to transfer
the money. How's he feeling?"

He nodded quietly, looking much older than his
nearly twenty-six years. Then he shot Sadie a glance,
his face turning red. "Don't say anything bad about
me," he said sternly into the phone, then handed it to
Sadie. "My sister wants to say hi."

Sadie took the phone, surprised. "Hello," she said
tentatively.

"Hi. This is Tessa. I suppose Caleb hasn't said much
about me." From the snap in her voice, Tessa was young
and on the sassy side.

"Well, um . . ."

"That's our Caleb. He likes to do his talking on the
mound. But that's why I'm here, to fill in a few blanks.
I just want you to know the kind of guy my brother is."

"I think I can figure that out."

"My brother," Tessa rode right over her, "is the kind
of guy who quit college to support us when our dad
wasn't around. He's the kind of guy who has always
been there for us. He's never let us down. Not once. Did
you know our mother abandoned us for some young
Italian stud? Did you know he used to change Teddy

and Frankie's diapers? Do you know what he does in the off-season, besides train his ass off?"

She knew that much, although the rest was new to her. "He's a stay at home brother?"

"Yes. He takes our bratty little brothers to school, he cooks dinner. Helps them with their homework. He lets me have a social life. That's the kind of guy he is. Do you see where I'm coming from?"

"You love your brother. I get it. He's a great guy."

"No. I don't just love him. I'd kill for my brother. If anyone hurt him, I'd be up there with a switchblade so fast, like supersonic."

At Sadie's horrified expression, Caleb snatched the phone back. "What did you say, Tessa?"

Sadie swallowed hard, imagining what it would be like to have someone as fierce as Tessa on her side. Maybe she should send her after Hamilton.

"Sorry," Caleb said after he'd hung up. "Tessa has the whole mother tiger thing down cold. It's been us against the world for a long time."

"Why didn't you tell me? About your mother and quitting college and all that?"

He shrugged. "Never really came up."

And that was another thing about Caleb. He possessed fearsome powers of compartmentalization. Baseball was baseball, family was family, Sadie was Sadie. He liked to keep things separate. But she wasn't going to let him.

"So tell me now. Tell me about your mother."

"Not much to tell." He set his jaw, the planes of his face stark and vulnerable. "When I was ten she hooked up with some sports car driver and ran off to Europe. She left me and Tessa a letter telling us how much she loved us and explaining that she couldn't afford a lawyer to fight for custody. We figured out later that she couldn't risk any attention from the law. We just weren't worth it."

"Oh, Caleb."

"Then there was our stepmother, Teddy and Frankie's mom. She was great, except she kept cheating with younger men. She was killed in a car accident while giving her boy toy a blow job. We never told the twins the full story. Not exactly your typical family history."

She shook her head with a low laugh. "Sometimes I think there's no such thing. My family's just as weird as yours, in our own way. My mother goes to sleep at the first hint of a crisis. Watching her made me want to *do* something with my life. Anything but sleep it away."

He picked up her hand, stroking one finger at a time. "I know what you mean. When Bingo went to prison I made up my mind to be different from all that craziness. No con games, no cheating. I like things straight-up and real. Solid. Caleb in control."

Caleb definitely liked to be in control.

She shivered, thinking of the hot scenes in the bedroom in which he completely took command. In bed, it totally worked.

Out of bed, she wanted more. She wanted everything. But for now she'd take what she could get. Knowing that Caleb wanted her, that he needed her in some way, made her heart sing with joy. Her impulse was to give him everything she had.

But she'd done that with Hamilton, and gotten decimated. Was it safe to give all her love to Caleb?

Did she have any choice?

Chapter 17

DONNA FILLED SADIE in on everything that had happened at the party after she and Caleb left.

"Three helicopters landed in the backyard. They were full of baseball players and the entire spring issue of Victoria's Secret."

"No way."

"Yep. They landed on the lawn in the back. Oh, and then Justin Timberlake showed up with his whole entourage. He sang a song for Crush. I heard he posted a bunch of photos on Instagram. Imagine that! Kilby on JT's Instagram!"

Sadie debated—JT or Caleb—and decided she'd gotten the better deal. "Was he as sexy in person?"

"More so," Donna said reverently. "Word must have gotten out because cars from town started showing up. It seemed like half of Kilby was there, at least the younger half."

"Hamilton?"

"I didn't see him, but maybe. I saw a few of his friends. They were playing naked glow-in-the-dark paintball with the models. Word is that all the church ladies are upset."

"Yup. Mayor Trent's been popping antacids all day.

She always looks so calm, but I think it might be just a front. Uh-oh. I gotta go."

The infamous red button was flashing. Sadie hurried into the mayor's office. She was on the phone, nodding patiently, and gave Sadie a signal to sit down. Sadie sat and waited, watching the rapid drum of her boss's fingernails across the desk.

Finally, the mayor hung up, slamming the receiver on the desk several times before replacing it in the cradle. "That damn man."

A curse and an act of violence against a phone. Not typical Mayor Trent behavior. "What happened?"

"He had to go throw a party, didn't he?" She unscrewed the cap of her bottle of antacids. "Not just any party, but a party that every wild young Kilby boy apparently crashed. All their mothers are calling me. And they're calling the Ladies' Auxiliary and they're signing that petition and not a single one of them cares about the horn-toed slugs." She chewed on a tablet, then downed a glass of water. "I wanted *no controversy*."

"We need to try harder. The cupcakes were such a hit. What about a calendar? All benefits would go to charity. Not just the slugs, but—I don't know—the library or something. We could get Caleb Hart to pose with a book."

For a moment Sadie lost herself in an erotic fantasy of Caleb, stark naked except for a book covering his privates.

"That's another thing. Mrs. Parrish actually tried to tell me that you were at the party holding hands with Caleb Hart. I told her that wasn't possible."

Stricken, Sadie stared at her boss. She couldn't lie to her. That would be a complete betrayal. But disappointing her was going to feel worse than a trip to the dentist.

"I was there. But I didn't know it was going to be Crush Taylor's party. And I left soon after I got there."

The mayor set down her antacid bottle with a sharp click. "You didn't know it was going to be his party?"

"I . . . I was with a friend. We ran into Mike Solo from the Catfish. He took us to the party, but it was kind of a . . . surprise." In the retelling, it sounded incredibly lame.

"So you went somewhere unknown with a member of the notorious Catfish? And then you held Caleb Hart's hand?"

She'd done so much more than that. Her face prickled with heat. "We're . . . dating."

The mayor drew in a shocked breath. "Dating a *Catfish player*?"

"I'm not happy about it either." The deep masculine voice had them both swinging around. Crush Taylor, black sunglasses firmly in place, lounged in the doorway. Instead of the sophisticated linen pants he'd been wearing at the party, he was back to ragged jeans and a misbuttoned shirt.

"Stop *doing* that," the mayor ground out, tightening her fist around her antacids. Sadie wouldn't have been surprised to see her wing the bottle at his head. "You're not welcome here."

"I'm a resident of Kilby and you're my mayor. I even voted for you."

The mayor gaped at him, as though stunned to hear that, and maybe not particularly happy about it.

"Women make excellent political leaders." Somehow, he made that statement sound patronizing. "And as far as I'm concerned, my star pitcher shouldn't be distracting himself with a local girl. He's got more important things to focus on. Like the fact that Ian Sullivan's been complaining of elbow pain."

Caleb had told Sadie about Ian Sullivan. He held down the third spot in the Friars rotation. As a lefty, Caleb would be the logical choice to replace him in case of injury. Sadie's heart slowly sank into her stomach. This was it. He'd be gone soon.

"Why are you here, Mr. Taylor?"

"I'm here, Mayor Trent, for two things. First, an apology. I usually manage to keep my parties private, but this one got out of hand. I know the ladies are upset, so I'd like to offer up some kind of gift to smooth things out."

"A gift. You think you can buy your way out of trouble?"

He lowered his sunglasses and peered over the tops with bloodshot eyes. "Everywhere except on the pitcher's mound, yes. My first thought was my standard apology, lingerie and flowers, but Ellington—my manager—talked me out of that."

Mayor Trent made a slight choking sound, making Sadie wonder if she'd gotten an antacid stuck in her throat.

"So, what would placate the Can the Catfish crew?" Crush asked. "A new church organ? A shrine to the Unknown Virgin? A quilting bee?"

"Yes!" The mayor came to her feet, her pink silk blouse rustling. "I'm sure the church ladies, as you refer to them, would love it if you and your players contributed to their latest quilting project. It's going to be auctioned off, with all proceeds going to needy children. Your participation would be most welcome."

Was that a look of shame on Taylor's face? Impossible. No, it must be a smirk. "I'll consider it," he said. "Now for my second problem. Why is Dean Wade leaving messages on my home phone?"

Sadie froze, and Mayor Trent went very still. Hadn't she mentioned something about Dean Wade running for mayor? "As you know, Dean Wade is a prominent local resident from one of the founding families of Kilby. He's a respected business and family man. As to why he's calling you, how could I possibly know that?"

"Hmm." Taylor yawned and replaced his sunglasses. "I detest local politics. If he's calling for my support in the next mayoral campaign, he's probably wasting his time. I'm happy enough with our current mayor. Or I would be if she liked me better."

He ambled out of the office then, leaving electric silence in his wake. Sadie ran through all the implications of what Crush had said. Obviously, Dean Wade was serious about running for mayor, if he was going to the trouble of courting Crush's support. No one could miss the hidden threat in his last statement. If Mayor Trent didn't warm up to him, he might actually support Dean Wade.

With the Wade family and Crush Taylor lined up against her, Sadie knew that Mayor Trent couldn't afford to keep her on her staff. She would be a terrible liability.

"I should quit."

The mayor rounded on her. "Don't you dare," she said fiercely. No one would see her as an ice queen now. "Crush Taylor can kiss my ass. So can the Wades."

"I didn't know she had it in her." Caleb smiled sleepily from under the corded forearm that shielded his eyes. A blanket stretched beneath them, sunshine caressed them from above. He'd taken her to the wooded Kilby State Park for a morning picnic before he had to report to the ballpark. The cheerful twittering of birdsong made it seem as if the air itself smiled on them.

"I'm nothing but bad news for her," said Sadie miserably. "And for you. Crush said I'm a distraction."

"Then he hasn't been looking at my stats."

"And he also said," this was the part she couldn't stop thinking about, "that you might get called up to the Friars soon."

All signs of sleepiness vanished. Caleb sat upright, pulling her along with him. "What are you talking about?"

She blinked at him, the sun forming a halo behind his head. "I thought you knew. He said that Ian Sullivan's been having elbow pain."

"Sullivan." Caleb ran a hand through his hair, then grabbed a water bottle and took a long swig. "He's been pitching okay, but they've been pulling him early."

"So it's not common knowledge?" Her heart sank. What if she'd just spilled some sort of Friars state secret?

"No, but it makes sense." With a sudden movement, he shifted onto his knees. A wild light burned in his eyes. "This could be my chance, Sadie. I've been solid for the last few weeks. I've even been hitting okay. I've worked through whatever fucked-up thing was going on in my head."

"What was it?"

"No idea. That doesn't matter now. I might be going back. Going back, Sadie! Back to the big leagues!"

She stretched her mouth into a wide smile, trying like hell to look happy for him. "That's fantastic!"

He gripped her upper arms. "Did he say what kind of pain Sullivan had? Sharp, intermittent pain, or more of a constant ache?"

"Geez, Caleb, he didn't get that detailed about it." She ducked under his arms and crawled across the blanket toward the picnic basket she'd picked up at the thrift store. Time to start packing up to go. But a warm hand on her waist pulled her back against his firm body.

"Sorry. I just want to know what he's dealing with.

Elbow problems are rough for a pitcher. Where are you going?"

"Nowhere." Now wasn't that the truth. Caleb would be off conquering the baseball world, while she'd still be here, typing memos for the mayor and waiting for Hamilton's next move.

"Wrong. You're coming with me." He shifted her into a sort of dip, as if they were spinning across a dance floor instead of lounging on a blanket. Under her back, his arms felt like steel rods, while his strong thighs supported her butt. The amount of sheer strength surrounding her made her want to swoon. But his words didn't make any sense.

"Excuse me?"

"You know I don't gamble, but if I did, I'd bet you a thousand bucks San Diego has a law school."

Her mouth dropped open. "It's going to take me years to save enough money for law school."

"Babe, you're with me now. If you want to go to law school, you go to law school. If Tessa wants to go to med school, she goes to med school. If the twins want karate lessons, they get them."

She pushed at his chest. "I couldn't take your money. Besides, you can't possibly afford all that."

"Well, not yet," he admitted. "I have two more years on this contract. I have to prove myself before that two years is up, so we can go into free agent negotiations. But I still have something left from my signing bonus. I invested a lot of it, and the fund's been doing well."

"It doesn't matter. That's *your* money."

"Sweetheart." He put a finger under her chin and lifted it so she couldn't escape his gaze. "What do you think we're doing here?"

She chewed on her lower lip. "We're hanging out. Getting to know each other. Having sex."

"Having great sex."

"Yes. But Caleb . . ." She fell silent again, then rolled off him. She stood up and brushed bits of grass off her shorts. "Do you ever feel like it isn't quite . . . real? Like we're in this romantic, beautiful bubble just floating through the air." She waved at the lovely birch trees arching overhead. "The bubble's going to bump into a tree or something."

"In your scenario, what's the tree? The fact that I'm a ballplayer who's probably—hopefully—going to leave town?"

"Maybe." She could think of so many other potential "trees," but that was an obvious one.

"I thought you wanted to leave Kilby."

"I *do* want to leave Kilby. I mean, I love Kilby. It's the only place I've ever lived. But with the Wades running things the way they do . . . I definitely want to get out of here, as long as my mother can handle it. She's been doing a lot better lately, but I still worry about her. But Caleb, it's not about where I go. It's about proving myself, proving I'm worth something."

"You're worth *everything*. Come here." He yanked her on top of him, making her huff in surprise. "I need you with me," he told her, fire burning deep in his eyes. "I can count my true friends on the fingers of one hand. But the ones I let inside . . . I'd die for them. I need you, Sadie. You make everything sparkle. You make me forget all the crap going on. I feel like Superman when I'm with you. I wish you could come on this road trip. God, I'm going to miss you."

And he pulled her into one of those all-consuming kisses that made her forget her own name.

But the Wade family would not forget her name, or the hard facts of her life. The next day a FedEx message arrived from Hamilton. It was addressed to "Slutty Merritt."

Her mother hovered over her shoulder as she debated whether to open it or burn it in the backyard burn barrel.

"It could be important," her mother said anxiously. "It looks so official."

Sadie tugged open the tab, feeling as if she was letting an evil genie out of its hiding place.

A bingo card dropped into her palm.

Her mother took the card from her suddenly boneless hand and puzzled over it, turning it this way and that, looking for the usual nasty message.

"This is just so very odd. We should call the police," she said fearfully.

"I don't think sending someone a bingo card is illegal. And have you forgotten who the police chief is?"

"Maybe it's a mistake. It must be a mistake, what could it even mean?"

But Sadie got the message just fine. Somehow Hamilton had figured out that Bingo Hartwell was Caleb's father. And if she didn't cut things off with him, the Wades would do something with that information.

She shut herself into her room, lay on her back and let her miserable thoughts go in circles along with the ceiling fan.

Hamilton had won. Again. She couldn't allow something bad to happen to Caleb because of her. If everyone knew that Bingo was his father, the press would show up, asking questions about him. Everyone in the stands would be talking about it. Opposing players would use it to rattle him. Opposing fans might hang banners in the stands making fun of the player with the ex-con dad. It would be a huge distraction from his game, just when he was getting his rhythm back.

Caleb trusted her enough to consider her one of his inner circle. She had to protect him, even if it cost her. She didn't even want to tell him about the bingo card, because he might go after Hamilton and make things worse. When he got back from the Catfish road trip, she'd figure out how to explain it, and maybe they could find a way to continue seeing each other.

So even though it felt like ripping her own heart out, she avoided Caleb's phone calls while he was away. She checked his schedule and made sure to return his calls when he was safely in the dugout, where no cell phones were allowed.

She delivered her own message to Hamilton, by way of Donna. Her best friend refused to let her get anywhere near Hamilton. Instead, she collared him at the Kilby Country Club, where she was taking the Shark to baby swimming lessons. The message was simple: "You win." Donna added her own flourish by tacking on several curse words.

"Sweetie, I think you're making a huge mistake," she told Sadie after the deed was done. "It's like giving in to terrorists. He'll think he can get anything he wants."

"He *can* get anything he wants," Sadie said dully.

"Except you."

"Well, not anymore."

"No wonder it's driving him crazy."

Every night during the Catfish road trip, Sadie listened to the local news report on the doings of the team. Trevor Stark was averaging two home runs a game, which was phenomenal. Off the field, his behavior was outrageous. He'd become a heartthrob across the state of Texas and beyond. Each town he went to, he'd appear on the local radio station and get girls to compete for a date with him. Trouble came when it turned out one of the winning girls was underage.

Luckily for the Catfish—not so luckily for the Can the Catfish petition—Trevor had figured it out pretty quickly and called her parents. He even managed to come out of it looking vaguely heroic.

In El Paso, Mike Solo and the entire infield entered a karaoke competition. They won it all with their sexed-up version of "Get It On." Paramedics had to be called to tend to three girls who fainted in the audience.

Jim Lieberman became briefly famous when he rescued a girl in Albuquerque from a rabid dog. Sadly, he got bitten during the struggle and fainted. When he came to, he was in a hospital bed, foaming at the mouth. Or at least he thought he was. Actually he was in the visitor's clubhouse, on a cot, with shaving cream dripping off his face and the Catfish laughing their asses off.

His reaction made every blooper sports show in the country. But he did get a date out of it, with the rescued girl.

The big news was Caleb's consistent, relentless performance. Just a matter of time, everyone said. Some were even placing bets on when he'd get called up.

Sadie cried herself to sleep every night of that road trip.

Chapter 18

WHEN THE CATFISH returned to Kilby, Caleb held onto a slim hope that Sadie planned to surprise him at the ballpark. She'd be waiting in her little Corolla to pick him up and whisk him off to Lake McGee or maybe a quiet hotel room where they could reunite properly. But the crowd in the parking lot didn't include any dark-haired, fire-eyed beauties. Nor did it include Bingo. Dispirited, he got into his Jeep and drove back to his apartment.

Bingo had left him a note: *Got a job! You can find me at the Sacred Grounds Café if you need me. Your mail is on the table.*

He flipped through it—maybe Sadie had left him a letter.

Nothing.

He wanted to pour his frustration into something, so he went after the supermarket circular and shredded it like confetti. Maybe Sadie didn't want him anymore. Maybe she'd been trying to break up with him at that last picnic and he'd been too dense to see it. That whole "bubble crashing into a tree" shit. Maybe they'd crashed right into it while he'd been away on his road trip. *Bam.*

He moved on from the circular to his bank statement. That got torn into shreds too, as did a notice from the landlord about a painting schedule. When most of his mail lay in crumpled scraps, he went into the bathroom, stripped off his clothes and took refuge in a shower. As the hot water pelted onto his back, his anger began to recede.

This was Sadie, not just any girl. Sadie was honest, intelligent, caring, and . . . wounded. She was just as wary as he was, and she had good reason too.

Something was going on. Now that he'd gotten his ego out of the way, he could see it. But how could he figure it out if she wouldn't talk to him? Then inspiration struck. Her friend, Donna. Mike had gotten her number, hadn't he?

Ten minutes later he was chasing down Donna at the playground. She waved when she saw him, barely pausing as she chased a gleeful little toddler across the woodchip-covered surface. The kid had no sense of direction, and seemed to be magnetically attracted to the protruding corners of the playground equipment.

"I have to watch him every second, so don't take it personally if I never look you in the eye," she warned him. "If this kid doesn't grow up to be a soccer player or something, I'll eat my cowboy hat. Or at least a cowboy."

"Is he always like this?"

"The Shark? Oh, he's worse at bedtime. I've clocked him at a hundred miles an hour running from his baby toothbrush . . . So, I suppose you're here about Sadie."

"She won't return my calls. Or rather, she returns them but never when I can actually talk to her. I know something's wrong."

Donna lunged forward to keep the Shark from bonking his little body on the frame of the swing. She plucked him into the air, his little legs wriggling a mile a minute. "Don't make me put you in the backpack, little motor man." The boy squirmed as she squished her nose into his chubby neck. Then she plopped him down. He immediately crawled toward Caleb and wrapped his arms around his leg.

Caleb laughed and lifted his leg a few inches off the ground, giving the little guy a ride that made him shriek with joy. He went up and down a few times, until it seemed the boy's grip was slipping, then he carefully set him on the ground. The Shark plopped onto his butt and dug his hands into the wood chips.

Caleb glanced up to find Donna watching him with an odd expression.

"You're a good guy, aren't you?"

"I don't know about that," he answered uncomfortably. "Pretty average, I guess." And that would be generous, in his opinion. After all, he'd grown up with a con man. How good could he be?

"I'm not supposed to say anything, but I'm going to. Because Sadie is my best friend in the world, besides the Shark, and he's useless when it comes to female conversation."

A strange combination of triumph and dread tightened Caleb's gut. "I knew something was going on. What is it?"

"Hamilton Wade sent Sadie a bingo card. I don't know what it means—she wouldn't tell me—but she asked me to tell him that 'he won.' That's all I know. Well, and that she hasn't figured out how to tell you and that she cries every night."

Caleb's fists clenched, once, twice. Rage worthy of the Incredible Hulk rushed through his veins. "I'm going to beat that guy into next year."

She snagged the back of his T-shirt, twisting it in

her fist. "Don't be an idiot. I didn't tell you this so you could go beat someone's brains out. Sadie's trying to protect you from the Wades. She'll be ten times more upset if you get hurt. And that family, they're like an old-style western gang or something. They don't know how to let things go."

"I don't either," he ground out through clenched teeth. "Ask anyone."

She wrapped the T-shirt even harder around her wrist. "I'm not going to let you go until you think of a better way to handle this. A way that won't hurt Sadie. She's been through enough."

He stared at her, wheels turning. Donna met his gaze for about two whole seconds before the Shark launched himself across the playground in a rapid crablike crawl. "You'd better go after him," Caleb said with a slow smile. "He's headed right for that slide. The one with the kids coming out like bullets."

She glared at him and edged toward the Shark, trying to pull Caleb along with her. Instead, he ripped off his T-shirt, freeing himself from her grasp and making her stumble. "You are a low-down scoundrel."

He strode off toward his Jeep. "Now that's a little more accurate," he called back to her. "But you have a point about not hurting Sadie. I'll get back to you."

Later, he called her again. "Tell Sadie I'm taking care of the situation and she can read about it in tomorrow's edition of the *Kilby Press-Herald*."

Sadie and her mother had long ago stopped getting the paper delivered, so she didn't see the headline until she passed through the metal detector at City Hall. The guard had his nose buried in the sports section, but by bending slightly, she saw the headline: CATFISH PITCHER REVEALS FAMILY SECRET.

Oh my God. She snatched the paper from the guard's hands. "Hey!" he protested.

"Aren't you supposed to be keeping an eye on people coming into the building, not reading the sports page?"

Quickly she scanned the article, which had Burwell Brown's byline.

Caleb Hart came forward with the stunning information that his real name is Caleb Hartwell and his father is Thurston Hartwell II, who just completed a six-year prison term for defrauding several widows of their life savings. Bingo has long been suspected of multiple forms of fraud, including illegal bookmaking. Hart told the *Press-Herald* that when his father was incarcerated, he assumed parental rights over his two younger brothers, who are still minors.

Said Hart, "I hope the fans can understand why I kept this personal family situation private. I play my heart out for them, and for the Catfish, and hopefully I will have the opportunity to help the San Diego Friars as well."

Hart has long had a reputation as a brilliant talent with an unpredictable streak. Asked if his inconsistency on the mound had any connection to his family's circumstances, he answered bluntly, "No."

Duke Ellington, the manager of the Catfish, had this to say about the surprise revelation and whether it would negatively impact the team: "Caleb Hart has our full support because he's earned it. Only an idiot would hold his father's actions against him."

However, the Ladies' Auxiliary, which is spearheading the so-called "Can the Catfish" movement, took a very different view. "Apparently we have an ex-con living right here in Kilby, thanks to the Catfish. One has to wonder whether it's safe for decent

families to attend the games, We call on Crush Taylor
to take a good, hard look at the sort of operation he's
running."

She dropped the paper, tears springing to her eyes.
Caleb had done this for her—for them.

She snatched up her phone and texted him: *What did
you do???*

The best thing for us. U okay?

Yes. As long as you are.

*Don't like bullies. Feel great. Want 2 see you. Bin-
go's working 2night. Come over?*

Yes!

She wished she could go right away, but Mayor Trent
was calling. *Oh fireballs.* Her stomach sank. Her boss
would not be happy about Caleb's interview. Or about
the fact that she had known about Bingo all along.

When Caleb opened the door of his apartment that
night, Sadie launched herself at him, wrapping both
arms and legs around his strong body. He nestled her
against him, hands on her ass, his warm mouth kissing
her neck. It felt so good to be next to him again—how
had she ever thought she could do without this giddy
bliss?

"Are you sure it's going to be okay?" she asked fearfully when the initial edge of her need to touch him had
been soothed. He turned and strode toward the bedroom, with her still wrapped around him.

"Everything will be fine. I thought long and hard
about it. I'd kept Bingo a secret because I didn't want
him doing any more damage to my life. But if someone
like Hamilton could use it to blackmail me, fuck that. I
owed Burwell Brown an interview anyway, remember?"

"Yes, but it was supposed to be about the slugs."

"I mentioned the slugs. Didn't he include that?"

She giggled into his warm neck, feeling the tendons flex as he walked. "No. I'm going to call and yell at him."

"Not now. You're going to talk to me first." He set her on the bed and fixed a stern gaze on her. "Why didn't you tell me about Hamilton's threat? He said the same thing to me before, but I just ignored the jackass."

"I didn't want to make trouble for you." She faltered under his steady stare, drawing up her legs and wrapping her arms around them. "The Wades have so many ways to hurt people. I couldn't bear it if they hurt you because of me. You're . . . you're very important to me." She ended in a whisper.

"You're important to me too. I figured you didn't quite believe that."

"They could ruin your baseball career. How could I live with myself if that happened?"

"How could I live if I lost you because of some freaking idiot who doesn't know when it's time to quit?" He tumbled her backward on the bed. "Next time, trust me, Sadie. You're not alone anymore. You understand?"

He rested his forehead on hers, and she felt as if her heart might explode into little tiny pieces of happiness. "I can't believe you told everyone about Bingo for me."

"I'd do a lot more than that for you, Sadie Merritt." He was kissing his way down her body, shoving aside clothing as he went. Every touch felt like a flame springing to life. When she was naked, she scrambled to her knees and turned the tables on him, pushing him onto his back. She straddled him and reached under his T-shirt, then pushed it up, revealing one hard ridge of muscle after the other. She danced her fingers up his chest, counting the lines of thick sinew.

"You have a six-pack times two," she told him. His eyes darkened as she stroked his skin. She reached his left arm, which bulged more thickly than his right. A strong vein ran along the inside of his bicep; she could feel his pulse through the skin. "I listened to all the games, you know. Every time you threw a pitch, I was so nervous I nearly threw up. Do you get nervous?"

"Nah," he said gruffly. "Not once I throw that first pitch. Before, sure. I have a method for dealing with it, though."

"Run to the bathroom?"

He laughed. "I haven't thrown up yet. No. It's silly. Just one of those superstitions we have."

"What is it?" She unsnapped the waistband of his jeans and began dragging them down his legs.

"Well, on my very first start, I was so nervous I thought I might die. Like, my heart would burst, or a blood vessel or something. And I thought, well, what do I want my last words to be if I do? So I texted Tessa and the boys. I said, 'Love you guys. See you on the flip side.'"

From halfway down his middle, she paused, resting her chin on his firm belly. "And?"

"And I won. I won my first two starts. On my third start, my phone battery was dead. I borrowed someone else's, but I still lost. So it only works if it's my phone."

"You probably just psyched yourself out."

"Maybe." He lifted his legs off the bed so she could slide his pants off. Already the crotch of his boxers was swelling, his penis pushing up the fabric. Heat pooled in her belly. He was so sexy with his strong thighs scattered with golden hairs. "But right before the worst game of my life, something happened that made me forget about the text. I didn't send one, not even from someone else's phone. And it was a disaster. I definitely learned my lesson. Always send the text. No matter what."

She ran her hand over his boxers, feeling the heat of his arousal burn through the thin cotton. "What happened? I mean, what was the thing that happened that made you forget to text?"

"I got a call from Bingo's lawyer that he was being released in a week."

Astounded, she stopped her stroking. "Maybe that's why the game was a disaster."

"Why?"

"Because you were distracted by the news about Bingo."

"Baby, when I'm on the mound, nothing distracts me." He lifted her so she sat with her sex directly on his swollen erection. "You could prance naked across the field and I'd still be staring at Mike Solo's crotch waiting for his call."

He pressed his thumb against her clit, and she shuddered from the pleasure. "Tha . . . that sounds like a challenge."

"It's not. Don't get any ideas. Not everyone has my level of focus." As if to demonstrate the power of his focus, he homed in on the tender flesh underneath his thumb, massaging it with the perfect amount of pressure. Those hands of his were magical.

"How do you make it feel so good?" she groaned, squirming back and forth on his increasingly hard boner.

He chuckled, deep in his chest, the way he sounded when he was completely turned on. "It's just like pitching. You gotta pay attention. Watch, listen, and learn. And focus."

Ripples of delight radiated from the spot between her legs where his attention was glued. She let her eyes fall halfway shut so all she saw was Caleb, his burning gaze, his ripped chest, his golden farmer's tan. That sweet intimate bubble formed around them again, as if it had never been broken.

She came in long, rolling waves, a soft, complete orgasm. She shuddered and let her head fall back, releasing a long sigh of bliss into the still air of his bedroom. Then he flipped them both over so she lay on her back, he on top, his elbows on either side of her head. She reached down and pushed his boxers off his straining penis. Taking him into her hand, she tugged lightly. "Come up here," she whispered. His eyes flared with heat.

Hamilton had always wanted her to do this, and she'd resisted. It was one of the justifications he gave for cheating on her. But for some reason, letting him penetrate her mouth had seemed dangerous to her. She'd never felt safe enough with him to feel comfortable doing it.

But with Caleb, things were completely different. He loved licking her; not only did he say so, but it was obvious from the massive erection the act gave him. And he never asked her to use her mouth, or demand she do anything. Sex with him was more like a big feast—a feast of desserts, from which she could pick and choose whatever she wanted.

And right now she wanted his beautiful cock in her mouth. He moved up her body and knelt over her mouth. "Yes?" he asked, scrutinizing her face. She felt flushed and decadent, as if they'd been doing this for hours.

"Oh, yes." She took his long, magnificent member in her hand and wrapped her lips around it. He let out a long groan.

"Oh Sadie, you have no idea . . ." But now it was her turn to focus on the beautiful piece of flesh filling her mouth. It slid so deliciously against her tongue, faintly salty, slightly sweet, maybe a little bit grassy, like a soccer meadow in the woods. Maybe all that time on the baseball diamond surrounded by grass had soaked into his skin. The thought made her smile, which made her mouth curve around his erection. He looked down, as if in agony.

"What?"

But she shook her head. His intimate scent was her secret, to be shared with no one, not even him.

"I can't . . ." With a low growl he pulled from her mouth and came in a burst into his own hand. The sight of him gripping his own member, every tendon of his body taut with effort, was unbearably erotic to her. "Sorry," he gasped. "No time to get to a condom."

"You could have . . ." She touched her mouth, which still tingled from his occupation of it. "I wouldn't mind."

"I wasn't sure. I wanted to ask but my mouth wasn't working." He rolled off her and padded, naked and magnificent, out of the room. She heard the water run. Running her tongue across her lips, she shut her eyes, wondering how this man could make her feel so wonderful. With him, she felt beautiful, sexy, and desirable. Never once, even with his penis deep in her mouth, did she feel slutty.

Sadie 1, Hamilton 0. Caleb Hart with the win.

Chapter 19

THE GUYS ON the team took Caleb's big revelation in stride.

"My father's a plumber," confided Mike Solo, stuffing a mile-high sandwich into his mouth after the next day's game. "In high school I had to borrow his van to pick up girls for dates. It had 'Your Shit Is Our Business' in bright red paint on it. Try scoring when you're driving something like that."

"My old man was a prison guard," threw in Ramirez from across the room. "Where was yours incarcerated? Maybe they know each other."

Caleb ignored that, because his attention was caught by Trevor Stark, who hadn't made a peep since the topic of fathers came up. It must be a sore spot, since silence was definitely not his normal M.O. He couldn't resist a chance to needle the cocky slugger. "How about you, Stark? What kind of work does your father do?"

"None of your fucking business," he growled as he snagged a slice of cheese off the deli plate. "I have a date. See you losers later."

"Hey Stark," Mike called after him.

"What?"

"Your ego called, it's waiting for you outside the ballpark. It was so big it couldn't fit inside."

"Kind of like your belly." Trevor gestured to the clubhouse attendant, who hurried to his side and shouldered his bag.

Mike thudded a fist against his midsection, which had maybe a few extra pounds of flesh on it. "Rock hard, baby. If you're talking size, you must be referring to the part a little lower down."

"I heard the word 'little.' That's all," Stark shot back.

Mike flipped Stark off as he followed the attendant out of the clubhouse. "Hart, you're lucky that guy is here. He makes you look good, even if your dad is a criminal."

"Gee, thanks."

"No problem. I'm ignoring that sarcastic undertone." Mike picked a leaf of lettuce out of his sandwich. "No greens. Unless it's a lime slurpee. And that green isn't found in nature, so it's okay."

"How's it going with Donna, by the way?" Caleb needled him. He knew from Sadie that Donna was having lots of fun torturing Mike.

Mike narrowed his eyes at him over his sandwich and pretended to be busy chewing.

Even the Kilby fans—the ones who came to the ballpark, not the ones who'd signed the Can the Catfish petition—seemed to support him. A wave of applause greeted him whenever he took the mound, even in the middle of the eighth inning when the annual "Crazy Catfish Whiskers" contest was being judged. A little girl in a pink dress won—she'd made her whiskers out of glitter-coated pipe cleaners. Caleb was given the honor of awarding her the prize, which was, unfortunately, a freshly caught catfish. When she opened the cooler to inspect her prize, she burst into tears.

Caleb whisked her into his arms and took her to the sidelines where the Catfish mascot was doing splits and handstands. Eventually she stopped crying and agreed to wave to the crowd, which gave a roar of approval. When he handed the girl back to her mother in the stands, she kissed him on the cheek. When that image flashed across the Jumbotron, everyone went crazy.

Caleb felt as if that one simple kiss on the cheek was like the keys to a city. Not the city of Kilby so much, but the City of Acceptance. The City of Not-hiding. It was an enormous relief to know that he wasn't keeping a secret anymore. He'd been doing it for so long that it was just part of life, something so habitual he didn't think about it—like walking with one foot after the other. But now that the secret was out, he felt light as popcorn. No more worries weighed him down.

Well, maybe one. He'd beaten Hamilton by taking away the power of his threat of exposure. But he knew damn well that wouldn't be the end of it. He didn't care what Hamilton did—or tried to do—to him. His big fear was that the Wades would take it out on Sadie by making her life even more miserable. To avoid giving them the opportunity, he made sure Sadie spent every extra minute of her time with him. This had the added benefit of . . . well, that she spent every extra minute of her time with him.

The next few weeks were the happiest of his life.

Even much of his anger toward Bingo leeched away. His father seemed to like his job at the coffee shop. He'd barely seen the man in the weeks since their meeting with Officer Kelly and he picked up no hint of trouble. Maybe he really had made a fresh start. One day his feeling of goodwill toward the entire world burst through the boundaries he'd thrown up between himself and his father.

"Tessa and the boys are going to drive down this weekend," he told Bingo over a cup of double espresso at Sacred Grounds. He'd stopped by to check things out for himself; he didn't completely trust Officer Kelly to resist Bingo's charm. He'd hung in the back for a while, hiding under a Twins cap, watching his father. What he saw gave him no cause for alarm, so he made the impulsive decision to give Bingo a second chance.

"Really? And I can see them?"

"Yes, you can see them. That's the whole point."

A funny look crossed his father's face. "Are you . . . I mean, what made you change your mind?"

Caleb sipped his double espresso with extra sugar; his dad had actually remembered how he liked his coffee. "The boys have been asking for it," he admitted. "They have a right to see their father."

Bingo wiped his hands on his barista apron, then adjusted his bow tie, then fluttered back to the apron. He looked like a nervous mother hen. "What if I screw it up?"

"Make sure you don't," said Caleb firmly. "I'll be watching every second, you can make sure of that. Except when I'm pitching. I'm scheduled to start in two days and I want you all to come."

Bingo sucked in a breath. "You'll let me in the ballpark?"

"Cut the drama, Bingo. You went whether I wanted it or not."

"But this time I'll be there with your permission. I won't have to purchase any strange sunglasses." He clasped his hands together. "This means so much, Caleb. I won't cause any trouble for you, I promise." His sky-blue eyes were so sincere, Caleb almost believed him. At the very least, he believed that Bingo didn't *want* to cause trouble. On the other hand, it seemed to follow him the way ducklings followed a mother duck.

"Has the press been calling?"

"Yes, but I've been telling them what you said, 'No comment. Please allow our family to get to know each other again in peace.'"

Caleb nearly choked on his espresso. "I didn't say that part. I told you to stick to 'No comment.'"

"A little embellishment. I had to give them something."

Caleb ground his teeth, but decided Bingo hadn't said anything too disastrous. "I don't want any press sniffing around when the kids are here."

"Absolutely not." The door jingled with a new arrival. "I'm not the one who went public, son. I was happy being Mr. Anonymous with the oddball sunglasses collection."

"Right. Well, sorry about that. It had to be done." He'd never explained the reason why, and he had no intention of doing so. It would mean revealing too much of Sadie's personal life. The degree of fierce protectiveness he felt toward Sadie continued to amaze him.

"I'm not complaining," Bingo said, squeezing Caleb's shoulder. "You did the right thing. You know what they say, 'The truth will set you free.'" He hurried off to take the new customer's order, leaving Caleb to drain the last dregs of his espresso and hope he was, in fact, doing the right thing.

His family arrived in a whirlwind of skateboards and oversized basketball jerseys and handheld electronics. Teddy and Frankie had grown two inches since the season started. They showed no awkwardness at all with Bingo, but immediately pelted him with questions about prison.

"How was the food? Did you ever see anyone get knifed? Did you learn how to make a shiv?"

When Bingo explained that he'd been in one of the nonviolent offender facilities nicknamed Club Feds, they moved on to baseball, and their ideas about how to change the game to make it more like basketball. "What if they put a basket at each base? The first baseman would have to like, do a slam dunk with the ball to get the runner out."

Bingo watched them with tears in his eyes, cutting occasional glances toward Tessa, who wouldn't say more than a stiff hello at first. For both Caleb and Tessa, the wounds ran much deeper, whereas the twins had been little kids at the time of the trial.

Tessa was more interested in talking about Sadie. She wrangled Caleb into helping her make chili while Bingo was playing Pictionary with the twins in the living room. "Will I like her? I'd better like her, because I've never heard you be so into a girl before."

Caleb focused his attention on the can of kidney beans he was opening. "She's coming to the game tonight. You can judge for yourself."

"She knows all about our crazy family?" Tessa pulled an embarrassed face.

"Sweetheart, everybody knows now. I did an interview in the local paper, and it got picked up everywhere there's a kid tossing around a baseball."

"I know *that*. But does she know everything? Does she know how he used us? Does she know about our mother and Teddy and Frankie's?"

"She knows most of it." The can opener got stuck; Caleb banged it on the counter to knock it loose. "She doesn't judge. She has problems of her own."

"Well, still, I hope she knows what she's getting into."

"Relax, would you?" Uncomfortable with the direction of this conversation, he dumped the beans into the

stew pot. "And don't start spilling any more family dirt.
I don't want you to scare her off."

Tessa gave him a scolding punch on the arm. "You're
going to have to share sometime. You can't put everything into separate little boxes."

"Yeah. Well. Are you sure about that?" It worked
for him, quite frankly. It's how he'd gotten so far in
baseball; the mound was his safe haven from all the
outside crap.

"Pretty sure. But I won't embarrass you in front of
your girlfriend." She put a hand on her heart. "Hartwell family vow."

Girlfriend. He let that word rumble through his
mind, and discovered he liked the way it sounded. Since
college, he'd had hookups, flings, one-night stands,
crushes, and more hookups, but he'd never had anyone
he would consider a "girlfriend." And yet, he wasn't
sure the word adequately described the emotions he felt
for Sadie. What did insatiable lust, fierce protectiveness, and a craving for her company add up to?

A strong wind swirled through the ballpark that night,
picking up dust devils in the bare-dirt corners of the
stadium. Every once in a while a fan's cap would get
whisked into the air and tumble across the bleachers,
making everyone duck and shriek. The flags—American
and state of Texas—flapped like sails in the wild gusts.
In the dugout, players buzzed with the possibility that
the game would be called due to the gusty, unpredictable wind and threat of thunderstorms. But the minor
league schedule was so packed, it took a lot to get the
umpires to call a game. The home team carried the responsibility for making that decision, which was why
Duke was deep in conversation with the groundskeeper
and the head umpire.

Caleb was too hyped-up to sit on the dugout bench, so he stood under the overhang, watching the wind play goofy tricks with the crowd's clothing and hairdos. Jim Lieberman joined him.

"Ever heard of the Magnus Effect?"

Caleb shot him a scornful look. "Of course." The Magnus Effect was a principle of physics that explained why pitches curved. It had to do with the flow of air over the ball, but that's about where his knowledge ended.

"And you know why it doesn't work on a knuckle-ball?"

"You got me." Caleb shrugged. "Don't throw many knuckleballs."

"You want to know, right? Do you want to know? Because sometimes I know things and people get all bent out of shape when I try to explain."

"Yeah, that's called the 'Know-It-All Effect.'"

At Bieberman's wounded reaction, Caleb clapped a hand on his shoulder. "Just kidding. Come on, en-lighten me. Why doesn't the Magnus Effect work on a knuckleball?"

Lieberman's face lit up. "Because the knuckleball has no spin. Its movement is caused by the way the seams catch the air. On a knuckleball's way to the plate, chaos theory takes over. Anything can happen. That's why they're so hard to hit, because they're unpredictable."

"Chaos theory, huh? No wonder I hate the knuck-leball. I like to know what my pitches are going to do when they leave my hand."

Lieberman popped one fist into the pocket of his glove, working it onto his hand. "You don't ever really know for sure." The dude had a point. "But with this kind of wind, imagine what a knuckleball pitcher could do."

Caleb stared across the dugout at the opposing team, the Salt Lake Bees. Ted Barstow was scheduled to pitch. He was a former fastballer who'd switched to the knuckleball when he'd had a bone chip removed from his elbow.

"Advantage Bees," Caleb murmured. "But I'd put good old-fashioned heat up against the junk any day of the week."

"It's not junk." Lieberman seemed genuinely wounded on behalf of the knuckleball. "You could say that since it's the only pitch without any spin on it, it's the least tricky. The knuckleball's only trick is catching the wind. You might say it goes with the flow. It surrenders to chaos."

Surrenders to chaos? Caleb snorted. "Bieberman? Get out of here."

Lieberman shrugged. A hot dog wrapper whipped across the field and slapped him in the face. He brushed it away with a grin. "Surrender to chaos, Hart. Surrender to chaos. It's going to win in the end, you know."

"The hell it will. I'll tell you what I believe in, Lieberman. I believe in *baseball*. I believe in numbers. Numbers are not chaos. I believe good luck comes from hard work. Respect the game and the game will respect you back. That's what I believe."

Lieberman gave a few rapid nods, his face lighting up like a pinball machine. Most of the guys mocked his attempts at philosophical communication, but Caleb occasionally threw him a bone. "All right. All right. How about this? 'Chaos is the law of nature. Order is the dream of man.' Henry Adams wrote that."

"You mean that pitcher for the Reds?" Caleb winked.

Lieberman laughed. "I'll give you that one because I know you're smart and not everyone has a photographic memory like me. Anyway, don't worry about the chaos.

As Deepak Chopra says, all great changes are preceded by chaos. When I saw the article in the paper about you, I thought about that quote."

Caleb stared at the baby-faced sprite. "Who the hell are you, anyway?"

"Jim Lieberman, shortstop. We've been playing together a few weeks now . . ."

"I know who you are, I mean—" Caleb broke off, having just spotted Tessa and Sadie making their way along the row of seats just behind home plate. The wind was playing havoc with Sadie's ponytail, whipping the long strands across her cheek. She wore a short-sleeved red blouse and jeans, and her radiant face glowed with laughter as she tried to keep the wind from snatching away the container of drinks she carried.

He couldn't understand why every single person in the ballpark wasn't staring at her. It made no sense.

In her wake trailed the twins. Teddy kept tossing peanuts over his shoulder for Frankie to catch in his mouth. Their coordination was impressive, despite the wind. Caleb wondered if the Magnus Effect applied to casually tossed peanuts. Bingo came last. He kept glancing nervously at the other crowd members. Maybe he felt self-conscious because of the article.

Not that he cared that much; his father had made his choices, and Caleb had made his. His gaze returned to Sadie, drawn like a homing pigeon. She was looking toward the dugout, shading her eyes against the evening slant of light and the occasional wafts of dust. He raised a hand to catch her attention. She waved eagerly and blew him a kiss.

He grinned and tapped his fist against his heart, as if she'd landed her kiss where it counted.

"There's no making out in the dugout, Hart," said

Sonny Barnes from behind him. "I learned that the hard way."

"Nobody's naked, Sonny," Caleb said, his gaze still locked with Sadie's. "It's all PG here."

"Not the way you're staring at her. Like you have X-ray vision, with a couple extra X's."

T.J. Gates piped up. "Is that your father, Caleb? Thurston Hartwell?"

Caleb hesitated only for a second. The secret was out, no need to dance around the subject. "That's him."

"Looks like you," said Trevor Stark, letting the dugout door slam shut behind him. "Would have recognized him anywhere. Matter of fact, I've seen him here a few times. Big baseball fan, is he?"

Caleb whipped his head back toward the group in the stands. *A few times?* But Bingo had promised not to come to the ballpark, and he'd claimed to be keeping that promise. "When?" he asked, his throat tightening.

Trevor shrugged as he slung his bat over his shoulders and twisted from side to side to warm up. "Last few days. I don't know. It's not my job to keep track of your family. Unless you include what's-her-name, Sadie. I'll keep track of *her* for you."

Caleb gave him a mental f-you finger and tuned out the rest of the team's ribbing. Trevor must be mistaken. Even in a minor league ballpark, so much smaller and more intimate than a big league stadium, it would be difficult to single out one attendee from another. He was being paranoid, and letting a mind-fucker like Stark mess with his focus.

Anyway, Bingo didn't matter anymore. His gaze traveled back to Sadie, who'd taken her seat and was distributing drinks to the rest of his family. Tenderhearted, sparkling, brave, brainy, sexy-as-hell Sadie. That's who mattered to him now.

The knowledge traveled through him like an electrical shock. He *loved* Sadie. She was the woman for him. No one else.

Love.

He loved her.

Holy knuckleball.

He felt a rush of air as Duke jogged past him on his way to the head umpire to deliver the lineup card. The opposing team's manager did the same from the other direction. A buzz traveled through the dugout and the crowd in the stands, and applause swelled. The game was on.

As Caleb discarded his warm-up jacket and prepared to take the field, he heard Lieberman whisper one more time, "All great changes are preceded by chaos."

For some reason, the words sounded like an omen, and he shivered. Or maybe it was the wind, which immediately tried to rip his cap from his head. He tugged it more firmly into place and jogged to the mound, ready to pitch in front of three thousand people, his ex-con father, his rambunctious twin brothers, his loyal sister, and the girl he'd fallen in love with.

It wasn't until his first windup that he realized that for the second time in his career, he hadn't texted his family before a game.

Chapter 20

Watching Caleb struggle for every pitch in that windstorm was a special kind of torture for Sadie. At one point, with the bases loaded and the count at two balls and two strikes, she found herself gripping Tessa's hand to the point of nearly snapping a few bones.

"Sorry," she muttered, pulling her hand away, then forgetting all about it and leaping to her feet with a scream when Caleb forced a pop-out. The ball soared high into the air, higher, higher, then descended in the craziest random pattern of dips and swirls she'd ever seen. The shortstop, Lieberman, had to hop like a bunny on speed to track the ball. His cap flew off, he stumbled, got to his feet, yelled something, and in the end made a diving catch when the ball ghosted left at the last moment.

Sadie sank into her seat, utterly exhausted. "How do you stand it?" she asked Tessa, who was grinning at her with that stunning smile all members of the family had.

"It helps to not be in love with him."

Sadie's face burned. God, was it that obvious? Yes, screaming like a banshee while Caleb pitched might be a giveaway. "Oh."

"Besides, this is Triple A. Save some of that emotion

for the big leagues. Playoffs? World Series? You might want to pace yourself."

"I don't think I'd be able to take it."

"Tessa, Bingo's taking us for some hot dogs," shouted one of the twins. Sadie couldn't tell them apart yet. "Want anything?"

Tessa lowered her voice. "Valium? Quaalude?"

Sadie laughed. "I'll be okay. Sweet offer, though."

They watched Bingo and the two boys make their way toward the aisle. Tessa narrowed her eyes at her father's retreating back. "I hope it wasn't a mistake to come here. He's acting weird. Then again, how would I really know, since I haven't seen him in six years?"

"You didn't visit him in prison?"

"Hell, no. I was too pissed off. Caleb went a few times. But Caleb's always been better at shutting things out. He can put on the blinders and just go. Me, every time I look at Bingo I get mad."

Sadie's attention was back on the game, where Caleb was working another deep count to get the third out. Either the wind was throwing him off or something else was, but he seemed to be fighting for every pitch. Finally, he forced the batter into a ground ball that skipped right at him. With an acrobatic move, he scooped it up and flung to the first baseman for the out.

Finally she could exhale, and ask the question that she didn't know how to ask Caleb. "I've been wondering. What do you think was throwing off his pitching when he first got sent down?"

"You mean the Game? When all hell broke loose?"

"Yeah. He doesn't ever talk about it. Ever. But I know it's on his mind. How could it not be?"

Tessa tilted her box of Cracker Jacks toward Sadie and propped her feet on the back of the empty seat in front of her. "Of course he doesn't. That's Caleb's way.

He'd probably see it as bad luck to *talk* about his bad luck. These guys are superstitious as hell."

"So that's all it was? Bad luck?"

"I'm sure there was more than that. Caleb keeps a lot hidden away, you know. He has a huge sense of responsibility. It's almost like he blames himself for what Bingo did. I don't really get it, honestly. I say, put the blame where it belongs. Caleb likes to shoulder everything. That's why he offered Bingo a place to stay when he got out. I thought that was nuts. But Caleb's always been that way, so I don't know why he fell apart during that game. It was around the time we found out that Bingo was getting released. But we knew it was going to happen soon, so I don't know why that would have thrown him for a loop." She shrugged, popping more Cracker Jacks in her mouth. "I told him he should see a sports psychologist, but he nearly blew me off the phone with his big fat 'Hell no.'" She shook her head mournfully. "Men. Good luck trying to tell them to do anything."

Sadie nodded sagely, though her knowledge of men was pretty limited. She'd hate to base it only on her experience with Hamilton.

Caleb was the first batter up. Adjusting his batting helmet, he stepped one foot inside the batter's box, staring at the opposing pitcher across those infamous sixty feet and six inches. He took a few preparatory swings, twisting his hips with his motion. She got wrapped up in watching his butt, which she could see only from the side but was fine from every angle. His wide shoulders and towering build made him look huge next to the stocky umpire standing behind the catcher. She had a sudden vision of him as a warrior, taking on every attack with the power of his body, his mind, his determination. Caleb Hart was . . . magnificent. Or maybe she was just crazy in love with him.

The sensation of someone watching her pulled her attention to the seats on the other side of the field. The sight of a silver-haired man in cowboy hat and denim shirt sent a chill through her. Dean Wade. Hamilton's uncle, who was considering a run for mayor. What was he doing at a Catfish game?

Dean gave her a courteous-enough nod and said something to his wife, who sat next to him. She laughed but didn't look at Sadie, so they didn't seem to be talking about her.

She cursed herself for her paranoia. What could be more normal than members of the Wade family attending a Catfish game? Everyone in town did so sooner or later, though football was most Kilbyites' first love. Especially if Dean was running for mayor, he'd make sure to show up at all the "hometown" places where people gathered. Why should it have anything to do with her? The Wade family had bigger fish to fry than tormenting the girl who'd dumped their favorite son. That was just a sideline.

"Everything okay?" Tessa was asking. "Don't worry, Caleb hits pretty well, but honestly, it doesn't really matter. When you can pitch like Caleb, a decent batting average is gravy."

A man two rows ahead of them gave a sudden jump that made everyone in the surrounding rows stare. He had a tiny pocket TV propped on his knee and an earbud hanging out of one ear. "Sullivan's been pulled," he said to no one in particular. "Looks like he's hurt. Oh man. Hart better start packing."

Tessa and Sadie glanced at each other in alarm. Tessa clambered over the row of seats until she was right behind him, watching the TV over his shoulder. "What are you talking about?"

"Ian Sullivan. Rumors been flying he's going to need

surgery. He's a lefty, so that means Hart's a shoo-in.
Especially the way he's been pitching. They'll let today
slide."

"He's pitching just fine today," Tessa said loyally.
But Sadie couldn't summon so much as a smile.

Caleb was about to get called up. He was leaving the
Catfish.

Leaving her.

He was going back. Caleb tried to hide the exultation
that surged through him as Duke delivered the news.

"They want you on the next plane to San Diego
for the upcoming home stand. Congratulations, Hart.
You've earned it."

The next plane. Crap. His grin slid a bit as he realized he wouldn't have time for more than a quick good-
bye to Sadie and his family.

Duke continued, "Unfortunately, the earliest flight
the travel office could find is tomorrow morning at eight.
Puddle-jumper from the Kilby airport to Houston."

"Got it. Thanks, Duke. Thanks for everything."

Duke stood up and shook his hand. "I don't want to
see you back here, Hart. Got it?"

"I don't intend to come back." But the words struck
the wrong note, like the ominous shake of a rattlesnake's tail. Leaving Kilby meant leaving Sadie, and
things weren't settled with her, not at all. She couldn't
just pick up and leave everything, no matter how much
he might want her to. And he didn't have anything solid
to offer her yet. He'd be staying in a hotel at first, until
he proved himself enough to secure a spot in the lineup.
Right now he was an injury replacement. He wouldn't
even sign a short-term lease until he had a better idea of
his chances of staying on.

The only guarantee in baseball was that nothing

was guaranteed, and you'd better be okay with things changing with one swing of a bat.

He left Duke and loped back to the clubhouse, where applause and a few pats on the butt greeted him. Somehow, he'd held his own against the wind and the Catfish had squeaked out a two-run victory. But more than that, everyone celebrated when someone got called up.

"You show 'em, Hart," said Mike Solo, giving him a chest bump. "And keep a spot in the dugout warm for me. I'll be right behind you."

Caleb grinned and went to his locker, where he stuffed his few personal items—iPod, extra jock strap, his phone, and a couple of T-shirts—in his bag. The clubhouse attendant would be responsible for removing the tape with his name and replacing it with that of the Double A guy who was right now getting the word that he was jumping up a level. That's how it went in baseball. One guy's bad luck meant a break for other guys all the way down the line.

Everything depended on what you *did* with that break. His stomach tightened. This time he wasn't going to mess up.

Bingo begged off from dinner that night, saying he felt some kind of flu coming on. Caleb and Sadie dropped him off at the apartment, then headed back into a gorgeous night the color of sapphire velvet. Tessa and the boys were going to meet them at Lone Star Pizza—as if they hadn't eaten enough ballpark food for an entire Boy Scout troop.

Sadie, sadness lurking around the edges of her smile, had given him a huge hug when he'd exited the ballpark. Now he drove with his right hand on her thigh, his fingers savoring the firm give of her muscles. Her hand rested on top of his. It wasn't a sexual connection, but more of a grounding one. He felt better when he had Sadie nearby, that was all there was to it.

"This doesn't change anything with us," he told her roughly, after they'd driven a few blocks in silence. "I promise."

"I suppose we can go back to the early days when we talked on the phone all the time." She offered him a smile that managed to look both brave and cheeky at the same time. "I've heard some people have a lot of fun with phone sex."

"Now you're talking, sweet cheeks. 'Course, I had my own version of phone sex going on back then. It was a little lonely, but it got the job done."

"You did not." She made to draw her hand away from his, but he grasped it in his and drew their clasped hands onto his own lap.

"Your voice is so sexy, it drove me crazy."

"But we didn't talk about anything like that. We were talking about . . . I don't know, slugs."

"You could talk about toilet cleaner and I'd probably get turned on." Even the subject of phone sex was getting him hot. He moved her hand toward the expanding bulge in his jeans. "Yep. Look at that."

"Caleb!" She sounded both scandalized and fascinated at the same time, which he found even more arousing. Exploring with her fingertips, she pressed the outlines of his erection. "I will never understand men."

"What's so hard to understand? You turn me on. I could pull over right now and show you how much."

"Don't you think your family will be a little worried when you turn up three minutes late?" She laughed at him, eyes sparkling in the light from the dashboard.

"Oh, you did it now. Three minutes?" He laughed maniacally. "I can make you come in two, and use the remaining minute for myself." He swung the steering wheel to the right and veered into the parking lot of a strip mall. None of the businesses were open, but a few people had left their cars overnight. One more wouldn't catch anyone's attention. He chose the darkest corner and braked to a stop. He turned off the lights, so soft darkness fell around them.

"Don't even think about it," she squeaked as he turned toward her, his eyes a glitter of sheer lust.

"Oh, I'm thinking about it. Actually, I'm done thinking about it." He disengaged his seat belt with a snap, then leaned over and did the same to hers. The fresh scent of his recent shower, mingled with the quintessentially masculine smell of his skin, made her let out a long, lascivious breath. "I heard that," he told her. "I know what that sigh means." He hovered over her, his nearness causing every hair on her arms to rise.

"What?" She laughed up at him. "Maybe it just means that it's good to get my seat belt off."

He pulled the lever on her seat, so she suddenly found herself nearly flat on her back. She made a goofy *eep* sound that he immediately mimicked.

"Eep. Eep."

"I suppose you know what 'eep' means too." Her breath was coming in skips and gasps as his hand roamed across her rib cage.

"Yes ma'am, I know what 'eep' means. It means 'Do me, Caleb. Do me hard and fast.'"

She wished she could say he was wrong, but his warm breath on her face and his exploratory, hungry hand were sending her into a kind of reverse coma, hyperawake instead of sleepy, ultrasensitized instead of unconscious. When he nestled his hand around her breast, she nearly moaned, but he caught the sound with his warm lips.

"Shh, my love. I think we're safe, but we don't know who's around. Same reason we're keeping our clothes on." He squeezed her breast through her tank top, making her bra scrape across her nipples.

"Oh God," she groaned. "If you want me to be quiet, you shouldn't make it feel so good."

"Sorry, no can do. I want you to feel the best you've ever felt." He nuzzled her neck while his hand traveled to the waistband of her shorts. She pressed up against him, crazy for him, wild for him, loving the way his big body hovered over her, all that strength restrained so she wouldn't get crushed. All that power about to explode.

"Caleb," she murmured. "How do you make me do these things? We're in a parking lot outside Betty Sue's Acrylic Nails and I want your hand inside my pants."

His expression tightened into predatory lust. "Is that a fact? All you had to do was say so." Deftly, with those talented pitcher's hands, he undid the top button and slid down her zipper. He cupped her outside her panties first, using the dampened fabric to make little circles over her clit. Then he slipped inside. Her wet sex was primed for his touch, and her legs fell open before she even realized what was happening.

"My hand's inside your pants, my love. What else do you want?"

"Move it," she said harshly. "Back and forth. The way you do. It feels so good."

"Yes it does," he said with heartfelt appreciation. "You feel like silk, like the softest thing I ever felt." But his hand wasn't soft; it was hard and callused, and he used those ridges of skin to create havoc on her nerve endings. She panted and twisted against the cloth-covered seat of the Jeep. The windows fogged up, creating an even greater feeling of intimacy. Outside, the steady whir of tires on pavement provided a soothing sort of white noise. She could stay here forever, immersed in this moment of pleasure, in the presence of this unexpected and miraculous man.

She came with one long, primitive groan, almost like a man, riding his hand for every last shivery spasm of sensation.

"Your . . . turn . . ." she gasped.

"I don't think—"

"Shut up and get back to your own seat."

With a snort of laughter, he returned to the driver's seat. She yanked down his zipper and worked her way on top of him, squeezing between his big body and the steering wheel. He pushed the seat farther back, his eyes pure silvery heat in the steamy darkness. She drank in the rapid rise and fall of his broad chest, the tightening tendons of his neck, the way his muscled thighs felt beneath her body, the scent of sex that hung between them. She freed his shaft from his boxers and impaled herself in one swift move.

"Know how much time it takes for a fastball to get over the plate?"

"What?"

"Four hundred milliseconds." And he exploded, taking her with him into a spiraling freefall that she never wanted to end.

Chapter 21

THE TICKLE OF a soft laugh against his ear pulled Caleb from his sex-induced coma. Sadie was still draped across him in the driver's seat. Laughing.

"What?"

"Why were you quoting baseball statistics while you came?"

Was he? He didn't quite remember what had flashed through his brain at that moment. "I'm pretty sure it was physics. Speed of a baseball, right?"

"You said it takes four hundred milliseconds for the ball to reach the plate. Just wondering why you brought up that piece of information at that exact moment." Her sparkling eyes laughed at him in the way that always made him feel juiced and jazzed and a little jangled up.

"Well . . ." He squinted, trying to remember why it had seemed significant. He traced the line of her jaw, the merry curve of her lips. This was how he loved to see Sadie—relaxed and happy and sexed up. "Because I don't think it even took that long for me to fall for you."

Her smile vanished. A sheen of tears caught the light of a passing car. "How'd I get so lucky?" she whispered. "Whatever happens after this, it's been the best thing in my life, knowing you."

"Don't talk that way, Sadie. It makes me nervous." He shifted her onto the passenger side and raised his seat back. He fastened his pants over his softening penis, then helped her adjust her clothing. "We're together. I'd like to see the Friars, the Wades, or anyone else fuck it up for us. Not going to happen, sweet cheeks. You're stuck with me. It just might take a little while for us to figure out how to fit together. I mean, out there." He gestured to the night, to the steady slipstream of traffic, the flow of the rest of existence. "In here, we fit together like a ball in a glove."

"I know, I know. I didn't mean to get maudlin. I just . . . I love you, Caleb."

The palms of his hands tingled. Mini shock waves ran through him. He opened his mouth to tell her the same thing—*I love you too. I just realized it today, at the ballpark. My heart is yours, only yours, forever*—when bright lights flashed in his eyes and a car pulled up next to them. He gave Sadie a quick once-over to make sure she was decent.

"We seem to have a weakness for close calls," he murmured to her as he turned the key in the ignition.

She shrank back against the seat. "I think they recognize you. They're waving."

In the big SUV next to them, two guys in Catfish caps were gesturing at him to roll down his window. "Caleb Hart?"

Not wanting to risk a long conversation, he called through the glass. "This isn't the right moment, dude. I'll catch you next time, okay?"

The guy didn't crack a smile. "Just want you to know I'm going to have a lot of explaining to do to my kid. You guys should think about that when you go for the easy money."

"What?" Caleb shot Sadie a puzzled glance. "I got

called up. That's what us minor leaguers work for. How's that easy money?"

But the guy just shook his head, as if he was utterly disappointed, and rolled up his window. Then the SUV backed out of the lot, as if they didn't even want to share a parking lot with him.

"What the hell?" Caleb stared after them, mystified. "Maybe they just read the article about Bingo."

"But . . . easy money? He made it sound like you did something wrong. Like you were the one who ripped off those women."

A horrible thought struck Caleb. What if Bingo had decided to talk about the way he'd used his kids as unwitting messengers? What if he'd lied and made it sound worse than it was? What if all the news outlets were now blabbing on about morals in sports and the latest athlete hero to take a fall?

His hand trembling, he turned on the radio and flipped to an AM station that carried late night sports news.

"The news about Thurston 'Bingo' Howell II's alleged illegal bookmaking at Catfish Stadium comes at a sensitive time for his son Caleb, who just got called up to the San Diego Friars. As we all know, Major League Baseball takes gambling charges very, very seriously. Hart could not be reached for comment tonight, but we'll be sure to have more on this developing story as soon as more information comes out."

For a moment the world went black around him, as if he'd been plunged into a dark vortex. He couldn't see, couldn't feel, couldn't hear anything except a pounding in his ears.

He became aware of a warm body hanging onto his arm. He wanted to shake it off, but some distant part of his brain told him that wasn't okay. The pounding kept going, a heartbeat of horror. A panicked voice penetrated the dense fog surrounding him.

"Stop it, Caleb. Please stop it. You'll hurt yourself."

Consciousness returned. He became aware that he was repeatedly slamming his fist against the steering wheel. His left fist; his pitching hand. The hand that was supposed to pitch for the San Diego Friars soon.

He snatched it away and plunged his fingers into his hair, digging into his scalp. The pain in his head brought him back. "I'll kill him. I swear I'll kill him. He promised," he choked in a thick voice.

"We have to find out more, Caleb. It's just allegations. Maybe he didn't do anything wrong, or maybe it's not that bad." Sadie's arms were wrapped around him, as if she was trying to keep him from hurting himself. Too late for that; he'd hurt himself by being born into a family of crooks.

"You don't understand, Sadie."

"Maybe I don't. Explain it to me, Caleb. Talk to me. Tell me what's going on in your head." She kept talking in this soft, *caring* voice that made him nuts. He didn't deserve *niceness* right now.

"You don't want to know," he told her harshly.

"Yes, I do."

He glanced down at her, so wide-eyed and concerned. She was still plastered against his side. He peeled her arms off him. "I have to get out of this car," he choked. Pushing open the door, he stumbled outside and took long gulps of the warm night air. He heard a car door slam and knew she must be coming after him.

No. No. He didn't want her around right now. He couldn't tell her, couldn't disillusion her. Couldn't bear it if she looked at him without that light in her eyes. At the edge of the parking lot, he whirled around. She stood in the garish pool of light from a streetlight.

"Here." He tossed her the keys. "Take the Jeep. Drive yourself home, do whatever you want. I need some time."

She let the keys fall to the asphalt. He steeled his heart against the stricken look on her face. "Caleb. Don't do this. I want to help, if I can."

"You can't. Not right now. I'll call you later. I promise. I just need to walk this off."

"Caleb!"

But he was already hurrying away from the parking lot. If he could have walked himself right out of his body, he would have.

After wiping her face clean of tears, Sadie drove the Jeep—radio off—to the Lone Star, where Tessa and the boys were digging into two large pepperoni pizzas in happy oblivion. As soon as Tessa saw the look on Sadie's face, she excused herself and the two of them hurried into the bathroom.

"A news story just broke about Bingo getting involved in some sort of gambling thing. Caleb's really upset and he went off by himself. He gave me his Jeep." Her voice was trembling so hard she sounded like a stroke victim. That's almost how she felt, having gone from sexual bliss to shock and horror so quickly.

"Shit. I should never have brought the boys here. I should have known." Tessa checked her watch. "I'm going to take them to a hotel. I'll get ahold of Caleb and pick him up when he's ready. He just needs some time, that's all. We've been through this before."

"But—" Sadie fought back a new threat of tears. Why wouldn't Caleb let her help? Why Tessa, but not her? Didn't he trust her? She forced herself to remember this wasn't about her. "Okay. Will you call me when you find him?"

"Of course. Can you get someone to help you with the Jeep?"

It was after eleven. She couldn't call her mother or Donna. Definitely not her boss. She cringed as she thought about Mayor Trent's likely reaction to this news. Not to mention that of the Ladies' Auxiliary.

"I'll figure it out. You guys take care of yourselves, okay?" She gave Tessa a swift hug. "I'm really glad I got to meet you."

"We'll see each other again," Tessa assured her. Sadie forced a smile. The way Caleb had acted, she wasn't so sure about that.

"I hope so," she murmured.

Back in the restaurant, she said a quick good-bye to the twins, who seemed unfazed by the change in plans. The poor Hartwell family must be used to crazy disasters striking out of nowhere.

In the end she called Caleb's friend, Mike Solo. He didn't hesitate or ask questions. He met her outside Caleb's apartment, where all the lights were off and there was no sign of either Bingo or Caleb. She left the Jeep, then texted Caleb that the keys were in the mailbox.

No answer.

Feeling numb and confused, she climbed into the passenger seat of Mike's old Chevy Cavalier. Mike's tousled hair looked as if a family of squirrels had spent the night there.

"I heard the news on the radio," he told her right away, to her enormous relief. She hadn't looked forward to filling him in. "This is going to really mess with Caleb. I know the dude pretty well, but there's a whole lotta shit that's off-limits with him."

"Yeah," Sadie said with a hint of bitterness. "I'm starting to figure that out."

They drove the rest of the way in silence. Sadie had

the sense that Mike was turning something over in his mind, but everything that wasn't Caleb seemed very far away and uninteresting to her. Had Tessa managed to find him? Were they having a heart-to-heart about their wayward father right now? Why wouldn't he even give her a chance? She kept remembering the way he'd tossed those keys at her, as if he didn't want her to come one step closer.

She directed Mike to her house, and as soon as they reached it, jumped out. Before she could close the door behind her, he leaned across the passenger seat. "Don't give up on him, Sadie. If you care about him, hang in there. He's going to need you, whether he knows it or not."

A thousand replies shot through her mind. How was she supposed to "hang in there" when he wouldn't even allow her to be "there"? If he turned to his sister during a crisis, what was she to him other than a fun time in bed? Of course she cared about him—she loved him. But that didn't mean he felt the same. Maybe she was just a . . . a driver of his car. A chauffeur with benefits.

She needed to get off this crazy train, fast. "Thanks for the ride, Mike. And the advice. Maybe I'll see you around."

He looked like he wanted to say more, but she didn't give him a chance, fleeing up the path to her front door and slipping inside. The dim glow under her mother's bedroom door told her the television was on, but Brenda often fell asleep to the tune of QVC shopping or late night *Law and Order* episodes. Not that her mother would be much help. Sadie could practically write the script for her.

I told you to stay away from boys. They might seem like smitten kittens at the beginning, but you can't trust that. It's after you've given them everything you

*have that you find out their true nature, Sadie. How
many times do we have to learn the same darn lesson,
a* *purple! How many times are you going to put me
through this?*

No, better to let her mom sleep. She'd get the news
soon enough, if not from the newspaper, then from the
ultimate source of news in Kilby. The Kroger checkout
counter.

The next morning, a text from Tessa told her that
Caleb was safe at home and she and the twins were
headed back to Plano. No matter how often she checked
her texts, nothing showed up from Caleb. With a leaden
feeling she drove to work at seven-thirty, a full hour
and a half early. Black coffee in hand, she spread the
newspaper out on her desk and plunged in. The main
article was written by Burwell Brown; the sight of his
byline felt like a stab in the back.

Thurston Hartwell II is still in custody in the Kilby
County Jail today, one day after the news broke that he
was allegedly spearheading a bookmaking operation
centered around minor league baseball. Bookmaking
is illegal in the state of Texas. At Caleb Hart's home,
detectives were seen removing a computer and other
files. None would comment on who the computer belongs to or why they were seizing it.

The accompanying photo of two uniformed police
officers leaving Caleb's house, loaded down with boxes
and a computer, made Sadie feel ill.

Gambling on baseball is legal, either through a
land-based or online sportsbook, though there has
never been much interest in large-scale betting on the
minor leagues. Proposition bets—on relatively trivial

issues such as who will get the first hit or how long an inning will last—are fairly common among the fans in the stands. Such gambling is considered harmless and entertaining.

As added concern in this case is that Hartwell is the father of an active player. It is against the rules for anyone connected with baseball to place any kind of wager on a game. The notorious case of Pete Rose still haunts Major League Baseball to this day. Many questions are still open. Did Caleb Hart's father use his access to a player to gain an edge in his illegal gambling schemes? Did Caleb Hart know what his father was doing? Did he ever succumb to the temptation to throw a game to benefit his father—or even his own pocketbook?

The general sense among Catfish fans calling into the local radio sports show this morning could be described as "wait-and-see" with a healthy dose of outrage.

"I'm not saying this happened, because no one's saying exactly what happened yet," said one longtime Kilby baseball fan who uses the name Dagwood, "but the way Hart was pitching, like he was on some kind of roller-coaster ride, it almost makes you wonder if there wasn't a reason for all those crappy starts. If he pitched bad just so he could collect his winnings, well, that's just darn pathetic."

None of Hart's teammates on the Catfish would comment. Crush Taylor, owner of the Catfish, had this to say: "In this country, you're innocent until proven guilty, and I hope everyone will remember that. I hope they get this sorted out fast so we can get back to playing the great game of baseball."

Mayor Trent could not be reached for comment either. The mayor has recently begun working with the Catfish on a promotional campaign on behalf of the endangered horn-toed slug. A representative of the group, reached late last night, said, "If this brings attention to the plight of the slugs, then maybe some good will come out of the situation."

Something else, perhaps not so good, has definitely come from the situation. Caleb Hart had been scheduled to join the San Diego Friars to fill the spot in the lineup left by injured pitcher Ian Sullivan, but a call to the San Diego front office revealed that those plans are now cancelled, pending more details about the case.

Oh, poor Caleb. Sadie dropped her head onto her desk, inhaling the scent of newsprint and coffee. Everything had just been ruined for him in one fell swoop. The news was much, much worse than she'd feared. Never in her most dire imaginings had she thought that Caleb himself might be implicated.

But he wasn't, not for sure. She scanned the article again. Everything was questions and speculation— there was nothing that actually said the authorities were looking into Caleb's possible involvement. Didn't they know he had a horrible relationship with his father? Didn't he tell them that? How could such a one-sided article go to print?

On impulse, she picked up her phone and called Burwell Brown. When he answered, her anger almost got the best of her. "Nice article."

"Thanks. What's up, kid? It's crazy over here today. I haven't gotten this much attention from an article since I reported on the UFO spottings over the bell tower."

The exultation in his voice made her even more furious. "That's what this is about for you, isn't it? Maybe you'll get your name in the national news. But if you'd done the least bit of actual investigating you'd know that your insinuations about Caleb are complete crap."

"Caleb Hart? What do you know about it? Ah, that's right. You've been working with him on the slug thing."

"Why didn't you call *me* for a comment? I could have told you that whatever Bingo did, it had nothing to do with Caleb. He doesn't even like his father. He's the furthest thing from a con man that he could be."

"Sadie—"

"I'll give you a comment right now. No way on God's green earth did Caleb do anything the least bit illegal. You should be ashamed of yourself, Burwell."

She realized her voice had risen nearly to a shout. Standing up, she glanced around the cubicle area, relieved to find she was still the only one at work.

"Are you . . . involved with Caleb Hart, Sadie?" Brown's voice had shifted, become more alert.

"Um . . . no comment." He couldn't print *that*. Quite honestly, she wasn't sure if she was involved with Caleb anymore. She might be nothing but his chauffeur with benefits.

"Because I have to warn you that it's not going to look good for you at the mayor's office. The slug connection is one thing, but if the mayor's assistant has been dating a Catfish player linked to a gambling scandal . . ." He whistled. "Hoo boy, things are gonna get nasty if that's the case."

"It isn't," she said quickly. "Like you said, I've been working with Caleb and I've gotten to know him. I'm just telling you what I know about him, that he has a lot of integrity and loves baseball and would never do anything to harm his career like that."

"Is this an official quote, as Mayor Trent's assistant? Because I would suggest you talk to your boss before you go making any public statement. I'll take a quote, don't get me wrong. But I'm looking out for you here, Sadie." His voice was kind, maybe kinder than she deserved after her accusations against him. "Do you want all the gossip to start up again?"

Oh fireballs. He was right. "I . . . I'd better wait and talk to the mayor."

She hung up, feeling about as low as she ever had in her life, as if she'd just abandoned Caleb when he needed her most.

Chapter 22

CALEB WAS TRAPPED in a nightmare, one he'd lived before. The cops knocking at the door. Carting off his stuff. Bingo taken to jail. Calls to lawyers. Calls from his agent. The press. Duke, Crush, Mike Solo.

Okay, some of the details had changed, but the essence hadn't. Once again his life had been thrown into chaos by Thurston "Bingo" Hartwell II.

The Friars put him on personal leave. They couldn't suspend him because there was no proof he'd done anything wrong. But still, it meant no baseball. No escape from the events unfolding around him. No safe haven where he could focus on ball, motion, glove.

He wanted to call Sadie, nearly called her a million times. Maybe more. But the bad news cascading around him made it impossible. He didn't want to drag her into his mess. That wouldn't be fair to her. If she was really smart, she'd use this as an opportunity to put him in the rearview mirror, like a bad taco joint that had given her a stomachache.

Against the advice of his lawyer, he visited Bingo in the Kilby jail, located in the Kilby County Courthouse, around the corner from City Hall. All on their own, his eyes scanned every inch of the blocks surrounding the city government structures. Was that her, the girl reflected in the window of the coffee shop? Or the girl jogging in place, staring up at the statue of Colonel Kilby on his rearing horse? Every flash of red clothing put him on alert; every time it didn't belong to Sadie, his heart fell.

It was for the best. He had Bingo to deal with, and she had a reputation to salvage. No matter how much he longed to see her—even a glimpse of her, from a distance—protecting her was more important.

So he put her from his mind and strode into the county jail. After following the all-too-familiar check-in procedure, he sat down at the designated table and waited.

Bingo looked rumpled and panicky, and he wore the same clothes he'd been wearing the last time Caleb saw him at the baseball game, which felt like a thousand years ago.

"You hate me," he said right away, stopping halfway across the room, the guard nearly stumbling onto his heels. His cerulean blue eyes were round as a baby's, or a naughty kid facing a spanking.

"What do you think?" Caleb ground out the words, because he didn't want to let Bingo off the hook, but it was so much more complicated than "hate." Hate would be easy. But this, this confusing stew of worry, shame, and fury . . .

"It's not what it looks like, Caleb. I swear it isn't." Bingo plopped down onto the seat across the table.

"Wow, this is going to be good. What are you talking about?"

"I'm innocent." A lying, choirboy face like that ought to be illegal.

"Good. Because the police are analyzing my computer right now. The computer I fucking forgot I even had, stuck in a box somewhere. They won't find anything because you're innocent, right? No bets, no bank transfers, no e-mails, nothing?"

Bingo blinked rapidly. "Okay, not that kind of innocent. But it's not what you think."

"Did you need the money that bad? What about your job at the coffee shop? Was that just a front? Something to throw me off the track?"

Bingo thrust his hands into his hair. "I wish I could explain."

"I'm not stopping you."

"I . . . I can't." He shook his head violently.

Of course he couldn't. Because there was no explanation besides the obvious one. *He was a freaking criminal.* "Just tell me this," he said savagely. "Did you bet against me, Bingo? Did you make a profit from my slump? That's all I want to know, then you and I are done."

"I didn't. No," Bingo said hoarsely, fixing his eyes desperately on Caleb. "I didn't make any profit." But then he snapped his mouth shut, his cheeks bulging with the air he'd just sucked in.

"No profit? I guess there's not much money to be made on a minor league fuck-up pitcher. I don't know why you even wasted your time on the Catfish. Why couldn't you keep your dirt out of baseball?"

Bingo clapped his hand over his mouth, every bit of his face turning red with strain. It looked like he was trying to physically keep something inside. More excuses? Explanations? Rationalizations? The webs this man could spin would put Spider-Man to shame.

Caleb decided he'd had enough. He rose to his feet. "I'm putting your stuff in storage. I asked about bail, but since you violated your parole with this crap, there's no chance of that. You're probably safer in jail anyway. Crush Taylor is one pissed-off owner right now."

Bingo dropped his hand, looking crushed. "I'm sorry, Caleb. I don't know what else to say. I wish I could say more, but I can't. It'd just be worse, trust me."

"Trust you? You betrayed me. I took you in, I gave you a second chance, and you screwed me to the wall. Who's supposed to take care of the kids now? Where's the money supposed to come from? I was heading to the Friars, and you fucked it up. Now you're sorry?" Incredulous, Caleb shook his head, then turned to go.

"You didn't," burst out Bingo.

"Didn't what?"

"You never gave me a second chance. You never will."

"You got that right."

After Caleb left the jail, he was too filled with adrenaline to do anything but walk, just as he had the night the news first broke. He walked fast and furious, picking empty side streets and vacant lots. The heat beat down on his head, generating a flow of sweat down his temples and the back of his neck. It felt good. He wanted to be wrung out. Exhausted. Spent.

He left the quaint downtown area in short order and found himself in a more run-down part of town, where kids played basketball in the middle of the street and no blade of grass felt the benefit of a sprinkler.

He shouldn't complain. He had a healthy body, a valuable skill, a baseball contract. Most people around the world would envy him. He wasn't complaining. But sometimes he felt that his entire life was a banquet he couldn't touch. He was a major league pitcher who couldn't pitch in the fucking majors. He was a man who fell for a woman he couldn't be with. A son who wanted so badly to help his father—but couldn't.

The truth of it struck him hard. Inviting Bingo to move in with him had been his way of trying to build a bridge between them. But once Bingo was there, he could barely look at him. Bingo was right. He'd never given his father a *real* second chance. He didn't want him to attend his games, he didn't spend any time with him. When he did—because sometimes he couldn't avoid it—he practically wanted to jump out of his skin.

Was this partly his fault, because he'd been so hard to get along with? If he'd been more welcoming to Bingo, if he'd hung around him more, maybe none of this would have happened. For one thing, his father wouldn't have had *time* to get into trouble. Damn, he should have hired the man as an assistant and kept an eye on him 24/7.

He paused next to a group of kids playing whiffle ball. One wore a Yankees shirt with the number 36. Beltran. Outstanding hitter, especially in the postseason. He could read the curve ball like nobody's business. Better to start him with a slider, or maybe a split-finger fastball. Always a chance he'd swing at an inside fastball.

He realized he'd spoken out loud when the kid stopped and stared at him. "This is whiffle ball, man. Ain't no inside fastball here."

"Yeah. Sorry. Have fun, guys." He walked on as the kids shrugged and went back to their game.

It might be whiffle ball, but it had a lot in common with baseball. The game went on, no matter what any one individual did. That thought lightened his mood a little. The game had survived Pete Rose, the Black Sox scandal, and the dead ball era. It would survive Bingo and Caleb Hart.

He might not be around to enjoy it, but it was something.

Mayor Trent was out of the office all morning, but as soon as she strode through the door around three, she beckoned Sadie to follow her into her private office. With her heart in her mouth, Sadie closed the file she was working on and joined the mayor inside. The tense silence was punctuated by the lazy buzzing of a fly that kept bumping into one of the windowpanes.

Finally the mayor stalked to the window and wrenched it open, allowing the fly to escape and a rush of warm air to enter the room. "Meetings all day, and the only thing anyone in this town wants to talk about is the Kilby Catfish." She slammed the window shut, making Sadie wince on behalf of the old glass.

The mayor lowered herself into her chair and crossed one leg over the other, her gray suit revealing a peek of her knee.

"People always like talking about the Catfish. They have a knack for getting themselves in the news."

The mayor gave her a sharp look. Apparently her stress level had graduated from finger-drumming to pen-tapping. Sadie watched her gold Cross pen bounce on the polished surface of her desk with metronomelike precision.

"We're going to have to put the Sluggers for Slugs initiative on hold."

Sadie nodded, already resigned to that. Among the worries facing her, that particular one ranked very low.

"I've already received several calls from the Ladies' Auxiliary. Let's just say that the Can the Catfish campaign has received a big boost. Luckily, that's not my problem, it's Crush Taylor's." A smile touched her lips.

"Have you spoken with him yet?"

"Not precisely."

Sadie lifted her eyebrows. The mayor looked as though she'd swallowed a dish of ice cream. "I did leave a message for him expressing my heartfelt sympathy for this embarrassing situation."

Mischief gleamed in her perfect eyes. For the hundredth time, Sadie wondered what was really going on between the mayor and the baseball legend. As far as she knew, her boss was single. Occasionally she attended official events with Drake Hannigan, a well-known local lawyer. But she'd never witnessed so much as a kiss on the cheek between them. And Drake never got Mayor Trent rattled the way Crush did.

The mayor's fleeting expression of amusement vanished. "But this is a serious dilemma for us. I had my doubts about associating with the Catfish, given their history, but I never imagined things would get this bad. We have to do whatever we can to disassociate this office from the team. I debated putting out a press release cancelling Sluggers for Slugs, but I think it's best for the campaign to quietly die out. We don't need to mention it. If anyone asks, we're putting it on hold until the ongoing legal case is settled. Let Brett Carlisle know." She waved at Sadie's notepad.

Sadie scribbled a notation—*Call Brett*—but her mind wasn't on what she was doing. "It's not like the Catfish themselves have done anything wrong," she pointed out. "Bingo Hartwell isn't a member of the team."

"Close enough. Besides, the way I read Brown's article, his son is one step from being indicted himself."

Sadie's stomach twisted. "That's just speculation. Caleb didn't do anything wrong."

The mayor fixed her with a stern look. "Now Sadie, don't make the classic mistake of thinking that a set of six-pack abs make the man. You should judge people by their actions, not their physiques."

"I am." A slow wave of outrage gave her courage. In most things, she bowed down to Mayor Trent. But in this instance her boss had it all wrong. "His abs have nothing to do with it. He's a good person. He's been taking care of his brothers and sister since his father went to jail. He was only nineteen when it happened."

The mayor narrowed her eyes. "It sounds like you two have become pretty close."

"Close enough so I know he didn't do anything wrong."

"Sadie. What did we talk about? You were supposed to keep a low profile and do nothing to embarrass this office."

"Embarrass this office?" Sadie made an agitated movement that knocked her notebook to the floor. She stooped to pick it up, using the moment to collect herself. Taking a deep breath, she rose to her feet. "What about not rushing to judgment? What about not assuming the worst about someone because people are spreading vicious lies about them?"

"Do you hear yourself, Sadie? Sit down."

Despite the mayor's imperious gesture, Sadie refused to take her seat. The emotions that had sparked that impetuous speech still coursed through her system. *Vicious lies.* They were vicious lies, and she couldn't stand by and let Caleb be hurt by them.

The mayor's voice gained a steely edge. "I went out on a limb hiring you, Sadie Merritt. Don't make me lose my faith in you."

"Don't make *me* lose my faith in *you*!" Oh my God, what was she saying? "You're jumping to conclusions and not waiting to hear all the facts."

The mayor slapped a hand onto her desk. "I'm not a judge. I'm a mayor with a political future to protect."

"And Caleb Hart is just collateral damage to you?"

"What is he to you, Sadie? That's what I want to know."

Sadie dropped her gaze to the polished wood-plank floor, where the afternoon sunlight caught a few dancing motes of dust. "My personal life isn't your business."

"I hired you *despite* your personal life. If your personal life causes trouble for me, it very much is my business. Welcome to politics, Sadie."

Politics. *Politics!* "It's not politics, it's gossip."

"It's a fine line sometimes. Now what are you going to do about this? You have a choice to make here, Sadie. Choose correctly. Now go give Brett Carlisle a heads-up about my decision." The mayor gave her a gesture of dismissal and turned back to her computer.

Sadie dragged herself across the office. Everything about this situation felt unfair. But when was anything fair? At the door, she turned back. Even though the mayor faced her computer, already focusing on the next task, she had to say her piece.

"What Hamilton did to me was horrible. I thought you were standing up for me when you hired me, and I was really grateful. I still am. But that doesn't mean I did anything wrong. I know you went out on a limb to hire me. But you shouldn't have had to, and you can't blame me for that." Was this making any sense at all? The mayor's head still hadn't moved in her direction. She looked like a marble statue, hands poised on her keyboard: *The Typist.*

Sadie tried again. "I'm overeducated and overqualified, and I've done this job better than anyone who's ever had it. Shouldn't that be the important thing, not how some messed-up ex-boyfriend violated my privacy?"

Still no response from the mayor. Sadie's shoulders slumped and she stepped out of her boss's office, closing the door behind her.

She made the call to Brett Carlisle, who expressed massive disappointment that they couldn't use the sudden media spotlight for the benefit of the slugs.

"Come on, Sadie. We can make this work. We'll change the name. 'Sinners for Slugs,' what about that? Gambling's one of the deadly sins, right? I kinda zoned out in Sunday school."

"The sad thing is, I don't think you're kidding."

"Scammers for Slugs?"

"Why don't you try 'Stoners for Slugs'? That would be pretty accurate." She slammed down the phone, ignoring Brett's gales of laughter.

And suddenly she couldn't stand to be away from Caleb one more minute. Not one more. He *needed* her. She knew it, on some sort of molecular level that blocked out the voice of reason, the memory of that key toss. And she needed to see him, to drink him in, to make sure he was okay.

She sent Mayor Trent a quick e-mail—*I need to leave early today*—but didn't wait for a response before dashing out the door.

Ten minutes later she screeched to a halt behind Caleb's Jeep and raced pell-mell up the steps. What if he wouldn't open the door? What if he really, truly didn't want to see her? *She couldn't think about that now.* She was here, and she wasn't leaving.

When he opened the door the barest crack, his face set in wary, exhausted lines, her heart nearly broke for him. He showed no reaction to the sight of her, other than a flicker of surprise in his steel-blue eyes. His physical presence nearly overwhelmed her, even through the narrow gap provided by the barely open door.

She thrust her hand against the door to keep it open, just in case he was considering shutting her out again.

"Caleb, listen to me. I'm here because I love you and I can't bear for you to go through this alone. But it's not just that. When Hamilton started his smear campaign against me, no one gave me the benefit of the doubt, except Donna. It was easy for people to think the worst. They wanted to, because it was convenient and it gave them a reason to suck up to the Wades."

She paused to draw in a necessary lungful of air. Her heart was beating so rapidly she could barely talk. Caleb's stony expression gave her no clues about his thoughts. *Maybe this was a mistake.*

Too late to stop now.

"I swore that I would never do that to anyone. I'd never leave them twisting in the wind with no support. I'd never assume something was true just because everyone was saying it. That's why I want to go to law school. To fight against that kind of thinking. So what I'm saying is . . ."

Wait. What was she saying, exactly? Whatever it was, she needed to figure it out fast, because Caleb had the funniest look on his face now.

"I need to be here with you. I need it for my own self-respect. It's not just because I love you, though I do, and I really wish you'd show maybe some tiny piece of a reaction when I say it. Just a little . . ." She pinched two fingers together to show just *how* little would satisfy her. "But that's okay, we can talk about that some other time. Or not. We don't have to. That's a tangent, really, and I don't even know what I'm saying anymore, except that—"

But Caleb saved her from finishing her sentence by hauling her against his body and sealing his mouth to hers.

Chapter 23

FOR A MAN who'd been through hell, Sadie in his arms came as close to heaven as Caleb ever expected to get. He devoured her sweet mouth, swallowing the murmurs that might have been more conversation. He didn't want more conversation. He got her point. He appreciated it. But right now he wanted her. In his arms, in his bed.

He kicked the front door shut behind her, thanking his lucky stars that the reporters had just left. Then he scooped her into his arms and carried her into his bedroom. His bed looked like the lair of a deranged bear, with its tangled sheets and rat's nest of blankets. He hadn't slept worth a damn since Bingo's arrest. He set Sadie on her feet and brushed an empty bag of chips off the end of the bed.

"I don't care about that," Sadie said, tugging his arm. "I don't care if we do it in a Dumpster. I just want you."

"You got me," he said roughly, tossing her onto the bed. "Be careful what you wish for," he added with a wink. "I might ravage you until you come to your senses."

"I dare you to try." She was wearing a blue short-sleeved sweater, very demure and proper, which she whipped off her body and tossed over the little TV that sat on his dresser. Underneath, she wore a sort of camisole that pushed her breasts together. His hands itched to touch them. He prowled toward her like a beast about to feed on his prey. Her pupils expanded, turning her eyes dark and desirous.

She spread her legs apart, so her flowery skirt rode up on her thighs. The contrast between her good-girl outfit and her come-hither manner just about drove him crazy. And—she still had her cowboy boots on.

Heaven, for sure.

He fell onto the bed, on his knees, as a goddess deserved. He reached under her skirt and pulled off her panties, desperate for a glance at the sweet triangle he craved. For a moment he feasted his eyes on the delicate patch of hair, the shadowed grove of soft, mysterious flesh. No matter how many times he made love to Sadie, he would always want her, always want more. Grasping her fine-boned thighs just above the knees, he pulled her toward him so her long legs were positioned on either side of him, her sex open before him.

"If I don't have you this second, I think I might die," he muttered.

She sat, pressing her chest against his, so they were heart-to-heart. With her arms and legs wrapped around him, he felt surrounded by her smooth skin. The scent of her perfume drifted from the hot skin of her neck, like wild strawberries in the sun. It took only a second to slip his cock inside her, for her inner heat to claim him.

"Sweet Sadie," he whispered. "I don't deserve you."

"Yes, you do," she said fiercely, nipping at his earlobe and working her hips to get him deeper within her. "We both deserve this. Forget the rest of the world. This is about me and you, Caleb. Screw everyone else."

He snorted; Sadie never used profanity like that. She must really mean what she said.

"You heard me." He felt her laughter as a vibration against his chest. Spreading his hands across her back, so narrow he could nearly span the width of her rib cage, he flexed his hips, going deeper.

He let out a groan, the sound drenched with equal parts anticipation and satisfaction. *This* was what he'd been craving, and he hadn't even known it. Sinking into Sadie's sweet heat was the only cure he needed. He pumped his hips, gripping her ass to angle her just so. She squirmed desperately against him, seeking something more.

He knew his Sadie, knew how much she liked friction against her clit. He snuck his palm between their bodies, where an ovenlike heat was developing. There it was, that plump little kernel begging for his touch. So juicy his mouth watered. He locked his hand into place, ignoring the pull on his wrist, letting the motion of their two bodies rocking against each other provide the pressure she needed.

He thrust deeper, feeling everything else fall away. Pleasure flooded his brain. He dragged her even closer against him, so they were sealed tight, impossible to peel apart. Her ragged breaths urged him onward, the pressure built in his spine, he wanted to come, but not yet . . . not until Sadie's body tightened around him, not until she threw her head back and wailed . . . Then he slipped the leash and detonated, soaring into a place where all was pleasure and no one would ever hurt them.

Sadie made him dinner. It was the cutest thing, because he had no ingredients for food in the house. He sat at the kitchen table and watched her like a puppy as she retrieved a can of tomato paste, some Ramen noodle soup, and a jar of pickles from his cupboards. The refrigerator yielded eggs and Miracle Whip.

"How do you live?"

"They feed us dinner at the ballpark." Of course, that didn't apply to him anymore. "I do better than most guys. They don't pay minor leaguers for shit, so you'll see guys living on mashed potatoes and whatever they can scrounge up at the restaurants that sponsor the team."

She whipped up an omelet with a filling of chopped pickles in mayo. "This looks like one of my mother's specialties. Anything with Miracle Whip makes her happy."

"Hard to disagree." He took a bite, suddenly starving. He'd forgotten about eating, which was pretty unusual for an active ballplayer. "Not bad."

"Once you finish that, the soup will be ready."

"You don't have to baby me." But it felt so good, having her hovering over him, tending to him.

"You have a funny definition of babying." She quirked her butt at him, which made his eyes glaze slightly. After sex, she'd pulled on a pair of his boxers, which now hung low on her hip bones. He eyed the opening designed for the penis to exit. He could just slide his cock right in through that slit, take her right there on the kitchen counter . . .

"Eat your food," she said sternly, hands on her hips. "You need to stay nourished."

"Yes, I do." He leered at her. "I'm going to need lots of energy to keep up with you."

She made a face at him. "I didn't come here for a sex marathon."

"What? All I heard was sex marathon. And I'm all for it."

"Caleb, be serious. You have to take care of yourself. When you opened the door, I nearly cried. You looked terrible."

He launched into the patented Hartwell grin, guaranteed to put stars in girls' eyes. "Look at me now. All better?"

From her spot at the stove, she peered at him, then blinked. "Now, that's just not fair."

He laughed, feeling on top of the world. "Dr. Sadie knows what she's doing."

"Seriously, Caleb. We need to talk." She poured the soup from the pot into a bowl, since he had nothing resembling a ladle. "All I know is what the papers are saying, and I don't trust a word of it. Not even what Burwell Brown is writing. This is one of the stories where people seem to forget the whole concept of journalistic ethics."

"Was it like that for you?" he asked as she carefully brought him the bowl. "With Hamilton?"

"I didn't make the papers, but it's the same idea. People just say anything and everything because it's so juicy. It's almost like they can't help it."

He blew on a spoonful of Ramen soup, which she'd thickened with the tomato paste and spiced with packets of salt and pepper left from a bag of takeout. "That must have been rough. I wish I'd been here then. I would have kicked some ass."

She shuddered. "I'm glad you weren't. Anyway, you wouldn't have met me. I mostly stayed in my room for about six months. Even that wasn't safe because I had a computer and I couldn't make myself stay off Facebook. I'd avoid it for about a week, but then I'd start wondering what disgusting thing he'd come up with next, and what was being said, and if anyone was making him stop. And I'd go online and get sick all over again."

He put his spoon down, suddenly unable to stomach food. The thought of her going through that experience alone made him ill.

"Don't look like that," she said quickly, sitting down next to him and rubbing her cheek against his shoulder like a cat. "I'm fine. It's behind me now. And I'm a lot stronger. Do you know what made me decide to stop hiding in my room and go look for a job? Besides, you know, needing to pay some bills and getting pretty bored and pissed off?"

He managed a smile. "What?"

"You're going to laugh."

"Good. I could use a laugh. What?" At her insistent gesture, he took a sip of his soup. Not bad.

"Believe it or not, I started watching the baseball playoffs. Last October. I couldn't watch regular TV because there was too much drama, too much relationship stuff. It would just make me cry. But then I'd switch to the playoffs and they kind of . . . lulled me. Like a lullaby."

"Baseball was like a lullaby?"

"Kind of. The announcers' voices were so soothing, and it felt kind of timeless, like I could be listening on the radio somewhere on a dock, my feet in the water. Then something big would happen and they'd get all excited and I'd get completely carried away. And then there were all the stories."

"Stories," he said blankly. All this time he'd been busting his ass on the mound for . . . a lullaby and some stories?

"Sure, stories. They kept talking about a player who was working his way back from surgery. I can't remember his name. Another whose wife had just had a baby, and he'd missed a game to be with her. Another one who finally made it to the Yankees coaching staff after pitching batter workouts."

"Throwing batting practice."

"Right." She made a face at him. "Anyway, I kept

thinking, batters get so many chances to hit the ball. And even if they strike out, they'll probably get another chance later in the game. Or the next game. There are always more chances, until you leave the game or, well, die. And I wasn't ready to die. Hamilton was one strike. Why shouldn't I get more chances, just like everyone in baseball?"

Caleb put down his spoon, a grin spreading across his face. "You are really something, you know that?"

"I am?" she asked dubiously.

"You've actually made me feel better, and not just with your amazing, sexy body." He pushed his chair away from the table and spun to face her, then pulled her onto his lap. Her legs fell open, all long, creamy gangliness. The slit in the front of his boxers gaped open, flashing him with an eyeful of her beautiful secret parts. "I want to tie you up and keep you here in my house with me. All we'll do is cook, eat, and fuck."

He danced his hand into the opening and brushed against her silky curls.

"That sounds like some kind of escapist male fantasy."

"You know it, babe. All the essentials. Pussy and pizza." He began stroking her softly, aware that her tissues were still engorged from their last go-around. "But no baseball."

"You'll be back in baseball," she said confidently. "It's your destiny."

"Is that right?" He swirled a thumb around her clit, feeling it warm to his touch. Her eyelids flickered. Her head fell back against his elbow. He tightened his arm to support her trusting weight. "I have a different thought," he whispered in her ear. "Maybe you're my destiny."

And that was it for conversation.

Caleb didn't start talking about Bingo's situation until they'd had sex three more times. By then, apparently, his defenses were finally down and all his appetites satisfied. They lay tangled in his big bed, the window partly open to let in the cooling evening air. They sure had a habit of steaming up places.

Caleb lay on his back, his powerful limbs akimbo, arms spread open. Sweat curled the hair on the back of his neck, and every one of his spectacular muscles seemed to purr with relaxation. She would never get a better opportunity than this. "Have you talked to Bingo yet?"

"I went to see him once. He kept insisting it wasn't what it looked like and he didn't want to hurt me. But Bingo's words have never been worth the spit it takes to say them."

"I wonder what he's talking about."

"Nothing. He just says what he thinks people want to hear. Do you think I want my father to be a crook? Hell no. But that's what he is. I wish he'd just tell the truth."

Sadie felt the tension enter his body again. She put one hand on his shoulder, hoping to calm him, only to get wrapped up in the magnificent architecture of that joint. So complicated, with sinews, bone, tendons and muscles, all united in one perfectly functioning unit, guided by the knowledge inside Caleb's brain. She smoothed two fingers down the outer slope of his arm to the knob of his elbow. He gave a little *mmm* of enjoyment.

"He has a lawyer, right?" she asked.

"Of course. Betsy Clark. She represented him last time. I retained her again right away. But he won't talk to her either. She says he seems afraid of something. She thinks maybe he's protecting someone else, a partner maybe."

"What do you think?"

Caleb made an impatient movement of his head. "I think he's full of shit, and I have problems of my own. He used my old computer. I can make a pretty good case that I exclusively use my laptop now, but it's a little iffy."

"But you aren't actually in any danger, are you?"

"I don't know. I didn't do anything, so I don't see how they can prove something that didn't happen. But Major League Baseball has no gray area when it comes to gambling. So I don't know. Hey, I can always go back to college. It's in my contract that they'll pay for my education."

The deadened tone of his voice alarmed her. She knew him well enough to know that walking away from his baseball career would rip the heart out of him.

"But couldn't Bingo clear you?"

"I told you, Bingo isn't talking."

She sat up, her hair spilling across her back. His eyes went immediately to her breasts, so she crossed her arms over her chest. She wasn't going to let him distract her from this conversation, not again. "We have to get him to talk. That's not fair, he can't get you into trouble then leave you hanging."

"Oh no?" With a sharp laugh, he pulled the covers off and swung his legs over the edge of the bed, his back to her. With his head buried in his hands, he said wearily, "There's a lot you don't know about Bingo and how far he'll go to save his skin. I didn't tell you this before, but he used me and Tessa. He put stuff in our name, had us deliver messages. Used us to create a picture of a perfect motherless family."

"That's horrible! But that's not your fault."

"We didn't stop him. We didn't warn anyone. I didn't know everything, but I always suspected something was off. I was too wrapped up in my own life, baseball and hanging out with my friends."

Sadie crawled across the bed so she was close enough to touch him. But she didn't. He might as well have had an electrified Keep Out fence around him. "He was your father. Kids tend to do what their parents say. You shouldn't blame yourself, Caleb."

"Well, I do. So maybe I deserve whatever's about to happen. I didn't get charged last time, so maybe it's catching up to me now."

"That is ridiculous," she said fiercely. "You didn't get charged because you didn't do anything wrong. You still haven't done anything wrong. Nothing's catching up to you. This is Bingo. It's all Bingo."

Caleb didn't move a muscle. At least he wasn't telling her to back off, but still . . . he looked so frozen and defeated. She knew that feeling; she'd lived it for a year. She had to wake him up, shock him.

She took a deep breath. "I'm going to talk to him."

That worked. "The hell you are." He swung around, fixing blazing steel eyes on her. "Didn't you hear what I just told you about him? You stay out of this. Bingo's more dangerous than he looks."

"He's not going to hurt me. He's in jail!"

He took her by the shoulders, his fingers digging into her flesh. "You can't trust the man. It's pointless talking to him because nothing he says is the truth."

"But even if he lies, it might be a clue. What if someone else is threatening him, like your lawyer says? Maybe we should try to find out if there's more to the story."

"Let it be, Sadie. Promise me. The police are on it, that's their job. Bingo has a lawyer. If he talks to anyone, it'll be her. She's good. Really good. One of those newfangled female lawyers I've been hearing about." A glimmer of a smile lightened his face. "You can talk to her, I don't mind that."

But his lawyer didn't know Kilby. She did. Maybe she could find out something neither the lawyer nor Caleb could. "When you talked to Bingo, did you even give him a chance to say anything, or were you just furious and yelling at him?"

He narrowed his eyes at her. "Are you saying he didn't deserve to be yelled at?"

"No. I'm saying maybe he didn't say anything useful because you were yelling at him."

"Stay away from him, Sadie. Promise me. He's bad news."

She raised her chin stubbornly. "You're doing it again. You're shutting me out. You're putting me in this little box over here labeled 'Sadie,' and Bingo in another box over there labeled 'Keep Out.' I don't want there to be any 'Keep Out' boxes, Caleb!"

They stared each other down, tension shimmering between them. Then his expression shifted. "So you want to get into all my boxes?"

"Ye-es."

"How about my boxers? I'll let you into those." A devilish light back in his eyes, he flipped her onto her back.

"*Don't distract me.*"

Too late.

Chapter 24

For Caleb the next week was split evenly between Heaven and Hell, with Hell taking place during the day and Heaven reigning at night, when Sadie came over. Thank God, she'd given up on the idea of trying to pry the truth out of Bingo. When she came over, they spent their time lolling in bed, talking about anything and everything *except* the case of Thurston Hartwell and the "Triple A Betting Scandal," as the media was calling it.

During the day, he made himself keep track of all the developments. The TV coverage had dug up the footage of him attacking Bingo in the stands and put a new spin on it—while replaying it in excruciating slow motion over and over again.

"Now that the mystery man has been identified as Thurston Hartwell, speculation is flying about the meaning of the incident. Some say it could indicate that Caleb Hart was trying to stop his father's illegal activities. Others point out that if he knew what was happening, he should have reported it to Catfish management. The fact that the woman in the video is the assistant to the mayor of Kilby brings another twist to the story. Is Sadie Merritt somehow involved in the scheme, or was it pure coincidence that she was so close to Bingo on that particular day?" The reporter droned on while Caleb's frustration mounted.

Why, *why did they* have to drag Sadie into this? Why had he lost it in such an idiotic way that day? Why did so many people have to carry iPhones around with them?

"I don't believe in coincidences," declared the head of the Ladies' Auxiliary, a fiery older woman with a turquoise pendant around her neck. "We're big supporters of Mayor Trent but I have to wonder if she knew what she was doing hiring Sadie Merritt. We believe this bears further investigation."

He picked up the phone and started to call Sadie, then put the phone back down. She had enough to deal with. She didn't need him bugging her. Instead, he put on workout clothes and went for a long, sweaty, pounding run.

"I need to take some time off from work," Sadie told Mayor Trent.

"Why?" The two of them were heading down the corridor to a press conference that had been arranged on the steps of City Hall. Fittingly, Sadie wore the same outfit in which she'd interviewed for the job. It felt like coming full circle, as if for a brief time she'd actually been a normal, legitimate person, and now her time was up.

"Because I'm becoming an issue. I don't want to be an issue. You told me to keep a low profile and now I'm on every news channel."

"That's my problem to worry about, not yours," said the mayor sharply.

"It *is* my problem. I work for you. My job is to help you, not hurt you." Since they were about to reach the door, she gripped the mayor's arm and tugged her to a halt. "Remember how you said to choose wisely? Well, I chose. I chose Caleb. I'm not going to walk away from him. I don't want that decision to create a problem for you."

The mayor scrutinized her for a long moment. "You're sacrificing your job for Caleb Hart?"

"I hope not. I'm not quitting. And hopefully you won't fire me. I just want to take time off, or maybe work from home. I can still do things for you behind the scenes. But for now, I don't want to be a lightning rod."

"You must really care for that ballplayer."

That was putting it mildly. "Yes. I do."

Mayor Trent released a big sigh as her sculptured face finally softened. "Fine, take some time off. I'll keep you on half-pay and I may have some projects for you to work on at home. And if the reporters ask, I'll say you're a wonderful assistant and are taking some time off to complete your law school applications. That ought to shut them up."

On impulse, Sadie gave her a quick hug. She'd never been in such close contact with her boss before, and she felt the older woman's automatic stiffening. She must have breached some sort of protocol with her spontaneous embrace. Maybe jostled her hair. "Sorry," she said, drawing back.

"No. It's fine." The mayor patted her cheek. "I'll miss having you around. I want to tell you something, Sadie. You have a fire and a light inside you that will always draw people, and always make other people want to tear you down. Do you understand me?"

Sadie frowned uncomfortably. She didn't think she had any fire or light.

"Oh yes, you do," Mayor Trent said, as if reading her mind. "I saw it the other day, when I lectured you about choosing wisely. You told me I was leaping to judgment, and you were right. You impressed me, Sadie. You stood up to me, and you can stand up to those others too."

"Do you mean . . . Hamilton?"

"Hamilton's one. He couldn't have you, so he tried to extinguish you. Don't let people like that win."

A shimmer of pain, so quick Sadie nearly missed it, marred the perfect surface of Mayor Trent's composure. Was she referring to some past experience? She knew so little about the mayor's life.

"I . . . I'm trying not to let him win."

"Not just him. Anyone. Anyone who wants you to be less than what you are—avoid those people, or at least ignore them. Promise me."

The door to the front steps opened a crack as one of the interns hurried in. "They're getting restless out there," he called to them. "What should I do?"

"I'm on my way." The mayor squeezed Sadie's shoulder, then gave her a wink. "Now go cheer up that Catfish of yours."

Sadie gathered up her things and left by the back door; everyone was too wrapped up in the mayor's press conference to notice her anyway. She pushed back the sadness that she wouldn't be part of this event, or the next or the horn-toed slug campaign or any other of the mayoral initiatives for a while. Maybe ever. After all, the mayor would need a new assistant.

But she knew it was the right thing to do, so she steeled herself and moved on to the next item on her agenda of complete disaster.

She went to the county jail to visit Bingo.

"Does Caleb know you're here?" the man asked eagerly, when he'd settled into the plastic seat on the other side of the table.

"Not exactly." No need to mention that he'd blow a fuse if he knew. She'd had to write her name in the visitors' book, and could only hope that Caleb didn't plan to visit again. Of course, if the reporters or Bingo's lawyer told him, he'd find out anyway.

Bingo's face crumpled, as if he were a toddler whose treat had just been taken away. "He hates me."

"Well, if he did, you couldn't really blame him, could you?"

He shook his head mournfully. "What a godfor-saken mess this is."

Ever since her conversation with Caleb the other night, Sadie's conviction had been growing that some-one else was pulling the strings in this situation. And since this was Kilby, and one family had a lock on the string-pulling in town, she had a strong suspicion she knew Bingo's puppet master. The trick would be getting him to tell her.

She leaned forward, creating more of an intimate space between them. The guard shifted his position. "Not too close there, miss."

"What do you think I'm going to do, pass him a cake with a key inside?" she snapped at him, forgetting for a moment that she was inside a jail and the guard carried an impressive-looking weapon. All this stress must be getting to her. "I mean, sorry, mister. Officer. Sir. I'm just here to talk."

She tried her meekest smile on him, which seemed to do the job.

She shifted her position enough to reassure the guard but not shatter the connection she'd formed with Bingo. "Bingo, I know you love Caleb. I can see it every time you're with him. I know you don't want to hurt him. Am I right?"

His baby blue eyes widened in alarm. "Why?"

"Because I think you're protecting someone. And if you don't speak up, Caleb might have to quit baseball. Or even go to jail."

Bingo shook his head rapidly. "No He won't. My lawyer said that wouldn't happen, no matter what."

Daru. Okay, time to get creative. "Well, I'm studying to be a lawyer, did Caleb tell you that? No? The thing is, your lawyer's job is to represent you. She's not representing Caleb. So are you sure you can trust what she says about him?"

He swallowed hard, his Adam's apple bobbing.

"Imagine that I'm Caleb's lawyer. As Caleb's lawyer, I'm telling you he's going to have trouble clearing his name unless the whole story comes out." That much was probably true. If a big mess of gossip and rumors hung around for too long, his reputation would be ruined for good.

"But he hasn't . . . he didn't—" Bingo snapped his mouth shut.

"You're not supposed to say anything, are you? Someone is threatening you so you'll keep quiet."

The convulsive movement of his head might have been a yes. Or it might have been a neck spasm. Hard to tell.

She glanced at the guard again. He was listening closely, which meant that chances were good anything Bingo said right now would get back to someone.

"I understand. I don't want to get you into trouble, I really don't. In fact, I understand what you're going through, even better than you think. It's hard *wading* through all the options of what to do in some situations. Like wading through a swamp, you know?" She winked at him, a quick, totally uncharacteristic gesture. Did he notice? She winked again, until finally she had his full attention. "It's like you have to pull on hip waders just to make your way through the muck."

Okay, had she said *wade* enough times? She felt a little ridiculous, as if she were playing secret agent. But maybe it would work. Again, she winked, then raised one eyebrow. "Know what I'm saying?"

Finally, after another darting glance at the guard, Bingo nodded. "That's a good way of putting it, Sadie. Exactly right. The kind of swamp where a cloud of mosquitoes follows you around wherever you wade."

There. He'd said the word back to her. That was confirmation, right? Did she need more? She sat back in her chair, laughing casually. "Someday we'll laugh about all this, while we're wading through a plate of fries and a bucket of margaritas."

He shook his head sadly. "That might take a miracle. You'll probably be dean of your law school before I get my life straightened out."

Dean. Adrenaline shot through her. Bingo had understood her code, confirmed her suspicions of the Wade family, and even added a first name. Dean Wade.

"Oh, Bingo, don't be so hard on yourself. I think we'll get everything sorted out before you know it. Hang in there, okay?" She gave him a big, beaming smile, and for the first time since she'd walked in, he unleashed his version of the Hartwell grin. Almost as lethal as Caleb's, but not quite, in her very biased opinion.

Her exhilaration faded as she stepped out the door of the county court building. Now that she knew Dean Wade was involved, what could she do with that information? Unless Bingo *actually* spoke—to the police, probably—all she had was a cryptic conversation about wading through mosquito-ridden swamps. Nope, she'd have to do better than that. She'd have to move on to the next unpleasant item on her How to Ruin Your Life checklist.

Hamilton Wade.

Dean was too smart; he'd never make a slip. But she

knew Hamilton, knew his many, many weak spots. She
shot him a quick text, asking him to meet her in the
park. Cringing, she texted the ultimate lie: *I miss you.*

Only a vain idiot would believe that. Since he fit that
description, she had no doubt that he'd show up.

A quick stop at Burwell Brown's office, to borrow one
of his little pocket recorders. Last step, a call to Donna.

"I'm going to see Hamilton." She headed for the
park, forcing her feet to carry her there. The few times
she'd seen him since the breakup had been accidental.
The idea of a deliberate, pre-planned encounter made
her nauseous.

"Why? Don't you dare, Sadie. Where are you right
now? Is Caleb with you? Does he know?"

Sometimes Donna's sharpness could be inconve-
nient. "Caleb? Why do you mention him?"

"Oh come on. Mike says you two are head over heels.
And I know it's true because I haven't heard a peep out
of you in days. You never answer my messages."

"Sorry. I've been swamped."

"Yes, swamped with hot baseball player sex. You're
blushing, aren't you? I can see from here."

Sadie instinctively put a hand to her cheek. Yep, definitely blushing. "That's not the point now. I can't get
into the details right now, but I need . . . I'm on my way
to meet Hamilton and I need some moral support."

"I'm going with you. Can you wait three hours until
I get the Shark to sleep?"

"No."

"Damn this kid and his lack of narcolepsy. Listen,
you'll be fine. Hamilton's an asshole and he's not fit to
lick the wart on your little toe. Just stay cool and make
sure you're in a crowded public place."

"We're meeting in the park downtown. Do me a
favor. Call me in half an hour in case I need an out."

"Done. Just like high school. Good luck, sweetie."

She ended the call, butterflies running rampant in her belly. Her footsteps slowed as she approached the park. It was still afternoon, the lazy, hazy heat of midday draining everyone of their energy. Old men dozed on benches, mothers desultorily pushed baby strollers shaded by umbrellas, and a small crowd had gathered around the food cart selling snow cones.

Crowded public place. Check. Unpredictable, cruel ex-boyfriend. Check. New red dress guaranteed to grab his attention, check. Her iPhone safe in her pocket, the pocket recorder on. Check. Check.

Hamilton stood under the old elm tree, scrolling through texts on his phone, his sunglasses resting at the base of his thick neck. She forced herself to smile as she stepped into conversational range. It had been over a year since she had willingly done that.

He glanced up as she came closer, and shoved his phone into his pocket. "Hey babe." He made to kiss her, but she tilted her head so his lips brushed against her cheek instead. Even that small contact gave her the shivers, but it was better than the alternative.

"Hi, Hamilton." She let her shoulders droop in the most woebegone manner possible, so that even Hamilton, not known for his sensitivity, would notice.

"You look like you've been rode hard and put away wet, Sadie. Things were a lot easier when you were with me, huh?"

"You're so right, Hamilton." The park had a lovely footpath that meandered around the edge, with one-half reserved for bicyclists, the other for pedestrians. "Can we walk a little?" She had a lot more confidence in her ability to deal with Hamilton when she wasn't looking him straight in the face.

"Sure, babe. But I don't have long. So get to the

point. You want to beg me to get back with you? Maybe
make another movie? The last one was such a monster
hit. Sorry, I have a new girlfriend and she's not too keen
on the extracurricular fun."

God, he was disgusting. "I'm glad you found someone, Ham. You deserve a good woman." No he didn't.
He deserved a good whipping. But she wasn't here for
truth telling.

"She'll do okay. The family likes her."

Perfect opening. She jumped on it. "I actually wanted
to see you because of your family."

Hamilton frowned. "Oh yeah? What about them?"

"I . . . well, this might sound weird, but I wanted to
thank them."

"For what?"

She waited until two skateboarders, both with back-
packs slung over their shoulders, had glided past, then
leaned close to Hamilton and whispered conspiratori-
ally, "For exposing the truth about Caleb Hart."

Something greedy and ugly flared in his eyes. "I don't
know what you're talking about."

"Oh." She made herself look crestfallen. "Never
mind. That was silly of me. I shouldn't . . . I shouldn't
have come here." With a fluttery wave of her hands to
indicate complete embarrassment, she turned to go.

"Wait." He snagged her with a hand on her shoulder.
"I didn't say you were wrong. I just said what are you
talking about?"

"Well . . . I was totally putting Caleb up on a pedestal.
I mean, he's a professional athlete, he's so handsome,
and he's going to make millions of dollars as soon as he
signs his next contract. He's like every woman's dream
man. But now that I know the truth . . ." She shook her
head, peering under her eyelashes at him. Had she made
him sufficiently envious of Caleb's attributes? Should

she mention he was also incredible in bed and made her feel things she'd never imagined?

Better not.

"He's got one flaw," Hamilton sneered. "Bad choice in fathers." Sadie wanted to smash his face in but ruthlessly suppressed the urge.

"Very true. I know it looks bad for Caleb. But I bet he'll come out of this okay. When there's that much talent at stake, I mean, people want to see him pitch. They say he's guaranteed to make it to the Hall of Fame someday, that's how good he is."

Crimson flamed up Hamilton's neck. "Don't count on it."

"Hmm? Oh, I know it's not *really* guaranteed. I mean, he still has to actually pitch, and hopefully not get injured, but everyone's saying his natural talent is so incredible that—"

"As long as his father is Bingo Hartwell, he doesn't stand a chance," said Hamilton nastily. "Which means, pretty much forever."

Sadie opened her eyes wide. "What do you mean? I don't understand."

"My uncle *owns* Bingo now. Owns him. Like, deep. Like, Bingo stumbled right into his trap. And I was the key. As soon as I figured out who Caleb's father was, my uncle roped him in. It was easy too."

"Because he needed the money?"

"No. Because Uncle Dean threatened to expose him to the press, which would hurt Caleb. By the time Caleb gave his big interview, it was too late. Bingo had already done the legwork on the gambling setup. Smart guy, in some ways. Stupid, in a whole lot of other ways."

Sadie nodded numbly. "But Hamilton, Bingo could just take all the blame and clear Caleb."

"Nope. He can try, but my pops has the evidence

room on speed dial. No sweat. We have lots of leverage. If that doesn't work, Bingo has other children besides Caleb. We saw them at that last game, where he fucked it all up and got himself busted. Must have been distracted. Right now, Bingo has two choices. Keep his mouth shut and take the fall, or watch bad things happen to his family. You know the kind of things we can do. Too bad for your hotshot pitcher. The only time he'll see the Hall of Fame is if he goes on a tour."

Oh my God. They *did* "own" Bingo with their nasty threats. It was sickening, the lengths the Wades would go to manipulate people.

Time to get out of here. Exit plan, exit plan . . .

Just then her phone rang. *Donna*. Thank you, Lord. She answered. "Hey Donna . . . oh no, the Shark's puking his guts out and you need a ride to the emergency room? Yeah yeah, I'll be right there." She hung up. "Sorry, Hamilton, I really have to go. Vomit emergency. You Wades have been such a help. I'll stay far away from the Hartwell family from now on."

She hurried off, feeling his gaze heavy on her retreating back. Quickly, she dialed Donna again. "I'm keeping you on the phone until I get out of the park, okay?"

"How did it go? What are you up to?"

"Oh, just doing a little story research for Burwell Brown. I think I got what I needed."

Chapter 25

CALEB DIDN'T WANT his pitching motion to get rusty, so he found a deserted, dead-end alley near his apartment and stood a pitching target near the back wall. He carefully measured off the regulation sixty feet and six inches. Every evening, he drove to the alley, blocked its entrance with his Jeep, and threw for at least an hour.

After he'd cleared away the broken glass and gotten used to the urine smell, it made a pretty good bullpen. In fact, it was therapeutic. A ball, a glove, a target. All the ingredients for catharsis. As he pitched, his imagination erased the dingy stucco walls and filled in other images. Bingo's face often appeared on his target, smiling with those false baby blues. Trevor Stark showed up now and then. The cocky bastard swung and missed over and over again. It was amazing how many times he struck Trevor out. How had the guy ever made it to Triple A, let alone the Friars? And Hamilton Wade got more than a brushback. He got a full-on fastball to the jaw.

Sometimes no one appeared at the plate, and his only opponent was himself. Explode faster off the mound. Hit that inside corner. Again. Again. In those moments, a sort of peace came over him and he knew that none of the bullshit mattered.

And in the audience, always, Sadie cheered him on, her bright smile lighting up the dreary alley.

So it was a shock when Sadie herself called to him from behind his Jeep while he was retrieving his balls after an especially satisfying curveball that brought Hamilton to his knees.

Sadie, in a sexy silver tank top, was waving at him from behind the Jeep. "Can you take a break?"

"Well, it is the bottom of the ninth and the bases are loaded," he explained, dropping his balls in his gym bag. "I have no idea how they loaded the bases when no one's been able to touch me."

He reached the Jeep, put down his bag and leaned across the hood. Their lips met in the middle. Electricity sizzled between them, nearly frying his brain. He almost expected his Jeep to rise into the air from the reflected magnetic pull.

"Really? No one's been able to touch you?" she whispered after he pulled away, heart racing.

"Just you. I have no defense against you."

"Good thing the opposing batters don't know that little secret," she joked. "All they have to do is walk to the mound and kiss you on the lips."

He eyed her suspiciously. Something was different; she practically glowed. "You look like you just won tickets to the World Series."

"Duke wants to see you. You weren't answering your phone so he called me."

At the sound of his manager's name, Caleb's stomach clenched and reality came rushing back. He took a longing glance at his lonely alley, with the pitching target a dim outline against the back wall. "That can't be good," he muttered.

"It *can* be. Come on. Do you need help with your stuff?"

"No, I got it. Where's your car? What are you doing out here at this time of night anyway? It's not safe."

"Would you relax? You're acting like an old man," she teased as he tossed his glove into his gym bag and flung it on the backseat.

"Is that right? That sounds like a challenge."

"You can prove your virility later. We should go see Duke now. I'll drive with you if you can take me back to my car later."

"Is your car at my place? Does that mean you'll come inside for some good old-fashioned virility-proving?"

"You have such a dirty mind."

"Only with you, babe. Only with you. What were you thinking, wearing that sleeveless thing? I can see your beautiful nipples through it."

"You can not."

"Then lift your top so I can."

They teased each other during the entire ride to the ballpark, which meant that by the time the stadium loomed into view, he wasn't nearly as tense as he would have been otherwise, and Sadie was flushed and giggling. The stadium lights were off; the game must have already ended.

"I hope everyone's gone," Caleb muttered as he pulled into the parking lot. "Oh, hell."

Plenty of cars still filled the lot. Not all the guys had cars; most minor leaguers scraped by on carpooling and walking. In the big leagues, a car service would take you to the game—some insurance issue. But here in the good old minor leagues, it was all do-it-yourself.

He'd been so close. *So close.*

Shoving the thought aside, he swung himself out of the Jeep. Sadie caught up with him, taking his hand in hers. It occurred to him that it was kind of odd that she was coming to a meeting with Duke.

"What exactly is this all about?"

"You'll see."

Despite the fact that her smile could have lit up the stadium by itself, a sense of foreboding filled him. He didn't like surprises. In his life, they had almost always been bad experiences. The knock of a detective on a door. A sudden move to a new town. The news that he was being traded. Then sent down.

He gripped Sadie's hand more tightly. On the other hand, being sent to Kilby might be the best surprise he'd ever gotten. She gave him a wide, sideways smile, and his heart expanded, like a sun bursting through the clouds.

And then things got very strange. When they walked through the door, Bieberman was waiting for them. "Duke's in the clubhouse. Says you're supposed to find him there."

"What are you still doing here? Shouldn't you be home watching *Brainiacs* by now?"

"I'm Tivoing it."

"Of course you are." The shortstop bobbed along beside them.

"So . . . did we win tonight?"

"Seven to four, Farrio with the win."

Farrio. That was strange. He should have been called up by now, taking Sullivan's spot. Maybe the Friars had traded for someone else. His heart sank. Maybe they'd traded for an already established lefty, meaning they'd given up on him, or anyone else from their farm system. It wouldn't be surprising. It was early August and the Friars were still in contention, one spot behind the San Francisco Giants. They needed to solidify their lineup for the last third of the season.

Maybe he could ask to be traded. Maybe he could get a job teaching baseball to kids. Coaching Little League.

Did those guys get paid or were they volunteers? He should find out as soon as possible. Well, as soon as formal charges were filed and he knew where he stood.

They'd reached the double doors at the entrance to the clubhouse. Sadie tugged at his hand, and he realized that during that crazy stream of thought, he'd started gripping it so tightly her hand probably stung. He looked down at her, apology on his lips, then realized they were standing in the exact same spot where he'd first seen her. Then, he'd thought she was cute but irritating. Now, he found her utterly beautiful and . . . essential.

Her eyes shone as she gestured to the door. "Go on."

Shrugging—what was all the fuss about?—he pushed it open. A roar of applause slammed him like a wave breaking on a beach. He looked around, bewildered. The Catfish filled the locker room, clustered around a long catering table, standing on benches, all staring at him. He took an instinctive step back, and heard Bieberman yelp. Sadie let go of his hand and started applauding along with everyone else.

What the hell?

Duke stepped forward, holding a newspaper. "Early edition of tomorrow's paper. Should I read it out loud, boys?"

"Woot," a few of the guys hooted, clapping some more. "You got the stuff, Duke." . . . "It ain't the comics, can you handle it?" . . . "One word at a time, skipper."

"How about some interpretive dance?" Bieberman added, earning a general mystified stare from the rest of the team.

Duke ignored them all and peered at the front page of the newspaper.

"They're on top of your head, Duke," called Stark.

With a grumble, Duke slid his glasses into place.

"The headline says, 'New Information Clears Catholic Pitcher.'"

The guys all stomped their feet and clapped their hands. Caleb wanted to snatch the paper from Duke's hands and devour the details, but stood frozen to the spot as Duke began to read.

"The *Kilby Press-Herald* has acquired explosive new information that has sent the investigation into the so-called 'Triple A Gambling Scandal' in a radical new direction. As this edition goes to print, the police are questioning members of the locally prominent Wade family in connection with a scheme to establish an illegal bookmaking operation. Police Chief Wade has recused himself from any involvement in the investigation.

When asked what this means for Thurston Hartwell II, the ex-convict at the center of the scheme, Betsy Clark, his lawyer, said, 'Details are still under wraps, but we are working on a plea agreement that will allow my client to tell the full truth.' She added, 'One thing we'd like to make clear is that Caleb Hart has never had any involvement in the situation and in fact knew nothing about it at any point. My client would have come forward earlier, but he was under threat from individuals who cannot be named yet. We urge the District Attorney to do a thorough investigation into all aspects of this case, including the threats made against my client, Thurston Hartwell.'

When asked what specific threats were made, Ms. Clark said only that they involved, among other things, planting evidence that would have implicated Caleb Hart.

These explosive charges have rocked City Hall and the political leadership of Kilby. The Wades have long been a very influential family, ever since they founded Kilby in its Wild West days. Some have accused the Wades of skirting the law, but no allegations against them have ever been proven. Now, Mayor Trent says, things are about to change.

'I was voted into office on a platform of preserving the Kilby way of life. The Kilby way of life should not include intimidating witnesses, unfairly influencing America's pastime for the sake of greed, or unnecessarily smearing a baseball player's reputation. I will be urging the authorities to take this case very seriously. On behalf of the City of Kilby, I'd like to apologize to Caleb Hart. He's an outstanding ballplayer and a fine human being, which he proved by donating his time and celebrity on behalf of the endangered horn-toed slugs. Caleb, I hope you knock it out of the park in San Diego.' "

At this, Duke looked up from the newspaper. The entire clubhouse seemed to be holding its breath. "I already faxed this to the GM. You're back in, Hart. I hope you still have your bags packed."

The applause erupted all over again, amid a din of foot-stomping and hooting and hollering. Caleb stared around the room at his teammates. Mike Solo grinned at him and held up two fists in a victory gesture. Trevor Stark's cool smile and lackadaisical clapping was about what he would have expected. Dwight Conner kept thumping a fist against his chest, then pointing at Caleb. Even though he'd only played with these guys for part of a season, they were cheering for him.

And then they were surging forward to shake his hand, pound his back, even hug him. Out of the corner of his eye he saw Sadie wipe away a tear and Bieberman hop up and down like a bunny.

"We got some extra grub to celebrate," Duke called over the din. "Italian place sent over some lasagna, and we got burritos from Tico Taco. Dig in, kids! Just go outside if you gotta fart."

More applause, then a virtual stampede as the players converged on the banquet table. "I'll get you some lasagna," whispered Sadie. He nodded, but when her hand slipped away from his, he regretted it. He'd rather have Sadie by his side than a lifetime of lasagna.

Bieberman joined the crowd at the table, but Mike Solo moved to Caleb's side. He drew him away, out of earshot, and lowered his voice.

"No one here believed any of the crap they were saying, but management ordered everyone to keep their mouths shut. Duke called a meeting and said it's easy for words to get twisted and the best thing we could do for you was shut the fuck up."

"It's all right, dude. It wasn't anyone else's problem anyway."

Trevor Stark, who'd been so recently starring in his pitching target, joined the two of them, ambling up with that tigerlike prowl that he used to intimidate pitchers. "Well, that's not exactly right, now, is it?"

Mike Solo elbowed the slugger. "Go away, Trevor. Why can't you ever lay off?"

"What are you talking about?" Caleb asked.

"You don't go on Facebook much, do you?" said Trevor.

"No."

"Stark, go eat a burrito," said Mike. "Suck down some beans and carne asada and stop being an asshole for two minutes."

"Just trying to make sure my man here is staying connected. I have ten thousand 'likes,' did you know that?"

"That's because they don't know you," growled Mike.

"Of course they don't know me. You don't know me." His menacing stare raised Caleb's hackles.

"Do you have a point here?" he asked. "Because I want to sit and eat lasagna with my girl and think about my upcoming trip to *San Diego*."

That dig hit home; Trevor's square-jawed face tightened. "Your girl? Do you mean this girl?" He whipped his phone out of his pocket in a gesture that was clearly pre-planned. A photo was already cued up. Caleb didn't want to look, he tried not to. He tried to keep his gaze fixed on Trevor's ice-green eyes. But the outline of Sadie's figure drew him irresistibly—it always did, whether in real life or in a photo. She stood in that little park downtown, wearing that sexy red dress of hers. She'd only bought it a few days ago; the photo must have been taken since then. Her head was tilted up, and Hamilton Wade was kissing her on the cheek.

"So the fuck what?" he growled at Trevor. "A kiss on the cheek. Am I supposed to be jealous? I'm not that kind of guy."

"That's sweet. But you didn't read the post."

Caleb pushed the phone away. "I don't need to read the post."

"Want me to get Duke back here for another dramatic reading? Nah, I can do it." Trevor started to read aloud, but Caleb snatched the phone away. Whatever nastiness it contained, he didn't want anyone else hearing it. He stared down at the phone, trying to get his eyes to focus on the small type.

Sadie and me about to make a NEW Sexxxx Tape! Didn't know she was going to take it to the reporters. Would have done something different with my mouth. Doesn't matter. We have good lawyers, but a slut is a slut to the end.

Caleb couldn't move, couldn't speak. It was a lie. Impossible. It had to be.

"A sex tape, how about that?" The nastiness dripped from every word Trevor spoke. "Someone e-mailed me a copy of it. Got it right here. Amateur hour, but then again, my standards are high. Check it out." Trevor took back the phone, pushed a button and a video popped onto the screen. Behind the play arrow at center screen, Caleb saw a blurred image of Sadie's bare torso and long dark hair.

Everything went red around the edges, the way it had when he climbed into the stands to confront Bingo. "Get that away from me," he said in a hoarse whisper.

"You haven't even seen it yet. I didn't know cupcake girl had it in her."

Trevor touched his thumb to the phone and a grainy video began to play. Sadie, unfastening her black lace bra. Her breasts popping out, to the sound of a wolf whistle and a "Work it, Sadie-baby." Lifting her arms and gyrating, stripper style, a little awkward, while Hamilton, his back to the camera, put his hand to his crotch.

Caleb swung at the phone to knock it away, but Trevor deftly whisked it into his pocket.

"Delete that shit," Caleb hissed.

"Sure, man. You got it. But it's getting e-mailed all over town. Figured you'd want to know how you got cleared. Did you send your girlfriend in to do your dirty work? A little slam-bam, thanks for the confession, man? Nice to have that kind of support, dude. Seriously, nice work."

Mike thrust himself between Caleb and Trevor.

"You made your point, Stark," the catcher said in a low, tense voice. "Now you're just being a dick."

"I was born a dick," he smirked. "Secret of my success."

But Caleb wasn't listening anymore. He looked over at Sadie, who stood at the long banquet table, chatting with T.J. Gates as she inserted a big serving fork under a piece of lasagna. She lifted it into the air, long strands of cheese dangling. She lifted it higher, higher, trying to break off the strings of cheese. But they wouldn't cooperate, and she started laughing at the ridiculous sight. When she made that throaty, delighted sound, no one around her could resist joining in. It was like some sort of magical gift. The Catfish around her also chuckled. A few shot her curious looks, and Caleb wondered how many of them had seen that video.

A sex tape. Sadie in the park, in her brand new red dress. Kissing Hamilton. *Sex tape*. Bare skin. Long hair. *SEX TAPE*.

He was drowning. Spiraling downward into a deep dark vortex where no light or laughter could reach. He flung himself away from Mike and Trevor, hearing Trevor's phone clatter onto the floor. Mike shouted something after him, and Trevor cackled, but none of that mattered. He needed air. Air and grass and dirt.

He ran down the corridor, then burst through the door that led into the dugout. The baseball field seemed smaller at night, tamed and sleepy. The only light came from the crescent moon just peeking over the stands and the utility lights in the dugouts.

When he reached the edge of the grass, he stopped, panting, shaking. It couldn't be true. It couldn't. Sadie wouldn't do that. There must be an explanation. *But he'd seen it*. He had to think. Had to figure this out.

"Caleb?"

Fuck. She'd followed him. He couldn't talk to her right now, couldn't look at her. If he spoke to her now, he'd say something bad. "Go away, Sadie."

Her quick indrawn breath felt like a dagger in his back. "What's the matter? Why aren't you celebrating?"

Celebrating? Yeah, he should celebrate being made a laughingstock. Celebrate Trevor Stark shoving that "sex tape" in his face. "Need a minute," he choked out. "Just give me a minute."

"But . . . talk to me, Caleb. Don't keep putting up a wall between us. I . . . I want to be part of it, whatever just happened. Whatever upset you."

He simmered on the edge of explosion. He didn't want to explode, didn't want to hurt her. But if she stayed one more second or said one more word, he might. He tried one more time. "*Later.*"

"Caleb—"

Boom. The dam broke. "You went to your ex." He couldn't say the name. Couldn't say the word "tape."

"Yes, I did, because—"

"You promised you'd stay out of it."

"I know, but—"

"You went behind my back. To that *asshole.*"

"I had to. I had to get him on tape."

"You made that tape."

"Yes. I had to. I know it's not admissible in court, and kind of a sleazy thing to do, but it was enough to use as leverage to get Dean Wade to make a deal. I made the tape to help you, Caleb. It's not as if I enjoyed it."

Every word she said made it worse. So it was true— she had made a tape. The words "Sexxxx Tape" flashed in his brain, mocking him. She'd made a sex tape with her evil ex-boyfriend. She'd betrayed him and made a fool out of him. *With Hamilton Wade.* He couldn't deal with this; couldn't hear anymore. Couldn't look at her. "Go, Sadie. Before I say something I can't take back."

"But—"

He turned, giving her a full blast of the hurt and disbelief churning through him. "Go! Just get the hell out!"

He caught a flash of her white, stunned face before she whirled around and ran off the field. The instant she disappeared, he started drowning all over again.

Chapter 26

Afterward, Sadie couldn't remember much about how she got home. She was pretty sure Mike Solo drove her back. She remembered a vague conversation about the slugs, of all things. As if the slugs mattered anymore. As if anything mattered. The look of scorn on Caleb's face and the contempt that dripped from his voice when he'd told her to get the hell out were branded on her soul with red-hot acid.

She didn't think she'd ever recover.

Just when she thought she'd regained a bit of self-respect, he'd ripped it away with one glance from those steel-blue eyes.

After sleepwalking into her bedroom, she couldn't even summon the energy to take off her clothes. She crawled under the covers and huddled in the far corner of her bed, her arms wrapped around Pugsley, the big goofy panda that her father had won at a carnival during one of their outings. At least Pugsley had never betrayed her, despite the hardened nail polish on his paw and the Oreo crumbs ground into his fur.

What did it say that she had better luck with a stuffed panda than with the real live men in her life? Nothing good, that was for sure.

Have you learned your lesson yet?

Tears coursed down her cheeks, but these were tears of anger, not pain. As they fell, it felt as if they hardened into amber, filling up the place Caleb had gutted.

Stupid, silly Sadie, she lectured herself. *From now on, here are the rules. You are not permitted to get involved with* any more men. *None. No matter how tempting. Go to law school. This is your mission. Get a degree. Get out of Kilby. Get a job. Take care of yourself. Take care of your mother. Get her out of town too. Do something useful. Help people.* No more men.

"Except you, Pugsley," she whispered. "You can stay."

Eventually she drifted into a shallow sleep, from which she awoke with hot, gritty eyes. Still in her clothes from last night, she wandered into the living room, where her mother was watching a crafts show on how to make bird feeders.

"Sadie! Don't you have work today?"

"Day off." She sat on the couch and stared vaguely at the TV, feeling her mother's questioning gaze on her.

"Is everything okay?"

"Sure," she said, automatically, because she knew better than to tell her mother the truth. The woman on the TV poked a hole in the bottom of a yogurt container. "Cool bird feeder."

They sat in silence for a moment as Sadie tried to summon the energy to pretend everything was really okay. On the TV, the bird feeder woman's hand movements were hypnotic and her instructions strangely soothing.

"We should make one of those," she told her mother.

"You think so?" Her mom sounded dubious, but Sadie could see it all now. The two of them could become bird feeder-crafting, man-avoiding, decoupaging shut-ins. It wouldn't be so bad.

She gave up and padded back to her bedroom.

The time was twelve-fifteen. Caleb must be on a plane to San Diego by now. Off to his wonderful career, partly made possible by her.

Another surge of fury left her shaking and holding onto the wall. She sank onto the floor, scrabbling for her purse. When she found her phone, she flipped through her contacts, found Caleb and blocked his number. There. She'd never have to talk to him again. He was just like everyone else—worse, because he'd claimed to be different. She'd trusted him and opened herself up to him, and then he'd judged her without listening to a word she said.

Forget him, she told herself savagely. *Erase every last speck of Caleb Hart from your mind. Gone. Gone for good.*

After blocking his number, she deleted his name. Seeing it disappear from her screen made something hot gather at the back of her throat, but she ignored it. A few people had called—Donna, for one—but she didn't check their messages. Instead, she dragged herself back into bed and curled up with Pugsley again.

Her mother knocked on the door, once, twice, then again later. She didn't answer.

She drifted off to sleep again. Sleep felt good. She could get used to sleep. She really needed to sleep more often. Like, all the time. Maybe her mother had it right after all.

When she awoke, it was dark and the house was empty. Feeling shivery and weak—when was the last time she'd eaten?—she made her way to the kitchen. In the dimness, she felt like a ghost. A ghost of the old Sadie. When she turned on the light, she saw a note from her mother, perched on top of a pile of mail: *Night shift at Kroger. Maybe you should look through some of these. Love you, Wonder-girl.*

Her mother hadn't called her Wonder-girl since fifth grade.

She peeked under the note to find a stack of law school catalogues. Brick buildings, shining faces, sober lettering. All this time, her mother had been hiding them. She'd never liked the idea of law school. She thought it would be too hard, or that Sadie would leave and never come back.

Now here was page after glossy page of . . . hope. An invitation to a future; permission from her mother.

As if a spigot had been turned on, a rush of hot tears flooded down her cheeks.

Sadie sat down with a thump and leafed through the catalogues. At first the snapshots of students in the library or delivering an answer in class were daunting. Everyone looked polished and perfect, not a shameful secret or a self-doubt to be found. But then one photo caught her eye. It portrayed a legal clinic where students volunteered. A young Latino girl and her mother were listening closely as a student showed them some paperwork.

Yes. She wanted that. Exactly that. She wanted to *know* something, to be an authority, to be respected, to help vulnerable people when they needed it most. She could *do* that. She could be that student in the photo explaining tenants' rights or how to file a restraining order.

A sense of power rushed through her. Hamilton had made her into a victim. She'd felt helpless against his smear campaign, completely out of her depth. But hadn't she turned the tables on him by getting that recording? Now *he* was the one scrambling to defend himself. So what if Caleb had a problem with it, which she *still* didn't understand. She'd gotten her revenge in a way that righted the scales of justice. If Caleb didn't like it, he could go screw himself.

The thought of Caleb brought a stab of pain so deep, she actually clutched her stomach and bent over, resting her forehead on the table. She took quick, shallow breaths, because that's all her suddenly tight chest would allow. In, out, in, out. The clock over the stove clicked to the next hour. A tiny red ant crawled over the rim of the table. The refrigerator hummed. In, out. In, out.

Caleb had delivered a blow so much deeper than anything Hamilton had. Ham had shamed her, humiliated her—but he hadn't broken her heart.

Caleb had.

Now she had to put the pieces together and figure out how to live.

Streeerike! Caleb savored the umpire's call and the satisfying pop of his fastball into the glove of Juan Patron, the Friar catcher. He caught the ball from Juan and paced around the mound, waiting for the next batter.

So far his first game as number 27 on the San Diego Friars was light-years from his first start as a Catfish. Strangely, he hadn't even been nervous when he took the mound. He'd been on fire since the first pitch, throwing with a sense of purpose and freedom that he hadn't experienced since he turned pro. The crowd was loving it. Big placards with giant K's—six of them—lined the railing to the right, but he tried to ignore them. One batter at a time. One pitch at a time.

The next batter came to the plate, a big right-handed slugger named Trask Brown. He crouched over the plate like an assassin, and for the first time Caleb faltered. The guy's stance reminded him of Trevor's, the way he crowded the plate, practically begging for a brushback. And his last name . . . Brown . . . just like the reporter back in Kilby.

Ball one went so high Patron had to jump for it. The catcher flashed him a "keep 'em down" sign before tossing the ball back.

Yeah. Keep it down. Genius advice.

Block it out. The guy wasn't Trevor, and this wasn't Kilby. He took a moment to scan Friar Stadium with its three-tier grandstands and massive scoreboards. Forty-two thousand people had come to the game tonight. Forty-two thousand people were watching him.

He couldn't afford to think about Kilby right now. Because Kilby equaled Sadie. And Sadie equaled . . .

Patron called for a curveball. Caleb reared back and delivered, but the batter swatted it like a mosquito and it bounced foul. Strike one.

The batter resumed his stance and twisted his cleats into the dirt, ready to wheel on his next pitch. Caleb saw his name, Brown, march across his wide shoulders. *Brown.* Why'd he have to be named that?

Patron called for a fastball, and he felt for the seams, placing his index and third finger on the stitches. Burwell Brown's article had cleared him of all suspicion of gambling. And Brown had based his article on exclusive information provided by "someone close to the Wade family."

Sadie.

The fastball spun past Brown, who swung so hard he nearly rotated in a complete circle. The crowd roared.

Caleb felt nothing. A sort of numbness came over him every time he thought about Sadie. None of it made any sense. He *knew* her, and yet maybe he didn't. Maybe they'd gotten involved too quickly. Maybe he'd fallen too fast. Was no one what they seemed? Was Bingo right, and everyone was a cheater? He still couldn't bring himself to think about that tape. He'd wanted to ask Mike to check into it, to get the full story. Maybe if he knew exactly what was on the tape, it wouldn't make him so crazy. But he'd been on a plane to San Diego before he got the chance. In less than a day he'd been on the mound, pitching in his all-important first start as a Friar.

Besides, Sadie had sounded proud of that tape. What was he supposed to do with *that*?

Even though Patron called for a curveball, Caleb ignored him—a big no-no because a catcher could get seriously hurt if he set up for the wrong pitch, and if the pitch went wild a base runner could easily score. But Caleb needed the speed, needed the release. He went for the heat, a sizzling fastball that Brown crushed into left field.

All eyes tracked the ball as it soared high above the third base line. Then it slowly descended, down, down . . . toward the bleachers . . . no, toward the field. Fans stood, craned their necks. The players watched, except for Brown, who was already racing past first. The left fielder practically climbed the wall, stuck out his glove, and made the play of the game by stabbing it out of the air. The entire ballpark erupted. Brown cursed loudly and stalked off the field.

The Friars jogged back to the dugout; Caleb felt a pat on the butt, heard an angry, "What the fuck?" from Patron, but absolutely none of it meant anything.

He felt nothing.

After the game, which the Friars won, he showered quickly and headed out of the clubhouse to meet up with Tessa and the twins. He'd flown them in to watch the game; they were going to stay overnight in his hotel. Even though every damn player on the team, every coach and assistant manager, offered congratulations and words of welcome, he still felt nothing.

He didn't feel anything until he'd run the gauntlet of

fans wanting autographs and saw the boys and Tessa
waiting at the back of the crowd outside the players'
exit. The twins flew to him with high fives, but Tessa
held back. When he was done goofing off with the boys,
he turned to her.

"No congratulations?"

"Sure." She gave him a quick, hard hug, then surprised him with a whack across the side of his head.
"Congratulations for being an asshole."

"*What?*"

"Boys, go get someone's autograph or something."

"Caleb, can we have your autograph?"

"Someone *else's*."

The twins raced off, leaving Tessa and Caleb alone.
"Mike Solo called me. He says Trevor's telling everyone
Sadie made a sex tape and you're not denying it."

He took a step backward. His shoulder throbbed
from the effects of a hundred and two pitches. "The sex
tape has nothing to do with me. It was someone else."

She looked like she wanted to whack him again,
but instead she stomped her foot. "Do you really think
Sadie would do something like that? Are you out of
your mind?"

He stared at his sister, her short blond hair ruffled
by the breeze coasting through the parking lot. Players were still exiting the stadium, to the pleas of "Will
you sign my baseball card?" from the waiting kids. The
rumble of cars leaving the lot mingled with the chatter
and laughter of happy fans: the atmosphere of a major
league ballpark. Kilby felt a million miles away. "I saw
it. Stark had it on his phone."

"You're getting your information from that jerk?
Without double-checking? I called Mike, and Mike
talked to Sadie's friend Donna. That tape is old news.
It's from when she was with her old boyfriend. He re-

corded it secretly, then started sending it to people after she broke up with him. According to Donna, Sadie was trying to give him his birthday wish. A silly striptease, which he taped because he's a jackass. It's one of the ways he tried to get revenge after she dumped him."

A horrible feeling settled in his gut. He remembered Sadie whispering in the gazebo at Crush Taylor's— something about a "really embarrassing tape." They'd never talked about it again, and quite frankly, he'd forgotten all about it.

But no, that couldn't be right. "No, Tessa. She admitted it. She *told* me she made a tape to get Hamilton's confession."

This time, Tessa gave him a little shove. "Yes, she made a tape. An *audiotape*. Did you even read the news coverage?"

"No. There wasn't time, I was on a plane that night."

"It says clear as day that it was a conversation held in a public park, recorded on a pocket recorder. Did you even give Sadie a chance to tell you all that?"

Sadie's face formed in his mind, the way she looked when he told her to get the hell out. Stricken, shocked, bewildered. White as the chalk on the infield lines. *What had he done?*

"Oh my God. I fucked up." He leaned over, hands on his knees, suddenly sick to the very pit of his stomach.

"I'll say."

"No, you don't understand." He'd *fucked up*. He'd done exactly the same thing to Sadie that everyone else had. Jumped to conclusions, judged harshly, condemned without giving her a chance. "She's never going to forgive me."

"Well, you'd better do something. Because I like Sadie. Right now I like her more than I like you."

Right now, he felt the same way. "I have to call her.

Where's your rental car? I'll meet you there. Just give me a few minutes."

She waved toward a vehicle, but he didn't even notice which one. He was already dialing Sadie's number. All he got was a busy signal. He paced around the lot for a few moments, kicking away a beer can and a carefully filled-out scorecard. Whatever that scorecard said, it was wrong.

The real score was Caleb Hart, big fat zero.

After a minute, he tried Sadie again. Busy signal. Two minutes later the same thing. Finally it sank in. She'd blocked his number.

He spotted the twins climbing into a Ford Taurus and ran to his family. "Tessa, I need your phone."

With a frown, she handed it over. This time he didn't get the busy signal, but he got Sadie's voice message, in her soft, husky voice. "Please leave me a message." The sound of her voice made his stomach go tight. How badly had he hurt her? "Sadie, it's Caleb. Call me back, please. I have to talk to you. Please. This is Tessa's phone. You can call her or me. Just please call. I'm sorry."

I'm sorry. That wasn't nearly enough. He should say more. A lot more. But he had to get this right. He couldn't do it on voice mail. Even doing it on the phone would be tough. He wanted to see her, touch her, throw himself at her feet.

He tossed the phone back to Tessa.

"Get in," she said, with the first glimmer of a smile. "You promised us dinner."

Numbly, he got in the passenger seat, but even that made him think of Sadie, and the time he'd crammed himself into her Corolla and they'd gone to the swimming hole to see the slugs' habitat.

Images steamrolled through his head. The shy way Sadie had stripped off her top and skipped into the water before he could fully appreciate her long, lanky form. The two of them kissing while his toes sank into the soft bottom of the lake. The way she'd huddled behind his legs, only her head above the surface, then trudged through the mud to retrieve her bra.

What about the way her lips had parted in shock when he pulled out the blindfold? The willing but naïve way she followed his sexual lead? A birthday striptease made sense. Deliberately making a sex tape behind his back—hell no. What had he been thinking? Tessa was right. The thought was ridiculous.

He groaned aloud.

"It's finally sinking in, isn't it?" Tessa jammed on the brakes just inches from an SUV with a bumper sticker that read: I HAVE NO LIFE. MY KIDS PLAY BASEBALL.

"I'm such an asshole."

In the backseat, the twins cracked up. For once, Tessa didn't scold him for the inappropriate language. Probably because at the moment it was completely appropriate.

"What are you going to do?"

"Keep calling. She has to talk to me eventually."

"No, she doesn't."

He shifted, trying to get his long legs to fit more comfortably into the Taurus. "What do you think I should do? I can't just fly back to Kilby. I'm with the Friars now. I have to work my butt off and show them I belong."

Tessa didn't answer while she maneuvered around the long line of vehicles exiting the stadium parking lot. The Friars had booked him a room at the nearby Millenium Hotel, just one difference between the major league lifestyle and what he was used to in the minors. In a few days they'd be getting on a charter jet to Atlanta for a three game series against the Braves.

But right now he couldn't care less about five-star hotels and fancy planes. The only thing that mattered was what Tessa would tell him to do about Sadie.

"It's up to you," she finally said as she pulled onto the freeway. "I know what this means to you, and to us. You deserve this shot. And now Bingo can't screw it up. I'm happy for you. You're going to do great. You'll get your contract, I don't have any doubts. This is your destiny, Caleb."

He waited for something more, something that would explain how he could make things right with Sadie. "That's it? You don't have anything else to say, any little lecture or piece of advice?"

"Nope. You got yourself into this mess. Good luck."

Chapter 27

"**Y**OU'D BETTER GET your butt over to the Roadhouse, this band is rocking!" Donna yelled over the phone, a thumping bass line nearly drowning her out.

"I'm in my pj's, Donna. Forget it." Sadie was peacefully stretched out on her bed, wearing sleep shorts and a tank top. She'd spent the day checking out law school applications online, scheduling her LSATs and pinching her left arm whenever she thought about Caleb. A painful method, but it was all she had. "Anyway, why all the partying lately? What's going on with you?"

A short silence, then, "Okay, there is something I've been wanting to tell you. Something important. Will you come to the Roadhouse?"

So there *was* something, and if she didn't jump on Donna's offer, she might miss her chance to get the story. "Fine. But why there? It's too loud."

"Because this is going to take some courage. The liquid kind."

"All right. Don't go anywhere. I'm on my way."

Sadie hung up, watched the hypnotic rotations of the ceiling fan for a moment, then sprang out of bed. A broken heart didn't mean death, after all. She was a strong, invincible woman. Take that, Caleb Hart.

It took more than ten minutes, but she finally walked into the Roadhouse in a killer outfit that included a ruffly Victorian-style top, a pair of lacy short shorts, and her favorite red cowboy boots, which always gave her confidence. Take *that*, Caleb Hart.

She paused at the entrance so the bouncer could stamp her hand. His appreciative wink gave her another shot of courage. *Take that, hotshot pitcher.* She sauntered inside, enjoying, for once, the glances that came her way. Just because she was going to be a highly successful lawyer didn't mean she couldn't have a little fun. After the year she'd had, and the crap she'd put up with, she deserved some fun. As soon as she saw someone halfway cute, she'd get out there on the dance floor and let loose. The band, a sort of ska-swing group with a killer brass section, was cranking. The beat pounded through her body, calling to her.

But first she scanned the bar for Donna. When she finally caught a glimpse of her friend's red hair gleaming under the lights, her heart plummeted. A familiar figure leaned over Donna, close enough to be menacing. Hamilton's cousin, Jared. On Donna's other side loomed another Wade cousin whose name she couldn't remember at the moment. She quickly surveyed the rest of the small knot of men surrounding Donna. All Wades, or "friends of Wade." Hamilton himself lurked at the edge of the group. And not a single one of them was smiling.

She hurried toward Donna, who caught sight of her and shook her head in warning, which she ignored. She wasn't going to let Donna face off with the Wades without any support. When Sadie didn't stop, Donna gave her a panicked *Go away* gesture. Jared noticed and swung toward Sadie. A sly grin crossed his face.

"Well, if it isn't Slutty Sadie all ready to par-tay."

The rest of the gang looked her way, a blur of hostile faces. She took a deep breath. This was a crowded bar. If they did anything too aggressive, someone would call the police. Out of the corner of her eye she saw that Todd was on duty. He wouldn't let things get out of hand.

"Hi guys," she said in voice that, miraculously, didn't shake. "What are you all doing here?"

"We saw Donna drinking alone. Couldn't let that happen."

Sadie addressed Donna. "Everything okay?"

"Sure," she said tensely, fiddling with the label on her Shiner. "It's a little Wade family gathering. All in good fun, right, guys?"

One of the other cousins spoke. "We have no problem with Donna, y'all, right? Too bad she hangs out with such a ho."

"Ain't it the truth." One of the hangers-on snorted. "You should pick your friends better, Donna." Typical lack of originality, Sadie thought. The hangers-on always just repeated whatever the Wades said.

"I could say the same for Hamilton," Donna answered tartly. "I don't know what he sees in you guys. All you do is follow him around like little serving boys."

Sadie cringed. She mouthed *Shut up* to Donna, who ignored her.

"You know, I'm kind of glad you came over here, boys," Donna said, tossing her hair down her back. "It gives me a chance to say something that's been on my mind for a while."

"Donna!" Sadie hissed fiercely.

"This oughta be good." Jared smiled without an ounce of humor. "Go ahead. Let it fly."

Donna, who definitely looked a little tipsy, heaved herself onto the bar, so she sat on the edge with her feet propped on the bar stool, "I've been waitin' a long time for this opportunity, so bear with me, y'all." She lifted her beer bottle and tapped a fork against it.

"Donna!" Sadie hissed, completely horrified. The atmosphere in the bar had taken on a wild, unpredictable edge. More of the Wades' friends had joined the group, and other people were craning their necks to check out the scene. "Get down from there."

"I'm not getting down. I'm going to say my piece and then these losers are going to leave you in peace."

Sadie clutched her head in despair. "I don't want this. Donna, I don't."

"Well, too bad. It's got to be said. All righty now, you guys got your listening caps on?" She tapped the bottle again. But before she could start, Todd the bartender leaned across the bar and tugged at her elbow.

"We don't really allow folks to sit on—" She aimed the business end of the fork at him. "Never mind. Carry on."

"As I was about to say, I've had enough of you Wades running your mouths off about my friend. Sadie didn't deserve to be treated like that just because she had the good sense to dump Hamilton."

An angry growl came from Hamilton's direction. Sadie stole a glance at him. His face was so red, it looked like it might explode right off his shoulders. He wore a *Wade's Hunting Gear* T-shirt and loose shorts. "That's not how it happened, Donna."

"Oh yes it is. She dumped you and you couldn't take it like a man, so you started smearing her good name. That's not something a man does. That's something a coward does."

Jared stepped closer and took hold of her ankle. "You better shut your mouth right now, Donna MacIntyre."

She kicked his hand off her ankle. "Or what? I got a

hundred witnesses right here. And Todd's probably got his fingers all set to dial 911. Am I right, Todd?"

"We don't want any trouble," Todd said loudly. But from the way his eyes darted back and forth, Sadie knew he was freaking out. Everyone in Kilby knew you didn't mess with the Wades. They'd get their revenge sooner or later. "Donna, take it easy," he added.

"Don't you tell me to take it easy. I've been watching my friend suffer because of these assholes long enough." She tossed her head so her red hair flowed over her back, like some kind of Amazon queen. "The Wades didn't use to be so low-down. Must be the next generation that turned into a bunch of sniveling, rotten losers."

Someone brushed against Sadie's back and she stumbled forward, bumping against Jared. Blindly, he thrust an arm behind him to keep her back. She ducked to the side or it would have hit her cheek. All the Wades and their friends looked furious enough to hit something. She didn't want it to be her.

The person she'd bumped into steadied her. "What's going on?" said a low voice in her ear. She glanced behind her to see Mike Solo. His usually mischievous face looked serious, and he kept glancing up at Donna, as though unable to believe what he was seeing.

"I think Donna's defending my honor," she said, with a catch in her voice. "But she's going to get herself hurt."

"Not if I have anything to do with it," Mike said grimly. "Stay here."

With a huge sense of relief, she edged to the side to let him squeeze by. Even though the Wade crew was made up of big, beefy guys, he had enough of the athlete's command to work his way through the crowd.

"Come on, guys," he said once he'd reached Donna's side—or the side of her legs, still resting on the bar stool. "No need for a scene. Why don't you all just move along now?"

"Who are you to tell us what to do, Catfish?" Hamilton said belligerently. "I've seen you here, with that pitcher."

"The criminal," added Jared.

"Excuse me!" Donna said loudly. "He's not a criminal. The Wades are the criminals and my friend Sadie proved it. So watch what you say, jerks."

The tension in the bar rose another big notch. The waves of body heat coming off the enraged Wades fanned against Sadie's face. Desperate and panicked, she looked around for help. Maybe Todd had called 911. Maybe the police were here. But instead of blue uniforms, she caught sight of someone completely unexpected. Crush Taylor stood watching the unfolding scene, arms crossed over his chest, alert and still.

With him were several other members of the Catfish. None of them held drinks; maybe they'd just arrived and hadn't even seen a waitress before spotting the crazy confrontation at the bar. A wild-haired redhead versus a gang of beefy good ol' boys. Sadie tried to get Crush's attention—maybe he could call the cops— but he didn't seem to notice her. He turned his head to say something to the big, tattooed Sonny Barnes, who in turn bent way down to whisper something to T. J. Gates and Lieberman, the little shortstop. Trevor was there too, his almost otherworldly handsome face set in wary lines.

For a moment the memory of Caleb in this place nearly brought her to her knees. They'd danced here. They'd talked and flirted, and he'd held her in his arms. And now he was gone.

The Catfish team members shook their heads and

turned away, probably deciding to take their business elsewhere, away from the local madhouse.

"She should never have made that tape!" shouted Hamilton. "Big mistake."

"Which tape?" Donna asked. "The one in which you run your fool mouth, or the one you just had to drag out of the archives again? You're so predictable, Hamilton. When in doubt, bring out the sex tape. You should be ashamed."

Oh fireballs. Sadie wanted to sink into the floor and die. Sex tape? Had Hamilton sent it to Caleb? Is that why Caleb had been so upset?

"Shut up, Donna!" Hamilton yelled.

"Is that all you got, big guy? You're just a bully, Hamilton Wade."

Mike Solo was now standing in front of Donna, his arms spread wide, using his body to shield her like a bodyguard for a celebrity. He seemed to have given up on getting her to stop talking.

"And everyone here who believed what Hamilton said about Sadie and never even asked if it was true, yeah, I'm talking to you guys over there, I see you Lucy-Belle, I see you Alison and Manny. You just let him bad-mouth her and no one said a thing. You let him plaster a private moment all over town. Two people were on that tape. Why's Sadie getting all the blame, instead of the asshole who leaked it? Is the entire city of Kilby really so scared of the Wades that they don't have the guts to say when they do something wrong? Well, that's bullshit. Wake up, Kilby!"

A sort of roar spread across the packed room. The band faltered and came to a stop. Dimly, Sadie heard the singer say, "We're going to take a short break. You might want to step outside for some fresh air."

But if anyone stepped outside for fresh air, twice as

many crowded toward their end of the bar. The scent of fight was in the air, electric and wild. More bodies pressed against Sadie's back, trapping her in the same little patch of floor. Maybe she could drop down and crawl out of there. That would be her only option for escape. But she couldn't leave Donna. Even though she wanted to whisk her away and yell at her that she was being stupid and reckless, there was no getting off this train now. Until it crashed off the rails.

"Kilby doesn't need you, Donna MacIntyre. Or your slutty friend Sadie," Jared was yelling.

"More name-calling! That's all you have, isn't it? You call people names and intimidate them so you can get what you want. You're a bunch of bullies. Wake up, Kilby!"

Good Lord, Donna sounded like some sort of rabble-rouser trying to get a union going.

"You want us to do more than call you names, we will," snarled Jared. "Come down off of there."

"She's not going anywhere," said Mike firmly, pressing his back against Donna's legs. "That's enough, y'all. Just step back, take it easy. What are you going to do, hit a woman? Let it go, guys."

For a moment Mike's voice of reason seemed to work. Jared stepped back and none of the other cousins said anything.

Then Hamilton raised his voice. "Are we going to let some baseball player tell us what to do? This is our town. To hell with the Catfish. He doesn't even live here."

A rumble of agreement swept through the group. Sadie's nails dug into the palms of her hands. How far would the Wades go in a public place like this? They weren't generally stupid. But Hamilton had never felt the sting of being publicly mortified, the way she had.

The bullish look on his face, the way even his forehead was turning as red as roast beef, made her extremely nervous.

He caught her looking at him, and something flashed in his eyes—a maddened, reckless cruelty. Over the temporary lull, Hamilton called to her.

"Hey, Slutty Sadie!" he shouted. "You're fucking a Catfish. Tell his friend to get out of our business."

Heads swerved toward her. Waves of heat and cold rippled across her body. The moment crystallized around her like a drop of hot sap hitting cold water. This was it, right here and now, everything that was wrong with Hamilton and everything that was wrong with her life. She took a deep breath and called back, in as loud and even a voice as possible.

"My private life is none of your business, Hamilton Wade. You keep your dirty, nasty, low-down insinuations to yourself."

"You tell him, Sadie!" Donna applauded, bringing her hands together over her head. "Tell him, girl!"

"She's just trying to get me back," Hamilton said to his smirking friends.

"Think what you like, Hamilton. But you'd better stop slandering me or I will sue. What you did is wrong. Just because I didn't want to be with you anymore doesn't mean you had the right to spread lies about me." Oh, this was dangerous. Hamilton was bigger, stronger, had more friends, and a lot more testosterone. But she couldn't stop now that she'd started. "I should have sued you long ago, but I was too naïve and I didn't know I could. But I know a lot more now, so you better watch yourself, Hamilton Wade."

For a moment a flash of shock crossed his face. Then he must have remembered that he was a Wade, and Wades never paid for their misdeeds. They paid people off, or they paid for expensive lawyers, but they never paid where it counted. "Dream on, slutty Sadie. I'm not going to pay for shit. You'd have to pay me to fuck you again. You weren't worth the—"

"Hey boss," shouted Mike Solo. "Have we had enough yet?"

Sadie jerked her head around. Crush Taylor was only a few feet away from her, his body vibrating with tension.

"Yep, I've reached my limit. One more word against Sadie Merritt and you boys will regret it," he called crisply. "I'm a born-and-bred Kilby resident, and I don't think much of this kind of behavior."

"Crush," Sadie hissed. "No. What are you doing?"

He ignored her, keeping his gaze fixed on Hamilton. "I think you and your friends should go home now." He nodded to the two men who had appeared behind Hamilton—Sonny Barnes and Dwight Conner, two of the most intimidating guys on the team. They each took one of Hamilton's arms.

"The hell with that!" Hamilton went wild and tried to rip away from the two Catfish players. He didn't get far with that, except to get dragged back a few inches. "You sleeping with the whole team, Sadie? You got all of them doing your dirty work now? Jared!" He jerked his head toward Mike Solo.

Jared drove his fist into Mike's jaw. Since he still had his arms spread apart to shield Donna, he couldn't protect himself. His head snapped back. Donna gave a little shriek and kicked Jared in the cheekbone with her high heel. He stumbled backward, snarling. Donna leaned down to whisper something in Mike's ear while he rubbed his jaw.

"Oh my God, oh my God," Sadie began chanting under her breath. "This is bad, this is very bad."

But no one else seemed to see it that way.

"That's it, team!" Crush roared. "Remember that thing I said about behaving yourselves and not getting into so much trouble? Well, forget about that! This one's on me, kids! Let her rip."

All hell broke loose, as if a dam had burst. The Catfish players seemed to materialize out of nowhere, popping up behind the Wades and their friends. Hamilton managed to free one arm and drove his fist into Barnes' stomach. Dwight Conner drilled Hamilton with a left jab, and the three of them started whaling on each other gleefully.

Mike and Jared went after each other in a whirlwind of fast punches and grunts. Donna took off her shoes and stood on the bar, then whipped a shoe right at Jared, opening up a cut over his right eye. Blood poured down his face.

"Stay back!" Mike Solo yelled to her.

"This is my fight!" she yelled back, scanning the melee, brandishing her other shoe. She caught Sadie's eye and waved enthusiastically at her. "Sadie! Throw me your shoes, girl!"

But Sadie was being buffeted every which way by the surging, yelling bodies around her. Lieberman jumped onto a Wade cousin's back and tried to cut off his air supply from behind. Ramirez and T.J. Gates used their bodies to form a barrier to protect the onlookers. Trevor Stark actually bonked two guys' heads together, the way she'd only seen in old westerns. Crush was magnificent, wading like an avenging angel into the crowd and plucking members of Ham's entourage out of the mess.

Sadie stumbled forward, then ducked to avoid an elbow. She nearly lost her balance and grabbed onto someone's shirt. Red and green plaid, she noticed. Very

Christmassy. Then something hit her hard in the back and she fell forward just as a fist slipped through from somewhere and slammed her in the face, and then everything swirled into a red and green kaleidoscope.

Desperate, she clung to the plaid shirt, trying to stay on her feet, but whoever it belonged to lunged forward and the shirt slid from her hands and then all she saw was the black-painted, filthy floor as it zoomed toward her face. Still she clung to a last shred of consciousness, knowing she couldn't stay on the floor, that she'd get trampled and crushed and . . . a brilliant stab of pain in her leg pushed her over the edge into the black void.

Chapter 28

CALEB HAD CALLED Sadie six times, left three messages of apology, and sent five text messages. He'd gotten zero response to any of them. The sickening truth was starting to sink in—he'd lost her with his idiotic behavior. Not only that, he deserved to lose her. How had he let Trevor get into his head like that? If he was on the mound, he would have known the dude was trying to psych him out. That's what batters did.

"So, do you have a plan?" Tessa asked as he drove them to the airport.

"Yes. My plan is to call her until she gets sick of me and picks up the phone. Then I'll apologize over and over and over until she gives in."

"Then what?"

"I'll . . . tell her I love her."

A big smile danced across Tessa's face. "You'd better."

He'd tell her more than that. He'd tell her that he'd never let anyone so close to his heart. He'd never trusted anyone enough, not since the disillusionments of his mother, stepmother, and Bingo. His automatic impulse to mistrust had kicked in at the worst possible moment.

"She'll understand," he said aloud, as if trying to

convince himself. "She loves me, she has to forgive me. Doesn't love mean never having to say you're sorry?"

"I don't even know what that means, but it sounds like something a man would say."

After dropping off Tessa and the boys and returning the rental car, he hopped in a Town Car, which took him to the stadium. The Friars were playing an afternoon doubleheader against the Giants. Sadie would call him back any minute now. She wouldn't hold a grudge. She'd told him she loved him. That wouldn't change because of one fuckup, would it? As long as he apologized enough?

Walking into the Friars clubhouse, which could have been the Taj Mahal compared to the Kilby clubhouse, made him feel a little better. The locker room was a picture of spacious luxury. The lockers ringed the perimeter, while a seating area with leather couches and blond wood coffee tables took up the center of the room. Separate rooms contained a whirlpool, spa, gym equipment, along with a dining room and kitchen, where a chef cooked for the team.

This time around the sheer level of luxury didn't throw him, as it had last time. Something had shifted inside him, so he no longer doubted that he belonged in this world, with these masters of the game. He scanned the names on the other lockers. Carlos Quentin. Huston Street. Joaquin Benoit. And then there was his. Caleb Hart. It looked like it belonged.

No one else had arrived yet, and the clubhouse attendant looked surprised to see him. He stopped folding freshly washed towels long enough to offer Caleb some coffee.

"Nah, I got it," he said, and stepped into the dining area where a coffeemaker gurgled in the corner.

"Want a paper?" the attendant offered, coming in

with a selection. "We have the *San Diego Tribune, Los Angeles Times, New York Times*."

"That's all right. I know we won last night, that's all that matters." He winked at the wiry Latino man.

"You got that right. Well, let me know if you need anything." Halfway out the door, he paused. "You just came up from Kilby, right?"

"Yup. I was a Catfish until a couple days ago." Even the name Kilby gave him a sharp jolt of sadness.

"You hear about the big brawl they had down there?"

"No. Did it start with a brushback? That's how it usually goes."

"No, this was off the field. The Catfish were out celebrating a big win, and they got into it with some locals. I don't know what it is with that team, they're a magnet for trouble."

"No kidding. I guess I missed out on all the fun." Caleb gestured toward the newspapers. "Is the story in there?"

"I don't know. It happened late last night. I saw it on ESPN. You want the papers after all?"

"Yeah. Thanks." Caleb took his mug of steaming black brew and the armful of newspapers to one of the couches in the clubhouse. God, the couches were comfortable. Perfect way to kick back after a tough game. The major league life . . . oh yeah, definitely for him. A quick leaf-through of the newspapers showed nothing about any brawl, and he wondered if the attendant had gotten it wrong.

Except that it sounded like something the Catfish would do.

"I think they're showing it again." The attendant turned on the overhead television and switched the channel to ESPN. A grainy, blurry video filled the screen. Caleb couldn't tell what was going on, except that arms were flailing and bodies colliding. He squinted, recognizing the downhome interior of the Roadhouse.

"Jesus," he said. "I think I've been to that place. Turn it up, would you?"

The reporter's voice filled the room. "The San Diego Friars are still not commenting on the late night brawl that involved most of their Triple A farm team, the Kilby Catfish. Several team members are still being examined for injuries. Catcher Mike Solo has three broken ribs and Trevor Stark may be put on the injured list with a sprained wrist. But the most serious injury was sustained by a bystander, a local woman who was trampled underfoot. Her name has not been released to the media, but we're told her condition is serious. As to what started the melee, Crush Taylor would only say this."

Crush Taylor's bruised face filled the screen. "It was a long time coming. I'm proud of the Catfish, and the Friars should be too. I take full responsibility for what happened. I'll pay for all damages and all medical bills. And if the Friars or the league wants to punish anyone, it should be me. No one else."

Caleb was on his feet, the coffee spilling onto the pile of newspapers. *A woman trampled underfoot.* Had Sadie been there? No. It couldn't be her. What were the chances? There were hundreds, thousands of girls more likely to be at the Roadhouse that night than Sadie.

But she hadn't answered any of his calls or texts. Not one.

He fumbled for his phone and called Sadie again. Once more it went to voice mail. Mike Solo's did the same. He didn't have Crush Taylor's number or any of the other guys on the team. But he had Sadie's friend Donna's number somewhere in his phone.

By the time he finished scrolling through two weeks'

worth of calls, he was about ready to tear his hair out. One of the assistant coaches came into the clubhouse and gave him a curious look. "Something wrong, Hart?"

"I think my . . ." What was Sadie? His girlfriend? The woman he loved but might have lost for good? ". . . girl might be hurt. I need to fly down to Kilby." He started calculating travel times and flights. No direct flights to Kilby from San Diego, but with luck he could get a red-eye into Houston and be there by late tomorrow morning.

"Did you call the hospital?"

This from Alex Stenholder, the right fielder, who was folding his long body onto the couch opposite him. Where had he come from? Caleb looked around. The clubhouse had started to fill with players. Game time was in a couple of hours and the guys were showing up for batting practice and their pregame rituals.

Caleb raked a hand through his hair. Terror pounded in his veins. This morning he'd been afraid he'd lost her love, but he'd never really doubted his ability to win her back. But if she was hurt, injured . . . God knew how badly . . . that changed everything. That could be . . . life or death.

Just then his phone rang. A Kilby number, one he didn't recognize. Oh God, what if it was the hospital . . . a doctor . . . Hands shaking, he answered the call with a grunt instead of a "Hello."

"Is this Caleb Hart?" The woman's voice sounded familiar, but he couldn't quite place it. His sense of dread deepened so that it felt as if everything was happening in slow motion.

"Yes." He managed.

"This is Brenda Merritt, Sadie's mother. I thought you might want to know that she's in the hospital."

The world turned ice cold. "Is . . . is she okay?"

"She's still unconscious."

But she was alive. He hung onto that thought with all his might. "I'm coming. Right away."

"If I hadn't been at work, I would have told her not to go. Those Wades—" Her voice broke. "I told her to stay away from men. I guess I just sound like a broken record these days. I almost didn't call you, except I know my daughter cares for you. And I'm hoping you're different."

"I am. Completely different." He'd spend the rest of his life proving it if he had to. "I'm on my way."

"Kilby Community Hospital. Room 203. The doctors say she should come out of it soon. If she doesn't . . ." Her voice shuddered with sobs; it sounded as if she'd been crying nonstop.

"She will," he said fiercely, trying to transmit all his determination to her. "She will. I'll be there soon. Just hang on."

"I hope I did the right thing, calling you," she said fretfully. "She seemed pretty upset. Really shook me up. I hated seeing my baby like that."

"I'm going to fix it. And Mrs. Merritt, thank you. Thank you for giving me another chance." He hung up. Kilby Community Hospital. What was the quickest way to get there? He was scanning through the flight options on his travel app when he realized the assistant coach was standing before him.

"Suit up, Hart. Pitching coach wants you to throw a bullpen today."

"Coach, I have to get to Kilby. I need some personal time. Just a couple days. I'll be back in time for my next start." Maybe. If Sadie were well enough.

The coach, an imposing African-American named

Tony Blaine who'd spent his entire career in the Friars organization, glowered at him. "You just got here, Hart. You're supposed to be in the dugout for every goddamn game until Sullivan gets back. You really want to mess with this?"

He could catch a flight to Houston in two hours if he left now. He clicked Purchase.

"I have to go, Coach."

"This is your career you're tanking. You can't just walk away. You need permission from the front office. I'm on your side here, son."

But Blaine wasn't on his side. He was in his way. He couldn't wait for permission. He had to be on that plane. Too much time had already passed. "What if I got suspended?"

If a player got suspended, he wasn't allowed in the clubhouse or anywhere in the ballpark—he couldn't even wear his uniform.

"Suspended. For what?"

The big right fielder, Stenholder, rose to his feet and ambled toward them. "I can think of something." He gestured to his stomach and nodded at Caleb, who shook his head, confused. The other ballplayer winked and pointed to a spot on his stomach. Really? He wanted him to . . . ? Without thinking too much more about it, Caleb strode forward and planted his fist in the outfielder's taut, muscled gut, right where he'd pointed.

"Two day suspension!" roared the coach. "Get out of here, Hart, and don't come back until Friday."

The coach shook his head at Stenholder, who doubled over in fake pain. He'd clenched his muscles so tight, it would have taken a bullet to hurt him. Caleb clapped a hand onto the man's back as he motored out of the clubhouse. The last thing he heard was the right fielder telling the coach, "I have a romantic streak, what can I say?"

Sadie surfaced through layers of pain. Even unconscious, she'd been tortured by painful images of Caleb, mocking her, kissing her, tossing her aside, turning away. Then Hamilton had joined in, pointing at her and laughing. Crowds of people backed him up like a herd of hyenas. As she slowly came to, the taunting visions gave way to physical pain. Her leg ached and throbbed, her head felt about twice its normal size, and, in fact, she couldn't locate a part of her body that didn't hurt.

Even her eyes stung as she dragged them open. Her mother sat nearby, reading a tabloid. For a moment Sadie simply watched her, taking in her mother's disheveled ponytail and rumpled blouse. The clothes she wore when she worked at Kroger. She looked exhausted. Had she left work to come tend to her?

A tear ran down her cheek, then another. Even the tears hurt her sensitized skin. She must have made a sound, because her mother looked up quickly. "Sadie! You're awake." She tossed aside the magazine—Sadie caught a headline about Jennifer Aniston—and hurried to the side of the bed. "How . . . how do you feel? I should call the nurse. They've been saying you'd wake up soon."

She sounded so tentative, so anxious. One flap of her blouse was untucked and she'd smeared cream cheese on the side of her skirt. Okay, so her mother wasn't put together and polished like Mayor Trent, but Sadie's heart swelled with love for her. "Sorry," she croaked.

Her mother's forehead creased. "For what, honey?"

"Should have listened to you." God, her body ached. "What happened to me?"

Brenda crossed to the Call button and pressed it.

"The nurse should probably explain everything, but you're going to be fine. The worst thing is that your right leg is broken. You'll be in a cast for about six weeks."

Cast. That big white thing suspended in the air above her bed, with her leg inside. *Hey, leg. You doing okay in there?*

"Oh." Her thoughts were moving so sluggishly and weirdly. "It hurts."

"Do you need more morphine? You can press that button right there. It's set so you can't overdose."

"Is that why . . . can't think?"

"Probably. But you don't have to think, sugarpie. Just rest."

Fatigue tugged at her like a friend who wanted to play. *Friend . . .* "Donna? Okay?"

"I am not happy with Donna MacIntyre right now. But she's fine. When she saw you fall to the floor, she yelled bloody murder. That's when the fire department came."

"I'm so sorry, Mom. I should have listened." Her chaotic thoughts careened from one sad topic to another. If she hadn't gone to the Roadhouse . . . if she hadn't been trying to forget Caleb . . . if she'd never gotten involved with Caleb . . . if she'd never accepted a date with Hamilton . . . if she'd never . . . She lost track of the thought, her gaze fixated on a vase that held a bouquet of bright sunflowers with rust-colored centers. The petals glowed with life against the pale beige of the hospital walls.

"I called Caleb."

Sadie dragged her attention back to her mother, who was looking a little blurry. She had to repeat the words in her mind, because at first they didn't make sense. Her mother called Caleb? Why would she do that? "What?"

"I thought you would want him to know."

Tentacles of exhaustion wrapped around her, but she fought against them. "Why?"

"Because I think you really love him, and he loves you."

"No," she managed, each word like dredging her feet through a mucky swamp. "Doesn't."

"He's on his way here."

Sadie struggled to sit up. "Don't want. Don't let him in."

"Honey, listen to me." Her mother hurried to her side and pressed her back down to the bed, which took shockingly little effort. "I was wrong. You shouldn't judge everyone in the world by Hamilton Wade. Or by your father. I know your father did what he could. Hamilton, that's a different story. He's bad, Sadie, bad to the bone. And he's been raised spoiled. But your Caleb, he's not like that. I should have kept my mind more open and not tried to scare you away from every single boy who came along. Caleb's good for you. You're more like your old self with him, full of life and laughter. More like my Wonder-girl."

"No." Sadie shook her head, trying to dislodge the hand her mother had fastened on her shoulder. How could she explain that her mom had been absolutely right, and that Caleb was just like Hamilton? That he'd plunged a knife into her heart and then twisted it with that horrible look of contempt?

"I know something happened between you two, but I bet you can work it out. Seeing you the way you've been the past couple of days really woke me up, Sadie. You've been stayin' in Kilby for me, haven't you? I've been holding you back. Keeping you in this town even when it isn't good for you. Keeping you from doing what you really want."

"Mom . . ."

"You don't need to take care of me, Sadie. I'm not going to let you. I'm going to take of myself so you don't have to worry, and you're going to go to law school like you want. Caleb's on his way and when Caleb gets here, I sure hope you'll listen to him."

Caleb. On his way here. Her heart raced at the thought of him walking through that door.

The door opened and someone charged in. Not Caleb, but a nurse. "What's going on here?" He went straight to the monitors, which were bleeping like mad. "How long has she been awake?"

Sadie grabbed at the nurse's wrist. "Don't . . . let . . . Caleb . . . in."

He gave her a worried look, adjusted something in the IV, and Sadie finally lost the battle. Sleep reached up and swallowed her whole.

Chapter 29

"**WHAT DO YOU** mean, she doesn't want to see me?" Caleb couldn't believe he'd traveled ten hours and potentially torpedoed his career only to hit a roadblock right outside her door.

"You're Caleb, right? She was pretty clear," explained the nurse, a young African-American man who looked to be in his mid-twenties, with a lightning bolt shaved into his hair. "About blew her stitches making sure I knew."

Caleb scrubbed a hand through his hair. "Is she going to be okay?"

"Yeah, she'll be fine, eventually. But she doesn't need any more drama-trauma, know what I mean? Getting trampled is bad enough. Then we got people coming here trying to make amends or whatever the hell else y'all are tryin' to do." The man was jotting down notes on a clipboard right outside Room 203. Just past that door lay Sadie. So close Caleb could feel her in every pore, but still so far.

"I just want to see her." He eyed the young man. "Any chance you're a baseball fan?"

"Don't even go there, dude."

"Football?" This was Texas, after all.

"You know how many concussions we get in here from football? Hell no."

"Basketball?" He knew guys in just about every pro sport played in America.

"You tryin' to bribe me? How's this for a mind-blower. I don't even like sports. So you'd better start gettin' creative."

Creative . . . creative . . . "Are you a fan of romance?"

The guy cocked his head, finally showing a spark of interest. "I do like a cute romantic comedy now and then. Good escape after a long shift. Go on, work it, my friend."

My friend. That was better than *dude.*

Caleb cleared his throat. "The only girl I've ever loved, and the only girl I ever will love, is in that room. She doesn't want to see me because I acted like a major league dick. But I know she loves me too, and if you'd just let me in so I can apologize—"

"Let him in." A quiet voice interrupted. Brenda Merritt had opened the door a crack. She beckoned to Caleb. "Really. It'll be okay," she reassured the nurse. "I promise."

Caleb didn't give Brenda a chance to change her mind. He slipped past her into the quiet beige room with the blinking monitors and the pervasive smell of disinfectant. On the bed lay Sadie, her dark hair rippling across the pillow, her face like something out of a nightmare. Her right cheek looked like a baby eggplant, purple and globular. Butterfly bandages held together the edges of a gash across her forehead. One leg, encased in layers of plaster, was propped on a pile of pillows.

God damn it.

He turned wildly to Brenda, who had just slipped

back into the room and closed the door. "What did they do to her?"

"There was a fight at the Kilby Roadhouse. She slipped and someone fell on her leg."

"How could that happen?"

"Shh."

He hadn't even realized that he'd been yelling. "Sorry." He clamped his jaw shut and stalked to the window, staring out at the overcast early morning sky. If he let his mouth open again, he didn't know what would come out. Some sort of howl of anguish, probably.

"Listen, I'm going to get some coffee," Brenda Merritt said. "She'll be out for a little while longer, I think. Do you want anything?"

Yes. A time machine so he could go back in time and fix this. He'd refuse to leave Kilby unless she came with him. She'd stay by his side where he could keep her safe. Nothing would ever hurt her again, except . . .

He had hurt her.

Agonized by that thought, he whirled around. Brenda was gone, the door just drifting shut. He dropped to his knees next to Sadie's bed and rested his forehead on the crisp bedcover.

"Sadie, I love you. I love you with every bonehead corner of my heart. I can't believe I acted the way I did. I was wrong. I know that. I think I even knew it then, but I'm a stupid asshole about some things. I don't like surprises, I'm not good with them. It's a funny thing for a baseball player to say, since you never know what's going to happen in a game. But baseball has rules, and life doesn't. I got so used to stuff coming out of nowhere and biting me in the ass that I just believe the worst so I don't get messed up. I like to think I'm in control, but when it comes to you, I might as well just throw that out the window."

He took her hand in his, just to feel her skin, even though he knew it wasn't really right or fair. If she were conscious, she'd probably hit him with that hand. But the sensation of her soft, warm skin eased the fear that had stalked him all the way from San Diego. No matter what, she was alive.

As long as she breathed, he still had a chance.

"I know you can't hear me, and if you could, I probably wouldn't even say these things because I'm not good at saying what's in my heart. I keep things inside, I know that. But here's the truth. I'm completely crazy about you. I love you so much, maybe it will soak right through your skin and into your heart. Maybe you'll wake up and know how much I love you. I should never have left without telling you. I should never have left, period. I belong with you, Sadie. Every second I was away from you felt empty and wrong. Even my first win as a Friar felt wrong. You should have been there. I kept thinking you *were* there, because I never stopped thinking about you, you were always there in my heart, every pitch I made. I know it probably sounds crazy, or it would if you could hear me, but—"

"Only . . . little."

He jerked his head up. Sadie's eyes were open—as open as they could be given the degree of swelling in her eyelids. But that precious Sadie sparkle danced in the dark brightness, and his heart cracked open.

"You were listening?"

"Yes. Wouldn't miss that." Her voice came slowly, more like the thick croak of a bull frog. But still, it was the most beautiful sound he'd ever heard.

"How much did you hear?"

"Why? Take it . . . back?"

He put her hand on his chest. "No way. I want to make sure you hear every word, and if you didn't, I'll repeat it over and over, I love you, Sadie. Did you catch that part?"

She smiled, then winced. Her mouth looked so dry and parched. He glanced around and located a plastic cup of water with a straw in it. He held it to her lips so she could take a long sip. Finally, she nodded, and he took it away.

"Sadie, I was terrible to you," he said, very seriously. "You didn't deserve it. I fucked up. I don't have any excuse, except I have a real problem with trust. I haven't trusted anyone outside of Tessa and the boys for a very, very long time. I trusted you, and when I thought you'd betrayed me, I lost my mind for a while. I was wrong, flat out wrong. I'm sorry. What's it going to take for you to forgive me?"

She curled her fingers against his chest, the scrape of her fingernails generating a hard thrill. "I trusted you too."

"I know you did. And I threw it back in your face like a prize asshole." He pulled her hand to his mouth and peppered it with kisses. "And then I thought it was too late, and I wanted to die. I don't want to live without you, Sadie. I want you with me, close as I can get you. I want you to marry me."

Oh sweet Lord. Where had that come from? Sheer panic froze him for a second, but then something seemed to burst in his chest, something bright and warm and wonderful, and he knew it was a stroke of genius.

"Marry me, Sadie," he said again.

"Caleb." The word came as a soft sigh. "You're feeling guilty. That's a guilt proposal."

"No. No way. It's the real thing, Sadie. You don't have to answer now. In fact, I don't want you to answer now. You've been mad at me, and I don't blame you.

Then you got hurt. Then I show up blubbering like an idiot and asking you to marry me."

She opened her mouth but he put a finger to her lips.

"Please. Just think about it. The question isn't going anywhere. I'll still want you to marry me tomorrow, or next week, or next month, or next year, if you want to wait that long. But you need to think hard about it, because being married to a baseball player can be tough. They move us around like chess pieces. And it can be a roller-coaster ride, one day you're the toast of the league, the next you're traded to a last place team. The wives put up with a lot of crap."

Wives. *Wives*. God, he really was serious about this. He wanted Sadie to be his *wife*. In fact, he wanted it desperately, because no one else in the world would do.

She was frowning, and it looked like she might be falling back to sleep. "So . . . chess . . . and roller coaster?"

He laughed, nestling her hand against his cheek. "Chess and roller coaster. That's baseball for you. With a dose of physics and a few dopey sayings. Want to know my favorite?"

"Hmm?" Yes, she was definitely fading.

"Babe Ruth. 'Every strike brings me closer to the next home run.' Works better for a batter than a pitcher. But you get the point. I struck out with you before, Sadie. That just means a gigantic home run is waiting to happen." Her eyes were drifting shut, but her lips were forming words. He leaned forward to catch them.

"Love . . . Caleb." And she was out. He'd just have to fill in the blanks the way he wanted.

When Sadie woke up the next time, she was almost a hundred percent sure that she'd hallucinated the entire visit from Caleb. But there he was, his powerful body

slumped in the armchair, his head propped on one
hand, dozing. She drank him in as if he were rain after
a long Texas summer. His legs were sprawled apart, the
denim of his jeans straining over the strong thigh muscles. His rumpled T-shirt had gotten pulled up on one
side, probably from when he'd slid deeper into the chair.
It revealed a glimpse of his lean waist and that ridge of
muscle that made her want to lick and bite and . . .

Well, apparently she was feeling better. She blinked
her eyes a few times, relieved to feel no pain. Gingerly,
she tried raising herself into a sitting position. That hurt a
little more, because she jostled her leg in the process. She
gave a slight gasp, and Caleb immediately came awake.

"What are you doing? You're not supposed to move.
What do you need? I'll get it. You should have woken
me up. That's what I'm here for. I shouldn't have fallen
asleep, damn it." He rubbed sleep out of his eyes, looking rumpled and confused and utterly adorable.

"Relax, Caleb. I'm okay. It's just a broken leg."

Last night, or whenever it was when she learned her
leg was broken, it had seemed like a catastrophe. Now,
she didn't mind so much. Because Caleb was here. And
he'd asked her to marry him. Marry him! She still didn't
entirely believe it. They were too young to get married,
weren't they? He had a baseball career to pursue, and
she had law school, and none of that mattered because
she loved him so much.

"Just a broken leg," he mumbled. "If I find whoever
broke your leg, they'll regret the day they ever walked
into the Roadhouse."

"Well, most people do, eventually," she said cheerfully. "Not me, though. I love the Roadhouse. We
danced there, remember?"

"Of course I remember. I told you, I remember everything. It's a curse."

"How many strikeouts did you get during your first start as a Friar?"

"Seven. That's not even a challenge."

"Okay. What was the sequence of pitches for the fourth strikeout?"

"Fastball up high. Curveball down and away. Cut fastball on the inside corner. Boom. Out. Batter was Jorge Dominguez, who's batting about .300 these days. How's your head?"

"Over my heels." She let a small smile play across her lips while he worked that one out. The flare in his steel-blue eyes satisfied her down to her bones.

"Head over heels, are you?"

"Completely." And it was true, so true. It was terminal, what she felt for Caleb. She'd never be cured of it.

"Have you been thinking about what I said?" He got to his feet, which had the tragic consequence of covering up that lickable section of torso she'd been eyeing.

"I've been unconscious," she said dryly. "So, not really."

"Oh." His crestfallen expression made her smile.

"Besides, it's not the kind of thing I have to think about too hard."

He raked a hand through his already disastrous hair. "I know I sprang it on you out of the blue. And then I told you all the ways the baseball life is tough. But don't say no too quick. It has some bright sides too. It's baseball. The best game in the world. And San Diego has a law school. I checked. I'll support you a hundred percent in that. I intend to get that big contract."

The nervous flow of his words made her smile. "Caleb, you're starting to make me mad."

"I am?"

"I know it's a tough life. I get it. But you know what's tougher?"

At the bewildered look on his face, she held out her arms. "Being away from you."

A wild look came over his face, as if he wanted to snatch her out of that bed and snuggle her tight against his chest. The intensity in his steel-blue eyes made her heart hurt. Life with Caleb wouldn't always be easy. She already knew that much. But she'd throw every ounce of her self into it.

He moved toward the bed and fell to his knees next to her. The stubble on his chin rubbed against her arm as he gathered her against him. "So you forgive me?"

"You really hurt me, Caleb."

"I know. Baby, I know. I screwed up. Royally. And then a couple hours later I was on an airplane to San Diego and pitching and—"

She struggled to sit up. "Caleb, what are you even doing here? You're supposed to be in San Diego!"

"I got suspended."

"*What?* Oh, Caleb, what happened? Is it Bingo? Did he do something else crazy?"

"It had nothing to do with Bingo. It was all me. I punched the right fielder in the stomach." At her gasp, he smiled. "Actually, it was the right transverse iliac muscle. You know, this one."

He stood up and lifted his shirt to reveal the rippling muscles of his abdomen. He indicated the ridge of muscle shaped like a V pointed toward a very important part of his anatomy.

She sucked in a breath. "You punched him there? Why?"

When he made to drop his T-shirt, she held up her hand. "Please don't. I'm in a hospital bed, you have to be nice to me. Take it off. Come on, hotshot. Pretend we're at the lake hunting slugs."

He narrowed his eyes at her but obliged, shucking

his shirt in one quick motion. She feasted her eyes on his powerful torso. "Okay, so why did you punch the right fielder?"

"So I'd be banned from the ballpark and no one would miss me if I came here."

"So you . . . compromised your baseball career to come and see me?"

"Well, a two-day suspension isn't the end of my career. But yes." He crouched down and cupped a callused hand around her cheek. "Without you, it's not worth anything, my love."

The tears came so quickly, she couldn't blink them away fast enough, and a few spilled down her cheeks, running across his hand. "I love you, Caleb. You have no idea how much. I was in a dark hole and then you came along and . . . everything got bright and wonderful."

Tenderly, he stroked the wetness from her cheek with his thumb, something deep and powerful glowing in his eyes. "Bright and wonderful, that's you, my sweet love. That's completely you."

"Then I thought it was all over. I could barely breathe."

"Not over. Never. Not in this lifetime."

They clung to each other for a long, piercingly sweet moment.

"But Caleb . . ." She had to force the words from her throat. "If you get famous, and you're with me, and someone digs up that . . . sex tape . . ."

"I don't give a rat's ass about that. I really don't. You didn't do anything wrong, Sadie. You didn't hurt anyone, you didn't break any laws. You were trying to give your boyfriend a nice, sexy birthday gift. It wasn't anyone else's business. Not mine, not anyone's."

Something inside her released, a sense of shame floating away like a loose balloon. Caleb was right. She hadn't done anything so terrible. More tears flowed down her face. "I was stupid. Naïve. I didn't ever think he would record it. Or do any of the things he did."

"Of course not." He leaned closer to put his arms around her. "Who would, except another jackass like him?"

"What is going on here?" The indignant voice of the nurse—the young black one named Randall—smashed the moment like a jackhammer. "I did not let you in here to strip naked in front of my patient."

Caleb straightened up to his full, gloriously bare-chested height. "I'm not naked."

"I asked him to," Sadie said at the same time.

"I don't care if you asked him to do a lap dance. This is a hospital. What's wrong with you people?"

"So no naked bodies are allowed in hospitals?" Caleb snatched up his shirt from the foot of the bed.

"Now now, what's going on here?" Another nurse stepped into the room, this one in her early forties, with cinnamon red hair, named Andie. Sadie liked her because she always joked about the food.

"This guy barged in here yesterday," Randall told her, "then spent the whole damn night here, now he's boppin' around with no shirt. Ain't that some kind of sanitation issue?"

The red-haired nurse looked at Randall, then at Caleb, who stood frozen, his shirt crumpled in one hand, each chiseled muscle of his spectacular torso standing out in the drab room.

"It certainly is," Andie said sternly. "Hospital regulations are very clear on this point. Patient safety comes first at Kilby Community Hospital."

"We have elderly patients here," Randall scolded. "Do you know what a sight like this could do to them?"

"Heart attack waiting to happen, Mr. Hart. You

really should be more considerate. Come on, hand it over." Andie gestured to Caleb's shirt. "I'm going to have to confiscate that."

"*Excuse me?*" Caleb's expression was priceless; Sadie had to bury her face in her pillow to keep from laughing out loud.

The two nurses burst out laughing and exchanged high-fives. "We're just having a little fun with you, Hart," said Randall. "Since Sadie's doing so much better, we can't complain too much." He winked. "Just keep it decent when you leave this room. We know how wild those Catfish are."

Caleb whooshed out a breath, the tension leaving his body. He scrubbed a hand across the back of his neck. "I think I'm going to miss Kilby. I really do."

Chapter 30

THE NEXT DAY was a whirlwind, since Caleb had to be back in San Diego in about twenty-four hours. Of course, the sports blogs reported on his suspension, along with speculation about whether he was going through the same kind of meltdown he'd experienced the last time he pitched in the majors. Words like "unstable" and "unpredictable" were tossed around, fortunately intermingled with words like "brilliant" and "sensational."

The talk didn't bother him, because this time he felt at peace with himself. And an encounter with Duke in Mike Solo's hospital room cemented that feeling. Caleb dropped in to check on his friend, who was sleeping, and instead ran into Duke. "Walk with me," the manager barked, and gestured for him to follow down the corridor.

Caleb's gut clenched. Had he been sent down again, and this was how the Friars were telling him? Had he pushed it too far with his two-day suspension, one day after getting on the roster?

He shoved aside the worry—no matter what, it was worth it—and strode alongside Duke as he waddled toward an outdoor courtyard where smoking was allowed. They stood in the hot sun as Duke lit a cigar, the spicy scent of tobacco rising into Caleb's nostrils.

Duke must have picked up on his anxiety, because he shoved his Catfish cap back on his head and squinted. "Don't worry, kid. You won't be back."

"You don't know that. Sullivan—"

"Sullivan's getting traded." He mimed the turn of a key in front of his lips. "Take that one to the tomb."

"Traded."

"Front office likes what they're seeing from you. You're the future, and they know it. I been telling them exactly that for long enough, they ought to know it by now."

Caleb struggled to contain the surge of emotion that threatened to capsize him. The spot was his. His destiny awaited him on that beautiful mound in Friars Stadium. "Thanks, Duke."

"You can thank me by going all in, Hart. All in. None of that chickenshit 'I'm doing this for my family' bull."

"Excuse me?"

"You heard me. Yeah, I know you want to take care of your family. I know you want a big contract. But this game doesn't work that way. You have to love it, you have to let it beat you up, knife you in the gut and leave you bleeding on the goddamn bathroom floor."

Caleb bit at the inside of his lip to keep from laughing at the image. "I've shed my share of blood."

"Yes, you have. And you came back for more. That's how I know you're going to make it this time." He shifted his cigar to his left hand and stuck out his right. A little bemused, Caleb shook it. Duke stubbed out the cigar on the cement block wall of the courtyard and swaggered back toward the door. "I told Crush my idea would work. Hope the man has learned his lesson by now. Always listen to the Duke."

Caleb followed close on his heels. "What idea?"

"You and that Can the Catfish petition. I told him it would help you out of your slump."

Caleb frowned. How the hell had that ridiculous petition helped him out of his slump? He'd gotten *himself* out, damn it. He'd toughed it out and stuck with it until his head straightened out. That's all there was to it. "I don't get it."

"Still don't get it, huh? You had a spell of what I call 'spotlight-itis.' A bad case. Most people don't have fathers in prison. You got up there and saw all those people watching and you got afraid they'd find out about your deep dark secret. You couldn't step into the spotlight because you were ashamed. Ruined your mojo."

"That's a load of bull." It had to be. He didn't believe in that psychological crap.

Duke ignored him. "You can't throw a decent fastball with the weight of the world on you, Hart. You gotta do it for love. I put you on the Can the Catfish petition so you'd start having fun again. That thing was so nutty it was guaranteed to be fun. Guaranteed to shake you up and bring a little crazy into your life."

A memory flashed into his mind, Bieberman talking about surrendering to chaos. Maybe there was something to Duke's theory. But he wasn't about to tell him that. "Duke, you are so full of shit, I'm surprised they don't hose you down and pat you with baby powder."

"Don't give my wife any ideas." He winked and rolled into Mike Solo's room.

After a quick snuggle with Sadie—he didn't want to be away from her more than a few minutes at a time—Caleb dropped in on Mike and got a complete rundown on what had happened at the Roadhouse. The story made his blood run cold.

"Thank God you guys were there."

"I'm telling you. They were out for blood, those Wades, especially after Donna got up there on the bar and lit into them." He shook his head, albeit carefully. "This isn't done, Hart. Those guys are nuts, and they're mad as hell that we whipped their asses."

"I'm going to get Sadie to come with me to San Diego," Caleb told him. "I don't want her in the same town as them."

Mike grinned. "So you got yourself a woman. Nice work, Hart."

"Yeah, and I nearly fucked it up for good."

"Good save, then. Way to go. So you're taking Sadie away from here. Wish you could take Donna too. I don't know what she was thinking, but she's put herself in the line of fire, for sure."

"I guess you'll have to watch out for her." Caleb gave Mike's shoulder a squeeze. "How long are you out for?"

"Couple days, max." Since one of his eyes was swollen shut and Ace bandages were wrapped tightly around his torso, keeping his broken ribs in place, that sounded optimistic to Caleb.

"That's the spirit. Shake it off, dude. Heal up and get yourself to San Diego. I can already see the fireworks for your first homer." Every time a Friar hit a home run, a ship's bell sounded and fireworks went off in center field. Total circus, and he was glad they didn't do it for visiting batters.

"Hold that good thought, bro." A quick grasp of each other's forearms, and Caleb went back to Sadie's room. She had a visitor—a very repentant Donna. Caleb didn't even have to glare before she leaped to her feet, full of apologies. Sort of.

"I'm not going to defend myself to you, Caleb, because you haven't had to live in this town with those . . . those . . . *criminals*. I just couldn't take it anymore, and I'm sorry the Catfish players got hurt, and I'm sorry Sadie got her leg broken, and I'm really sorry about Mike, I never meant any of that to happen, and—"

"You should apologize in person. Mike's three doors down."

An uneasy expression crossed her face. "I don't know if he really wants to see me."

Caleb wasn't sure either, but he hid his doubt behind a reassuring smile. "Of course he does."

After Donna left, Caleb sank onto Sadie's bed and gathered her into his arms. It felt like coming home after a trip around the world. "God, I missed you."

"I missed you." They both laughed, since they'd only been apart for, what . . . ten minutes?

After a long, luxurious snuggle, Sadie murmured, "Hmm. Donna still hasn't told me what's going on with her. That's what I went to the Roadhouse for."

"She'll have to tell you by phone, then. I want you with me as soon as possible. Did the doctor say when you can travel?"

"As soon as I feel up to it."

"Good. I want you to come back with me to San Diego. Please."

She drew back and held his face in her hands, her brilliant dark eyes beaming light right into his soul. "You're worried."

"Hell, yes." Of course he was worried. It felt like leaving her alone in a war zone.

"Don't be. It's going to be fine. Nothing can really hurt me now. Not where it counts."

That was all well and good, he thought as he peppered her face with kisses. But he wanted her physically intact as well.

"Can you take me to City Hall? Mayor Trent wants to see me."

He frowned, annoyed. "She should come here."

"They're releasing me in an hour anyway. I told the mayor we'd stop by on our way home."

He liked that "we." He wanted to hear more of that. "Fine. But if you get tired or need more painkillers or a backrub or a—"

"Striptease?"

"No. Leave me some dignity, would you?"

An hour and a half later Caleb opened the door to the mayor's office so Sadie could swing through on her crutches. Pain nagged at her leg, but even so it felt good to be back at City Hall, where everyone greeted her with hugs and worried exclamations. As the door shut behind them, Mayor Trent rose to her feet, immaculate as always in a black suit with a crisp, fuchsia scarf at her neck. She came around the desk to embrace Sadie, who was so stunned by the sight of the other man in the room that she barely managed a hello.

Roy Wade, Hamilton's father, sat in the "supplicant's chair" before the mayor's desk.

"What are . . . what is . . ." She looked at the mayor, totally puzzled.

Caleb's hand tightened on her elbow. He probably didn't know who Roy was, but he easily picked up on her shock.

"I invited Mr. Wade here today because I believe I've come up with a solution to our problem."

Roy stood up too. He had Hamilton's football player build, with an extra pillow of fat around the middle. He wore a bolo tie and a loose cotton jacket. "We might not agree on the source of the problem, but we agree on the solution. A one-way ticket out of Kilby."

Sadie stiffened. The mayor held up a finger, like a scolding kindergarten teacher. "Now Mr. Wade, don't forget the potential lawsuits you're trying to avoid. If you anger Sadie, she might not agree to drop her claim against Hamilton."

Claim against Hamilton . . . She looked up at Caleb, but he simply moved closer to her, so she felt his warm solid strength at her back.

"You and I know that claim is a load of cow turd."

"If that's so, why are you here?" The steely note in the mayor's voice made him snap his mouth shut. "Let's move past the cow turd phase of this conversation. Sadie, I've made a proposal on your behalf, but it's up to you whether or not you'll accept it. If you want to take your case against Hamilton Wade all the way to court, I'll make sure it gets tried outside of Kilby. You should have an excellent chance. Hamilton went too far this time, and everyone knows it. Brett Carlisle—you know him, from Save Our Slugs—is willing to testify that Hamilton deliberately thrust his foot onto your leg in an attempt to break it."

Sadie noticed she didn't say that Hamilton actually did that. She didn't remember who had broken her leg but did not doubt that the ultimate blame for the brawl lay with Hamilton. Caleb steadied her, his warm breath ruffling the top of her hair. "What's the proposal?" he asked the mayor. "It better be something really good."

"Mr. Wade has offered to pay Sadie's tuition at the law school of her choice. As long as it's not in Kilby, which isn't a problem since we don't have a law school. He thinks Hamilton could use some distance and perspective."

"What's Texas coming to when you can't get into a barroom brawl without lawsuits flying?" Roy Wade grumbled under his breath. "We need a new mayor in this town, that's what we need."

Sadie ignored him, still stunned by the offer Mayor

Trent had made. *Law school tuition . . .* She could actually go to law school—assuming she got in. On the other hand, were the Wades paying her to leave Kilby? She didn't like the sound of that.

"In addition, he will donate a substantial sum to the Save Our Slugs group."

Roy coughed, burying the word "payoff" in the scratchy sound.

Mayor Trent gave him a sharp stare. "I'm tempted to add room and board—"

"That's not necessary," Caleb said, the rumble of his chest against her back making her shiver. "I can take care of it. All of it. Sadie, you don't have to take this deal. I can afford law school. Or I will be able to, as soon as the next contract—"

"Hey!" Sadie tilted her face to his. "I don't want to be one more person depending on your contract. If I marry you, it'll be because I love you and want to be with you, not so you can support me."

"*If?*" His eyes turned stormy. "Didn't we already settle that?"

"When," she corrected herself. "I meant when. But my point is—"

"Your point is valid," interrupted the mayor. "What you and Caleb work out between you has nothing to do with this deal. This is the Wade family paying for their horrendous behavior, which culminated in my assistant being physically assaulted by their offspring. Quite frankly, you're letting them off easy if you take this deal. But it will avoid a big, messy court case and your name in the papers, and I know you've had enough notoriety over the past year. But it's completely up to you, my dear."

Sadie sent Caleb a silent question. *What do you think?* Take their money? File a lawsuit? He looked steadily back at her, but gave no clue as to what he thought. Her leg throbbed. She needed to get home. She turned back to the other two.

"So basically you're offering to pay me to become a lawyer, so if Hamilton ever tries some other sleazy move, I can go after him with all the legal skills I'll possess by that point? And I can help anyone else he messes with? Or I can help other people who have nothing to do with Hamilton?"

Roy Wade shrugged. "Take it or leave it. I don't care."

"For the sake of irony alone, I'll take it."

Mayor Trent smiled triumphantly. "Good. I knew we could work this out. Sadie, you should get home. Thanks for stopping by." She leaned in to kiss her on the cheek. "I'm going to miss the best assistant I ever had." Turning to Caleb, she added, "I bet the Catfish will miss you too. For a very brief moment in time, the team actually looked good."

From across the room, Roy gave an unpleasant snort. "Another thing you and your church ladies are about to ruin."

"Excuse me?" Mayor Trent swung around with a frown. "What are you talking about?"

"The league's fed up with Crush Taylor. They want him out. If he goes, the team will move somewhere else. He only keeps it here because Kilby's his hometown. Anyone else would move it to a bigger city."

The mayor tapped her fingers against her side in a rapid rhythm. *Stress.* Sadie recognized it. "We'll see," she finally said. "Crush Taylor has a way of coming out on top."

Was Sadie the only one who noticed how worried Wendy Trent suddenly seemed?

"Something's going on between Crush Taylor and

the mayor," she whispered to Caleb as they made their way back to his rental car. "I'd kill to know exactly what."

"No way. They're complete opposites. And Crush is always lecturing the players about not getting serious about girls."

"Oh really?" She gave him a teasing nudge, just because it felt so good to touch him. "Didn't you propose to me not long ago? You just don't listen, do you?"

He winked back at her. "Nope. I'm a rebel, baby. A rebel with a cause."

"What cause?"

"The best. Getting into your pants."

Accidentally-on-purpose, she grazed his foot with her crutch.

"Did I say get into your pants? I meant . . . win your undying love." His broad grin nearly knocked her off her crutches. He gazed down at her, eyes shining in the darkening twilight, his big body angled protectively toward her, adjusting to the pace of her crutches.

Well, if that was all he wanted . . . mission accomplished.

While Sadie slept off the effects of that dramatic meeting, Caleb visited Bingo in jail.

"Tell me the whole thing, beginning to end," he told his father. "I need to hear it."

So the story spun out in all its sad absurdity. Bingo had been drawn to the ballpark because that's where Caleb spent his time, but he'd gotten tempted by the ubiquitous prop bets. It seemed harmless. But once the Wades wanted to turn his just-for-fun sideline into a full-service bookmaking operation—and threatened to publicly reveal his connection to Caleb if he didn't—he felt trapped. "After you gave that newspaper interview,

I tried to get out. But they said they'd make it look like you gambled on the games yourself, which would be even worse."

That made a certain sort of sense, although something still bothered him.

"Why did you want to bring the kids here? Were you going to use them somehow, the way you used me and Tessa?"

"No. I swear it, Caleb. I wanted to see them. It had nothing to do with the Wades. I wish they'd never seen the boys and Tessa. One more thing to threaten me over, and I never saw it coming. I would have gone to prison for twice as long if that's what it took to keep them away from our family." He shook his head miserably. "I didn't want to make trouble for you. Turns out, I made plenty without even meaning to. Do you hate me?"

"I don't. No. I wish you hadn't started in with the prop bets."

"Christ, so do I," Bingo groaned.

"But it was partly my fault. I should have given you more of a chance. Invited you to the ballpark. Opened up to you more. Besides, once you got caught, you tried to protect Tessa and the boys, and I'm with you on that."

"Don't give me too much credit, Caleb. I have a knack for trouble. But I don't want my family paying for that. No more than you already have."

"Well, I can't argue with any of that." Caleb couldn't help smiling; he was too happy to hold onto his resentment. "Maybe you should figure out a way to make trouble legally."

Bingo peered up at him hopefully. "Good thought, son. Good thought. I'm going to work on that."

Thurston Howell II—a man it was impossible to stay angry with. "Here, I almost forgot." From his pocket,

Caleb pulled out a handful of his brand new San Diego Friars baseball cards, already signed. "We're working on a probation agreement. In the meantime, just in case you need to tell anyone about your sort-of-famous son, take these."

He pushed them across the table. Bingo touched them as if they were made of gold. "Really? You don't mind?"

"I don't mind. See you soon, Bingo."

Late September

Even in a meaningless game—the Friars had fallen behind too far to have any chance of making the playoffs—the atmosphere inside Friar Stadium was un- believable. Caleb scuffed his cleats against the mound, carving it the way he wanted, with a little extra groove for his left foot. This was his office now, and even though the season was about to end, he planned to come back with a vengeance next year. When he had it just right, he took one quick glance over his shoulder for a 360-degree view of his domain. He loved the open air stadium, with its stucco surfaces, dark blue seats, and exposed steel beams painted white. The buildings of downtown San Diego soared behind the bleachers, and beyond them he caught a glimpse of the blue waters of the bay.

If you could pitch in a ship at sea, that would be Friar Stadium.

And Caleb loved every moment he spent on that mound. Even the tough ones. Because, now that he thought about it, maybe that was the point. Win or lose, beat or get beaten, you had to give yourself com- pletely. No shame, no doubt, no worry, no mistrust—

just put it all out there and take what comes. Even if what comes is chaos.

Turning his attention back to home plate, where the Nationals' Ian Garner was assuming his stance, he accepted the one-finger call for a fastball. Turn, lift, *explode*. The ball sizzled through the air and into the catcher's mitt. *Strike*. Garner shook his head, muttering to himself.

Meaningless game? No such thing. Not in baseball. Not for the players, because every pitch and every at-bat counted toward your stats. Every pitch was a moment that mattered.

But with a 10-2 lead, he could at least let his gaze wander toward Section 113 in the Infield Box down the first base line. The front row seat meant for Sadie had been empty at the beginning of the game, and since then he'd been busy keeping the Nationals to two runs. But now, with two outs and Garner at 0-2, he allowed himself to glance in that direction.

There she was. Sadie, in a red top and shorts that showed most of one long, sleek leg and the black brace on the other. She stepped carefully down the aisle, wearing a small backpack and holding a box of Cracker Jacks. The breeze played with her dark hair, sending it in whimsical little flyaways.

Joy flooded him. *There she was*. Alive. With him. *With him*. He wasn't alone anymore. Sadie was with him. No matter what curveballs his career or his family threw his way, Sadie would be with him. She was his home plate, his dugout, and his Cy Young Award all wrapped into one sexy, delicious package.

The next pitch he threw, a knuckleball, took chaos to a whole new level, dancing and whirling like a demented hornet. Garner, incredible hitter that he was, got a piece of it and crunched out a fifty-five footer.

Caleb snagged it, tossed it to first ahead of Garner for out number three, then, instead of heading toward the home dugout with the rest of the team, he kept on going.

It happened in a blur, the way it had last time. One minute he was on the field, completing the one-three play to end the inning, the next he was over the dark-blue-padded barrier and scrambling toward Sadie. Then she was in his arms, her Cracker Jacks flying into the air, her smile setting his world on fire.

He kissed her with passionate hunger while Cracker Jacks cascaded onto their heads. It wasn't as if everything else disappeared. He heard the roar of voices all around, felt the trembling of the stadium floor as fans stampeded to get a good shot of them. The breeze kissed them with the scent of peanuts and salty ocean. The moment held all those things, and he loved them all, because Sadie was in his arms and he loved *her*.

The voice of the play-by-play announcer from someone's radio caught his attention. "He's done it again! Shades of Caleb Hart's infamous attack in the stands down in Kilby. This doesn't look like the same kind of thing, but even so, the Friars have to be wondering just how stable Hart is. They're pinning their hopes for next season on his missile launcher arm. But can they count on him to stay on the darn field?"

One of the Fox color commentary girls came running up, along with a cameraman, who aimed the camera at them. The red light warned them they were live on the Jumbotron.

"Caleb Hart, can you explain what's happening?"

Sadie, shaking with laughter, buried her face against his chest. He wrapped one arm tightly around her. "I haven't seen my fiancée in a while, and I guess I got a little carried away."

"So this is your fiancée?"

Sadie angled her head at Caleb, wrinkling her nose in a way that promised sweet vengeance later on. Then she too turned to the reporter. "Hi. I'm Sadie Merritt." She gave a little wave to the camera.

He loved the way she said her name, so proud. Maybe she'd shaken off her ghosts too.

"How do you feel about your future husband joining the Friars pitching roster?"

"Anyone would be lucky to have Caleb on their team. I'm not saying that just because I love him, even though I'm crazy about him. He's a great player, and the thing is, he's just getting started. All you Friars fans should sit back and enjoy the ride. Next season's going to be amazing."

A cheer went up around them. Caleb squeezed her shoulder, so touched he couldn't say anything. So this was what it felt like to have someone *with* him.

"How did the two of you meet? Mind telling us the story?"

Sadie turned and met Caleb's gaze, tossing that question to him. He knew a besotted smile had spread across his face and he probably looked ridiculous up on those Jumbotrons. He didn't care. He bent down and brushed a soft kiss across her lips. "She tried to kick me out of Kilby. She didn't know what a stubborn guy I am."

"Are all the stories about the Kilby Catfish true?"

The Nationals were taking the field, and a few catcalls floated toward them. The first Friars batter was moving toward home plate, limbering up. Caleb had to get back to the dugout before he caused any more of a disruption. "Gotta go. Enjoy the game, everyone!" He waved and turned to Sadie, who gave him one last radiant smile.

"See you after the game," he whispered, for her ears only.

"I'll be here."

And that, it turned out, was all he needed.